S0-ABO-510

Write Letter to Billy

Write Letter to Billy

a novel by Toby Olson

COFFEE HOUSE PRESS

COPYRIGHT © 2000 by Toby Olson
COVER PHOTOGRAPH © Daniel Proctor/Photonica
AUTHOR PHOTOGRAPH © Robert A. Lisak
COVER + BOOK DESIGN Kelly Kofron and Linda S. Koutsky

COFFEE HOUSE PRESS is an independent nonprofit literary publisher supported in part by a grant provided by the Minnesota State Arts Board,
through an appropriation by the Minnesota State Legislature, and in part
by a grant from the National Endowment for the Arts. Significant support
has also been provided by the Bush Foundation; Elmer L. & Eleanor J.
Andersen Foundation; General Mills Foundation; Honeywell Foundation; James R. Thorpe Foundation; Lila Wallace-Reader's Digest Fund;
McKnight Foundation; Medtronic; The Pentair Foundation; Patrick and
Aimee Butler Family Foundation; the law firm of Schwegman, Lundberg,
Woessner & Kluth, P.A.; The St. Paul Companies Foundation, Inc.; Star
Tribune Foundation; Target Foundation; West Group; and many individ-
ual donors. To you and our many readers across the country, we send our
thanks for your continuing support.

COFFEE HOUSE PRESS books are available to the trade through our primary
distributor, Consortium Book Sales & Distribution, 1045 Westgate Drive,
Saint Paul, MN 55114. For personal orders, catalogs, or other information,
write to us at 27 North Fourth Street, Suite 400, Minneapolis, MN 55401.

LIBRARY OF CONGRESS CATALOGING-IN-PUBLICATION INFORMATION
Olson, Toby.
    Write letter to Billy : a novel / by Toby Olson.
        p. cm.
    ISBN 1-56689-103-5 (ALK. PAPER)
        1. Fathers and sons—Fiction. 2. Fathers and daughters—Fiction.
        3. California, Southern—Fiction. 4. Divers—Fiction. I. Title.
PS3565.L84 W75 2000
813'.54—DC21   00-043100

10 9 8 7 6 5 4 3 2 1
FIRST EDITION / FIRST PRINTING

PRINTED IN CANADA

*This book is for
Jill Bates and Jack Olson*

The author thanks Peter and remembers Roberta Markman, his good friends, and thanks Toshie Sweeney and Scott Wauben for the pleasures of Catalina Island.

The story does not ultimately depend upon what is said, upon what we, projecting onto the world something of our own cultural paranoia, call its *plot*. The story does not depend upon any fixed repertoire of ideas and habits: it depends on its stride over spaces. In these spaces lies the meaning it bestows on events.

—John Berger

My Father's List

1. Look into blossom gradation and etching.
2. Go over it with Bev again.
3. Laguna: check local newspaper morgue.
4. Leonard has batteries.
5. Rennert: why Susan?
6. Could it really have been Housewares?
7. Weather: moon, wind, tides.
8. The question of the sheet.
9. Write letter to Billy.
10. The History of the American Theater (TAT: Its History) what?
11. Time longer than rope.
12. Go see Blevins.

Prologue

When I was a child, my father took us to the Arrowhead Hotel, near San Bernardino, where the palm trees looked like people, and it was there I witnessed his failed experiments with flying.

We stayed together in a small and modest room on the second floor, my narrow bed under a gauze-curtained window, and looking out I could see a broad expanse of tailored grounds, gravel paths, and squares of cultivated garden flowers: lilies, I think, and clustered campion. Dichondra curled at the edge of a cottage porch, the earth turned slowly for a week, and the slopes at Big Bear rose above the feathery palm heads in the distance.

My mother spent our time at the Arrowhead with movie magazines and plays. My father had brought his planes along, large and variously altered replicas of those models hanging from the ceiling in my room at home, and I remember the way he limped down gentle slopes, Pipers lifting from his fingertips and into air, only to fall to earth just yards from their ascension.

In the crisp evenings, when the breeze died down, sun came at a slant and lit fires at the palms' feet, something I didn't see then— I was nine years old—but it comes up in memory that way, as if the tree might flee, hop out of the fire and leave me exposed there, watching my father where he sat under a eucalyptus tree, taking careful notes among the wreckage.

He was not really my father, nor Beverly my mother. He was tall, gently serious, and she was vibrantly beautiful as I've come to see them, though they were in their early sixties even then. Nineteen-forty-nine in El Monte, California, and yet they'd called me a love child, not knowing what that meant, but that they'd "chosen" me when I was only six months old, somewhere near Chicago.

And there were trails at the Arrowhead, and a small lake for swimming and a recreation room. And there was a wood fire in the evenings, music and other children, even an early TV set in the tattered lobby. Yet my thoughts were with my father and his experiments, and I did little at the Arrowhead but linger at his side and watch him, even as I lingered then at the deck rail. It was nearing the end of June, an unseasonably cool evening. No moon, but a sky full of stars, and I was wondering about family.

"What are you *doing* there?" she said.

Her name was Beverly too, and it was that and the fact they'd be leaving the next morning, a similar family trip, just the three of them, a little fishing and some time together, that took me back to the Arrowhead and my mother and father.

I turned from the deck rail to face her and saw Jason standing at the sliding glass doors beside his father, as a man should stand, though slightly awkward when he gestured, his thirteen-year-old energy still beyond him. He was blond, like me, and taller than Aaron was.

"My big boy!" Beverly said brightly. Aaron saw us looking, and he winked.

"Let's get another drink," I said.

She pushed away from the rail then, and I followed her into the house and to the kitchen, a large country kitchen on a farm in Wisconsin. The gin stood on the butcher block, the tonic beside it, and juice drained from the cut lime staining the wood. Then Beverly was at the sink, washing the lettuce and potatoes, and I was speaking tentatively again.

"There isn't any anger. Just a vague sort of hollowness, as if I'd lost all that time."

TOBY OLSON

"So have they," she said, her voice muffled in the running water. "Anyway, it's bound to be interesting. I'd think a little more than that though."

"Yes," I said. "But I'm not really sure I'm ready just yet."

"How could you be?"

Her voice had the humor of some promise in it, and in the silence that followed we could hear the muffled laughter of father and son. Good old Aaron, I thought, remembering the time when he had saved my life.

It had been twelve years before when we were stationed together at the Philadelphia Naval Yard. Jason had just been born and Beverly was with him in Wisconsin, holding the family farm together until Aaron's discharge. He'd done eight years and thought he'd be staying in, like I, until retirement. But then Beverly had come along, his parents had quit the farm and moved into Madison, and Aaron's plans had changed.

Philly was a good city for sailors even in those heated sixties, if they'd been in for a while and were no longer on the lookout for a fast life. Cheap, off-base housing was available in those days, and there were jazz bars, something that brought Aaron and me together as much as work did and his loneliness without Beverly and his son. He spoke of home and farming, boyhood times, plans for the future. He was biding his time, and though I knew I'd be staying in, his stories with their promise of a solid civilian life drew me and we spent a lot of time together, listening to music and talking. I was at a loss for any future even then, though without concern for one, safe in the bosom of mother Navy.

We were working a massive carrier they'd brought in, but not to dry dock. Most of the refitting was above water line, and those few things below, spot welding mostly, were for us. We'd charted the hull and voids in wet suits and tanks, had taken a skittery engineer down with us to mark each fault with bright fluorescent paint. Then in a week we took the gear down, tanks, torches, power sanders, and the rest. I was the master welder in a heavy diving suit. Aaron wore lighter gear, and it was his job to move the tanks and torches and keep the lines clear. I was piped into the ship and could stay down indefinitely, but Aaron had to go up from time to time to get fresh tanks of air. When he was gone I did absolutely nothing, just stood in the murky water looking along the endless hull.

I had a head lamp, but its focus was only a tight circle, and while pieces of dead weed floated across my helmet glass from time to time, the water was heavy and lifeless, the carrier's hull no more than a stationary dark wall a few feet from my face. It was a two-week job, the work boring and mechanical, and after a few days it felt as if we were in some half-lit cabin above decks, not under-water a good sixty feet down.

We grew complacent, and when the sudden storm came, a stiff wind and driving rain out of the north, we didn't answer the sig-nal quickly enough, the massive hull shifted, fouling my air line, then crushing it and the backup too. I remember turning my head, searching for Aaron through my helmet's side port, then sucking for air. Only sixty feet, but I knew in that moment it would be enough to end me. They'd winch up my heavy suit, but not soon enough. Then I was gone, and only later did I learn that Aaron had gotten my helmet off, had buddied me up with his own air line as they'd hoisted me.

He came to the hospital to visit, though I was only there for a few days. He brought flowers along. Then he'd left the Navy and headed back to Wisconsin, and I'd not seen him since.

"Time will tell," Beverly said, then turned from the sink to grin at me, well aware of her cliché and its obvious truth.

Over our dinner of steak, salad, and potatoes, Aaron spoke to Jason of their morning trip to Crivitz.

"Again?" Beverly said, rolling her eyes and smiling.

"Yes!" Aaron said. "And bluegills big as hubcaps! A pike or two if we're lucky. Maybe even a muskie."

TOBY OLSON

Jason grinned, urging him on, the child in him believing his father. There was baby fat in his cheeks, under the downy beginnings of a beard.

"What time?" I said, and Jason spoke for the three of them.

"We're out of here by four-thirty. Right?"

"That's right," said Aaron. "Up and out."

"I won't be leaving that early."

"Of course not!" said Beverly. "An ungodly hour. And you have plenty of time."

"All the time in the world," I said, and Beverly gazed at me from across the table.

That night that marked the end of certain things, I lay below a quilt that Beverly had cut and sewn, my fingers in a field of various flower squares, Wisconsin violet, buttercup, and morning glory. Petals in a boy's room? A kind of question I had never asked before. I lay flat as a coffined corpse, uncommon for me, watching the stars' lights in the ceiling where Jason had pasted them, or someone else had, to fake a dim galaxy for any imagination. A hollow bell in the distance: how now brown cow, my mother's voice, and the declamations in my father's awkwardly soothing one of us in our egocentricity. This, at the edge where sleep came to me and in the twitter of a night bird on breeze at the window, feminine and almost recognizable.

1.

It's a long story.

I'd driven to Wisconsin from Philadelphia, where I'd finished up my twenty years plus three and been discharged into retirement at forty. I was just seventeen when I entered the Navy in San Diego, 1958, and though my time had spanned those infamous war years, I'd been a landlocked and domestic sailor for the most part.

Time in New London and Corpus Christi, Great Lakes in Chicago, a brief stint in Seattle, those two tours in Philadelphia, and only a year at Guantanamo, and that in peacetime.

When I'd returned to Philly, eight years after being with Aaron there, I had rank and age. Younger, hotshot divers were available, and I managed a recruitment position for myself, spending my last hitch on Broad Street, just a few blocks from City Hall.

I sat behind a desk under fluorescents in a razor-sharp dress uniform, the backs of full-sized cardboard cutouts in the front window across the room. Viewed from the street, they were happy sailors, outlined in sea-green neon. That was something. The modern Navy. And yet those who stumbled through the door, hesitant and bright-eyed, seemed no different from the self I'd been, all those years ago.

I was no lost child then. Though my parents were older, well into their seventies when I enlisted, they'd managed to stay with the ways of youth through connection to the sources of memory and the world outside and had stayed close to me that way. My father, Andy, was an information hound. Our house in El Monte was full of instruction manuals and specialty magazines. The radio, tuned to news shows, spilled constant information, and once he'd retired from Ball Brothers Glass, where he'd supervised an assembly line, my father had focused on experiment, trying out those things he'd been gathering facts about over the years.

It was through him I'd gotten a taste for underwater work. He'd taught me welding and brazing, his thorough enthusiasm for the mechanical, just anything with moving parts, and once he'd found an old regulator, repaired it, and rigged up a tank. He'd checked it out in the bathtub, head down at the drain and bubbles rising. Then he'd given me a chance, holding the tank up off my back as I drifted under; then I found I could breathe in water. And I remember sitting beside him in the evenings, studying deep-diving magazines, his voice full of seductive details, our fingers on all those glossy photographs.

I suspect he got my mother's initial attention in a similar way, not through good looks surely, or wealth. He'd been a poor boy, and though he was tall and lean, he had that slight limp, an unfortunate overbite, and hardly any chin at all. His attraction was all in his pure interest in everything. He was a very good listener.

My mother was a few years younger than my father and had been a successful ingenue when she was a girl. And she'd managed, even through some serious drinking and early aging skin, to get such roles into her thirties. She'd come to Los Angeles from a farm in South Dakota against the wishes of her parents around 1910. Magazines, songbooks, and a few biographies: star-struck, she said. It was one of those stories.

She'd gotten a few bit parts in silent films, but it was the legitimate theater that drew her, small repertory companies in Hollywood and Pasadena at that time. Then came the twenties, the fast life and drink, and by the time she was forty she was finished. It was not that she couldn't act, couldn't have taken on the personality of mature women. She was that. It was her face and a certain way with gesture and articulation that couldn't seem to change, to step forward into appropriate age.

She had a pure youthful enthusiasm, one that had come to its visual qualities on stage but was deeper in her than that. It was in her eyes and smile, her quick expressions even when she was in her sixties. It had something to do with constant wonder and surprise. She wore a younger face, just under those lines that marked her maturity, and that face was clearly visible when she spoke, smiled, or laughed. Seen from a distance or without knowing her, she seemed insincere, but though it was that perception that took her off the stage, it was a false one. It was not that her emotional development had been arrested, nor that the growing richness of mind brought naturally through age was not hers. It was her heart, I think, that remained fresh, something to do with an utter lack of cynicism.

There was a prized photograph. It hung with many others on the wall near the foot of my parents' bed. It was taken on the evening they met for the first time, in the lobby of a small avant-garde theater in Pasadena, an opening of *The Pelican* in 1935.

It was intermission, and the lobby was crowded, but off to the side near the concession table you could find my mother. She wore a long, dark dress, a clinging knit, I think, and had a wine glass in her hand. She was leaning against a pillar, her head cocked to the side coyly but a clear attention in her face. My father stood before her, thin and straight and wearing a stylish suit. He was speaking, his hands forming something in the air between them.

Theater was just another of my father's interests. He'd come across an article in *Popular Mechanics*, something to do with hydraulic pulley-and-chain mechanisms used to mount some extravagant opera in New York City. He'd devoured that, moved forward to set design, its history, then to various acting techniques. In a while he was applying his knowledge to live performances, studying stage management, the influence of famous, dead actors on those currently at work. He'd read something about my mother, various reviews written more than ten years before. She'd worked mostly in the experimental theater then, and that had grabbed his interest too, as well as all the rest.

"Andy listened," she was fond of saying. "And when he finally spoke, he knew everything. All those years and plays. They came alive again for me. I knew at once I'd never let him go."

He had just turned fifty when they met, she was forty-seven, a first marriage for both of them. She was down-and-out, living on borrowed money. He took her to his house in El Monte, set up a theater room for her, a place for photographs, albums, and clippings. And in the evenings they'd talk about the theater. She'd tell her stories, bright-eyed and young again, and he'd fill in those details of history and mechanics, providing the solid stage on which her stories could turn and vibrate.

She'd get a little drunk at times; she always had bottles in the house, but that was okay with my father. "It's the theater," he once said to me. "A highly charged and emotional life. Like diving. There's a constant tension when you're doing it, then opening up to relaxation afterward." I remember his blinking as he looked at me, aware that the analogy might set me off in a wrong direction.

"It could be eating too much," he said, "reading, some other obsessive activity. Just a little excess to relieve tension." He leaned on the word *obsessive*. He was reading Freud and others at the time.

It was late in the thirties when they decided on adoption. Both were over fifty by then, and though they made an exhaustive search of agencies all up and down the California coast, their circumstance was frowned upon and they had no luck. But there was my father and his exhaustive study. They didn't give up, and in time he found some connection near Chicago, not quite legal, I think, and probably expensive. They had little funds. Neither of them cared much for savings. But they managed somehow, and in 1940 I joined them, my memory of life beginning in that cluttered house in El Monte.

There'd been a Navy recruiter when I was a high school junior. They came to high schools looking for prospects in those days. He'd had bright eyes, like my father, energetic in that way, and when he learned of my interest in deep-diving, he'd looked into that, then sent me information, and I'd spent most of my senior year anticipating, reading, and taking scuba lessons at the local pool. I'd enlisted the day after graduation.

It was not all that hard to leave home. My parents had been so whole in their lives, my mother even past one life when I'd come to them, that through the years they'd managed a distance from me that I've come to feel as respectful. They were there when I needed them, but they gave me room of the same kind they gave each other. We were close, but never in a pathological way. Our evenings were like a gathering of very good friends, two of whom were lovers, for purposes of rich discussion, some tender council, enjoyment, and learning.

I'd been in seven years, was twenty-four years old and stationed in Corpus Christi, Texas, when they died, my mother, then my father only a few days after. They were in their late seventies and cancer had gotten her, a mercifully brief illness. I don't know what the cause was in my father's case. "He just seemed to fold his tent when she was gone," the doctor said. She'd died in the hospital in her sleep, and they'd found my father at home beside her empty bed. I'd tried to call him with my travel plans for her funeral, then had called the doctor when I couldn't reach him. The medical reports and a brief, joint obituary held the story, though not nearly in as much detail as my father would have approved.

I flew home and buried them, then spent a week cleaning the house out and listed it with a Realtor. As a place, it held nothing for me without them. They'd left a brief will: the car and house went to me, my mother's clothing and jewelry, anything I wanted of my father's. My mother's past, contained neatly in albums and file folders, went to the El Monte Historical Society. I kept that one picture, the two of them meeting for the first time at the theater, and I packed my father's gear in boxes, sixty-two of them, in as careful categories as I could manage. He would have liked that. I drove them to a warehouse on the outskirts of town, sold the old car at a lot across the street, then walked back with the money and paid for five years of storage. I took a bus to the airport, a good long ride. The Realtor had a couple of interested buyers. I'd call him as soon as I got back to Corpus.

Dead and supposedly gone, and yet it was no more than a week after my return that I met and took up with Carol, who was not at all unlike my mother. She was a Wave, a lab technician at the Naval Hospital, just a month short of discharge. She'd done her four years, used them to find herself. She'd enlisted after an abortion. Her father had thrown her out.

"I was a little loose in high school," she told me after I'd met her at the NCO club, took her to dinner and a movie, then in a few days slept with her. I was twenty-four, she just a year younger. "Bill," she said, as we danced a cowboy foxtrot at a downtown bar, "let's just go somewhere and do it."

We went at it hot and heavy for a few weeks, but we managed to talk about things too. I'd be staying in. She knew that, and she had a job lined up at a small lab in Bloomington, Indiana. She was not going back to her parents' place in Racine, not for a while at least.

When the day of her discharge came, I drove her to the airport and kissed her good-bye at the gate. She smiled when she looked up at me, no wish for lingering in her expression. She'd gotten rid of her uniform and was wearing a simple and efficient dress. Everything was in front of her, and I was already in the past.

From Corpus, I was transferred to Seattle and some interesting work. All my training was behind me by then, but I picked up things on my own. It was my father's influence, I guess. I studied metallurgy and hydroelectricity, the physics of volume

TOBY OLSON

and pressure. When I dove down for repairs, I knew things that other divers didn't know, and while such knowledge might not have made me more efficient, it certainly made the work more interesting.

Then there was scuba and free diving. Nothing in Philadelphia or Chicago, but by the time I had my year at Guantanamo I'd been in for a while, was a first-class petty officer with some authority, my own room, and considerable liberty. I took leave and headed for some islands in the Bahamas, where I dove for an entire month, stripping myself slowly of all gear until I was down to only flippers, weight belt, snorkel, and mask. I made ninety-five feet by the end of that month, and from then on every leave was a diving one. When I was close to discharge and was sitting behind that desk on Broad Street, I had plans for a year in the Netherlands Antilles—Aruba and Bonaire. No future beyond that counted for much. I'd have a good enough pension and I'd saved the money I'd gotten from the sale of my parents' house. With interest and the few bonds I'd purchased over the years, I'd be all right for a long while.

I had a cheap apartment, the top floor of Mrs. Venuti's house in South Philadelphia, and a new car. I'd be free of the Navy soon and all other care. Then the letter came.

2.

I think I knew the letter was from Carol even before I opened it, though I had no memory of her handwriting. Our time together had been based in other intimacies, and even those had faded from me over the years, a full fifteen. Still, I knew, and I felt a certain rush inserting the thin blade of the opener. The postmark was Racine, my address care of the Naval Yard; she'd guessed at rank, one notch above where I found myself, waiting for discharge.

We'd exchanged letters in the first month after she'd left Corpus for Bloomington. Long and detailed ones at first, hers full of excitement and anticipation, those followed by a brief note or two, the last one from me, as I remember. Then I was leaving for another place again, and when I got there she was behind me, just one of the many pasts in a sailor's life.

She spent the first two paragraphs speaking of her time in Bloomington, edging up to the letter's purpose slowly. She'd had a child, been married, had worked in a lab there for nine years. Her husband had been a doctor, a radiologist, and it seemed she mentioned his position with the satisfaction of a poor girl who's made good. But he had died quite suddenly three years ago. He'd left something, and she'd finally moved back to Racine and made peace with her family. He'd been a gentle and understanding man, she wrote, much older than she. And he'd accepted her little girl too, treating her as if she were his own child.

"Your child," she wrote. "Jennifer. She's fifteen now. She wants to meet you."

I'd written back, and then the girl herself had written, a long adolescent letter on pale blue paper, faint dry scent of flowered perfume rising from the pages. She'd seen some photograph I'd given Carol. But I would have changed by now, she knew that. She included a picture, "taken with Bell and Bob in the back yard," and then a date, only a month before. They were border collies, small and alert, and she'd penciled in an asterisk beside one of them, another after the word "Bob" on the photo's back.

She was standing under the shadow of a grape arbor, one small dog to either side of her, both at heel and looking up at the camera. Shadows fell across her long legs and the dog's haunches. She seemed to have dressed up for the portrait. She wore a pale flowered dress, a woman's dress, buttoned to the neck, and her hair was light, like mine, and cut short, a bobbing at her ears and straight, serious bangs. The dress was tightly belted at her waist, and I could see the slight rise of her budding breasts. She had my father's body, lean and straight, a hint of his overbite. I thought I saw my mother in her faint smile, but I knew it was a wish only, unaccounted for. She was looking directly into the camera lens, at me, and I knew she'd had the picture made for this specific purpose and that Carol had taken it, perhaps reluctantly.

She was a true love child, not chosen in the way I'd been. Love is often like that, I thought sentimentally, full of accident and regret. But she was so real there, so established in the camera frame. She was the product of intense moments, yet uncalled for, but my daughter now, and her steady stare held no hint of accusation, only a beckoning.

There had been other letters, filling in the details of her life. They were written carefully, and I was sure she'd worked them and made many drafts. Still, her youth came through in exclama-

28   TOBY OLSON

tion points, underlining, the way she sometimes jumped to recent vivid events, dropped her careful narrative for energy of the here and now. She'd taken diving lessons at her school, had a beginner's certificate.

Carol wrote too at first, but in a while her letters stopped, as if she'd been no more than a go-between, a matchmaker. She said she looked forward to seeing me again, but there was nothing but plain fact in her saying it.

And I wrote back to both of them, holding myself away from Carol as best I could, but taking up Jennifer's enthusiasm in short and emphatic sentences. And when she said she had the summer, nothing to do, and could we go someplace together, travel, see things, I knew it was coming, and I found it hard to hold back. I called Carol then, and we talked for a long time. "It's what she wants. She thinks so, at least." I said I could come, stay in the town. "We can give it a few days," she said, "then we'll see. You can stay here. We've plenty of room."

It was not a friendly offer, but an order, a way for her to keep an eye on both of us and how we'd be together. She wasn't happy about any of it, but she was quickly taking charge, and I remembered that quality of control from the past. She'd been in charge of our brief relationship as well, and I'd felt a certain comfort in being a follower.

I was discharged on the fifteenth of June, a matter only of signing some papers and clearing my few personal items out of the Broad Street recruiting station. I felt no need of occasion. My mind was on the future, and Jennifer, and my work for the past three years had been civilianlike, night watch only once a month, a nine-to-five job from which I went home to my apartment at Mrs. Venuti's house.

I'd found Aaron's number near Madison, then had called him. He was surprised. We'd not been in touch for a long time, and when he heard I was coming to Wisconsin, he said I'd certainly have to stay with them, for a few days at least, Beverly insisted. "I do too."

I stripped my bed, covered the stereo with a pillow case, then packed my clothing and the numerous maps I'd studied in planning a tentative trip for Jennifer and me. I hadn't marked them. Nothing could be sure yet. We'd have to see, or she would. It's up to her, Carol had said.

I put my diving gear in the back of the closet. The Antilles would have to wait. Then I gave Mrs. Venuti a book of signed checks for the bills and told her I'd be calling about the other mail. I gave her the address of the Navy recruitment office in Racine, asking her to send the end-of-the-month stuff there. I was expecting a few pieces of discharge mail, nothing important. I bought her a basket of fruit, thanking her in advance. She stood at the door, like a mother, as I drove away.

TOBY OLSON

3.

I knew the drive from Aaron's farm to Racine was a short one, still I got there earlier than I'd planned. Feeling like a high school boy setting out hesitantly on a first date, I drove through the town slowly, looking at buildings and houses, wandering down side streets. I found the Johnson Wax complex, one of Frank Lloyd Wright's larger accomplishments, and parked near the kiosk at the gate. I got out and looked at the buildings for a while. Then I located the Navy recruiting office, a storefront on a busy street at the edge of a run-down neighborhood. There were lights in the windows, a few figures moving inside. I'd been gone close to a week, and there could be mail. Mrs. Venuti was efficient that way. Her husband was always out and around, her son grown, and now her pleasure was in cooking, cleaning, and schedules. I passed the place. I'd give it another day.

Racine was lazy and small, and in an hour I'd seen most of it. Then it was time, just after noon, and I drove to Carol's street, found the house, and parked at the curb across from it. It was brick and had two large bay windows flanking the entranceway. It sat well back from the street, at the end of a brick path. It was large and substantial, with carefully tended old trees and flower beds under the bays. It seemed Carol had done well for herself, at least when it came to money.

She opened the door, then squinted slightly as she looked out at me through the screen. She was smaller than I remembered, but just as lean, and her dark hair was not all that different, though longer and more carefully ordered, and I thought I saw streaks of gray near her temples. She was wearing jeans and a loose green blouse. An expensive thin gold chain dangled down between her full breasts. I remembered her thin, pointed nose, her chin, large dark eyes.

"Well, you haven't changed," she said. "Not much."

"Enough," I said, reaching involuntarily toward my face. "But not you. You're the same."

We got by that. I could see her acknowledge it, then pause for a moment before she reached out and opened the screen door. She stood back to the side then, raised her arm, and ushered me in. I stepped over the sill and didn't know what to do. I put my hand out, turning toward her as I entered. She smiled, reached out and took it, shaking it in a parody of a handshake, then pulled me toward her slightly, stood on her toes, and kissed my cheek. I felt her breast brush against my arm. Still holding my hand, she led me through the foyer and into the large living room. I saw the two dogs, Bell and Bob. They were lying on the floor near the couch, and their heads came up to look at me as I entered. I smelled onions cooking, heard a soft thud from somewhere above on the second floor. I sat down on the couch, sinking in deeper than I wanted. I'd need to get up when she entered, be agile, and it wouldn't be easy. Carol sat in a large wing chair, arms crossed at the wrists over her knee, leaning forward slightly.

"Jen will be down soon," she said. "I'll call her. Can you relax?"

My feet were planted beside each other, and when I looked at my hands gripping my knees, I could see a whiteness at the knuckles. I released my hold and opened them. They were shaking slightly.

"I didn't expect this," I said.

"What *did* you expect?"

"That's it," I laughed. "I didn't know."

"Well, look," she said, "we'll have lunch. A little pasta and salad. Then I thought we'd take a walk. There's a park at the end of the street. I'll be here when she comes down, and for the walk. Then

TOBY OLSON

maybe this evening you two can go off together, to the mall. Shopping might be good, things for your trip?"

"Do you think we'll be going?"

"I do," she said. "I hope so. If you don't, it'll be because of something unfortunate. But take it easy. Let it happen."

Her words had a slight plea in them, but she was smiling thinly, reassuring me. I was trying hard to place her, myself too in that past we'd shared. We'd gotten into nothing that had to do with the fact that she'd kept my daughter from me for fifteen years, nor had we dealt with that in letters or on the phone. The idea was that I should be angry, the wronged father, but it made no difference to me just then, and though I'd thought of it before this, it was only the idea that was troublesome. I'd missed much of her childhood, but I'd not known I was missing it. I could feel no anger or blame, only a little guilt in the fact that I really didn't care. I would have had a different life had I known of her. I'd thought of that, troubling my complacency, not finding the idea very attractive at all.

"Can I call her now?"

"Yes," I said. "I'm ready."

I saw the dogs' heads come up, alert and looking toward the hallway before I heard her, that limping soft step, tripping slightly on the stair carpeting as she came down. It was my father's step, some vague memory without content. Then she was standing in the living room doorway, the dogs rising and wagging their tails, trotting over to her. She was like her picture, but even taller. As tall as I am, I thought. Carol had risen, and I was pushing on the couch arm and cushion, struggling to my feet.

We ate lunch in the sun room, a large screened-in porch off the kitchen. Jennifer sat across from me, Carol at the table's end, and I wondered about inheritance, my father who was not my father and his limp. She had it, almost a replica, a rare childhood nerve condition Carol had told me about, a slight atrophy in her left thigh. But gestures too, ones I might have taken on as a child; could that be inherited? My mother's thin nose, at least as I remembered it, recognizing it could be no more than accident.

I felt that familiar pain in my side where the birth scars were, found myself looking at her side to find them there, then saw that guard against her awkwardness, those tight little movements as she swirled the pasta in her spoon, lifted the tall tea glass to her lips, her eyes on me for a moment, a blush rising as she glanced beyond me where I knew there was nothing, only the kitchen behind me.

Her hair was short, a little wispy at her ears, and when she turned her head it fanned out there, caught the window light, and turned red at the tips. She wore the same dress as in that portrait photo she'd sent me, a flower print, buttoned up to her neck. I saw her only jewelry, a thick, beaded bracelet, and I recognized that the birthday ring I'd bought her was the wrong thing entirely. Next Thursday, I thought, we'll be on the road and I'll have to find something right. Will we? I couldn't really tell yet. She was reticent, embarrassed, and it was up to Carol to carry the conversation. Yet we watched each other as we could, and once we smiled, each catching the other's look. School, life in Racine, talk about her dead husband even, Jennifer's father, but like mine, I thought, not really that, it's *me*.

After lunch Jennifer left us, her chair rocking slightly as she pushed it back too quickly, and went to change. Carol looked hard at me once she was gone, and I recognized I was grinning.

"You don't really know her at all," she said, tapping the butt of her fork on the tablecloth.

"I know," I said. "I know that."

"Well," she said.

"But I think . . ."

"She's not fragile, you know. She's had to be tough."

"Her father," I said.

"No. Not that. She's smart, and the boys don't go for that."

TOBY OLSON

I'd misunderstood. It was a mother's concern, maybe only that, and for the first time in their house I managed to get beyond myself a little, to see it her way. There'd been an assumed intimacy between us, one *I'd* assumed because of that heated time we'd had together so long ago. I recognized I didn't know her at all really, how life might have changed her. She knows me, though, I thought, feeling something like jealousy. The Navy. Maybe I'd missed a certain richness, been complacent, was the same one I'd been back then, in Corpus.

Jennifer came down wearing jeans and a man's white shirt, her other father's, I thought, the tails hanging loose at her thighs. No bracelet on her wrist now, but a pale band of skin where a watch had been below the rolled-up cuff. Bob rose again, then Bell, and she leaned down, her fingers tapping at her knees, called to them softly in some private language. They were under and around her long legs then. Bob slipped between them and she held him with her knees, his wagging tail brushing at her calves. We were in the living room again, and when she came erect she was smiling. She might have said "these sweet, dear dogs," but Carol was at the door and had it open, and the two of us turned that way, Jennifer bumping her lame leg against Bell's haunches, and I followed my daughter and her mother and the dogs out.

The park was a series of block-long rectangles, a parkway really, edged by tree-shaded streets and rows of old houses. A gravel trail wound through the first one, among shrubs and thick old oaks, then broadened into a hard dirt pathway that dropped gently into an open meadow, which we entered, Jennifer ahead of us, the dogs running away from her, then returning.

The second park was meadow only, encircled by a cinder jogging path, a few runners in the distance. I saw Jennifer reach down for a stick, then stiffen for a moment when she rose. Two boys were throwing a Frisbee, off at the park's end. She threw the stick, and Bob and Bell rushed off, their tails wagging. Bell returned with it, head high, Bob banging his long nose against her muzzle. I turned and looked at Carol.

"Does she know them?"

"Oh, no, I don't think so. Her school's on the other side of town. It's just boys, you know." She smiled. "Can you remember when you were fifteen?"

I wasn't sure I could. I saw the smooth, hard muscles in her neck as she threw the stick again. I didn't think I'd ever looked at an adolescent girl so closely, not in this way at least. She had narrow hips, no woman's rise there yet, but I could see her small breasts bob as the stick came up, and caught myself imagining her armpit: would there be any hair there yet, would it be as blond as mine?

I remembered the foreign but sweet smell of my mother's perfume, a night when my parents were going out. They were dressed to the nines, as my father put it, so formal in fact that they seemed like visitors in the house, just leaving after some pleasant invited evening. My mother had kissed me, once on each cheek. She'd giggled, then kissed me full on the mouth in the way she had when I was a little boy, and in that mix of slightly comic acting, given my age, her perfume and the last kiss—she'd put her hand on my head—I'd lurched away from her, then seen that moment of concern in her eyes replaced by a certain recognition: that I was getting to be a man, was getting too old for that. I think we saw it at the same time in each other's eyes. I'd blushed and turned away. Then my father had reached out to shake my hand, and we were all laughing. I was fifteen. They were going to the theater, a play my mother had starred in many years before, Eugene O'Neill, I think. She'd played yet another young woman. I'd seen a picture of her in an album. She was dressed in a similar way, I think, and the smell of her perfume seemed to come to me from another time, musty, the way the boxes of old photos and clippings smelled when we sat on the couch beside each other and opened them. I'd hear her sweet, girlish voice, then

36   TOBY OLSON

feel her breath upon my cheek as she'd told her stories. I'd said, *Good-bye, please come again,* and they'd waved and nodded as they'd closed the door.

We'd stopped walking. Jennifer was throwing the stick, clapping for the dogs. I thought I saw the boys look over at us, but they were a long way off and I couldn't be sure. One of them missed an easy catch and the Frisbee skidded passed him across the grass.

"I can remember *that,*" I said, and Carol smiled. "But *you'd* be the one in this case."

"I should have been," she said. "I've tried to give her something different from that."

"Sweeter?"

"Not exactly. Just more conventional."

"Is that possible?" I asked.

"Oh, I don't know. But look at her."

The dogs were at her legs now, jumping up. She held the stick at her cheek, then faked a throw. They didn't go for it. She shook her short hair, laughing, speaking to them, then hopped back, her limp far less pronounced now that she was engaged and away from me. The dogs nipped at her knees. I wondered if there were some right way to grow up, some measure in another of one's own experience, then recognized it was a father's way to wonder. At least I thought so, but felt foolish, a know-nothing, which I was.

"How long has she known?" I asked. Carol was still watching her, in what I thought was a mother's way to do that.

"From very early on," she said. "She had no father, after all, before I married. I told her the first time she asked."

"What, exactly?"

"The truth, of course. There wasn't much of it. That you were probably alive somewhere. That you'd been okay."

"And that's it?" I said.

"Yes. And it was only after he died that she began to get ideas, to ask questions."

"And why didn't you tell *me?*" I said. "When she was born. You could have found me."

"It was none of your business, I felt, in the beginning. Then, by the time I had second thoughts, she was too old for that. To have your rooting into her life, I mean. Not unless it was her idea. But do you wish I had? Told you, I mean? Would you really have wanted that?"

"I don't know," I said.

"Well, when you figure it out, you can let me know and get angry about it."

"So there's really nothing for me to fill in, I guess. About us, that is."

"That's right. But you better damn well be fucking careful with her. There's that. And you better take me very seriously." Her anger rose up, impenetrable between us, and I knew I could say nothing at all right then to remove it.

It was later, at the mall, that Jennifer and I began to talk. She'd changed again, this time into a skirt and loafers, a loose paisley blouse. She'd brushed her hair, put on another bracelet, and I could smell the soap she'd washed her face with, lavender, I thought.

The mall was large, broad interior walkways lined with stores, benches against huge wooden planters, escalators and a second-level terrace, the two stories above us open to a glass sky.

Our shopping organized our trip. Jennifer was selective about the tents. She'd been to a rough, outdoorsy camp, "when I was a child," she said, and she knew about such things, ones easy to assemble, roomy and waterproof. We bought sleeping bags, a Coleman stove, various cooking utensils, canteens, and in another store got slickers, swimming suits, even a couple of beach chairs. We carried it all out to my car, laughing as we stumbled awkwardly, then returned, found a bookstore, and bought a road atlas. We'd have three weeks together, maybe a little more. That was the plan, to have her back with Carol by the first of August at the latest.

TOBY OLSON

"Let's eat," I said. "Where should we eat?"

"It's all junk food here," Jennifer said disapprovingly, then laughed. "But, what the hell," she winked a little shyly. "There's a Hofbrau, that's something."

"Okay," I said. "We need a table. We can check the map."

She touched me for the first time then, on the arm.

"But not yet. I have a surprise." She tugged at my sleeve. "Come on."

It was a diving shop; rather incredible, I thought, that there should be one here, in this mall in the Midwest. It was something she knew little about, though she'd had those high school classes and was interested, or at least wanted to hear me talk about things.

A young man who knew nothing but what he'd read in a few brochures waited on us. He addressed himself to me but was clearly trying to impress Jennifer. She stood close, took my arm at times, looked up unblinkingly as I explained tanks and regulators and the use of other paraphernalia. I knew I was showing off, competing with the young man, but Jennifer was not part of our possible triangle. It seemed something like a mild fear that got her close to me. He wasn't really flirting with her, but his presence was a bother, something she didn't know quite how to deal with. Still, she was really listening to the content of what I said. She was getting interested, and soon the young man left us, went to other customers, and I was telling her a diving story, then about my father and that first time, in the bathtub, when he'd shown me how to breath underwater.

"He wasn't really my father," I said.

We were sitting at our table at the Hofbrau. We'd eaten and now had the atlas open between us. I'd pulled my chair over, so I could sit beside her. That scent of lavender had faded. Her finger was tracing an easterly route, but it curled back to her palm when she heard my words.

"Neither was mine," she said.

"The two of us," I said. "Was it hard when he died? I mean, I know it must have been, but how was it?"

I'd forgotten she was only a girl, my daughter, forgotten that sense of appropriateness I knew I'd manufactured as the right way to talk to her, knowing even as I spoke that I had no real sense of what was right, wasn't even sure yet of the circumstance, though I could give names to it. I started to speak about my own father, tried to withdraw the raw question, but she was answering it, saying what I thought I might have said.

"He was not really my father, but I think he wished for children of his own. And then my mother, with me, and though he was older and busy in his work, well, he took time for me. I'd go to his office after school. He'd be reading x-rays, and he'd show me how to do that, white shapes on the film, irregularities. He came home late, mostly, and he needed his time alone and to be with my mother.

"There was one vacation when I didn't go to camp, in winter. We were in the Rockies, Aspen, and he was going to teach us to ski. We had a mountain cabin, and one evening we sat around a fire and talked. He told stories about when he was a boy, my age. I was twelve or so. But then a call came, some emergency, and he had to go back. My mother and I stayed on for a few days, shopping in the town, watching the skiers.

"One evening he didn't come home. There was a call, and then my mother telling me.

"I guess I trusted him. He was never angry. I think I knew, always, what he would do. I missed him at breakfast, for a while, the sound of the car door after dark. When he died there was nothing left to do that hadn't been done between us. How you can love a grandparent? My mother's father? He's dead too now. He was always happy to see me, and there was nothing much for us to figure out together."

She'd leaned back in her chair, and as she spoke it was as if she'd rehearsed it all, was calling the words up out of some place in memory where they were already formed, waiting for some special time, this specific one, when we would have space and time together. She didn't look at me, but back somewhere over my shoulder, and as I listened I felt I was her father, the name only, but ready to be filled up with particulars of relationship. They were still to come, but I was moved to a wish that, after time, when *I* died, she'd have another way of remembrance. It's up to me to get us there, I thought. What a strange desire. Then she lowered her eyes, turned her head slightly, and smiled at me, her face suddenly flushed.

"You're blushing," she said. "Don't you want me to talk this way?"

I touched my face, then reached my hand across the table and squeezed her index finger. Her thumb pressed my nail.

"Jen," I said. "Can I call you that? You can call me Bill."

4.

Our plan was to head north along the western shore of Lake Michigan and into the Upper Peninsula. We'd cross at Sault Sainte Marie, make our slow way to Quebec, then drop down into Maine and drive the Atlantic shoreline as long as we felt like it. We'd be going places neither of us had been, making shared discoveries. I'd be no fatherly guide, at least so far as the outside world went, though I had a thought that we might finish our trip in Philadelphia. I could show her my apartment, that city I'd finished a certain part of my life in. It seemed an empty life right then, the past twenty-three years of it at least.

We left late, near eleven, and Carol stood on the porch, Bell and Bob at her legs, and watched us go. Jen had lugged her own bags out to the car, then had returned and hugged her mother for a long time. I was at the wheel, giving them their moment. Carol released her in a while, and Jen knelt down and kissed each of the dogs, then rose and kissed her mother a last time. I could see the three still standing there, Carol's hand shading her eyes as we drove away.

It was one o'clock by the time we left Racine. We'd decided on a late breakfast and had found a place, a workingman's diner directly across the street from the Navy recruiting station. We sat in a booth at a window, going over the terms of our first day's journey, the map between us, and in a while I saw the sailor, a Chief Petty Officer in his carefully pressed tan uniform, unlock the station door. He looked in both directions down the street, then entered, and in a few moments I saw the lights come on, the neon outlines of those happy sailors standing in the broad windows. Jen caught me looking.

"Oh, it's open!" she said. Our egg leavings were already hardening on our plates.

"That's right," I said. "We'll soon be on the road."

I didn't take her in with me, but left her at the wheel. She had a learner's permit, good only in Wisconsin, and when I'd suggested that she drive, take us at least to the state line, her eyes had brightened.

"I am a good driver," she'd said quite somberly, then caught her own tone, and we both laughed.

"Nevertheless," I said, "I plan to buckle up."

The Chief was a good deal older than I, gray at the temples, and there were five hash marks on his sleeve. He held the thick manila envelope Mrs. Venuti had sent, but he wasn't handing it over yet.

"Very few come in," he said. "It gets boring, you know. But it's almost like civilian life. My wife is here, my kids grown up and gone."

"Will you stay in?"

"Just for a little while more. I mean, what's on the outside?"

"I can't tell yet," I said. "I just got there. That's my daughter out in the car. We're going on a trip."

He seemed to hear me, the slightly gratuitous statement and the gentle urge in it.

"Well, okay," he said, handing the envelope over. "Any time. I'll be right here. Have a good vacation."

We skirted Milwaukee, then drove east and up the lakeshore as far as Two Rivers, where we headed northwest to Green Bay. It was still too early for many tourists, and though we passed through lakeshore towns, traffic was sparse and we made good time. After Green Bay, the air changed.

"It's tougher, somehow," Jen said. "Maybe a little harder?"

TOBY OLSON

Beyond towns and into countryside, she drove with her right wrist at the wheel, her hand dangling down. The way her mother does, I thought.

We could have crossed into Michigan at Marinette, but I suggested that we head a little west again. We could stay in Wisconsin for a while and she could keep driving, something she was clearly finding pleasure in, taking her father on a trip.

We weren't talking very much at all, but I don't think she minded that. I know I didn't. Silence seemed our luxury. We had a good long way to go together, plenty of time for everything.

Dusk was coming on when I took the wheel and we crossed over at Niagara. We'd decided on Bark River, only another forty miles or so, but we kept to back roads, drove slowly through thick forests, past cold-looking lakes and small villages, and by the time we'd found a place and had settled in it was seven-thirty and getting dark.

"There," she'd said, and I'd slowed and turned in, a half-moon of cabins at the shoreline of a small lake. It was a fishing resort, a few cars with roof racks holding poles and other gear. We'd gotten a cabin, two bedrooms and a small kitchen, dark knotty pine walls and furniture. Carol had packed food for us, a lunch we hadn't eaten, and we sat on the cabin's porch facing the lake, munching and watching the half-moon rise and shimmer on the dark water.

"To our first day," she said, lifting her Coke can. I clicked mine against hers, then watched her take a big bite from her sandwich and tilt the can for a deep drink. A curl of hair touched into her ear, and she shook her head against the tickle. Then she settled deep into her canvas chair, her feet up on another. I was about to speak, to tell her something about my life, I thought, or ask something about hers. But then she lifted her soda can, held its side against her opening lips, stifling a yawn.

"I'm *so* tired!" she said.

I saw her to bed awkwardly. She'd taken the back bedroom, a window looking out on a thick stand of pine. I stood in the room with her. Her small suitcase was open on the bed, cosmetics bag on the crude pine table, and she was hanging a dress in the closet, the only dress she'd brought along. "In case," she said, then looked back over her shoulder to see me standing there near the room's center, hands hanging down, waiting for something. To tuck her in? I thought. Sweat pants and a long white T-shirt lay on the bed beside the open case. Well, good night then; see you in the morning; sleep well: something like that.

Then I left her, closing the door behind me, and stood in the small kitchenette, drew a glass of water from the tap, then moved to the center of the narrow living room that faced out onto the lake. I glanced at her closed door, then around the room at the dark furniture. I don't know how long I stood there, hearing the muffled sounds of her movement, watching the line of light seeping out under her door. But then the door opened and she came out, and when I turned to face her, I felt a stiffness in my legs and knew I'd been standing still there for a long time.

She was barefoot, wearing the baggy sweatpants and the long white T-shirt, and her head was tilted and down slightly, a faint smile on her face as she came to me. She stopped short, stumbled just a bit as her upper body continued to lean my way, and when she touched my arm she was bent a little awkwardly at the waist. I could smell the Ivory soap. Her cheeks were rosy, fresh scrubbed. She squeezed my arm then and kissed me on the cheek. I hadn't shaved, and I drew back, then lifted my hand and touched her near the ear and kissed her too.

"Our first day's over," she said. "Thanks for letting me drive so long." She giggled then, just a brief trill. "Good night, Bill."

I sat out on the open porch in one of the canvas chairs. There was a yellow bug light above the door, dim, but strong enough to see by. I'd fixed a bourbon. There'd been no ice in the small freezer, but the tap water was cold. And the night was pleasantly cool too. A light breeze moved in the pines, and above that almost subliminal whisper I heard occasional night birds and once the sharp cry of a loon. Jennifer slept, and I was the waking guard of our new life together, feeling that I dare not sleep, for a while at least, that I must hold the past two days for us in clear memory and not the vicissitudes of possible dreaming.

The half-moon hung out over the lake, brightly visible below the porch eaves, and a broad wash glimmered like a pathway from the lake's center to the still shoreline just a few yards beyond the steps. My drink rested on a small log table at my elbow, and beside it was the thick manila envelope Mrs. Venuti had sent ahead to Racine. I though I'd better call her soon, though I knew there'd be little mail from now on. The entanglements of my life in the Navy were over, and I'd not yet started another life, though maybe I was on my way to doing that. Would mail be a good measure? There was Aaron and Beverly now, and I could write something to Carol. Time too that I'd probably be writing to Jennifer, but I didn't want to think about that just yet.

The envelope contained a few bill receipts, gas, electric, and telephone, and a half-dozen advertising flyers—she'd sent the fourth class along as well. A bank statement, something from a hotel in the Netherlands Antilles, room rates and amenities, the windward island of Bonaire, and a thin catalog from the dive shop in Philadelphia. The last were three identical looking letters stamped with the Navy's official seal, two postmarked in Philadelphia, the third, oddly, from Corpus Christi. I put that aside and opened the other two. One contained information about medical benefits, ways to continue with them now that I was retired; in the other was a form letter invitation to join the NCO club at the Naval Yard. They had a retiree's rate, a party every year.

When I opened the Corpus letter, I found another one inside, a rather battered envelope, smaller than legal size, with my name and address typed in. The letter had been mailed to Corpus, and neither my rank nor rate was listed. I checked the postmark, a little shocked to see that it had been sent from El Monte, California, over a year ago. There was a small stapled tab over the return address, a list of printed notes with little boxes to the right, a check mark in the one beside *damaged in transit*. Though the letter was smudged, there was really nothing wrong with it, and I thought they'd gotten the wrong box and should have checked *lost in the mail*. I lifted the tab. The return was a street address only: a number, then Slaughter Avenue. The typing was uneven, an old manual machine. I recognized the street, and when I opened the thing I wasn't surprised to see the place's name rubber-stamped at the top of the brief note. The date heading was April of '79. I had two years left of what I'd paid ahead on the storage fee. That would be refunded. The place was coming down. There'd be a new shopping center there. I had a year to make other arrangements. They couldn't be responsible for things left in storage after that. I lifted the note up higher in the dim light, reached to the table for my drink. Jennifer's birthday was Thursday, the third of July. Tomorrow was Sunday, June twenty-ninth, the deadline date in the letter.

I could see my father's boxes, the side of the building gaping open. I read the letter again. The typed-in name with the signature above it had no title designation below, but there was a phone number under the stamped-in address at the top. I got up, still holding the letter in my fingers, and went to the porch rail. A thin cloud had drifted in over the lake, veiling the half-moon. The shimmering pathway was gone now, but the moon's shape and solidity were still apparent behind that misty curtain, and the whole of the lake now reflected a dull shine. Most of it did at least. The dark shapes of the trees I'd seen on the other side were gone now, and there was only a darkness at the end of my vision. Well, I thought, she's never been to California. I lifted my arm and looked at my watch. Ten-thirty. Then I went down the porch steps, still holding the letter and my drink, and walked in the dark to where I'd seen the pay phone beside the lodge, and called Carol.

TOBY OLSON

5.

My father liked to go to estate sales, for "research," he would say. Mostly they were subdued and quiet affairs, prices attached to furniture and carpets, tables thick with small personal objects, to be haggled about gently.

My parents had little money and our house was small and full. It held the things my father had gathered before their marriage, my mother's memorabilia, and the few new pieces of furniture they'd purchased when I'd come along.

The garage was for my father's stuff, his file boxes and those pieces of machinery, odd and often indistinguishable, that he'd found discarded or bought for close to nothing at dingy shops or going-out-of-business sales. We needed nothing, but my father was drawn to gathering, and though for years my mother refused to go along, I'd caught his interest. This had pleased him, and he would rub his hands together, smile at me, and say, "Let's go!"

Mostly we'd go to Hollywood, Silverlake, at times up into the San Gabriels. He'd have checked the paper, looking for large old places. I was young then, maybe eight or ten, and those running the sales would often look askance as I entered the crowded rooms. My father would tell them it was okay, okay, I was experienced; I wouldn't break anything. He'd strike up a conversation then, and if the salesman or woman was a remnant of the family, he'd get involved with them, learning what he could of the history of the place and people. Maybe he'd come out with some faded documents, a few photographs, maybe nothing. When those running the show were only brokers, he'd stay with them long enough to get entrance to the basement or the attic. Then he'd be gone for a long time, and I was left to wander the many floors and rooms, to study the heavy furniture and the numerous objects that had been taken from dark drawers and placed thickly on table and dresser tops. I'd shop for my mother, and when we'd get back, the trunk stuffed with magazines and boxes, I'd present her with a fan, a piece of lace, or an old postcard, things she had little use for, but always accepted with a smile and a kiss.

Once we were in West Hollywood, a good distance from home. The house was large and sprawling, and I could see the attentive pleasure in my father's quick strides as he walked up the gently curving drive in front of me. His limp was more pronounced when he was in a hurry, as if he'd forgotten he had one, was too concerned with where he was headed to mask it in any way. When he got to the open door, he didn't hesitate, and when we were inside he didn't look for the sellers, but went quickly through the foyer, into the living room, then up the curving, hanging staircase to the second floor. He'd spoken not a word to me, hadn't reassured anyone about my presence, and I was left standing stiffly at the room's center, feeling awkward and small among the adults, who moved slowly, touching furniture and lamps and checking price tags on curios. But he was back in only a few moments. I saw his broad smile as he limped down the stairs, and when he reached me he took my arm. "Let's get your mother," he said, and then we were out of there, driving at a good clip, heading for home.

When we got back, he took my mother into their bedroom. I heard her muffled laughter from beyond the door, drawers opening, and their footsteps as they moved around. He'd asked me to wait. "Would you sit here for a little while, Billy? We'll all be going out again soon."

TOBY OLSON

When they returned they were dressed as if for an evening on the town. My father had replaced his casual clothing with a dark suit and tie and a white handkerchief that peeked out of his jacket pocket and was half-covered by the cape that draped his shoulders, black on the outside, but rich purple where it curled out along his arm. He held the edges with his fingers, opened it slightly when he saw me looking at him from my chair, then limped slowly around in a circle.

My mother wore a long, knit dress, dark also. It fit tight at the neck, clung to her body, and I remember the soft curve of her belly, the place at her calf where the dress ended and her white stocking began. Her shoes were red, shiny as the thick silver necklace that hung down between the two soft mounds of her small breasts. She had her hair up, stuck there dramatically with a large red comb, and her lips were bright red also.

They stood there for me, turning, presenting themselves. At least it seemed that way then, but I think now it was each other they were turning for, my father with knowledge in his eyes, my mother once again the ingenue, ready to be guided bright-eyed into some new experience.

"Shouldn't I dress up too?"

I'm not sure that's exactly what I said, but I remember their laughter, my father dramatically sweeping me up out of the chair with a broad gesture. Then we were driving, I in the backseat now, my mother sitting close to my father up front.

It was the same house, the one they had arrived at separately only a week after their first meeting, a theater party, after yet another opening. And it had been an opening for them too. My father, though he had quickly "researched" her, knew where she lived and what the course of her days was like, had been shyly reluctant to call.

"I'm not sure I would have."

"But . . . maybe?"

My mother would look over at him with her eyes lowered, the

ingenue, when he brought it up. It was a thing between them, a little joke to relieve any sternness in the air, and it always worked.

They stood then among the others in the living room, those who when they entered had glanced at them curiously. But this was Hollywood. Nothing all that odd. And in a while they moved into other rooms. I trailed them, watched them fold into postures beside tables and chairs, look at each other and speak in intimate ways, words I couldn't hear and didn't try to hear, satisfied with their reenactment. I somehow knew it was that, not that name, but simply a display of something in their lives before I'd come to them or they'd found me and brought me away with them. It was history. It felt like my own. At least a kind of centering of who I was, which was being with them, living that way.

I saw the curves of fine modern tables and mirrors, vine-twisted wrought iron floor lamps, those objects gathered as always on dressers, but all this only as reflected in their brief tableaus, taken to them as enlivened furniture, specific reference in events and arrangements, a slowly structured plan for a beginning between them, tentative at first, but growing sure as time passed, glasses were brought to lips, common associations discovered.

Once they actually did raise glasses, thick crystal champagne tulips, a mime of drinking. They were standing in a room that had been a library, the low shelves empty of books now and nothing but a rich geometric carpet over the parquet floor. There was a fireplace at the end, elongated figures of naked white marble women in relief to either side, holding up the mantle where my father leaned, his right arm at the edge. My mother stood back from the mantle a little, hip slung, the curves of her body close to that of the marble women beside her. She held her right elbow in her left hand, that arm crossing her stomach, held her tulip glass between finger and thumb at the stem. My father was leaning slightly forward at the waist, bright-eyed, telling her things. His cape hung down rakishly from his left shoulder.

TOBY OLSON

I stood at the doorway watching them, and in a while I recognized that I had seen them this way before, but in a photograph, that one taken in the lobby of the theater at their first meeting. Then I recognized that they were wearing the same things, the same dress and suit, and that my mother's bright red shoes were probably the same also, though in the photograph they had appeared black. Had he worn the cape? I couldn't remember, though I had looked at the photo often over the years. But they stood there in the same way, talking, getting thoroughly interested in one another, and what at first was acting soon became real again, as it had been years before.

I stood and watched them for a long time, beginning in a while to feel that they had forgotten about me, totally, not just my being there then, but my place in their life with them. I don't think I shuffled my feet or made another movement, but I can't be sure. Anyway, just as I began to feel a certain vague anxiety rise up as slow heat in my cheeks, my mother lowered her tulip glass, reached out with it, and touched my father's hand where it hung down at the mantle's edge. She nodded, almost imperceptibly, and they both turned toward me. They were grinning, and my father lifted the edge of his cape, revealing that rich purple underside, bowed deeply in my directing, then called out my name. "Billy," he said. "Isn't your mother beautiful? This is the exact place where I got her."

"I don't see it," Jennifer said, as she held up the photo.

She was sitting on one of the cartons, a large wooden one my father had hammered together from scrap, and I was perched on another, a good distance from her near the center of the warehouse loft. Ten or more boxes sat askew in a rough circle around the one I occupied, dull, smog-filtered sun washing across them and lighting dust motes in the air and on the stained wooden floor. They'd ripped out the wide windows and roof supports, a good ten feet of the roof itself, but the bottom third of the wall was still there.

I could see out into the broad rectangle of open air for a good distance, out over Slaughter Avenue, three floors below. The low buildings at the town center in El Monte were vaguely smudged outlines far off, but there was little between them now and where we were, nothing I could identify from when I'd lived here, ridden my bike along Slaughter, then up Valley Boulevard to school. Nothing now but empty fields and rubble, new streets and curbing, a few leveled plots where the shopping mall would grow. The sky was thick with a smoky haze, and my eyes burned.

"Bring it over here," I said, voice echoing off the blank back wall, and Jennifer got to her feet. She was wearing baggy shorts, sneakers, and a loose yellow T-shirt, ready for California, though there was a hint of coolness in the air. We'd had to be careful coming up the ladders. The staircases were gone, the large open elevators half dismantled, and the crane that would soon get down to the serious work of demolition was ready at the back side of the building. It was Tuesday, near noon, only a couple of days until Jen's sixteenth birthday.

Carol had started to argue, then had backed off. I could almost hear her mind clicking. She would give her this, reluctantly, though she insisted that Jennifer call before we left.

"*If* we leave," I'd said, standing in the glass phone booth beside the lodge. Her voice was distant, though she was only a state away. "I have to try to call the place, tomorrow."

"Sunday?"

"Nothing else I can do," I said. "I won't mention anything, not until I find out. Get her hopes up, if she has any."

"She will," Carol said. "California, after all."

I'd called the next morning, while we were eating breakfast at the lodge. It was ten o'clock, eight in California. Early, but the woman sounded wide awake when she answered.

"What would you have done otherwise?" I remember asking her.

TOBY OLSON

She hadn't known. Her father had died, and she'd inherited the building two years ago. Then the plan for the shopping mall had been proposed and she'd done the work of contacting the storage tenants herself. Most had been local, and she'd found the others without much difficulty. I was the only one who hadn't responded. She lived in Pasadena, didn't think she'd ever even been to El Monte, but for the one time she'd gone to see the building after her father had died, and even then she hadn't gone in. I though I had a contract somewhere, back in Philadelphia, but I wasn't sure.

On the way back to the table, I had second thoughts. Surely I could call someone, get the thing done long distance. It might be a bit of a hassle—the woman hadn't sounded too responsible—but it could be accomplished. There was more to it, though, and even the idea of taking Jennifer far away, a real surprise for her in our travel, wasn't it. It was those things in storage, the life of my mother and father and of myself there. I wanted *that* for Jen, urged onward in this new possibility by our still tentative being together.

I'd told her a few stories about myself at her age. And it was, I was coming to see, my only vivid life, that one out there in California. Tales I'd told about my time in the Navy had been no more than anecdotes. There had been no matrix connecting them, and the more I'd felt that lack, and had searched for it, the more disconnected from that past I'd begun to feel. There was nothing I could find there from which to make some larger story, the story of my life? I was wondering what I'd done for those twenty years and more. Where had the people been? Only in story, set aside from any past or future. Even with Carol, her mother, it had been that way. We'd each moved on, cut off from the other completely, even after such intensity.

We spent Sunday at Bark River getting ready, I on the phone, Jen repacking her things in the car trunk, writing a few letters.

"You know," she said, while we were eating sandwiches in our cabin in the early afternoon, "I thought I'd have a *lot* of letters to write, about California. But there's only these three, girls at school."

Did she wish there was a boy?

The arrangements had taken a while, most of the day in fact. I called Carol again and told her I'd be in touch once we got west and settled in. Jennifer would call her from O'Hare; we had a long lay-over there. She took in the information without much comment.

"Carol," I said, "it's okay. I'll take good care of her. Tomorrow you can talk with her. You'll have a long time."

"Okay, okay. But, do I know you?"

"I don't know that," I said. "But you can trust me."

"I fucking well better be able to," she said. "And there's one other thing. I didn't think to mention it before. But now."

"What is it?" I said.

"She sleepwalks. Once in a while."

I felt a touch of anxiety that immediately seems unreasonable.

"What would I do?"

"There's nothing much to do. Just walk her around. Don't try to wake her too quickly. It won't last. It probably won't happen at all. It's just an occasional thing."

I hung up, then lifted the phone again and called Mrs. Venuti in Philadelphia, asked her to just hold onto the mail. I'd call again from the West Coast, once I was settled somewhere.

Both Jen and I felt some distaste at the idea of driving back the way we'd come.

"We've just started!" Jen said.

So we decided on Iron Mountain, and I managed to line up a flight from there, a small plane to Chicago, then connections from there to Los Angeles where there'd be a rental car waiting. I'd leave my own car in Iron Mountain, had found a place close to the air-port, long-term parking at a gas station, open twenty-four hours every day, they'd assured me. I was concerned about the new car, but when I went over all the gear in the trunk I realized there really wasn't much, mostly the camping stuff and the clothing we'd leave behind. We could outfit ourself again in California. "We'll be traveling light," I said, and Jen's eyes lit up at the idea.

"Like vagabonds!"

She crossed the dusty floor to where I sat and turned the picture for me. He wasn't wearing the cape, but his suit and my mother's dress were the same as I remembered.

"You're right," I said. "Did you find anything else?"

I'd picked the box out right away, though I didn't remember the large B I'd drawn on the side and top. It was stuff of my parents' that had been most precious to me, at least when I'd packed it, right after their deaths. It was smaller than I remembered, but chockfull, and when I'd picked it out for her and we'd opened it, I'd seen the felt folds tucked in at the side, my mother's jewelry. I hadn't opened them, but had handed them over to Jen, saying she could have what she wanted, trying for some reason to soften the possible drama of the gift.

"And the box too? Can I look through that?"

We'd gotten there early and had a good three hours before the movers were due to arrive. When I'd seen the state of the place and the steep ladders, I'd called them and made arrangements for ropes and pulleys. The new storage situation was in La Puente, only a few miles away, one of those long metal buildings I guessed, recognizing the name as part of a chain. The cost was reasonable, but I'd taken a month only. I thought that before we left California I'd find something else.

I'd counted the boxes. All sixty-two were there, and none seemed seriously damaged. Most of them had my father's markings on the sides, numbered lists of what they contained. It had been up to me to pack the "active" materials, papers he'd kept in two battered file cabinets beside his heavy workbench in the garage. There had been a time he'd kept the car in there, but not in my memory. He'd closed the garage door off, built broad shelves from floor to ceiling. That's where the boxes had been stacked. I'd left Jen alone with the special one and began looking through the others, each yielding pieces of memory or small surprises, areas into which my father had entered that I hadn't know about or had forgotten. The five I'd packed up after they died had no writing on the sides, only large check marks. I'd had wits enough to do that, though I remembered nothing of what was in them. I'd been pretty numb in those few days I'd spent at the house, mechanically busy with arrangements for the disposition of things and for the funeral. There'd been no hitch, nothing to keep me there longer, no edgy event that burned things into my memory. It was all over too quickly, and before I knew it I was underwater again, off the coast of Padre Island in Corpus Christi.

After I'd finished checking the writing on most of the boxes, dipping into the contents of ones that held some interest, I got to those last five and went through them with more care. I'd moved the others over closer to the ladder, and Jen had glanced up from her lap, where she had the jewelry folds open. Colors sparkled on her thighs.

"Won't the movers take care of that?"

"Yes," I said. "Did you find anything?"

"These things," she said. "They're beautiful!"

"You could try them on."

"Should I?"

"Well, they're yours now," I said.

I looked away. I wasn't really sure I wanted to give them to her, and I didn't want her to see my hesitation. I heard the dull, heavy click of a chain, a rustle of shifting links.

The sun was reaching its zenith, and the smoky light coming in at the ripped-away wall was softer now. I could see Jen's shadow,

TOBY OLSON

long and thin, like a wind compass needle, shifting back and forth off center across the floor.

The five boxes held stories of natural disasters, and it soon became clear that my father's study of volcanos, floods, hurricanes, and fires was background material to a closer focus, on earthquakes, their history, prediction, and aftermath, all specific to California. One full box contained material on the San Andreas and other faults. He'd taken that study back to plate shifts and even physics, a few very technical articles that were covered with his marginal notes. There was a thick folder on civil defense, a rough L.A. county map of fallout shelters and evacuation routes, and I remembered crawling under my desk in grammar school, the siren's sound and the principal's measured voice through that tinny speaker.

My father had been clearly focused on the business at hand, and the voluminous information he'd gathered suggested he'd been at it for a long while. But nothing suggested an experiment, though he'd always been one for such things, had often tested out what he read in some practice.

I was working my way through the last box, where his dated sheets of notes held material gathered only weeks before his death, when I came upon a thin manila folder that seemed misfiled. It contained information about a disaster, but a very local and personal one, photographs, news clips, and two follow-up articles about the death of a woman by drowning. What first drew my eye was the place, Laguna Beach. I'd made a call there the night before from our motel in Pasadena, had lined up a set of rooms at a resort hotel on the beach. It would be Jen's first chance at the Pacific Ocean. Three days there, including her birthday, then we'd head down to San Diego and into Mexico.

I was fingering through the file, looking at the photographs and the page of numbered notes my father had written in his small, careful hand, when I heard the sound of a motor coming from the street below us. When I looked up, Jen was crossing the room, smiling and holding out a handful of magazines and brochures. I could see the cover of one hanging down, that view of a high mountain lake somewhere in Mexico. I remembered sitting beside my father, his quiet voice as we turned the pages, the thrill of those photos of divers in deep, murky water. They held up encrusted pots and shards, those ancient artifacts cast into the lake centuries before as offerings to the gods. I'd wanted to be there. Even those thoughts of ancient retribution, something ready and waiting below the tips of the divers' flippers, drew me. And my father knew this, would put his hand on my knee, speak of technical things, aspects of gear, depth gauges, weight belts, and buoyancy.

I closed the file and got to my feet. Jen heard the motor too. "Oh," she said, lowering the papers. I noticed the rings on her fingers, the one silver earring hanging down from her lobe. She'd picked out my mother's best pair, those she often wore on evenings when they were going someplace special, an opening or the reprise of a play my mother had acted in years before. "Can this be possible?" my father would always say when she presented herself to us.

He'd have dressed early and would be sitting in the living room beside me. We'd talk about the play, and he'd often speak of my mother's career as if she were a star still, someone we were fortunate to know. We'd speak as I knew adults did, even when I was quite young, and there was never a hint of irony in my father's tone.

Then, in a while, my mother would come out and turn in the middle of the room for us, and he would say that, "Can this be possible? That I have won such a beauty?"

I wondered where the other earring was. Jen saw me looking, then lifted her free hand and opened her palm. The earring dangled down over the pad of her thumb.

We crossed the room to where the open box was, and after she'd slipped the magazines and brochures back among the other files, she took the jewelry off and rolled it back into the folds. I carried that one thin file, and when she'd finished I slipped it down

TOBY OLSON

beside the jewelry at the end of the box. We could hear the movers rigging up their pulleys and hoists, and we went together to the end of the room, where the steep ladders began. I climbed over the lip where the floor ended, and Jen pushed the box to the edge, tilting it down to me when I was ready.

"Be careful," I said, looking up at her. "Both hands on the rungs. And don't look down."

"Oh, Bill!" she said.

6.

"Tall and thin. Not much of a chin. And he would have asked a lot of questions."

"Around '64, you say?"

"No. Exactly then. Right after the drowning, about a week or so."

"*That* was something," he said. "Correcting that. Everyone assumed she was a hippie-type, or that one did it. We must have had about ten or so. Pathetic creatures. You should see the letters we got. That we were commies? This was a stupid place back then. San Clemente's just down the coast, you know."

"And he had a limp."

"Right. But we're talking fifteen years!"

"More," I said.

"Okay. He would have had to sign for them. What was the name again?"

"Andrew," I said. "Andrew Stewart."

He got up and lifted a section of the counter and went through the doorway to a back room. I turned in the swivel chair and looked out the windows to the Pacific Coast Highway, really no more than a busy town street as it passed through Laguna Beach. The newspaper office was on the ocean side, in a building that had once been a store of some kind, but very long ago, and the tall display windows gave me a broad view. I could see a restaurant, a surf shop beside it, and an expensive-looking clothing store. Beach goers crossed at the corner, heading down to one of the only public entrances to Main Beach.

Jen would be out there now, sitting on a blanket or in one of the beach chairs the hotel provided. We'd had a little argument, our first, that had started out as joking. She'd given me her "Oh, Bill!" when I'd insisted that she not go into the water until I got there. It was hot and calm, the surf was down, and she'd pointed out her hotel window to show me. The beach was pretty crowded. People, mostly kids, were playing in the water, and a few surfers sat on swells a good distance out, sunning themselves, no rides available. It had gotten to the point where I thought she might stamp her foot, and she must have seen my eyes widen at her clearly childish behavior. She laughed then, pulling herself up into a semblance of adult dignity, and agreed to wait.

The way she'd acted had unsettled me. In my awkwardness, I'd been treating her as an equal, which in a way she was. But she was also a child, something I knew but had not seen in her behavior, and I'd felt a rush of unspecifiable responsibility. It had lasted only a moment, but its remnant was still with me. I thought I could trust her, though, that she'd wait for me. Then we'd go swimming together, father and daughter, very near the place where the woman drowned, over fifteen years ago.

Her name was Susan Rennert. She was twenty-six years old and had been working for a year as a chambermaid at one of the fancier hotels along the beach. She had a California driver's license but no car, a social security card, and a few dollars in the canvas purse that was still clutched in her hand when the tide washed her up, if she did wash up.

She lived at the hotel itself in a basement room, a small and primitive place, one room only, a hot plate and the use of a toilet and stall shower down the hall. Nothing odd about that. Laguna was expensive, even then, and that was part of the deal, free rent and leftover dinner food late in the evening. There were a number of rooms down there and other chambermaids living in them.

In her room they'd found very little, some clothing and a clean uniform, the usual cosmetics and a small box containing costume

TOBY OLSON

jewelry and a few pens, and when they'd spoken to her fellow workers, most of them Mexican, they'd learned little more. One of the articles quoted some women to the effect that they'd noticed nothing, she was a private type, but didn't seem depressed, there was no boyfriend, and no one knew anything about her past. None of them had been there very long. She was older than most, efficient, but reticent. She knew how to make a bed quickly, how to clean, but none of them socialized with her. She'd been a good swimmer and had taken her solitary pleasure in that way.

For a few weeks she'd become a celebrity, a mystery woman, and there were questions about her death. It was not evidence, but the lack of it. Nothing suggested suicide, but neither did they have anything that pointed to foul play. The police ran her fingerprints, checked the license and social security card. She'd been born near San Diego, in Encinitas, but her parents seemed to have left there shortly after her birth. At least there was no trace of them. Nor were there any relatives listed in the area.

There was just one thing, the sheet, and I think I might have passed over it as insignificant had I not found it listed on my father's page of notes: "The question of the sheet." It was well down in his list, but he'd pushed hard with the pencil writing those words, and the next entry read "Write letter to Billy."

The sheet was mentioned in the paper. It had been found in the surf a short distance down the beach from where she'd drown, right in front of the hotel itself, and the blood that stained it had not been washed completely away. It was a hotel sheet, at least the same brand, for a double bed, but even before the news of it had made the papers, the police had checked it out.

There'd been no blood on her, the type on the sheet was different, and the medical examination proved anyway that she'd not had her period. Nor was there any evidence of something else, someone injured in the hotel or any of the others along the beach. Nothing from the town either, and the police had checked along the coast and inland for a good distance. It was mentioned in the follow-up articles, but as a curiosity only, a bit of titillation. The police continued to investigate, but the sheet seemed to have nothing at all to do with her.

In the photograph, it was as if she had just reclined there, face down, in a shallow and still pool contained between an offshore sandbar and the wash near the summer berm. Her dress was thin and light yellow, and it formed the shape of a perfect bell, her thin legs together below it, like a clapper, her splayed feet in dark shoes. Her hair was as light as her dress was, and long, and it formed a crescent on the water around her small head, the scalp visible, and where her hair ended there was no discernible line, only a slight color change, a darkening, and at the end of the fingers of her left hand, to shoreside—her arms floating out in the shape of crucifixion—there was a long curl of kelp. It was as if she'd held the end of it, the other licking at the sand, as if it were a ribbon used in dancing, then had let it go, her fingers relaxing, in order to look down those few inches to the bottom, where there might have been something. She'd lost a ring as the salt had shrunk her finger, or in the dance had lost an earring, something, and she was gazing intently down to find it, being very still in order not to stir the water, to bring some veil across her vision. Her right hand clutched the purse, which floated in the shape of a Portuguese man-of-war beyond her knuckles.

It was early morning, dawn. The sand across the beach was softly lit and sparkling, and the sun had reached her shoes. They shone like patent leather, as did the tip of kelp that was drying on the sand beyond the wash. But she and the pool she rested in were still in night's last shadow.

I looked up from her figure, out to the distant sea; swells were rising, a few gulls riding them, and to their left five women stood in uniform, their feet invisible beneath the water. Their uniforms were white, buttoned to the neck, and each had her hair gathered, held in place with pins. Where the inset photo had cut their feet

TOBY OLSON

away were words. They placed her at the left end of the group, a photo one of the chambermaids had come up with; it had been her birthday party, about a month before, and they had gathered close together in sun near the service entrance, the edge of a dumpster visible only a few inches from Susan Rennert's shoulder. The photo had been taken from a good distance, in order to get them all in. Her posture seemed a little stiff, unlike the others, and she was not touching the woman beside her. I could get nothing from her face but that her smile seemed forced, as if she suffered such community and didn't wish to be there.

There was another photo, in one of the follow-up articles, and though she seemed younger and more at ease in it, she was still wearing a service uniform, though a different one, some emblem or other over her breast. Her hair was again gathered, but more neatly here, pulled tightly back, and she or someone had draped the long ponytail over her left shoulder. The light was such that her head appeared like a slick dome, her blonde brows almost invisible, which exaggerated the broad plain of her forehead, hardened it into a semblance of white granite. Her thin nose was a slick promontory, and on either side of it her eyes were milky blue pools. She was not smiling, though her thin lips curled up at the edges. Below them, her chin was tucked back a little, close to the yolk of her dress. Her whole head was down slightly, as if at the moment of flash she'd tried to avoid it. It was her driver's license photo. Susan Rennert, I thought, drawn to her in a way I didn't understand.

I heard a bump behind me, and when I swung back around in the swivel chair, he was lowering the countertop, then moving toward me. He carried a large ledger and dropped it on the desk between us before sitting down. I saw a white marker sticking up from the spine.

"Well, it took a while," he said, his hands flat on the desk to either side of the thin book. "I couldn't find the damn thing. Misfiled."

"Yes," I said.

There was a gleam of sweat on his upper lip, and I saw an oozing high on his brow in what wispy silver hair remained there. Must be close to seventy, I thought. He was slight and very thin, but he sat up straight as he opened the ledger. He wore no glasses, but he had to back up in the chair a little to make out the writing.

"It's hot in there. I don't know why. Doesn't get the sun."

"Ventilation, maybe?"

I was eager for something but didn't want to push it, altogether unsure of where it might lead. I wanted to get it over with, get back to Jen. But I also felt my father vividly again, in those careful notes, his way of beginning something that wouldn't end until it was exhausted, until he'd contained its growing complexity, come to an end with it and gathered it into his life. Into that garage, I thought, and his way of being with my mother and with me.

"Well, he was here all right," the man said. He had a white handkerchief out now and was wiping his brow and head. "But it's curious."

"How do you mean?"

"Well, you came here about the Rennert matter. *That's* curious. It's been so long ago. But he didn't come here about that."

"But he *was* here."

"Yes, yes, no doubt about that. His name's here. Twice in fact. He must have come back. Lucky I found it. It was in those two weeks, the full flush of stories we ran about her, but he must have been after something else. I've got him checking out material on shipping, both commercial and tourist. We used to run the schedules. It was a holdover from when people needed that information. Then it became something quaint and a bit of promotion for the coast along here, that it had a serious history? We quit in the early seventies. It seemed ridiculous to continue. I mean, look at this place. It's all tourists and the rich now. The sea's no more than a plaything."

"What, specifically, was he after, do you think?"

TOBY OLSON

"Oh, well, now there's no way to tell that. We didn't have our morgue microfilmed then, didn't even have a decent Xerox machine. We're just a little town paper. Not the *Times!*"

"Go on," I said.

"Well, he checked out everything we had, a week each side of the Rennert death. I mean, not just what we ran in the paper, but the lists themselves, the ones the shipping lines provided."

"And he took them?"

"*Now* we do. Some things. We have a policy. A little money to cover use of our copy machine. But at that time, he'd have sat over there." He pointed toward the bay windows behind me. "We had a desk. He couldn't take them away, but he could read them, make notes."

There had been no notes, nothing in my father's file of that kind. Only the newspaper clippings and his list of short phrases, things to remember and do. One of the entries had read, "Laguna: check local newspaper morgue." That's what had gotten me there. Others were "Rennert: why Susan?"; "Weather: moon, wind, tides"; "Go over it with Bev again"; "Could it really have been housewares?" Then there were the two that had first gotten my attention, "The question of the sheet" and "Write letter to Billy."

"Do you still have them?"

"We might. Everything's on microfilm now, but when we switched to that we put some things aside. I can easily check. But if they aren't on film, it could take some time."

He was back in a few minutes, shaking his head.

"Okay," I said. "I'll be heading south for a while, but I can come back."

"I'll get on it," he said. "We've got a kid for the summer, from Long Beach State. A good job for her, learning how a paper's morgue can work, used to at least."

7.

I walked along the Pacific Coast Highway to the corner and used the public access path to get down to the beach, then sat on a bench where the concrete met the sand, and took my shoes and socks off. The sea looked calm and clear, and only when I reached the dark and harder sand where the lapping wash receded did I see the kelp bed in the distance, lifted in a brown swell.

The sea was on my right, and beyond the flat open beach the string of resort hotels started, tall and aggressive, each with ascending scallops of hanging balconies facing the water. Ours was the fifth one down, two beyond the one where Susan Rennert had worked as a chambermaid. The beach thinned where the hotels began, and I could see ripples of fabric at the edges of umbrellas in the distance, sun glinting off metal beach chairs, and clusters of people standing together, figures moving away from time to time, heading down to the water.

When I reached our place, I looked for Jen but couldn't find her and felt an edge of anxiety as I scanned the figures around me. I might have been looking right at her; I didn't know her body yet, hadn't seen her in her swim suit. Then I looked over to where the hotel's doorway opened out to the beach and realized it was the wrong place. They looked very much the same, as did the people who had spilled out of them. I moved between blankets and around small enclaves, and when I reached sand in front of the next place, I recognized Jen's yellow T-shirt. It was lifting just a little in the breeze, becoming a flag, then falling down along the oar around which it was tied. The oar was driven upright into the sand, and when I got to it I saw the faint wax writing running down its blade: *Dad—Gone to the room—Jen.*

"You're her father?"

I turned to his voice, having to lift my hand up in the sun. He was tall and fit, as blond as she was, and wore almost nothing, just a thin band of black trunks below his navel. Early twenties, I thought, feeling a tightening in my shoulders. But he was smiling, and he'd taken off the dark glasses that would have guarded his eyes from me. I nodded, started to say something, but he beat me to it.

"I lent her the oar," he said. "We thought the shirt would be good. That you'd know it."

"And the wax?"

"For my kayak," he said. "Over there."

It was turned up in the sand, long, thin, and efficient looking, its prow aiming at the sea.

"Well," he said. "She was feeling the sun."

"Were you swimming?"

"Oh, no!" His smile broadened. "Couldn't get her to go in."

"Right," I said, searching for something appropriate. He shuffled in the sand, then abruptly lifted his arm. I could do nothing but take his hand. His grip was brief but sure, and when I released him he smiled again, then lifted his glasses up and put them on. Then he nodded and turned and headed down to his boat and blanket.

When I got to my room, the door between ours was open, and on the glass table near the balcony sliders was a small wooden bowl of fruit and a full pitcher holding some light-brown liquid. The drapes had been pulled aside so that the pitcher stood in the bright sun, the fruit bowl in shadow.

"So-la-ti," she said. She had heard me and come to the open doorway. She wore the white terry robe the hotel provided and her hair was wet, her face flushed, both from the sun and a good rubbing.

TOBY OLSON

"Hi," I said. "What do you mean?" She'd written "Dad" on the oar blade, a tastefully guarded acknowledgment. Neither of us would speak of it, being tasteful.

"You know, do-re-me-so-la-ti. Solar tee, so-la-ti."

"Oh!" I said.

Her eyes brightened.

"You *don't* know! Mom makes it all the time in summer since I can remember. There were some tea bags here. In my bathroom, with the little pot and packages of coffee?"

"Tell me," I said.

She gathered her robe tight around her and moved into my room and to the table. The robe was too short for her, and I could see the smooth tendons behind her knees as she reached over and adjusted the pitcher, pushing it into the brightest wash of sun.

"Well, it's nothing," she said. "You just use cold tap water, throw in a few bags, then put it in the sun. Takes a couple of hours only, if the sun's hot. It's good because you don't bruise the tea with boiling water. At least that's what mom says. But it *is* good."

I sat on my small balcony, sipping the icy tea and eating a banana. The hotel bags were cheap, processed stuff, with mint added, but the tea tasted fine. I could see the full extent of the kelp bed now. Our rooms were on the sixth floor, high enough so that I'd have to lean over the rail to view the beach. The bed was a good hundred yards wide, extending as far as the eye could see along the shore in both directions, about a quarter mile out. White gulls dotted it, pearls dropped on jade brocade. The sun was still high. The breeze lifted, carrying a faint scent of rotting kelp and something else just under it. I suspected air pollution, but the sky out over the placid sea was clear.

Jen had said she'd dress, then come back, and we could talk about our plans for the evening. I could tell she had some idea or other and was holding onto it, waiting for the right time. It was close to four, just eight hours until her sixteenth birthday. I still had no present for her. I'd been watching and listening, trying to figure out the right thing. I knew I was making too much of it, but I felt that if I were mistaken, got her something of the wrong taste or style or interest, it would mark a distance between us just when we were starting to come to know each other.

I sat for a while longer, waiting for her, then got up and went back into the room and over to her half-open door.

"Jen?" I called out tentatively. No sounds came from the bathroom. I could only hear the distant wash of sea. I waited a moment, then spoke her name again.

"Oh! Bill!" Her voice sounded rusty, distant. "I got fixated! Come in, come in."

I pushed the door open, then saw her standing at the side of her bed, leaning over it slightly, though she'd raised her head up and was smiling wistfully at me. The bed was covered with the magazines and diving brochures she'd found in the box we'd taken from the storage place. She'd opened them, then placed them in rows on the spread, four rows running all the way from the foot to the rise of pillows and up over them too. She'd been careful not to flatten the more delicate spines, and the pages formed waves, sunlight-brightened photographs of this and other oceans and seas.

"Diving," I said softly. "It can be something."

"God, yes!" she said. "Look at this one."

I crossed to the foot of the bed and stood beside her. She was looking down at the slick center spread of a magazine, two butted-together pages, showing a woman in free dive, in a wet suit, her legs scissoring, long hair drifting above her head in a column ending in an opening spray. She wore a mask and snorkel and a weight belt squeezed tight around her waist. Her chin was raised, her back arched slightly, and her arms extended straight out from her shoulders, as if she were the poised figurehead of a sailing ship. Only a few feet below her, tubes and fans of dark coral hills were rising, small luminescent fish swimming in and out of their crevices. Her body shadow draped over the

74   TOBY OLSON

coral a few feet below and in front of her, as if her earthbound skin had leached away, freeing her aquatic dolphin self. And there was another shadow, almost as large as hers, drifting over a sandy reef break ahead. It was that of the giant halibut she perused, and looking up from the shadow apparitions, we could see the two in tandem, her extended fingers only inches from the broad, transparent fan of the fish's tail.

"Do you see in the back?" I said. "Where it's darker? Those are caves. You can barely see them here. The way the light filters. She's a good forty feet down. Not a difficult dive at all. You need wind, but you need to be relaxed too. That way you save air, and energy."

"But how do you know?" Jen said, her breath touching my cheek. "I mean the caves? I can't really make them out."

"That's Cabo San Quintin," I said softly. "Just a little way down in the Baja, below Ensenada. I used to dive there. Sometimes. We can go there."

"Can we?" She was looking down at the woman's body.

"Would you like that? For your birthday?"

"Oh, yes!" she said. "God, yes!"

We decided on dinner in the hotel dining room. I didn't know Laguna much at all, and anyway we thought to save something special for the next day, her birthday, either there or maybe even in Mexico, if we headed out early enough. She'd never been to another country, and I knew we could have a fancy and somewhat exotic feast in Tijuana or below there.

When we had our menus, and even before I'd opened mine, Jen said she thought something light, maybe a salad, and I looked up to catch her eyes lowering to the menu cover.

"Okay," I said. "What's going on?"

She forced her head back up and held my eyes in a steady stare. Hers were watering a little, and I could tell she was uncertain, wanted to look away. She waited a moment, then got it out in resolute and carefully measured words.

"There's a private party down the beach. A cookout. They have one every week, around eight. The food's all there. I've been invited, you too. You met that boy on the beach, Tod? He lent me his oar? He lives down there. The party's at his place. He invited us."

"You mean the older guy?"

"He's not *older*. He's twenty!"

"I doubt that," I said. "And anyway, you're fifteen."

"Just for a few more hours."

Her voice grew plaintive. She was asking me, and like a daughter, and I could still hear my own clipped words, the ridiculous sternness in them. They reeked of jealousy and unearned authority. I wondered if her other father had ever spoken to her in that way, and thought not, was sure her hesitancy and discomfort had in part to do with the newness of the situation. But I couldn't get myself to stop.

"Look," I said. "I've got a responsibility here. You're only sixteen years old. That guy, whatever his name is, is a man."

I was halfway through the words when I heard what I was saying, then managed to lift my brows, elevate and harden my tone into parody. By the time I was finished I'd put what I thought was a father's face on, something pompous and garrulous. Her face slowly lit up as she watched me, and when she spoke, her words came through a smile that was breaking into a soft laughter.

"Tod," she said. "A rather goofy name, as far as I'm concerned. And only one D—he said that. Very California, don't you think?"

We were both laughing then.

"I think you did that quite well."

Her words had a critic's tone and our laughter rose up, and when we settled down and into silence we were awkward with each other. We weren't quite out of it yet, and neither of us seemed to know how to continue.

The waiter came and gave us a formal moment then, a brief interlude in which we could gather ourselves and begin again. Jen ordered a fruit salad, and though I was hungry and wanted more, I

TOBY OLSON

chose the same, a tacit acceptance of the party and that we'd be going there together.

"We'd better talk about this, though," I said. "I mean, later, I'll be there. It could be awkward, couldn't it?"

She was very quick.

"He's attractive. I mean he's nice. It wasn't a date or anything. We just talked about where I'd come from, that I was traveling with my father. He said I should come to a beach party, that *you* should come. I should have that experience. I think that's all there was to it. But I *do* want to go."

There'll be other guys there, I thought, but I knew I was cooking myself up again, and I didn't say it. Then I blurted out the real question.

"Did you ever?"

Her eyes opened wide, and I felt the heat in my cheeks but didn't look away. Neither did she. There was a moment in which it could have turned sour. I could feel that on the back of my tongue and thought she was feeling it too. We both held on, waiting for the words to settle. Then she answered.

"Mom and I have talked. She was very good with that, judging by my friends and *their* mothers. No, I haven't, not even a little. Well, a little once, my freshman year. Just kissing and things. Is there anything you want to tell me?"

What in the world could I tell her, something about sex with her mother? I knew nothing, and yet I'd opened the subject and was now trapped by it.

"Yes," I said. "But only when you have a question, anything, just ask me. It could be embarrassing. But that's okay. I'll tell you what I know, and if I don't know, I'll tell you that too."

I'd expected a few kids only and that I'd feel out of place, but there were fifty people there at least, some clearly over forty. They lounged on blankets and in beach chairs, sat on benches that had been fitted into cuts in the low escarpment, above which the house sat, the glass in its many windows holding a rose tint, the final wash of the sinking sun.

Tod was at the fire, in shorts and a dark blue butcher's apron, no shirt and barefoot, and the real cook, a slight Asian man, stood beside him in a dun-colored jumpsuit. Both were looking at the coals. The stove consisted of two halves of a large oil drum cut the long way, thick pipe legs welded onto them. In tandem, they spanned a good eight feet, and I could see they'd been recently painted with a dull red primer, probably not for the first time. The cooking grates were wide and long, and at the end of the stove a large wooden table had been anchored in the sand. It was heaped with packages and two large coolers.

When Tod saw us, he grinned, handed the metal fork he'd been poking the fire with to the smaller man, then crossed the sand to where we were standing, close to the final surf line. Jen held my arm, squeezing and then releasing it when he got close. In just the short time of his coming over, the sun sank beyond horizon, the sand darkened into shadows, and all the bright clothing around us lost its color.

"We'll have fires in the sand," he said, looking at Jen. "I'm glad you came."

"This is my father," she said. "Bill."

We shook hands, passed a few clumsy words, then he took Jen to see the stove, what there'd be to eat and drink. I stayed there, looking around, then in a moment Jen came back with a can of beer.

"Is this okay?" she said.

Her face was in shadow, but I could see a tightness in her brow and knew she meant more than that.

"The beer? Fine. Thank you. Go ahead, go on. I'll find something, someone."

"Thanks," she said, really meaning it, and made her way back to Tod. He was no longer at the stove but was standing in a cluster of

78   TOBY OLSON

others, people his own age. Jen was wearing jeans and her loose paisley shirt, the tails hanging down over her hips. I saw her kick her sandals off as she touched Tod on the shoulder. He turned to her, then drew her in and introduced her to the others.

It was a perfect night, thick stars in a clear sky, the dull waxing moon, and no wind at all. The stars and moonlight were enough, but a few large candles were lit, and once the food was ready—burgers and dogs, an iron cauldron of chili, corn, and large wooden bowls of California salad—log fires were started in the sand, and people gathered into tight little groups, bright animated faces near the fires' light and laughter in darkness from those on the periphery.

I made my way awkwardly, talked briefly with a few people, then occupied myself with eating, getting the food and another can of beer from the cooler. The talk was about a predicted inversion, trouble expected inland in a few days. A smog alert, but not a warning yet. That, and the earthquakes. There'd been tremors noted to the north. "Maybe," a man said to me. "But then, they never get it right." "But they *do* get it wrong," a woman said, and there was laughter.

I caught Jen's eye from time to time and we smiled at each other. But once the fires were going strong and people had settled in, I found myself alone, standing in the sand on the ocean side, just a few feet from the water. Up the low hill, I could see lights in the house now and occasionally a couple, arm in arm, or a group of people, heading up the wooden steps to it. I could hear music, faintly, soft rock, and could see figures moving slowly beyond the glass. I wasn't sure where Jen might be and was getting ready to head closer to the fire. Then I heard the woman's voice, coming out of a soft splashing, and when I turned she was stepping from the surf and smiling up at me.

We moved back toward the fire and around the ring of blankets to a bench at the escarpment. I caught her face and figure in the light, a small, rather plain-looking woman, but with beautiful Asian eyes that turned inky black when we reached the shadows. She was wearing loose, drawstring pants and a baggy black T-shirt, the image of a full moon and a few points of bright stars rippling over the rise of her small breasts when she moved her arms and shoulders. Her name was Lin, and when she turned a little on the bench to face me I saw she was older than I was, maybe forty-five. She said she'd been to a number of these things, going back a good three years.

"A family story?"

"It was his father," she said. "Then his parents found a place in Hawaii and moved there permanently. I understand they're here from time to time, but I've never seen them. Then his brother took it up while Tod was in college. Now it's his thing. It's not as loose as it looks. There's security. Never any trouble, though, at least that I've heard of."

"Relaxed California dreamin'?"

She laughed. I'd heard the hint of an accent.

"Not here in Laguna. There's money, and it's a tight-assed place."

"You're not from here," I said. "What do you do?"

"Across the sea," she said. "Originally. I drift."

Her head tilted slightly as she spoke, the edge of a smile asking me something. I must have pulled back from it. She didn't wait for me, but continued on.

"But I've been here, rather stagnant, for almost four years." She had a cigarette now at her lips, and the match was a brief flash in the darkness. "Soon enough, I'll be leaving. And you?"

I told her about Jen, but not much. Just that she was my daughter and that we were traveling. I mentioned the Navy, my getting out, and that I'd lived in California when I was young.

"Don't worry about Tod," she said. "He's okay. This is only the summers for him. He's at Stanford, I think. Really, he's quite serious, not one of these funky California amoral types."

I told her where we were staying and that we'd be heading out soon, probably tomorrow.

TOBY OLSON

"Well, that's interesting," she said. "I work close to there, just down the beach. I do travel. Day trips, the airlines, the whole number."

"For four years?"

"Right. But for a second time. I was in San Francisco with an agency, before that Denver. But years ago, I was right where I am now, though down in the basement. I had a thing then, with one of the managers. Brief, but memorable. Then, when I learned travel and called him, well, here I am!"

"The basement?"

"I was a chambermaid. I was thirty years old then, and I'd just been drifting."

"Susan Rennert? Were you there for that?"

"Oh, God, yes!" she said. "Susan."

Her cigarette hand dropped to her knee, a wisp of smoke fading quickly into darkness, and she shifted on the bench. I wanted to get to the sheet, but my question registered and she raised her head quickly.

"But why in the world?" she said. "That was years ago."

"Sixteen."

I told her about my father, just enough, then mentioned the list he'd made, the entry about the sheet. She picked up quickly on the possible intrigue, something she seemed to like, and soon she was talking like a gossip. She'd slipped over a little closer to me and lowered her voice, though there was no one within hearing distance of us, and I liked that. It had been a long time since I'd had a private talk with a woman. The fires were no longer blazing but had settled down to a bright coal glow. It was getting late. A few people were leaving, starting down the beach.

It was a kind of game, Lin said. For a while they even had betting pools, both in and between hotels along the strip for major weekends. It was something chambermaids, she thought, had always talked about, part of the culture of the job, those stained sheets. There were other things, of course, found in rooms. People might shift the furniture, steal things, leave some telltale sign—towels soaking in the tub, a smear of Vaseline on the glass surface of a table. She'd heard once of a length of rope, one end tied to the metal bed frame, a leather cuff at the other, forgotten under a pile of pillows. The sheets, though, were better, a more perfect measure. "I mean, every bed had them, and the unstained ones that had been slept between were an accurate measure. The betting pools had to do with percentages, with only the bottom, fitted sheets considered.

"But it was more complex than that, once it got beyond the chambermaids and into the broader hotel staff. They began even to give points for the degree of stain, and if it was blood or semen. Consideration too of other body fluids, as long as they could be identified and connected to sex. That part grew absurd after a while, representatives from the various hotels arguing in the laundry, encrusted sheets all around them, draped over the metal folding tables. That's why it petered out, I think, went back to what it was, a more simple measurement, in-house, only chambermaids involved.

"So when Susan Rennert drowned and the sheet was found, there were whispers, but they didn't have to do with foul play or any other connection to her death. It was more a question of her life, the irony in the fact that she'd been offended by the sheet business, would have nothing to do with the talk or the betting, and that such a thing should happen, then be connected to her death in the newspapers."

"But what *about* that sheet?"

She hesitated, looked away from me and out toward the fire, working to remember. Then she lifted her cigarette. It had died out, and she tossed it on the sand. She reached into her baggy pants and got out a crumpled pack, extracted another one, and pulled it through her fingers, straightening it. Then she raised it to her lips but didn't light it, and soon it was between her fingers on her knee. She opened her mouth then, about to speak, then closed it, her black eyes still on the fire or beyond it on the surf that now sparkled occasionally, phosphorescent.

82   TOBY OLSON

"There is something," she said finally. "But I can't quite find it, something about that. A story? I don't know. But her death? That's pretty clear. We all thought it was suicide. She was a good swimmer. That was known. But it was easy to take the way she was a loner, that meager life of hers, as depression or some other kind of craziness. We guessed she was hiding something, the way she'd seemed to have cut her past life off completely. She never talked about such things at all, would grow silent or simply leave if it came up. She wasn't unfriendly, just kind of vacant. There were no men that anyone knew of. She spent a lot of time in her little room, reading magazines, I guess. They found nothing much when they went through her things, as far as I know."

"That's right," I said. "Almost nothing."

"It's a long time ago. Another life for me." She lit the cigarette, then shook her head as if clearing her ears after a swim. "I wish I could *get* that damn thing. Was it some theory?"

"What about weather?" I said. "Moon, wind, or tides."

She thought for a moment.

"No, I don't think so. Wasn't it in summer? I think I remember it was a busy season."

"July," I said. "The fifteenth." Then I tried another entry from my father's list. "What about housewares?"

"Housewares? What do you mean?"

"I don't know," I said. "Pots and pans? Linens? Cooking utensils? Bathroom stuff?"

The cigarette was moving toward her mouth again, but she stopped, her hand at her chest, the small burning tip illuminating the full moon there.

"Wait!" she said. "Yes! That's it. Yes, yes, yes, I've got it. It was a magazine. One of those monthly journals. *House Beautiful, American Home?* Something like that."

"Go on," I said.

"A magazine. That's right. One of the girls found it in the little lounge we had. There was a table piled with them. Fashion. Travel. Movie star stuff. You know the thing. We'd read them, then drop them there, and others would pick them up. But there was *this* one, some home magazine. She came across it much later. Two months, maybe? At least I remember it was after things had cooled down. I mean, the newspapers had given up the story by then, and there was no more talk in the hotels either. Oh, maybe an occasional mention, but very few. But after she found it, word got around and we were talking again, for a little while at least."

I started to say something, to push her to it, but she continued. People were singing now, a few soft and tentative voices in awkward harmony and darkness beyond the fire light.

"Susan Rennert had written things in that magazine. Little notes and check marks. We had to fill out chits in the job, at least at that hotel, make lists occasionally, supplies and things. The girl who found it recognized her writing, but in the story that got around she said she might not have, but for the places of the notes. Check marks and underlinings too, I think. They were all on pages of linen ads, in the margins and beside price lists. She'd made notes about sheets, and it was that of course that got us all talking again."

"What happened then?"

"Well, nothing really. She took the magazine to the police. I remember that. I remember us waiting for some news. I think I remember someone got the spunk up to call them about it. After time had passed and we hadn't heard anything. Beyond that? Well, nothing. Life goes on. I was out of there before long, off to Seattle, then San Francisco."

I suspected she must have left her heart there, or at least something. It was the way she named the place, soft and slowly, by syllable, her tongue lingering on the letters. She was somewhere else now, a long way from Susan Rennert. She reached for another cigarette, as if that might do something for her, then changed her

TOBY OLSON

mind. Then she turned toward me, expectant, but must have seen something. Her look told me, even before I knew it, that there was nothing there.

"Well," she said, lifting her shoulders slightly, then hugging herself, "It's getting chilly. That's Laguna for you. It must be late."

"I don't know," I said, disconnecting now and wondering about Jen. "I have to be going."

There was a slight apology in her words, as if there might have been something between us, that we might be going together.

"Well," I said, "good luck," then put out my hand in a way that felt quite stupid. She took it up with grace, then rose and walked off down the beach. I looked at my hand, and when I looked up again, the darkness had swallowed her.

I got up off the bench and made my way around the periphery of those gathered near the fire. Jen wasn't there, so I headed for the wooden steps that led up to the house. There was light still in the windows, but dimmer than it had been, and no figures were moving behind the glass.

The steps ended at a broad wooden deck, dark shapes of large ceramic planters resting along its length, and across the deck were sliding glass doors, tall windows to the sides of them, separated only by thick wooden panels.

I was in darkness there, and I moved carefully across the boards, then stood a few feet from the glass doors and looked into the large living room. There were leather couches there and easy chairs set in groupings as in hotel lobbies; rich carpets covered the brown tile floor, and the walls were hung with large abstract paintings. I could hear music, faintly, and saw the expensive stereo equipment in its glass cabinet. The room seemed empty, but then I heard Jen's laughter, saw her head rise up over a couch back, then go down again. The couch faced away from me, into the room, and for a few long moments I could see nothing. Then I saw a foot, not hers, stick out at the couch arm, the toe pointed up.

I felt a chill in my shoulders, something behind me, and though I knew it was only a sea breeze, it brought me back fully to myself, standing there, a voyeur, watching what I shouldn't be watching, though I could see nothing. Still, I found I couldn't move, not just yet. I thought of Carol, brought that up, my responsibility, now that I was Jen's father. I heard her laugh again, heard *his* laugh, saw somebody's fingers grab into the couch arm at the other end, squeeze and release it. A virgin. Jennifer, but not Stewart. What was his name, her last name? I'd forgotten, though I'd written her many letters using it.

I could move then, aware as I did so that it was that vacant name that released me, a benefit to her of the absent father. This, at least, I could give her. I turned and made my way silently across the deck, then moved down the wooden steps to the beach. There were only a few people left on the blankets now, and the fires were no more than a rich coal glow. The small Asian man in his uniform was wire-brushing the cooking grates, but quietly, and I saw his head turn, his bright teeth, as he heard me and smiled.

"What a night!" I said, as I moved to the end of the dark stove and stood there.

"Much like many." He almost whispered it. "This is California!"

I nodded and smiled back at him, then moved to an empty beach chair close to the dying embers. A figure, a woman on a blanket with others, raised her hand and I lifted my fingers and waved to her. Then I leaned back and looked up into the sky, and though the stars were bright and compelling, it was not the night's face that I saw then, but that of Susan Rennert, her image in that cheap photo in the newspaper. There had been something about it, about her, that I'd found beautiful, strongly attracting and very sexual. But that life, so tight and barren, at least as I'd been receiving it. She's gone, I thought, and for many years, and it's no good falling in love with the dead.

A creak and a sandy shuffling, then it was Jennifer's face, slipping in front of the stars, looking down at me. I had her even before my

TOBY OLSON

eyes pulled back to focus, knew the shape of her chin and lips. She was smiling, squinting against the fading firelight. Her body seemed poised, expectant.

"Is it time?" I said, extending my arm up toward her. "Give me a hand."

She laughed lightly, that same laugh I'd heard through the glass doors, then reached down and took hold of my wrist. I took hers, then slumped down in the chair, making it hard for her. She dug her heels into the sand, then took our linked arms in her other hand and leaned back. She was much stronger than I would have thought, and I rose up out of the chair easily.

We started down the beach then, barefoot, our shoes tied together by the laces and draped over my shoulder, our toes in the surf. Starlight lit the way.

"Did you have a good time?" I said.

"Oh, Bill! How could I not? It's twelve-thirty! I'm sixteen years old!"

"A woman!" I said, and reached over and took her in my arms and kissed her cheek and forehead.

We continued on then, hand in hand. She kicked at the surf and at times leaned down to pick up a shell, examine it, then cast it away. She held my hand tightly, but she didn't talk much, and I was sure her thoughts were elsewhere.

In a while we could see the hotel's night lights bathing the beach before it, and I dropped her hand at the same time as she released mine. Had anyone seen us coming along the beach that way, they would have thought we were lovers. I think we both recognized that. We stepped a little away from each other, and Jen did a child-ish, limping hop as we moved up into light at the hotel doorway.

8.

It was her birthday.

I had showered and shaved and was in my white hotel robe when I heard her tentative knock on the door separating our rooms, and when I opened it she was standing there, holding up a fistful of red roses, some tight in their buds, others opening in the morning sun as she had, her eyes glistening above her broad smile. She wore her birthday dress, a spill of calla lilies falling in a wave across her breast and hip on the yellow field. I saw my mother's necklace at her throat, large silver discs with gems set into them.

"And a telegram!" she said, stepping lightly across the sill in her fine shoes.

We got the glass pitcher, dumped out the dregs of solar tea, and filled it with fresh water. I dressed in the bathroom while she arranged the flowers. Then we called Carol.

"What's the plan?"

"Brunch," I said. "Then we'll drive down to San Diego." I looked over at Jennifer and winked. She was standing near the room's center, and I could see the roses behind her shoulder on the glass table.

"Then over into Tijuana for a big birthday dinner. After that, we're not sure yet." We *were,* but it was nothing I could handle over the phone. I knew I'd be taking liberties I'd not earned. I'd heard Jen mention the beach party to her mother, but she'd said nothing at all about Tod. She'd glanced over at me, then quickly lowered her eyes. We're in cahoots, I thought. I doubted Carol would have found it funny.

"So how can I reach you? I mean, in the next few days. When will you be coming back?"

"Well," I said, "we'll call tomorrow. We'll have a place by then."

"Call any time," she said. "I'll be waiting for a call."

"Everything's going great," I said.

"That's good. I've been wondering about all this. I can tell you that."

"Why, then?"

"Because she has rights. And she wanted this."

"You're a good mother," I said, aware of my presumptuous fool-ishness the moment the words were out.

"Bullshit, Bill. But that remains to be seen. As much as how you'll be as a father."

Her birthday brunch was a sumptuous buffet, mounds of vari-ous California salads, seafood, and fruit. The conventional stuff was there too, french toast, eggs, bacon and sausage. There was orange juice, champagne, and a pastry table, quiet music from a trio across the room.

Jen tried most everything, getting up and moving to the tables often, delighted that her empty plate had been cleared away while she was gone. During one of her trips, I'd spoken to our waitress, and when we finished eating and were sipping coffee— espresso for me and a cappuccino for Jen—the waitress arrived with a tall napoleon. It rested on a circle of white paper with scalloped edges on a fine china plate. A red 16 was sugared in on the shiny surface, one number above the other, and a thin unlit candle stood up at the corner.

"Happy birthday," the waitress said, discreetly, as she bent down and adjusted the plate beside Jen's coffee cup.

"Oh, Bill!" Jen said, just a little flustered, caught between thank-ing the waitress and me at the same time.

I reached over and lit the candle. The waitress stood there smil-ing. Jen looked up at her, then back at me. Then she put her palms at the table's edge, leaned over, and gently blew at the flame. It fell

TOBY OLSON

to the horizontal for a moment, then it went out, and a thin line of smoke curled up and quickly dissipated in the air.

We stayed there for a while. Jen nibbled at the napoleon, eating around the 16. We ordered more coffee, regular American stuff, and I told her about the woman I'd met at the beach party and some of the things she'd had to say about Susan Rennert and the bloody sheet, but not about the sheet lottery.

"What do you make of the letter?" Jen said. "That he would include that in his notes? To write to *you,* I mean."

We'd talked about my father on our drive to Laguna Beach, his sheet of notes and the fact that my name was on it. "Just curiosity," I'd said, before I'd gone to the newspaper office. We'd discussed my meager findings afterward, but only briefly.

But now we were going to leave Laguna, if only for a while, and I felt a force of unfinished business pulling at me. I didn't even have good questions yet, ones I could leave here, then return to after our trip. The bother was only a mild irritant, but I felt if I kept it to myself, it might grow into infection. I knew I couldn't have that, not now, just as the two of us were starting out. It seemed we'd been starting out for a while now, each day bringing something new. This could be another thing, my father, and my mother too, in those notes along with me.

"I don't know," I said. "That's something, though. I mean, he had me in this. Whatever it might be. But this damn list of his! The bugger's full of questions."

I'd removed it from the file and put it in my jacket pocket, feeling a need to have it close, and I took it out, unfolded it, and smoothed it flat on the table cloth. Then I got up and moved my chair so I could sit at Jen's elbow. The sheet curled up a little, and I put the salt and pepper shakers at its upper corners and held the bottom edges down with my fingertips. Jen leaned forward slightly, reading down the column:

1. Look into blossom gradation and etching.
2. Go over it with Bev again.
3. Laguna: check local newspaper morgue.
4. Leonard has batteries.
5. Rennert: why Susan?
6. Could it really have been Housewares?
7. Weather: moon, wind, tides.
8. The question of the sheet.
9. Write letter to Billy.
10. The History of the American Theater
    (TAT: Its History) what?
11. Time longer than Rope.
12. Go see Blevins.

"Who's Blevins?" she said.

"I have no idea."

She ran her finger down the list, stopping at the tenth entry.

"That could be a book. Is there anything else?"

"Well, yes," I said, "the obvious things. My mother and me, Rennert, though why the question mark I don't know. There's that housewares one, maybe a magazine. And there's Leonard. Someone my father knew. I remember him from years ago."

We troubled the entries for a while, but not in any order, guessing and asking questions. The table had been cleared, and only the circle of Jen's 16, the snuffed candle, and our empty coffee cups remained.

"Isn't it getting late?" she said.

We seemed to be running out of steam then anyway, and I nodded and pushed back from the table.

"Yes," I said. "We best get out of here. We have some shopping to do."

She moved the salt and pepper shakers, then lifted my father's list and handed it to me, and while I was folding the paper, she slid

TOBY OLSON

the scalloped napkin out from under the remaining circle of napoleon and slipped it inside the menu she'd held onto. She picked up the little candle, hesitated for a moment, then stuck it somewhat dramatically behind her ear.

"These I'll keep," she said. "But this . . . !"

She reached out with her fingers, lifted her 16, and popped it into her mouth.

9.

I'd dived near Cabo San Quintin only twice, and that had been close to twenty years before, when I was home on leave and still in the first flush of being a Navy man, and I'd taken my father with me the first time.

He'd had me stop in San Diego so he could check into a newspaper office, then Tijuana and Ensenada, where he spent some time digging through junk shops. He knew where they were, and before long the trunk was full of things he'd purchased, pieces of various machinery that I couldn't identify.

"Do you really *need* this stuff?" I'd asked.

"You can never tell," he said.

Once below Ensenada, virgin territory for him, we'd made better time, though he kept his eyes open and had me stop for a few minutes at a small, roadside cantina. I waited in the car, and before long he limped out with a handful of old magazines, holding them up and shaking them, a broad grin on his face.

"Something for your mother," he said. And I saw they were Mexican theater magazines, a woman in full Victorian costume in midgesture on the cover of one of them.

By the time we reached Cabo San Quintin it was early afternoon, and though at times a snorkel would appear and blow, the few free divers present were hugging the underwater peninsula off to the left and the sea directly in front of us was empty. There was a clear sandy bottom running out a good fifty feet, then darker water, the steep drop that would take me deeper, down to where the caves pictured behind the woman in the glossy photograph were. We'd read up on the place the night before. I'd sat beside my father as I had as a child, but this time it was I who did most of the talking.

We'd brought the tank and regulator he had rigged for me so many years before. He'd kept it oiled against corrosion, and once he was in bed I checked it out completely. It was old and jerry-rigged, awkwardly fitted, but carefully so, and the lines were sufficiently pliable and I could find no rot.

My father wore a blue swimsuit that reached down almost to his knees, and when he took his shirt off I was shocked by the look of him. He was seventy-six then, and I'd not seen him close to naked for a good ten years, though he was not modest about his body. I remember standing beside him at his garage bench in the heat of summer. He'd taken his shirt and pants off and was dismantling some small engine in his underwear. Sweat dripped from his arms and shoulders, a few drops splashing on my own bare arms as he showed me the inner workings. He was always thin, but there'd been hard sinew visible in his chest and arms, and his hairless legs had looked like white, cured wood.

But now his skin hung loose. The bones at the tips of his shoulders, even his clavicles, were skeletally distinct, as if they might soon break through their almost transparent covering. The calf on his game side held no definition at all. His leg, from knobby knee to ankle, was like a broomstick.

I was standing in the surf looking back at him, my mask in place, leaning toward him awkwardly under the heavy weight of the old air tank. His own mask sat like a strange hat on his forehead, the snorkel a fat pencil behind his ear. He couldn't see my face, and I remember thinking that was good. Surely my mouth had opened at the sight of him, my eyes holding a sad recognition.

I must have lifted my arm then and waved him on, for he

TOBY OLSON

grinned, lowered his mask to cover his face, and began to limp through the heavy sand toward the surf line. He was nimble, light and quick on his feet the way I remembered, and even his thin arms took on a certain sure strength that reassured me. I was able to turn away from him and wade out into deeper water, knowing he would be safe as he followed me.

We'd rigged a makeshift weight belt out of an Army surplus rifle strap and sawed off pieces of iron pipe, which we'd weighed on his scale in the garage, cutting shorter or longer lengths as necessary, and though as I sank water washed into the hollow cylinders and tried to turn me, the weight was right, and I fell at a good speed, my arms and legs extended, and had sufficient time to clear the pressure through my eustachian tubes.

When I was close to what I guessed was forty feet, my sinking slowed, then stopped, and I was buoyed up. The reef was ten or more feet below me, pipe fish and others cutting into crevices, and back against the steep wall I'd descended along I could see the small cave openings. I kicked out, heading that way, and when I got there I dipped into a few. They were shallow and without interest, though one was deep enough for me to disappear into for a moment.

I was performing for my father, feeling both silly and exhilarated, showing him my grace and comfort in deep water. The regulator was laboring, the valves worn and awkward in their technology, but I was in no danger. Even if the thing quit I could make it up without trouble, but I wanted it all to be right: this mechanism my father had made for me, long ago, that I was now using as a professional.

I could see him hanging there above, a thin water spider, his arms and legs extended and waving like ribbons of kelp in the sun's refraction. The clear water above me lightened gradually as sun reached down into it, and at the surface an aura glimmered around his limbs and torso. I was sure it was my father, that he was alive and floating there, watching me. Still, when I extended my arm and waved, I was relieved to see his answering gesture, no more than the ripple of a sea snake.

"Are we almost there?" Jen said.

"Pretty soon. Just a few more miles."

We'd made it to San Diego by late afternoon and had driven immediately to the ship's store at the Naval base. It was my first real act as a retiree, and I took some pleasure in showing my card and escorting Jen into a Navy world, really no different from other large department stores, though there were men in uniform shopping among the service wives and other dependents.

We found the sporting goods section and got down to Jen's birthday shopping. When I looked at the bill, then handed over my credit card, I felt a little guilty, wondering what Carol might think of the implied commitment. Jen's eyes had opened wider as the things we selected piled up on the counter.

"It's okay," I said. "Half of this is for me. This is good stuff that I've been needing."

We loaded it all into the car trunk, though Jen held back her mask and snorkel.

"I have to fiddle with this," she said. "Adjust the straps."

We crossed the border, and since it was still light we drove through Tijuana and made our way south to Rosarita Beach, where we found a nice waterfront hotel for the night. I called Carol and told her where we were and that we'd be heading farther south in the morning and would call again tomorrow. Jen spoke to her for a few moments. She didn't mention the diving. Then we drove to a restaurant at another hotel, where we ate Jen's birthday dinner, guacamole and bean salad, followed by fresh halibut steaks and avocados stuffed with crab.

"No birthday stuff, okay?"

"Of course, sure," I said.

We ate like two adults out on a friendly date. I lifted my brandy to Jen's Coke over dessert, a toast to the evening only.

The rutted road dipped down, then emptied into a grassy meadow close to the sea. The beach was wide and flat there, its quiet surf line visible beyond the low winter berm, and standing beside the car we could see the broad peninsula jutting out for a good distance on our left, a foam spray where waves hit at its terminus.

Jen carried the heavy Navy blanket, the flippers and masks, and I lugged our two tanks, going back for the wet suits and belts while she found a good place and spread the blanket, securing the corners with stones. There was just a little breeze, enough to cut the heat.

"We're certainly not the first," she said, pointing to a fire remnant, charred logs and a couple of beer cans behind us where the berm rose.

I'd seen that and other bits of trash along the path but hadn't wanted to acknowledge it.

"But nobody now," I said. "It's all ours."

She was fussing with her mask and snorkel again, clearly nervous, anticipating, glancing over at the peninsula from time to time.

"Let's check the water," I said.

We stripped down to our suits, then went to the water's edge and got our legs wet. It was warm and we wouldn't need our wet suits, but I helped her into hers anyway, letting her pull the zipper up between her breasts. Then we got our snorkels, masks, and flippers and waded out into deeper water.

Jen was a good swimmer, and in just a few minutes she'd learned to let the flippers do their work, more important here than in the still pool where she'd had her beginner's lessons. We stayed in shallow water, and I taught her how to clear her mask and blow her snorkel, things she already knew about, but hadn't practiced in a while. The water was clear to the sandy bottom, and when we went down together and I hit her mask rim, breaking the seal, I could see her distinctly as she readjusted it, rolled over on her side, and cleared it. We tried that a few times, then swam out a little, where we could dive deeper, enough so she could feel pressure, practice blowing her eustachian tubes. We worked for about a half hour, and though I could tell she was getting impatient, she was also enjoying the learning, that it was I who was teaching her. Then we got the tanks, moved to shallow water again, and worked with them.

I showed her how to breathe, to take it easy with that, keep her adrenaline down. While she was under I shut her valve, letting her get the feel of her air supply dwindling. I taught her how to buddy me up. I could see her bright eyes through the glass as she handed me her mouthpiece, watched her suck at mine when we changed over. In a while, we were back on the blanket, sharing a Coke.

"You're a good teacher," she said, passing the can. The sun was behind her, and I couldn't see her face clearly. She'd taken her wet suit off and was adjusting the clasp on her weight belt. Her hips were tight and slim where her black, one-piece suit ended, and I wondered when her woman's spread would start. Wasn't it time for that?

"Oh, I don't know," I said.

"But you *are*."

She was indulging me. I had taught her some things, but her lessons had been good ones, and much of what I'd shown her she'd already known.

"Well, my father maybe. He was a good teacher."

She'd gotten a broad-brimmed straw hat in Ensenada, insisting that she pay for it herself. I'd started to argue, but had seen that she was serious. Then she'd bought me one, a silly thing I knew I wouldn't wear. It didn't look silly on her, though, and once she had it on and her face was visible again, I could see the bright anticipation in her eyes. I'd wanted to speak of my father, to tell her more.

"Okay," I said. "Let's go!"

We left the tanks on the blanket and free dived the peninsula, drifting on the surface along its leeward length and sinking down a good twenty feet at times to where the reef curved out from the vertical into a narrow shelf before it descended again into deeper water. Twenty feet was the most that she seemed able to make at first, but she was fighting down too quickly, forgetting what I had taught her, and I touched her shoulder at the surface, pulled my mask away, and told her to take it easy, easy, she'd have plenty of air if she conserved it. In a while she relaxed and got it and could make her way just feet above the shelf with slow scissor kicks, staying down for long seconds, concerned with what was there rather than with breath.

There really wasn't very much there, though for her it must have been startling. The fish that dipped into the crevices were drab in color, but plentiful, and I saw her point when a thick pad of weed drifted by, pipe fish hanging in a cluster under it. We saw a white sea snake draped over dark rock on the shelf, the aggressive face of a moray eel peek out from the vertical wall. A lone barracuda passed below us to seaside, his eye on Jen as she turned in the water to watch him. A hundred yards out, the sea's tide grew stronger, pushing us closer to the wall, and soon we had to start back. I tried one of the hand signals I'd taught her. She got it and turned gracefully in a slow arc. I'd watched her closely all the while and was pretty sure she was ready for the tanks. Only forty feet or so, I reassured myself. Even if something went wrong, we'd be okay.

We moved along the shelf again for twenty minutes. I'd had her put her wet suit and weight belt on and fixed her underwater light to its hook. I'd tied the length of treated nylon rope to my own belt. I was swimming to her side, at the shelf's edge, and when I thought she was ready, I reached out, touched her shoulder, and waited for her to turn. Then I pointed down, kicked slowly away, and dropped along the descending reef into deeper water, sidestroking so I could look back and watch her.

The shelf was a tubular hernia, and after a few feet the reef cut back and under it. We were a good twenty yards from its vertical wall. Watching Jen closely, I worked back under the shelf, then drifted in place until she was at my side. I pointed up when she got there, and we rolled over. We were in the reef now, and the undersurface of the shelf was rich with sea life, far more colorful and various than it had been above. We drifted there and watched it for a while, then I touched her again and pointed back into the darkness, where I knew the caves were. I made the light gesture, but she didn't get it. So I took hold of the torch at her belt and pulled at it, then pointed ahead. She nodded deeply and lifted the light free of the hook, got it turned, and pushed the switch. The cave openings were visible then, but only as jagged outlines back in the dimness, where light and sun couldn't reach. I saw the one I wanted, remembering it clearly even though it had been a very long time since I'd been there. I pointed ahead. Jen moved the beam, and we stroked slowly toward the descending wall.

I'd told her about the caves, the ones she'd seen behind the woman in the diving magazine, but that I knew of better ones and that we'd go into one of them. Still I watched her, looking for any hesitation and finding none. She reached the cave opening first and started into it. I had to stroke forward quickly, reach out, and tug at her flipper. She backed away, came up to the vertical, and treaded water beside me. I waved a finger at her and saw a crinkling at the corners of her eyes.

The rope was unnecessary, but since it was there, I'd brought it along as a lesson. I had a hundred feet, but I could remember no sudden turns or false passages. The rise would be about forty-five or fifty, gradual at first, then a steep tube of ascension. I found a thick hook of rock near the cave opening, tested it, then tied a firm knot at the rope's end around it. Again I touched Jen, and we both grabbed the rope, leaned back as best we could and pulled it, making sure it was well fixed. Then I took the light and went ahead of her, playing the rope out as I entered the cave. I jerked it once, making sure she had hold of it behind me.

TOBY OLSON

Once into the cave, I could feel the sea current pushing me, its force accelerating as the mouth narrowed and funneled back into the reef. The torch light played on the rock walls, variegated at first, then washed to a white, granite-like smoothness by the current's increasing force as I went deeper in. At first I could turn easily, see Jen gripping the rope and sliding in behind me, but then the passage tightened, my tank scraped rock above me, and I had a brief moment of concern that I had misjudged, that this was the wrong place.

I was looking at the floor of the cave a few feet in front of me, then quickly craned my neck back and pointed the torch ahead. There was light there, maybe twenty feet away, and the rock cave widened into a ball-like chamber that I remembered. Air bubbles rose and swirled in the chamber, as in a huge champagne glass. The space would clear for a moment, then the current would pull again, and the water would turn milky in turbulent swirls. There was no longer any need to stroke. I touched the smooth wall to my side, holding myself in place, then tested the rope with a jerk, and felt Jen's returning tug. Then I took my hand from the wall and drifted forward and into the chamber.

Bubbles bounced off my mask. I was pulled upright, then buffeted gently as the current turned and shivered me. Then the water cleared and stilled, and I hung for a moment in suspension, the torch turned off now and hanging in my hand along my side. Light entered the chamber from above, a bright wash filtering through the water, illuminating the curves of white walls, and when I looked up, I could see the bowel-like ascension, a long smooth tube arching up and forward, then bending back slightly, a shimmering foam of opaque glow where I knew it ended.

Then the water in the chamber turned milky again, the current pushed at my flippers, and I was rising quickly. The rope tightened in my hand, and I dropped a few coils, then rose again. The walls of the narrow tube were perfectly smooth and I couldn't judge my speed accurately, but soon the rope grew taut, and this time I dropped all of it. I'd tied the end to my weight belt, and I let that bring it up.

I was rising with the water and could feel no pressure against my body as I flowed. At times the current receded, and I slowed and was suspended. Then the silent rush would come again and I'd be rising more quickly. Finally I felt the pop of bubbles against my face and arms and knew I was racing upward. I looked up then, into the heart of the fountain, and before I could prepare myself, I was out of the water to my waist and falling. I landed in soft sand, rolled over, and jerked my mask away.

The fountain had receded into a low bubbling pool, but in moments it rose up again, slowly and like a geyser, into a thick, four-foot shaft, plumes spilling out in arcs at its top. Then Jen rose from its center, arms over her breasts, one hand gripping the rope that snaked along the sand to where it was tied at my belt. Her back was arched, as if she were diving upward, beginning a swan, the fountain's plumes forming a billowing skirt at her waist. She rose up to her knees and I saw her hands come up, her palms beside her head. Then she was sailing out of the fountain as I had.

She hit the sand beside me with a thud, and I reached out for her, concerned that she might be hurt, then helped her turn over and come up to a sitting position. She pulled her mask and snorkel away, spat out her air-line mouthpiece. She was grinning, her eyes clear and like round, full moons.

"Oh, Bill!" she said. "Wow! Oh, wow!"

I'd brought a couple of granola bars and two cans of soda packed tight in a waterproof pouch strapped at the small of my back. We'd moved away from the fountain, found a place of some comfort against the rock wall, then leaned back against our upright tanks, our legs in the sand.

We were inside the peninsula we'd drifted along, above the waterline, and sunlight washed the curved ceiling in an even glow, its refraction bounced through mirroring tubes and planes from somewhere above. The walls and ceilings were white, blasted when storm had lifted tides to cover the peninsula, dumping sand in rain waves, flooding the chamber, then at recession swiftly draining it in abrasive cauldron swirls that ate away sharp edges.

"Everything's round," Jen said, her mouth full of granola. She was eating greedily, guzzling the Coke.

"Even the sand," I answered.

It rose in a circle like a large donut, the fountain geysering, then falling at its center. The rope was still secure at my weight belt, its lengths in a coil at my hip. I'd pulled it tight across the sand and could feel the vibrations, the sucking and release as it was moved in the tube through which we'd risen. I wondered now if in our descent we'd need it, thinking that we surely would, Jen would. I was glad we'd used it but couldn't quite remember any difficulty in my descent years ago. I'd been younger then, however. Could that be it? Am I risking her life here? I couldn't push the thought away, the sudden guilt and the slowly growing dark fantasy, my dead daughter, floating facedown in the place of Susan Rennert. Then I turned to her, saw her bright face, her still wonder-struck flush. She's *so* alive, I thought.

We sat there for a while, eating and drinking, listening to the vague rumble of surf, the sharp squawk of an occasional gull, continually surprising because it came from open air, the deep shush of the rising fountain that blocked the rest out. We could count the seconds of stillness, ten at least, then it would geyser again.

"I thought I wished I had my camera," Jen said. She was studying the glowing ceiling. "But it's all light. I couldn't get a picture. And even if I did, it wouldn't be the same. I mean the getting here. Do you think anyone else has been here?"

"We could leave a note," I said. "One of these cans?"

There was no human evidence in the place at all.

"Will we ever come back?"

She touched my arm, and I looked along the length of her seated body beside me. She'd taken off her wet suit. "To be really *in* this place," she'd said, and I could see her small, high breasts, the prominent bones of her clavicles. I wanted to take her in my arms and hold her like a baby. I recognized I'd never held a baby and couldn't quite imagine it.

"I doubt it," I said. "But there are other places, just as good, where we can use a camera. We can get one and go to them. There'll be beautiful fish, coral. We can go much deeper, find very strange things. We can dive to sunken ships, ancient ones, even sunken cities."

"Oh, Bill," she said, "I love this! I mean this diving. This is what I want to do!"

We packed the candy wrappers and the cans. Then I showed her how to test her regulator, her tubes and tank, telling her she must always do so before going down. She stood up, and I reached out to help her into her wet suit, but she pushed my hands away, saying "Let me! I have to learn." She wouldn't let me hold her tank, so I showed her how to slip her arms through the straps, to get it on by herself. When she was ready, her mask at her forehead and her flippered feet splayed out where she stood, I got quickly into my own gear, and we crossed the rise of sand together and sat near the mouth of the fountain. It was still, then it was boiling, then the thick column of water rose, spilled over, and drenched us. Jen laughed, then lowered her mask over her face and seated it.

We'd decided to replicate our coming up. Jen would go first, then after a count of five I'd follow. "If anything," I'd said, "any trouble." She could rise up again, grab my flipper, we could come back to the chamber. I'd showed her how to use the rope, hand over hand, at her stomach.

We waited through two more drenchings, then when the fountain had receded and the water at its mouth was a still pool, Jen

TOBY OLSON

turned and slipped her legs over the edge and pushed off. I watched her head disappear in a cloud of air bubbles as she sank down into the rock tube, then leaned back and waited for the geyser.

In a few seconds I saw the water begin to roil, then watched as the fountain's thick column lifted. It rose in a smooth cylinder, then opened like a flower at the top. Jen was in it, her head ascending, then her torso and tank. I saw the billowing water dress at her waist. Then she was sinking down through the column, her hands moving on the rope between her breasts. She was gone down into the tube before the fountain receded, and when I looked into the still water, I could see only a sandy turbulence.

I slipped over the edge, pulling at the rope, my flippers hitting the tube's side, and went down. In moments the rising water was pulling at me, tightening the rope. It took effort just to stay in place, suspended. Then the rising pressure stilled, and I pulled myself slowly down, looking at the blank curve of white wall, unable to judge the speed of my descent. The tube was too tight for me to dip my head, find the shape of Jen's body below my flippers, but I could feel her tug, like a fish on the line. We pulled, then paused, then moved down again in a kind of peristalsis.

Then, after what seemed a very long time, the wall moved away from me, opening into the ball-like chamber near the cave mouth. I pushed the rope to arm's length so as not to tangle it, tucked and rolled over until I was facing the opening, a jagged archway off in the distance, weed and a few fish moving beyond it. I kicked from my ankles, gathering the rope as I went, and in moments I was out in the sea and swimming toward Jen. She stood up in the water waiting, her arms and legs waving slowly, keeping her in place. When I reached her, I pointed toward shore. Then we swam beside each other, our arms at our sides, using slow and deep scissor kicks, as if we were professionals returning from a day's salvage work.

It was later, when we were packing our gear into the trunk, that we spoke of the days ahead. It was late afternoon and the sun was beginning to sink, the peninsula already in shadow, so we decided we'd spend that night in Mexico, in Ensenada. It was the Fourth of July, but neither of us had mentioned it.

"What then?" she said.

"Well, Laguna again. If that's okay. There's one thing. Then I thought we'd drive to El Monte. I can show you where I grew up. Maybe we can go to Big Bear, in the mountains, maybe the desert, Palm Springs. We could even head to Las Vegas."

"We could do more diving."

"There's that too," I said.

"It's that Susan Rennert. Isn't it?"

It seemed to come from nowhere, and I was taken aback. "Well, yes," I answered. "There *are* some things. But why do you think of that? Did I say something?"

"No," she said, "not that."

It had grown cool as the sun sank. The half-moon had risen, growing toward full, and the meadow grass near the car was touched with faint silver. She'd put a sweater on and was hugging herself.

"It was the coming down. Hand over hand. It seemed to take so long."

"I don't get it," I said.

"It's your father's list. Don't you remember? *Time longer than rope?*"

10.

Her other father came to her when she was ten years old and left to go to death when she was ready for her freshman year, just thirteen, and living with the two of them in Racine. They left Bloomington in summer, after she had taken the proof of him, that she *had* a father now, to school in the shape of fractures on film, to be held up in the light for a science project.

"It was always the explaining. Where is your father? I didn't have one. Then I did."

Then she didn't, and quite suddenly, and she would have to explain again, receive that formal sympathy that bewildered and enraged her.

"Mom never cried. Not in front of me at least. She talked of plans they'd had, a third anniversary party, trips to foreign places when his work slowed down."

Of a future, missing something that had never been. Not him so much. But who the hell was I to make such judgment, he who'd had no thought of missing things, had felt whole in my life? Until recently at least, and the past twenty years revealed as an emptiness. But for my father and mother, their gone lives I'd thought finished and behind me.

Only then, when he was gone, had she thought to find me. She didn't know, but she thought "my father," not to take me off to school, "though I might do that now," the diving, but she'd wanted. . . She really didn't know. "Talking? taking our *own* trips?

grandparents?" Maybe it was her mother and her own longing for a lost future.

"I can't say that. That I loved her," I said. "We knew each other then, a little at least."

"I know. I know," Jen said.

We'd left Ensenada in the early morning, after a light breakfast of fruit and corn tortillas, had crossed the border at Tijuana, then started north and a little inland on the superhighway to make better time. The radio spoke of the smog alert, still not a warning. The schools remained open, but the elderly were advised to take precautions, stay at home if possible. We could see it through the windshield as we headed away from the coast, not yet a blanketing but a high haze that thickened off in the distance.

Jen had talked to Carol the night before, had mentioned diving, but nothing of our recent experience. "I know!" I'd heard her say, "I *will* be careful."

She'd brought the Laguna newspaper to the breakfast table on the patio of the small, old hotel we'd managed to locate. Ensenada had changed, was thick with tourists now, but once off the main byways we'd found old Mexico. The place was clean and simple, the patio lush with potted plants and flowers. "Things sure grow like hell out here!" Jen had said. She'd folded the newspaper carefully, and when she turned it and pushed it across the table toward me, she kept her finger in place among the classified ads.

"What do you think? I have some money." Her look was quite serious, asking for real judgment.

I read the ad: a crash course in scuba diving for intermediates, four six-hour days, with a weekend junket to Catalina Island at the end.

"Catalina used to be nice," I said. "Some decent diving."

"Well?"

"It's expensive."

"I have money."

She really wanted it, that was clear. And I was taken with her

TOBY OLSON

enthusiasm about diving, that she would desire to enter into my life and past that way. But it was more than that, and better. I'd seen her, her quick grasp of things. She had a knack for it, a natural comfort in the water. I wanted it as a matter of genes, though knowing I could never be sure of that. It was enough that she seemed truly in love with it, even though she had only just started out. But a very *good* start, I thought, pleased with myself.

"Well," I said. "Let's figure it this way. The Catalina part. What if I go along for that? I don't mean to dive or anything, or get in the way. But that can be part of our trip together. I'll cover that. I *could* take care of it all. I have money too."

"No," she said sternly, but beginning to smile at the prospect. "It's *my* school. I want to pay."

"Okay. But how about the Catalina business?"

"What you said. That's good. I agree with that."

"But I'll have to check it out. The teacher. The course of study."

"Oh, Bill!" she said, knowing it had become her thing to say, a term of endearment when I acted like her father.

We reached Laguna Beach at four, the air clearing as we dropped down out of the foothills. It was a bright, sunny Saturday along the coast and the town was crowded with those taking refuge from the growing inland pollution. We tried for the same hotel, but without luck, then checked a few others on the oceanfront and found the same thing. We had to drive a few blocks back from the beach, and even there we found no vacancy signs. We finally settled on an old motel, a slightly seedy one, well off the beaten path.

"Tomorrow," I said. "The crowds will clear out and we can move to something better."

We had to share a room, two sagging double beds with only a thin space between them. The man in the office looked at me knowingly, but I stared him down.

"Yuk!" Jen said, when she saw the stained dresser top, then got a clean towel from her suitcase and spread it neatly over the surface.

It was five-thirty by the time we got to the dive shop. There was a sign in the window, a blowup of the classified ad. They'd Scotch-taped a photograph above it, a man in full scuba gear drifting over a coral reef. Jen said she'd check the shop next door, then wait outside. She didn't want to be there when I asked my questions, standing beside me like an awkward daughter.

"But stay close," I said. "You'll probably have to sign something." But it was I who did.

The owner was the teacher, a man my age, and it was only moments after I'd begun my questions that he began to smile. He was small and rugged, a little weird in sideburns that came straight out of the sixties. The shop was small and full to the rafters with diving gear, all of it in perfect order on racks and along the walls.

"The Navy," he said. "Am I right?"

He'd been a frogman and had done a hitch in San Diego, one in Corpus. His name was Michael Higgins, and his hair was Irish red.

"Padre Island was pretty good in those days. When you were there?"

"The same," I said.

We got into enough diving talk for me to be sure of him, and once I'd signed the papers, I went to the door and called Jen in, then introduced him to her. He was friendly but reserved, appropriately so, no joking or bluster. Even when we struggled with the money—should we use a credit card? would she write a check?—he stood patiently behind the counter, waiting for us to get straight with each other. Then we talked a little about Catalina, the weekend dive plans. There were some good coves, diving down to wrecks at the mouth of Avalon. They'd cruise to the backside, have a cookout on the beach. He'd hold the class to ten. They'd all meet at Main Beach on Monday morning at nine o'clock. Lunch was provided, during which there'd be lectures, then three hours to apply them in the water in the afternoon. She'd be finished at four.

TOBY OLSON

That night we stayed out of the motel room as long as possible. We drove to a good but conventional restaurant on the Pacific Coast Highway a few miles south of town, and though we lingered over dinner, we were finished by nine. We were both tired from the trip up from Mexico, but we stayed away a little longer, dipping into a few Laguna Beach shops when we got back there.

"I can't do this," Jen said after a while, then yawned so deeply her whole body shook.

"Okay," I said. "We can throw a towel over the lamp, let the shadows hide the stains."

We did that, and Jen had to lie near the edge of her bed, propped up on pillows and leaning slightly, to go over the Xeroxed instructional book Higgins had handed her before we'd left the dive shop.

"You've got tomorrow," I said, sitting up in my own bed in shadow just a few feet from her. I'd brought no pajamas, so had dressed in a T-shirt and a pair of khaki shorts for sleeping. Jen wore a long nightshirt, thin cotton and sleeveless, for the warm weather.

"You're right," she said. Then reached up under the towel and turned the light off, thrusting the room into a deep darkness. I heard her punch her pillows, slip down in the bed.

"Well, good night," she said, her voice muffled but very close, and I answered, though I didn't settle in. I waited for my pupils to open, to get the room and our placements in it, have that before turning. Good God, I thought, here I am, going to sleep beside my daughter.

Light entered in a while, a rich dark glow at the heavy drapes, coming from the bulb outside the door and the stronger lighting of the parking lot. The drapes wouldn't fit tight, though I'd pulled them, and a bright silver line stood at their joining, casting a thin rectangle between our two beds broad enough to touch the edge of both blankets, connecting and separating us at the same time. Light with the quality of moon on water, as if the blankets' ripples were the edges of a wave trough spilling toward a common center.

Wait a minute, I thought, stiffening slightly. And though I slipped to the far side of the bed and got up, the trick of light stayed the same, that image of a sea surface between our beds.

I heard Jen move, a deep sigh.

"Are you asleep?" I whispered.

She didn't answer, and I stood at the bedside for a few moments, then spoke again, making sure she was asleep. Then I slipped my shoes on, lifted the room and car keys from the bedside table, and made my way softly to the door. I tested the knob, then opened the door quickly and slipped through, careful to close it without sound.

It was raining, a soft steady rain, suprising in California in July. The parking lot was glistening under bright light, and I hurried to the car and climbed in behind the wheel. My father's file was under the driver's seat. I got it out, then reached to the overhead light and turned it on. That's right, I thought, when I found the newspaper entry. It was a sheet for a double bed, like those in the room I could barely see through the rain-washed windshield. "The question of the sheet," my father had written. Was that it? Could it have possibly come from that hotel, the one Susan Rennert had worked in? Any of the others along the beach? It had been the mid-sixties. Still, they were fancy places then, queen and king, and I didn't think so. But was it really double? Was the term generic? It was another thing to check on, something to do while Jen was at her class.

I sat in the car, mulling it over, but in a short while tiredness began to overtake me. The rain slackened and the drapes beyond the room's windows materialized through the windshield. I went back to the room then and slipped quietly into my bed. The darkness was total. I couldn't see the wave trough, but I could imagine it, knowing it would appear again if I gave my eyes some time. I could hear Jen breathing, a light adult snoring. I turned over in the darkness and fell quickly into sleep and dreaming.

We were on a lake in winter, moving, with something on our feet. Ice, but there was snow too, a light dusting that gusts of wind

TOBY OLSON

kicked into swirls of clouds, blinding me, then dropping down to a kind of billowing skirt at my waist, at Jen's waist, only a few feet off. I saw a strapping at her ankles, a kind of snowshoe, but ski-like, thick ice moving under it.

It was Bark River, that small lake we had started out from, dark shapes of trees on the other side I'd seen from the small porch in moonlight, opening that letter that had taken us west. In the dream, I couldn't see the other side, though the moon was full this time and not at half and waxing.

Jen was growing, or straightening, her arms lifted away from her sides, back arching, moving ahead. I was struggling to keep up. My shoes were loosening, and I had to gather my toes to hold the leather or rubber. We were bundled in heavy coats and hats, and my long scarf tapped at my knees.

Then there was light ahead, an opening in the snow cloud, and when I looked to Jen's feet, I could see the ice thinning under them. I knew we'd reach a place, soon, where the ice would end. We'd be near the middle of the lake, and there'd be bone-chilling water, small waves licking at the jagged ice edges. Jen was heading there. I had to reach her and push her. Or else I had to get to her, take her arm, and pull her to me.

And even in the dreamlike banality of the dream, I knew I was her father and what the dream was about. That I had risked her life in getting to that chamber near Cabo San Quintin, that at any moment she might have panicked, lost her air, been trapped in that rock tube. I'd been a fool, had wanted to relive, somehow, my own father and me, the time we'd gone there. But I had not earned the right to be a father, as he had.

Still, I kicked hard in the dream, fighting as if I did not understand it was only a dream, to get to her, save her. My hand was extended, my glove gone, and I reached out. I could see under her left arm. The fabric of her coat and undergarments were gone there, and I thrust my rigid index finger up into her armpit. I could feel her soft virginal hair, sweat as sweet and fresh as morning dew, and I wanted to pull my finger back, to smell and taste it, touch my cheek as if with tears. The folds of her baby flesh were smooth, gathering troughs. I could feel her rib, a yield of tendon, a deep, steady pulse that told me she trusted me, that I could lift her that way, with a finger.

I saw the ice where it ended in water, a narrow lighted rectangle, like the one between our beds. I'd be safe at the edge of it, but Jen was heading for it. Then in the distance, where the rectangle ended in a snow cloud, I saw Susan Rennert, that square photograph, flat, but enlarged to life-size and animated, vision in her still eyes, ambiguous, but beckoning, not of the dream at all, but in it, her intrusion strangely neutral, as if from another dream, or real life, misplaced here, but starkly present. I was in love with her, at least drawn forward by her. I wanted to enter into her eyes, be the only one for them, and I felt myself rising, and that deep familiar aching in my side. Jen saw her too. I knew that, but didn't know how I knew. She was not looking at me, but ahead now, unaware of the ice's ending.

I pressed my finger up into her armpit, to lift her, despairing as I did so, felt a tightness in my stomach, then a flooding and a wetness. My legs were wet, something sticky. The rectangle of water was roiling, and up from its depths something was rising—a fish?—oval shape of a fish, then breaking, bubbling up to spread over the surface, the tiny waves brightening into red curls, and I turned, my finger slipping out, arm crossing my chest. I was reaching for something, then my hand came to rest in a thick and bloody wetness.

She was standing at the side of my bed in the wave trough, first hint of early dawn's light washing through dimly at the draped windows, touching her pointed shoulders, the blond down on her arms. Her hands held her breast and her smooth cheek. I couldn't see her face clearly, and I lifted my hand to my brow, then looked into my palm. It was red with blood. But I

116   TOBY OLSON could see her eyes now, milky white globes. She was sleeping, standing there, swaying slightly, breath of a quiet talking, indistinguishable words coming from somewhere deep in her chest.

I was still supine, on my side, the deep ache vibrant there, and I pushed up to my elbow, then looked down from her face. Below where her arms had gathered the nightshirt and it billowed, a bloody fold draped over the sheet where my hand had come to rest. The stain started at her sex, a deep red congealing, then spilled in fanning steaks along the fabric covering her legs, feathering out to pink and continuing below the bed's edge, where I could not see.

"Jen," I said softly, shaking my head, pushing sleep away, but she didn't seem to hear me. Still, she released her breasts, her hands opened, and she slowly lowered them down over her stomach, smoothing the nightshirt. Her head was turning from side to side now, as if she were looking for something, heard only dimly, or a thing in distant light, a place of wakefulness. But she was still sleeping, I could tell that, and though I spoke her name again, louder this time, she continued to sleep.

I reached out and took her hand. She'd slipped it over her sex, and she jerked it back. So I reached to the other, hanging beyond any volition along her leg now, and squeezed it, but she didn't respond. I slipped my legs over the bedside and sat up, then stood in the wave trough beside her. I could still see it, though only as a dry sparkle of dimly lit dust motes floating around my legs, her long nightshirt drifting among them as she swayed. I could see her bare, white feet on the dark carpet, her toes, droplets of blood at her ankles.

I was waking, the sun was rising, and beyond my daughter's monotonous movement and humming, the close smell of her blood, the room was materializing, taking shape out of darkness: the scarred and tilted dresser, soiled coverlet, brown stains dripping among faded flowers on the wall. I could see the bathroom doorway, the ripped shower curtain. I still held her hand, and I squeezed it, but there was no response, though she was shaking now, and the half-formed words she uttered were emphatic, part of a conversation, I thought, with someone who was leaving, irrevocably so, and she was trying with words to bring him back, bring her back.

I leaned against her, got close to her ear, and called her name. She cocked her head for a moment, became still, then shook it and started to quake again.

"Jen," I said. "Wake up, wake up." Then I reached down and got my arm behind her knees and lifted her. She was tall and strong and felt heavy then, and as I struggled with her toward the bathroom, her head relaxed against my chest, though she was still speaking, and I could feel her breath against my chin. I smelled the sweet congealed blood, those forming membranes broken as I lifted her, the scent rising from her sex and legs.

In the bathroom, my feet on the cold tile, Jen sitting on the cracked toilet seat. "Jen!" Insistent, but still softly. I wet a thin white towel, held my hand briefly under the spigot, and washed her blood away. She'd smeared her cheek with it, and she tilted her head and let me wipe it, her eyes with pupils now, though fully dilated in the bright light, still unseeing. Then I pressed the rolled towel against the back of her neck, cold water. She shuddered, shook her head, tried to speak. "I . . ." only, then a sucking in of breath, as if after a moan. Then a deep moan. "Jen! Jen! wake up!"

But not yet. I touched her shoulder, holding her there, her head down now, hands on her knees, then released her for a moment and pulled my shirt off. "Stay there." I stumbled out into the room, grabbed the thick beach towel she'd spread on the dresser top, then came back, got her to her feet again, pulled towels from the racks, piling them on the toilet seat.

In the shower then, hot water beating down on both of us, soaking my shorts and her nightgown. In a tub, and I could stand behind her, hold her waist and shoulder, face her into the flood.

TOBY OLSON

Blood swirled pink at the drain. "Oh, I can't get back!" her voice plaintive and distant in the rush, then a coughing, spitting out water. I squeezed her hip at the small rise, bent down and got the hem, then lifted her soaked nightshirt. She felt it, and like a child raised her arms so I could get it up and off. The heart of her buttocks, two dimples, her spine, the clear outlines of her scapulas. I reached past her waist, my fingers brushing her small breast, and turned the handle, colder water. But something hot. I looked down between her spread knees, my foot between hers, a red foot, clots and fresh blood, then washed away, then another splashing, a rose wash on the insides of her thighs. I pushed beyond the plastic curtain, grabbed a towel, then reached around her waist again and pressed it up into her groin. I felt her hand over my own, slipped mine away, and let her hold it. "Oh, Bill!" she said, but there was no embarrassment, and I knew she wasn't back yet, though she was talking.

I turned her and held her, reached past her, and twisted the handle again. The water was cold now, but not icy, a sea cold, and I ran my hand over her back, gripped her tightly at the waist, and spoke through the water in her ear. "Jen," I said. "I'm here. Your father's here. It's okay, okay."

We stood there like that for a long time, the water beating down on her back, spraying out to hit my arms and cheeks. She stopped quaking in a while. I could feel her slack lips on my shoulder and against my neck, her fingers on the scar tissue deep in my left side. She'd stopped talking, and in a while her breath was regular and deep, and I thought she might be falling into a real sleep. I pressed my head into hers then, and she groaned, shuddered deeply, then raised her head away. I reached behind her and turned the shower off, then pushed past the curtain again and got a towel. I knew I had to look at her face, to see that she was truly awake, but I was reluctant, not sure at all what I would find there. Then I moved back slightly from her body, slipped the towel between us, covering her breasts, and looked into her eyes. They were clear now, the pupils properly contracted, but her lips remained slack, and her eyes held a certain wonder, one that had nothing at all to do with our positions or the circumstance.

"Oh," she said. "I've never . . . I don't understand."

11.

"Your period," I said. "Do you remember?"

I was looking into a gathering of daisies on the stained wall. Then I reached into the paper bag to get the soup.

I'd helped her to the bed, then into a T-shirt, and had turned away while she took care of herself. She was calm, but still dazed, and after she'd handed me the towel, I sat on the edge of my bed and watched her fall asleep. It was brighter in the room by then, and I could hear traffic sounds. The rain had stopped, but tires shushed on the wet streets.

Jen had slept until eleven, and when she'd awakened and glanced at her travel clock, she'd said "my class!" I told her it was Sunday, not until tomorrow. It would be all right. I'd watched to see that she was steady, then had left her for the restaurant, hurrying back with hard rolls and soup. She was sitting up in the bed, reading her diving book when I returned.

"It wasn't that," she said. "I've never, not like this."

"The sleepwalking? Your mother and I spoke of that."

She looked up sharply, jealous of that intimacy. The book was open on her lap.

"You had me in the shower, didn't you? I remember. I just *couldn't* wake up! And there was something in your side, ridges. I don't know."

"Just a scar," I said.

My mother had called it my birth medallion, some valiant struggle in coming out, and there were times when she had eased the aching with a pad and lotion, acting the part of a careful nurse in tragic circumstances.

"What was it then? Can you tell me?"

"Well, yes," she said, "It was a dream, a diving dream." She lowered her eyes and put her hand on the open book, pausing for a moment to gather it again. I opened the bag of rolls, scraped away the excess butter with the plastic knife.

"I was diving. It was that place we dove yesterday. The day before that? But it was not the same. I mean, I was alone, and there was no cave or reef, just open and clear water and a deep sandy bottom. And no fish or seaweed either. Nothing really, but I was happy. I could move when I wanted to, go deeper, but I wasn't kicking or using my arms or anything. I had them at my sides, and I could just turn my head and look somewhere. Then I'd be going there."

I carried the plastic tray over to the side of her bed. She moved the book, and I placed it on her lap, then sat down at the bed's edge. She shifted a little and I saw her brows knit. Then she blew at the surface of the soup carefully and sipped from it.

"That seemed a long time, that drifting and turning, and it seemed I was doing something or something was happening. What was it? I was swimming and in doing that was finding it. Or defining it. I don't know. But in a while I knew I was dreaming. That I could stop dreaming. The space in the water was mine, my own thing, and I could stay there and have it, and when I wanted to I could let it go, wake up, then think back about it. I don't know. Does it make any sense?"

"Go on," I said. "Is that it?"

"No, no!" she said. "Just the beginning."

She was shaking a little, the cup vibrating at her lips.

"Eat something," I said. "Have some roll."

She took a bite, chewed it, forcing herself back to something. Her effort seemed physical. Maybe the thing itself was. That it could hurt her, that she could slip back into it again. She put the roll back down on the tray and I reached for her hand and squeezed and held it tightly.

TOBY OLSON

"Then the sandy bottom was moving, sliding. I don't know how I knew that. It was so flat and so much the same. But I did, and a huge shape slid down under me, way down, and when I turned my head to look at it, I dipped that way and began to go there.

"How can I say it? The thing was not part of my dream, that place I had and could wake up from. It was something else, *from* somewhere else. I don't know. But it got clearer. It was like some sort of house underwater. It had windows, a door, other places, like crevices, or the cave we went up into. All rusty and dark, but very hard and very distinct. It was not part of my dream. It didn't belong there.

"But I dove down to it, not really wanting to, just going where I looked, and when I reached the side of it I turned and drifted along its length toward where a corner turned. I passed a doorway and windows, places where the metal was twisted and sticking out, a place where I saw a dim light through an opening. Then I reached the corner. My body bent and I went around it. More windows, rusted metal, another wall off in the distance. I was looking to my side, into openings in the wall I slid along, but then I looked ahead. Another window where the wall turned. I saw her then, that picture, but much larger, filling the whole frame. It was Susan Rennert, that woman, fixed and dead there, in that picture taken before she died. Her hair was pulled back tight. She was almost smiling, yet in pain. But she was not dead, just slowly dying, and she had come into my dream from somewhere else and was not part of it."

"My God," I said, in a whisper. She was holding *my* hand now, and I felt myself slipping, had to plant my feet more firmly on the carpet.

"But that's not it," she said.

She'd been looking away, over my shoulder, but now she turned her head slightly and looked into my eyes.

"It was you," she said. "You killed her. But it was not you."

"What do you mean?" I said. "Tell me."

"I got up quickly, then was standing, the water draining away from me, standing in a puddle. I was out of the dream, a feeling, but

I couldn't wake up. It was something not quite finished, that you had killed her, a terrible feeling, but that it was not you. I was in the middle of that, between it somehow. I couldn't turn one way or the other. I couldn't wake up."

She was finished, and the telling had calmed her down a little. But I was not calm.

"Is it over?"

"It never did. It was that you brought me away from it, in the shower? Talking to me. I don't feel it now, but I think I could if I worked at it. I don't want to."

We drank our soup and nibbled at the rolls, and when I thought she was ready I told her my own dream, how a similar thing had happened, and how I'd awakened to find her standing there beside the bed.

"In mine I didn't kill her, though."

"It's so *weird!*" she said.

It was early afternoon and we were sitting beside each other at the small Formica table, my father's file and list and the notes I'd made between us.

Jen had dressed but was still propped up in her bed reading the diving book when I left to find us another place. I'd gone to the same hotel we'd stayed in and had rented an even better pair of rooms. They wouldn't be ready until four.

Once she was showered and dressed, we spoke again, not about the dreams and their aftermath, but Susan Rennert. It didn't take long. I knew it couldn't be a casual thing for me anymore, and I soon found out the same was true for Jen. She was free of the dream's influence completely by then, but not of the issue.

"Our vacation," she had laughed. "We'll be the diving detectives!"

"That's right. But first you have to *learn* to dive."

"Oh, Bill!"

"We'll study the first lesson later this evening. You can get a head start."

I'd lifted from my father's list those things we knew something of or at least had specific questions about, then had made notes under each entry, including things we might do to begin with. At the bottom, I'd ordered those items that still meant nothing, and we tussled with them for a while.

3. Laguna: check local newspaper morgue.
   - done once.
   - check on shipping schedules tomorrow, Mon.
4. Leonard has batteries.
   - El Monte, dad's friend, Tues. (or Wed.)
   - still alive?
   - is Leonard first name, or last?
6. Could it really have been Housewares?
   - Laguna police, Mon.
   - did he mean the magazine itself,
     or her linen markings?
8. The question of the sheet.
   - find woman from Tod's beach party.
     Lin, Mon. (or Tues.)
   - hotel travel agent, which hotel?
   - double bed sheets, did hotels have them?
   - anything else.
11. Time longer than Rope.
   - Jen's idea, something to do with water?

1. Look into blossom gradation and etching.
2. Go over it with Bev again.
5. Rennert: why Susan?
7. Weather: moon, wind, tides.
9. Write letter to Billy.
10. The History of the American Theater
    (TAT: Its History) what?
12. Go see Blevins.

"Well, it's a start," I said.

"What about me? I don't see *my* name there."

"Once," I said. "The rope business."

"I mean, to do something."

"Well, you've got your diving class." I nudged her, and she pushed back. "But maybe El Monte, when I look for Leonard, you could hit the museum, my mother's papers."

"Wednesday afternoon? After class?"

"Maybe even Tuesday, if you aren't too tired. I'll call, see if they're open in the evening. We can see how it goes."

"Two things," she said. "Bev, and the American Theater business."

"That's right. What else do you think?"

"Well, what we said before. Seven is water. And then the rope."

"Scissors, rock, and paper?"

"Well, it *could* be in some order. I mean, things that follow each other. Do you think?"

"I can't really figure that. Maybe. But it wouldn't seem so. It would be like my father, though, to do that."

"How do you mean?"

"Well, orderly. He was that way."

"What about Blevins?"

"God knows. We could be fooled by Leonard, that Blevins is someone's name too."

"And the American Theater?"

"I don't know," I said. "As curious as the Rennert one. 'why Susan,' what's that?"

"Go ask Blevins," she said, poking me.

"Or write Billy a letter. Ask *him*."

"Or might as well be a local blossom and look into history at Leonard's."

"Ask the moon in its Housewares tide."

"Or check a TAT."

We struggled with the list a little longer, but got no farther, both

TOBY OLSON

realizing, I think, that any yielding would come only step by step as we did those things we had to do. I'd start tomorrow, at the newspaper office. Then we'd see. El Monte and Leonard, if he was still there, had possibilities. But I needed questions, good ones, should I find him. I'd met him only once or twice and hardly remembered him. He'd been no family friend, just someone my father had come across in his "research." I thought he'd been younger than my parents, but I wasn't sure. If even by ten years, he'd still be in his mid-eighties. Or he'd be dead, and I'd have to look elsewhere for the answers.

"I'm so hungry!" Jen said, nudging me again, though still looking down at the list. A shadow darkened the corner of the paper, and when I looked at my watch, I saw it was close to five.

"Let's get the hell out of here," I said.

Jen had packed, and while I shoved things into my suitcase, she slipped the list back in my father's file, then went around the room and ordered it, settled the pillows, and pulled the covers up neatly over the beds.

"You don't have to do that," I said.

"Oh, yes I do. It's for the chambermaid, for those who come after."

"Well, maybe you're right," I said. "And it is the Navy way."

"*I'm* not in the Navy!"

"But you're traveling with a sailor. Used to be, at least."

"And a diver. I'll be one of those!"

I carried our things to the car, and when I got back, Jen was coming out the door.

"Anything we forgot? Did you check?"

"Yes," she said. "But I *do* feel I've left something."

"Never mind," I said. "We've got everything we need."

She looked back in. "Good-bye, stinky room," then pulled the door closed and turned away.

Our new rooms were on a high floor, and when I leaned out on my balcony, I could see Main Beach off in the distance, the lifeguard tower where Jen would meet her class and teacher.

"Is that it?" Jen said, and when I turned, she was standing only a few feet away on her own balcony. She'd showered again, but had not dressed for dinner. She wore jeans and a clean, black T-shirt. Her hair was shining in the wash of the failing sun, and I could see the ovals of silver on her new Mexican belt.

"That's it," I said. "But what about dinner?"

"How about pizza? It's been a while."

"And beer," I said. "I could go for a beer."

We found a trendy place near the center of town, the menu posted under a light beside the door. Designer stuff, fancy mushrooms, spinach.

"Yuk," Jen said. "Can't we do a little better?"

So we headed away from town, back in the direction of the seedy motel, until we came upon a small, storefront place, the sign above the windows as wide as they were, PIZZA, and ordered a large pie with everything, a six-pack, and two Cokes for Jen.

We sat in my room, side by side again at the oval glass table, and while we ate I went over the first lesson with her. It was simple, things she'd already learned to do, but Higgins had laid them out step by step, which was good. At the end of the chapter was a list of things that could go wrong, and when I looked ahead in the book, I saw that such a list ended each chapter, things dropped from previous lists and new ones added. The text explained that one or more problems would arise each day but that the students wouldn't know which or when. That was the way with accident. You'd never know while diving. It was a good teaching idea, and before we finished, I went over the list at the end of the first chapter, explaining each potential difficulty. Jen was very serious. She asked good questions, pressed me to explain again when things weren't clear. "Okay," I said in a while. "We've got to leave something for the class. Bed, don't you think?"

It was only ten, but I was tired, and I thought she must be too. It had been a various day, not to mention night.

TOBY OLSON

"Okay," she said. "Will you wake me up?"

"What time?"

"Well, seven, I guess. Shouldn't I eat?"

"A little something, sure. They'll have lunch."

"God knows what. Probably sprouts. Vegetables. Yogurt."

"Hey," I said. "This is California!"

We both stood, and Jen reached down and got her diving book.

"Maybe a little bedtime reading," she said, then reached to my shoulder, leaned over, and kissed me on the cheek.

"Are you all right?"

"Yes, yes, I am. I'm fine. Thank you."

"For what?" I said.

"Oh. Well. For being a good father."

"Am I?" I said. "I hope I am."

"Good night," Jen said, then leaned over and kissed me once again, then pinched my arm. "Don't let the bedbugs bite!"

Sleep wouldn't come, so I got up and had a glass of water, pulled the drapes aside and let starlight flood into the room, then lay on my back watching the dancing sparkles on the ceiling. I'd opened a glass door to the sea and could hear surf and feel a faint salt wash along my arms. I had my hands together over my stomach. I lay like a dead man in a coffin.

"Rennert: why Susan?" my father had written. In Jen's dream I had killed her, but had not, and it was that, she had said, two exactly equal possibilities, which had held her suspended between sleep and waking. But more. It was the way Susan Rennert had entered the dreams, not of them, but from somewhere outside of them, and in the same form, that photograph from her driver's license. We'd both seen it. That could explain part of it, her being there, though not the experience of her entrance. And it had been I and not Jen who had been so strongly drawn to her, just looking at her picture, as if I'd been remembering her, still wanting her somehow, though she was gone.

My mother. I'd never been close to another woman in that way, not until Jen in the shower, blood on her legs, who was a woman in a girl still, though menstrual, to have cared for her even in that ultimate privacy, biology of a woman flooding from a child's body.

But she'd been suspended, neither awake nor sleeping, half dreaming. Had she known anything of that release? Had her suspension freed her? She'd stood at the side of my bed bleeding, in a gesture of asking. And I'd given her what help I could and a recognition she knew nothing of. At least we'd not spoken of that, what she might have remembered, but of the dreams only as cause of such aftermath.

I could feel my mother slipping into the bed behind me. I was eleven years old and had a fever. I'd been climbing and had fallen, a wooden picket driven into my back. Infection, the tenderness under the thick bandaging she moved against, making a spoon of herself, folding into me, and the scent of bourbon. Asleep or waking? The heat of her moon stomach warming the bandaging, the wound soothed.

She'd sung a song for me, her mouth touching my ear, a light comic show tune, about animals and crops. I could see her ingenue's face, or I could remember it from times she'd sung for my father and me, lifting her skirt in the living room, taking a bow at the end of it. My father and I applauding, her cradling the imaginary flowers he'd handed her.

It was a child's face, full of wonder and delight, but it contained a craftiness, that visible knowledge that it was not of a child, but of a girl, one soon to become something else. My mother sang to me that comic tune, a child's voice in an aging woman, and only the promise of something other in between.

I fell asleep and dreamed again, that I had risen and taken my father's file into the bathroom, had removed the photo of Susan Rennert and looked at it while I masturbated. It was something I'd seldom done with such intensity and focus, but when I was finished I felt no significant relief, only a dull longing, and for a dead woman I had never known or seen. I woke once in the night, my hand sticky and damp, and when I touched it to my side, the ache seemed to ease.

12.

I had Jen at Main Beach by quarter to nine. We drove there, and I helped her lug her gear down to the lifeguard tower. Michael Higgins had arrived, and three young men were messing with tanks and wet suits on blankets. Jen eyed them furtively, but then the others arrived, a middle-aged couple, another woman, and an old man, short and lean, who was quick to take his shirt off. He had a tight, muscular chest and hard, veiny arms. He smiled at Jen in a fatherly way, "Ready for the fun?" And she joked back at him, grinning.

Then Higgins called them all around him at the tower's side, held up a regulator, and began talking about it. He was dressed in a wet suit, the rubber hood resting behind his neck like a monk's cowl. The young men stood, hands on hips, but the others, Jen beside the old man, sat on blankets at his feet, their faces turned up attentively, and I left.

When I got to the newspaper office, the man I'd spoken to wasn't there, but a woman was, a young girl really, and I guessed she was the student he'd told me about.

"Oh," she said. "He isn't here. Out on assignment."

She said the last in what she seemed to think was a newspaper way, enthusiastically, then offered me the same seat I'd sat in before.

I told her why I'd come, and her eyes lit up.

"I've *done* that work," she said, then raised a finger for me to wait and went into the back room, returning quickly with a thin sheaf of papers.

"This is it. You can sit over there, take all the time you need."

There were shoppers on the street already, and beachgoers, and though none looked in, I felt I was sitting on a kind of stage. The desk was close to the bay windows, and I could see a good way down the sidewalk in both directions. It was only nine-thirty, but most of the shops were open and ready for business.

The lists held much more than the newspaper had printed. They'd selected out the more exotic passages, ships with foreign-sounding names or odd cargoes, the fancier cruise ships, even when they didn't make a stop near Laguna. It was clear from the printed clippings tucked in at the back of the sheaf that the list-ings held no practical purpose at all near the end, when my father had come there.

But the lists themselves, twenty single-spaced sheets, seemed complete, an accounting of all traffic that had passed by, at least those crafts that were over a certain tonnage.

I didn't know where to start, so I checked the dates at the begin-ning, four weeks before my father had come there, then looked at the end of the last sheet he'd examined. The date was the same as the one he'd logged in, and I went back to the beginning and read down the list. There was something in the middle of the first page, a smudge or small pencil mark, a little dot beside a cruise ship entry, and I moved ahead, looking for others and finding them. Tiny markings, but each was beside a ship in the King of Norway line, four of them, *King of Norway V, III, VII* and *II,* and when I checked the other entries, I found they were the only ones with that name. I made a note of each, writing down the dates of passage, then went through the lists again, but could find nothing else.

"Would you know anything about this?" I asked the girl.

She was sitting at the desk going through some papers and clip-pings, and I put my finger beside one of the dots and turned the top list toward her. She studied it intently for a moment, and when I showed her the others, she looked hard at them also.

TOBY OLSON

"Well, I don't know," she said. "Looks like pencil. But I surely didn't do them. Maybe when things were selected for the paper?"

"It isn't that," I said. "I checked that. These are listed, but so are others of the same kind, and no dots there."

"He'll be back in a while. You could call, or I could call you? Do you have a number?"

I gave her the name of our hotel and my room number, thanked her, and then left. I was convinced the markings were my father's. It was his way, just those tiny dots. He'd never soil important information, and to him it was *all* important.

I walked the beach back to the hotel, and at Main I shaded my eyes and looked out to sea. A high, thin haze lay over it, softening the sun, and I could see them clearly. They were close to shore, bobbing around the large inner tubes Higgins had lashed together. I couldn't find Jen. They were all in wet suits, hoods tight around their heads and as such looked identical, women indistinguishable from men. I smelled something on the light breeze, scent of an aftermath of burning.

When I got back to the hotel, I went through the adjoining door into Jen's room and got the box we'd taken from the storage place in El Monte. I carried it back into my own room and placed it on the freshly made bed. The chambermaid had been around, and I thought briefly of my sheets, wondering if she'd noted the stains. I'd turned the radio on, and after a brief and ominous interview with some scientist about earthquakes, they were talking again about the smog. It seemed it had thickened; school closings were pending.

Jen had taken the jewelry folds from the box and locked them in her suitcase, and the manila file folders were no longer tightly jammed together. I sat on the bed, removed each file, and looked carefully through it. There must have been twenty, some thick with offprints and articles that had been carefully cut from magazines. It was mostly that disaster and civil defense material, nothing at all that had to do with the Rennert matter, and no letter to Billy. I lingered over the diving files, two of them: printed instructions, a few vacation brochures, advertisements for gear. After an hour or so I was finished, and once I'd settled the box in a corner of the room, I turned off the radio and went to the phone and called Carol.

"She's diving."

There was a silence, and I followed up quickly.

"It's a class. Middle-aged women, even, and an old man. I checked it out. Don't worry."

"I'm trying not to," she said. "What's next on the agenda?"

I told her about Catalina, that we'd be going there, then told her we were looking into some things my father had left behind. I mentioned my mother's jewelry, that I'd given it to her, that Jen had liked it, then I asked her about dreaming.

"No, nothing extreme. Did she have one?"

"Yes," I said. "A nightmare. Nothing to do with the trip, I don't think." I was lying to her, but it was too much to explain.

"Has she had her period? She's due. Would you know about that?"

She was very direct in saying it, as if she were speaking to her husband, I thought, to Jen's father, but I wasn't sure if she was making that kind of connection.

"Dreaming?" I said.

"No, nothing like that. It's easy for her. But I thought, some embarrassment? You know, with you there. That kind of thing."

"Well, she has," I said. "Just yesterday. I don't think she's bothered by my knowing. I think it's okay."

"A child," she said. "She's still a child."

"I know that."

We spoke of other things. I told her it was making sense that we not plan far ahead. Jen seemed to like that. We were set for the rest of the week, with diving class and Catalina at the end of it. I didn't know what would follow, but so far that kind of thing seemed fine. I said we'd keep in touch, of course, let her know what was coming.

"Do you know how long you'll be out there?"

"I don't know. Maybe a few days, before we come back east. She seems to like it here." Then I asked her what she was doing.

"Reading. Shopping. Wondering what's going on out there."

"I know," I said.

"No," she said. "You certainly don't."

"You're right," I said, feeling we might get into an argument, say something we might regret.

"Look. I'm not blaming you for anything. It's just that it's not easy."

I pressed my lips together, holding back any statement of false understanding. I *didn't* know how she might feel. Not at all. And I recognized that my ignorance went beyond these specifics, that I'd really had little occasion to be empathetic, wasn't even sure I was capable of that. Once again the emptiness of the past twenty years flooded in on me, and what I had thought of as a certain comfortable aloneness in my life now felt like loneliness, even waste.

"Well," I said. "Please don't worry. Whatever else, I'll take good care of her."

When Carol and I were finished, I called Mrs. Venuti, catching her on the way out. "To the Italian Market," she said, "There's no rush," and I waited while she got my mail.

There was nothing there, only some junk flyers and a few unimportant bills, magazine subscriptions, and yet another brochure from a place in the Netherlands Antilles. *That* would be a place for us to dive, I thought. I asked Mrs. Venuti to just hold onto things, that I'd get back to her again soon.

"My son," she said. "Larry? Did I tell you he got chairman of his department now?"

"No," I said. "That's good news!"

"Yes it is," she said. "But Bill, are you having a good time with your daughter out there?"

I'd told her about Jen, that we'd be taking a trip together.

"Yes," I said. "A *very* good time."

It was noon by the time I reached the police station, an efficient modern looking building with plenty of glass, on Third Street near Laguna Canyon Road in the foothills above the town. The fire department was housed next to it, the nose of a freshly washed red engine poised in the tall, open bay. There were two squad cars near the station entrance, but no others, and when I pulled in beside them, I checked to see that I'd be legal there.

Beyond the glass doors, the place was quiet and seemed empty. I walked the short corridor, bulletin boards like those in high school on the walls, community announcements, summer art fairs and drama productions. The brief hallway ended, and I turned into a wider one, at the end of which a tall counter cut off the entrance to a large, sunny room. It was full of desks, computers, and copying machines, low lateral file cabinets lining the walls. There were chairs to the counter's side, small tables covered with magazines. It was only when I reached the counter and looked over it that I saw the uniformed man sitting at a desk below. He was fingering through a sheaf of papers, a pair of wire-rimmed half glasses parked near the tip of his nose. He jumped in his seat a little, my shadow or a squeak of sole, then got to his feet, took the glasses off, and dropped them onto the papers. He was smiling.

"Shit," he said. "You scared me."

"I'm sorry."

"It's that way at lunch. The place gets kinda quiet."

"Are you alone?" I said.

"Oh, no. They're off in the other wings. But the walls are thick."

He was small, very neat in his freshly pressed uniform, maybe early thirties, and when he put his hands on the counter I could see his clean, manicured nails.

"What can I do for you?"

"Well," I said. "A rather strange request."

I told him about my father and the way he was, some of his interests, the Rennert file and the list he'd made.

The officer's name was Sanchez, and he remembered Susan Rennert's death, had even looked into it himself, though he'd been a teenager when it happened.

He was local, getting ready to graduate from high school, and knew he'd be taking the civil service test. The death had been a mystery, even talked about in classes, and when he joined the force at twenty-one, he'd gotten out the file and studied it. There was still some investigation going then, though halfhearted, and it was given up completely shortly after his rookie year.

"It's curious," he said.

He'd found the thick file and the magazine without much trouble. Even at this late date they'd kept it handy, though he didn't think it had been looked at in many years. It was no longer an irritant, but no one chose to put it in the inactive. He wasn't sure of the sheet or her few belongings. Certainly not in the evidence room, though there'd been little and it wouldn't have taken much space.

He'd given me a desk off in a corner, had gone through the file carefully himself. Anything confidential, he'd have to remove that. But there'd been nothing. He said, a little apologetically, that he'd have to watch me, and he asked me to be careful turning the pages. He had me wash my hands in the bathroom down the hall. He stood at my shoulder, but in a while sat at the desk across from me.

"Why curious?" I said. "Do you mean that it was never solved?" I was looking down at the magazine cover, an old issue of *House and Garden,* a view across a flagstone patio and through glass sliders, elegant country furniture in a sitting room.

He started to say something, but the sound of footsteps beyond the counter pulled him away. He got up and headed there. I heard the squeak of leather, a clink of metal, then saw the countertop lifting, a uniformed figure, ominous in dark glasses and metal helmet, another behind him. He took the glasses off and looked at me, then lifted the helmet away. His hair was gray, slicked down around his scalp. He smiled and nodded, and the other motorcycle policeman, younger and less heavy, moved up beside him. They turned and spoke quietly to Sanchez. Then they went to a desk across the room and began working on some report or other. Their voices remained subdued, as if they were avoiding disturbing me. I heard more footsteps, others returning from lunch or just checking in. Sanchez was busy at the counter now. He'd given up watching me. I lowered my eyes to the magazine again and began going through it.

Using the tips of my fingers, I turned the pages carefully, then folded them over with the palm of my hand. The spine had dried out and was cracked and a few pages had broken from the glue. What looked like coffee stains darkened bedrooms and gardens, rippling the paper into parchment, and I thought much of the damage had happened earlier, before the death of Susan Rennert, when the magazine was communal on that table in the chambermaids' lounge.

I passed advertisements, photos of smug and smiling couples in dream-house settings, a few brief articles printed in large type. Near the center, I came to a thicker page, the one I knew about. Someone had slipped a glassine sleeve over it, and there were Susan Rennert's pencil markings beside a photo of a large, made-up bed and small inset ones showing various sheet designs, edges folded back, revealing patterns. Her letters were printed, small and very carefully, and she'd listed figures in some places, prices, and those code designations relating to color and design. I read through a column, losing my addition halfway, drawn to letter and number shapes, the fact that she'd written these things, as if some unfolding articulation of motive and thought were still alive there, that she was alive there, more real even than in the photographs I'd seen of her. The writing pulled at me in a way I couldn't quite locate, something about its care and guardedness, as if there were a thing behind or under it held in tenuous control, a more real self, something sexual.

And I was rising, had to shift a little in the chair, then slackened, as I recognized that I'd been reaching in a kind of vacant fantasy for

TOBY OLSON

some union with the dead. I leaned back in the chair, looked up at the ceiling, and rotated my head. My neck cracked, loud to me, but no one in the now-full room seemed to hear it. They were sitting at tables or standing beside them, each in uniform, and I lowered my head and looked once again at the page.

Prices of sheets and pillowcases, various designs calculated along with others; checking the code numbers, I found they were all king and queen. What was she doing? Some fantasy of a better life? She'd selected the most expensive, placed one color against another. The figures went on and on, but I could find no development or conclusion in them, and in a while I folded the page over, looked at the beginning of an article on the back of it, then continued on, nothing but more of the same, and I had to force myself to move slowly.

I was near the end of the magazine, looking at another linen ad, a half page this time and with none of Susan Rennert's writing in the margins, when I noticed the restaurant advertisement below it. It was an ad for a national chain of upscale steakhouses, and to the left of the fancy scripted title, below which was a small picture of an elegant dining room, white tablecloths, good china and crystal, there was a list of cities. "Each of the same high quality and quiet elegance," the ad said, and below those words was a small map of streets and freeways near Los Angeles, a little square noting the location of the steakhouse there. They must have worked the ad in a regional way, I thought, different insets for different places. The map was very simple, a half dozen streets stylized into thick straight lines. Only the freeways showed curves, the proper exits marked with arrows.

I was ready to turn the page, had my fingers at the corner, then stopped, seeing either the small pencil marking or the street name. I wasn't sure which had stopped me, but there it was, just a little dot, a pencil point rotated to make it. Was it my father's signature? *Could it really have been Housewares?* That was on his list. He might have been here. But only if he had seen the dot and not made it would he have listed that last entry. At least that seemed right. *Go see Blevins*. It was not a person, but a street name, Blevins Street, and near the map's perimeter, nothing at all to do with the restaurant, that small pencil dot beside the B.

When I was ten, my father took me Japanese kite fishing at a small lake in the San Gabriel Mountains above Los Angeles. He had careful maps, and though the lake was lined with expensive homes and was private, he'd found an abandoned firebreak near the far end and was able to chug the old Oldsmobile down through deep ruts to within thirty yards of the water's edge. He parked among trees, out of sight, and we lugged the line and kite and the small, hand-cranked generator down to the shore. He'd handed me books and articles, and on the way there I'd read what I could and had looked at the pictures. I'd asked questions, and he'd known all the answers, even about the history of the thing, the sources of those who had started it. "But Billy," he'd said, "We're gonna make a little advance on it." Then he explained the workings of the generator, how I'd have to give it a good crank and watch the needle, where the button was, and that his signal would be simply "push." He said we'd have to "research" it a little, "the size of the fish."

The line was a braided twist of electrical wire, thick kite string and fishing filament, and my father had been careful to keep it light, even though the kite was a big and stable one, something he'd made himself, using the same materials he'd cobbled his planes together with. He'd checked with the weather service before leaving. I'd heard him on the phone, calling the man by his first name, talking about family.

He limped along the waterline, checking the overhang of trees behind us, looking for the best place, and when he found it, he helped me position the generator firmly in the sand. Then he handed me the line end, a few inches of electrical wire extended below the braided portion. He watched me twist the bare wires around the terminal posts, something he'd taught me to do, positive and negative, then grinned and nodded when I was finished and looked up from where I was kneeling.

The breeze was stiff and blowing out from shore, and when he lifted the box kite, his back to me, it rose immediately and sat above his head on a tight tether, then drifted slowly away over the water as he played out the line from coils held at his chest. I could see the length of braid descending from the kite strut, the fish hook and dangling bait. It swayed a few feet above the lake surface, and he held it there, working the kite out until it hung over deep-enough water. Then he turned his head and smiled at me and nodded. The breeze had lifted his shirt collar and it tapped against his cheek at the corner of his eye, causing a mad winking. He threw his head back to get it away, then turned toward the lake again.

I grabbed the wooden handle and started to crank, watching the needle jump. It was tough at first, but as my speed and momentum increased, it got easier and the needle rose more quickly. I cranked until it hit the number we'd decided upon, then called out to my father. He yelled in return, the breeze swallowing all but the sound. Then I saw the line grow taut, the kite tip, and the bait move down toward the lake's surface. It plunked when it hit, then went under, and when he had it a good ten feet below, he slackened his grip, held the kite in place, and we waited, my father poised and ready, his game leg bent at the knee, all his weight on the stiff other, my finger on the metal beside the small red button.

We waited a long time, at least it felt that way to me. I watched the kite for as long as I could manage, then shifted my eyes to the generator, its bolts and rivets. Then I looked across the lake at the distant houses, wondered what it might be like to live in one of them. I even turned and glanced back into the woods, found an edge of the Oldsmobile's gray fender peeking out from the leaves. I began thinking about home, wondering what my mother might be doing. It was Saturday. She was probably reading, listening to show tunes on the radio. Maybe . . . "Hang in there, Billy! It won't be long now!" He hadn't turned, but he'd known somehow that I'd been drifting. I checked my finger placement beside the red button, then looked back and found the kite. It was still, where it hung in the air, but then, amazingly to me, it lurched down, and when I looked below it, I saw the braid snap taut.

"Push!" my father yelled, and I poked the red button.

The first one was a bass, a big one, and it fought hard against the kite's rising. The two were in stalemate for a while, the line vibrating and the kite shaking angrily. But then my father got the kite up, and I watched the fish pop through the surface. It flopped and wiggled at the hook and was still jumping when we got it in and on the sand. My father stood over it, hands on his hips, watching its gills move, then looked to where I now stood beside the generator. His brow was creased, and I saw it was the dying fish he was concerned with.

"Billy, these are bigger fish than I thought they'd be out there. I'm afraid we've tortured this one. More juice, I guess. Let's jump it up to ten."

He loaded fresh bait, then shook the sand off the kite and had me hold it as it rose up at the lake's edge, while he untwisted the braid and coiled it again. Then he leaned down over the generator and checked the terminals. The breeze was pulling hard at the kite, and I had to hop a little to the side and pull toward the woods to hold it. I got my foot wet in the wash. The lake was warm, and the water flooding my tennis shoe felt good. My father limped quickly over when he saw my struggle, but he didn't take the kite line from me. He grabbed my shoulders, leaning with me, and when he spoke, his mouth was at my ear.

"Can you feel it in your arms, Billy? That's nature's power. It's like sailing. Even flying. I've been researching that. Related to kites. Maybe we'll try that soon!"

He got the kite out over the lake again, the fish line above the water. I was already cranking, working to get the needle up to ten.

TOBY OLSON

It was hard going. I was turning furiously but couldn't get above eight. I had to reach into myself, get my shoulder and back into it, press down on the generator housing with my free hand to keep it steady. Then the needle did rise, slowly but steadily, and when it reached the mark, I jerked my hand away, sucked air into my burning lungs, and watched the still-spinning crank slow down. I wanted to call out, but I had no breath, and when my father looked back at me, I simply nodded and shook the hand that was at my brow, wiping the sweat away. He turned to the lake again, and I watched the kite dip and sink in the air, the bait enter the water as it had before. Again we waited, my finger beside the red button, my father poised at the lake edge, but not for long this time.

The line jerked, the kite rustled and fell. I saw my father play the fish line for a moment, then hear him yell out again. "Push!" and I hit the red button.

There was a crackling in the air. I saw a blue light outlining the kite struts, then gathering into a tube of blue that shot down the line and into the water. Wisps of smoke rose from the struts, a smell of wood burning, and there was a bubbling at the surface where the line entered. The hair on my father's head had risen into spiky tufts, and I saw his game leg shaking, his toe slapping at the sand. He stumbled, and the kite rose up again, flames in its paper box now. It lifted the fish up out of the water, another large bass, but this one still and dead, hanging from the hook. The fish stood up in the air for a moment, but then began to lower again, and I saw the bodies of other dead fish on the surface where it fell and floated, and when I looked back up at the kite, it was no more than a skeleton, flesh of a few strips of flapping red paper curling into ash as it drifted to the side and began to fall.

"Christ!" my father yelled, hopping around to look at me. Ash fell from his brows, his leg was still vibrating, but he was grinning, his hair like meringue. "Too much juice!" he laughed. "No question about it! But Billy, wasn't that a pisser!"

My father stripped down to his underwear and waded out with the net. I stayed on shore, disconnected the wires from the generator, and pulled the kite, no more than a few charred sticks now, up onto the sand. The water was deep where the fish were, and my father had to sidestroke out to them. He treaded and turned, sweeping the net along the surface, herding them into it. There were fifteen, including the large bass. Most were just a little bigger than minnows, though there were two almost respectable perch among them.

It was early evening by the time we got back. My mother was waiting at the open doorway, and she welcomed us home, theatrically, as The Fishermen. I saw her look at my father's brows, but she didn't comment. It was their way. He'd tell her about it later, and I knew he'd grow enthusiastic in the telling, reliving it all.

"The catch?" she said, seeing the gunnysack I was holding. It hung like a long empty sock at my side, and when we reached the kitchen, my father held the mouth while I searched around the bottom, finding the fish, then lifting the sack high up, dumping them into the sink. We stood close together, looking down at them.

"Well, we killed them," my father said. "But it was quick, and I'm sure they didn't feel it. The way seems now impractical. I mean, how account for size? Right, Billy? Still, they'll make an adequate dinner. Don't you think so, Bev?"

She *did* think so, and after we'd gutted and cleaned them, my father using his surgical instruments and a jeweler's head-held magnifier on the smallest ones, my mother dipped them in egg and bread crumbs, then lowered all fifteen into the large, black skillet, where they sizzled and fried.

We ate them with boiled potatoes, fresh coleslaw, sliced tomatoes, and a crisp french bread my mother had bought during the day, then warmed in the oven. Both my parents made smacking sounds, nodded at each other with full mouths.

I remember my mother touching her napkin delicately to the side of her mouth.

"You know," she said, "I haven't had better fish since that trout almandine. Our dinner at The Brown Derby, after we saw *Ghosts?*"

"I remember it well," my father said, "That purple dress!" He speared a minnow and held it up on his fork, then shook it and smiled at me.

"But Billy, what do *you* think?"

13.

It was three-fifteen by the time I got to the Main Beach parking lot, and though many of the day's sun lovers were packing trunks and pulling out, other cars were slowly cruising the lot, grabbing spaces as soon as they became vacant. It took me a good ten minutes to find one. Something was going on. I saw a white truck with a TV station logo on the side, parked illegally, two men in coveralls dragging thick loops of cable from the back. I crossed the lot and found an empty bench on the blacktop path where the beach started. I could see the lifeguard tower from there and beyond it the edge of surf where the sand sloped down. People stood knee-deep in the water or sat on blankets, but there weren't many now, and when I looked out beyond the few inshore swimmers, I could see the fat, trussed-up inner tubes of Jen's diving class, dark figures bobbing beside them.

Once I'd discovered Blevins Street, I'd closed the magazine and gone through the file. The newspaper articles had been thorough, and though the police reports were more detailed, there was nothing in them that added significantly to the picture. Susan Rennert's early past seemed empty, or at least irretrievable.

A glassine folder held her social security card, driver's license, and a facsimile of her baptismal certificate. Her birth was documented by a notarized letter that mentioned the date and time, taken from some official log, and included a statement about water damage. There were lab and autopsy reports, a sheet of careful notation written by the officer who had first arrived at the scene, transcripts of interviews, and a careful narrative that had been gathered from all this.

She'd worked at the hotel for close to a year. There was a written reference through which they'd traced her to her last job, at a place in Los Angeles where she'd done the same kind of work. She'd been there four years. Then there was two years they couldn't account for. They'd found her at nineteen, just a few months at some coffee shop in Rosemead. Before that, there was nothing, not since her childhood, when her parents had disappeared from Encinitas. They'd checked the Rennert name throughout the state, had even put it out on the wire, but they'd come up with nothing. They'd found a remnant of unpaid bills in Encinitas during the year of Susan Rennert's birth, but only a hint of her parents having lived there. The address listed in her birth document was now that of a shopping mall. They had her parents' first names, but no living relatives whom they could find.

When I was finished with the file, Sanchez came over. He was carrying a log book, his hand stuck in between the pages. He opened it on the desk across from me and turned it, his finger on the page.

"Your father," he said. "He was a newspaper man?"

I looked down at the sheet and quickly caught the entry, then looked up at him and smiled.

"Well, sometimes," I said.

My father had gotten a press card through the *El Monte Sentinel*. He was known there, always doing research, and there were those at the police and fire stations who knew him as well.

"Anyway. He was here."

He got another book and had me sign it. I included both the hotel address and that of my apartment in Philadelphia. I thanked him as I was leaving, and he wished me luck.

At twenty to four I saw the inner tubes moving in, a line of bodies to seaside pushing them. Then they were all up and standing in the sluggish surf, lugging the tubes out of the water, awkward in their tanks and flippers. I could see Jen, the old man behind her holding her tank while she slipped out of the straps. Then he turned, and she helped him. The young men helped the older women. Then they all kicked their flippers off, trudged up the beach, and gathered around Higgins at the lifeguard tower. One of the young men sat near Jen, and I thought he was leaning toward her, saying things. I saw Higgins's hands moving in the air as he explained something. Then in a while he leaned a little toward them and clapped his hands. They were all clapping then, and after that they stood and gathered up their gear. The young men waved to Jen as she started up the beach toward me, her tank, flippers, and wet suit hanging heavily from her shoulder. Her head was up and looking, and I stood at the bench and waved until she found me.

"Bill!" she said when she reached me and I was helping her with her stuff.

"How was it?" I said.

She was flushed and full of it all, her hair pressed tight around her head like a cap. A red line from the wet suit hood made a circle around her forehead and cheeks, and the whites of her eyes were pink from the salt water.

"Oh, it was glorious! I'll tell you all of it! But there's something else."

She was sitting on the bench now, brushing the sand from her feet with a towel. I stood above her, watching her bare shoulders.

"And what's that?" I said.

"Beach volleyball! They're professionals! Even TV! Just down there." She raised her towel-draped hand and pointed.

"And you want to go."

"Oh, Bill, could I? Those nice boys, my diving mates? They've got tickets. They invited me!"

She looked up at my face then, less awkwardly than she had when asking about Tod's beach party, and I felt pleased. Not so much that I'd be an easy touch, but that she trusted she knew me, was sure of my response, even the next question, which she answered before I asked it.

"They really *are* nice boys, and it's over before dark. By eight o'clock. I could meet you here, right at this bench. It's just down the beach. I can eat there, burgers and such."

I started to ask her about clothing, but I'd seen a bit of beach volleyball on television. Many in the audience were in swimming suits, those with fine and intimidating bodies.

"You can wear your wet suit top if it gets chilly," I said. "There's a certain classiness in that. They'll know you're a diver, almost as good as being a surfer."

She started to say *Oh, Bill,* but ended up just grinning. Then she reached out and pulled at my pant leg and laughed.

After I'd loaded Jen's gear into the car, I drove back to the hotel but didn't go to the room. I crossed the lobby to the concierge's desk, where I asked directions to the travel service, a small office down a short hallway at the lobby's streetside corner. A large woman sat at a desk covered with phones and papers.

"Lin? Oh, sure," she said, and gave me directions, even turned and pointed through the wall behind her.

It was the third hotel down from ours, in the direction of Main Beach, and I took the beachside walkway, a twisting strip of blacktop. People still lingered on blankets on the sand, but most had shirts on now or towels over their shoulders. The sun was still high, but a slow, cool breeze blew down from the foothills, carrying a hint of smog from inland, a faintly acrid smell. Jen had a towel as well as her wet suit top, but I thought I'd better get there earlier than eight, just in case. It was close to five, still a good few hours until sunset.

I saw Lin crossing the lobby as I came through the glass doors from the beach. She wore a tight, tailored suit, nylons, and low heels, and there was a colorful scarf tied at her neck. I followed behind her. She moved quickly and seemed stiffer than she had that night on the beach. This is business, I thought, and when she'd entered her office, moved around the desk and sat down, she saw me at the door but raised her finger, then grabbed for the phone and began talking quickly. She was at it for a good long while, arrangements for some flight or other, and I stood there awkwardly, waiting until she finally hung up the phone.

"I can come back," I said.

"No, no," she said. "That's done. That's it for a while."

But work wasn't done. She'd be there until after nine, a big Catalina package.

"Half of the largest hotel in Avalon. Christ, the needs of these people."

I sat down across from her at the desk. Her computer screen was visible at the L, thick with phrases and figures, and between phone calls we talked again about the sheets. There was none of the slow seductiveness in her that I'd seen at Tod's party. She seemed harder and much more efficient than I would have thought then.

"Nothing but king and queen. When they have a third in the room, it's a single, either a pullout couch or something they roll there."

"Even then?" I asked.

"Oh, sure. There's just no reason to do it otherwise. Nobody *prefers* a double."

"The maid's quarters?"

"Well, I don't know," she said. "If they were very old, I guess. But then they'd have to find those sheets among the hundreds of others, or wash them separately. Wouldn't want to get to a room with some that didn't fit. Then again, they *might* segregate the single size, though they'd be much easier to find, and I'd doubt that. I could find out."

"Now?"

"Sure," she said. "This one, at least. Right now."

She got on the phone and called the laundry. I heard her ask for someone. We both waited, and she smiled at me, then put her hand over the mouthpiece.

"You're really into this thing, aren't you?"

"I guess I am," I said, then started to say more. But she raised her hand to stop me and spoke into the phone. She listened and in a few moments was nodding. I heard her ask about other hotels along the beach. She waited again, then said, "Okay, thanks." Then she hung up.

"Well," she said. "It's as I thought. Not a double in sight. Though he can't be positive about the other places, he'd bet on it. And he's been here twenty years."

I left the hotel by the front entrance, saw the liquor store across the street, and wove between the waiting cars to get there. All four lanes were stalled, and car horns were blowing. I could see something up ahead, a truck, I thought, sitting at an odd angle.

I got a bottle of bourbon and a bag of ice, then walked back to the hotel and took the elevator to our floor. There was a chambermaid's cart in the hall, piled with sheets and towels and holding various packets and small plastic bottles in wire compartments. I passed it and the open door, heard her singing softly as I reached for my key.

The light was blinking on the phone, and I put the bottle down, spilled the ice into the insulated container, then lifted the receiver and called down for the message. An officer named Sanchez had asked me to return his call, and I wrote the information on the pad beside the phone, hung up, and dialed the number. It was a little after six and he wasn't there. I could try him again tomorrow. He'd be in at eight in the morning. I hung up, then lifted the phone again and called room service and ordered a sandwich and salad. I'd eaten nothing since our skimpy breakfast and was feeling tired and a little woozy. I fixed a tall bourbon and water, then flicked the TV to the six o'clock news, sat down on the couch, and watched it.

It was typical local stuff, fire and crime, and a long report about the smog. It was listed as a warning now. Schools would be closing, some businesses, and they interviewed a few specialists who gave detailed instructions about ways to seal up windows and doors, what kinds of breathing apparatuses were available. I sipped my drink and waited for my dinner. Near the end, they brought an earthquake scientist on camera, but only for a few moments. The smog was now the big story, and the ominous tremors could wait. I checked through the *TV-Guide*, looking for a good movie.

When I got to Main Beach at quarter to eight, Jen was waiting in the parking lot. It was still light, but the sun was sinking, sending blood-red streaks through wispy clouds at the sea's horizon behind her. She wore her black wet suit top, her white towel like a scarf over her shoulder.

"Goose bumps!" she said, as she slid her naked legs into the seat.

I could see them along her thighs. Her hair was scruffy and matted, and tiny salt crystals stuck to wisps at her ears.

"You're early," I said. "How was it? Did you eat?"

"It was great!" she said. "A women's tournament. I *don't* see how they can run around like that in the sand!"

"How about the boys?"

"The ones I went with? They were fine. Jimmy? The old man in my class? He was there too. We ate together. Burgers and french fries. I was *so* embarrassed!"

"Why?"

"Well, I didn't have any money!"

"Oh, shit," I said. "I didn't think of that."

"But he was great! He *insisted* that it not be a loan. He said it was like a date. He was taking me to dinner."

"Where was it?" I said.

"Just a truck vendor. But it was good stuff. The fries were great! Oh!" she said, wriggling in the seat, "do I need a *shower!*"

Traffic was still thick on the main drag, and I crossed it and headed west, figuring to take side streets south, then dip back down to the coast near our hotel. I'd drunk a little too much on an empty stomach and was careful to drive slowly and keep both hands on the wheel. Jen looked out the window. She'd been energized by the day's rich experiences and had told me snatches of things about the diving and the volleyball, but in a while she fell silent, her adrenaline waning, and I thought she'd be ready for sleep early.

She headed for the adjoining door, yanking at her wet suit top, as soon as we got into my room. She had the rubber bunched above her bare waist as she went through, but in moments I heard her muffled voice call out to me. She was standing beside her bed when I got there, the suit a dry bundle above her breasts, her head hidden in its folds. Her distant voice called "Help me! Get the arms!" One of them was standing out at her shoulder, her hand opening and closing.

I grabbed the rubber at her wrist and pulled but had no luck. Then I got behind her, slid my hands up, under, and across her bare back, pulling her suit strap loose in the process, and worked my fingers to her armpits, then over her shoulders, lifting the rubber with my knuckles. Jen reached to her hood with both hands, and together we got the thing over her head, her swimsuit top coming away with it.

"Oh!" she breathed, but not at her exposure. "It was dark in there!"

She dropped the wet suit on the bed, her back still to me, and retrieved her top and put it on. I tied the straps. She turned then, reached up and squeezed my shoulders, and kissed me on the lips.

"God! Thanks!" she said. "What a mess!"

"Maybe next time into the shower with it. Much easier when they're wet."

"Oh," she said, "of course. How stupid." The suit had lifted her hair into gnarled spikes.

TOBY OLSON

"Not really," I said. "You wanted that shower." I reached to her shoulders, gripped them tightly, and turned her. "Go to it," I said, and she walked quickly toward the bathroom.

"Crackers and cheese?" She called over her shoulder. "A couple of Cokes?"

"I'll get it," I said, and watched her enter and close the door. Then I went back into my own room and called down.

"Could we put it off till Wednesday?" Jen said.

It was ten to nine and she was sitting at the edge of the cushion, poking through the glass bowl for the right strawberry. I'd ordered those as well as the cheese and drinks. I'd told her about Blevins, my father's marks beside the *King of Norway*. Then I'd mentioned tomorrow's trip to El Monte.

"Why?" I said.

She'd dressed in loose, white cotton pants and matching blouse, and she'd put on one of my mother's necklaces, linked silver disks and green stones. Her face was shining from her shower, her hair fluffy from toweling. She looks beautiful, I thought, quiet sophistication, and for some reason I felt proud.

"Well, it's the volleyball again." She laughed lightly, cocking her head and looking at me, the strawberry tipped with sugar in her fingers. "Tomorrow night's the finals."

I felt a mix of things, that she'd betrayed our pact, that I'd been foolish to draw her into it, that this was a pulling away from me.

"Of course," I said. "Maybe even Thursday. It's only a kind of game, after all. This is our vacation!"

"Well, *that's* not true," she said. "I don't think it's a game." She bit the tip off the strawberry. "And not Thursday, either. Wednesday, for sure."

"All right," I said. "I'll check out Blevins Street."

"That's it!" she laughed. "Go see Blevins."

The movie was one I hadn't seen before and was quite compelling. Jen sat beside me on the couch, and we both sipped at our drinks as the credits came up over a smoggy cityscape that we soon learned was Los Angeles.

A woman and a man were trying to untangle and understand their feelings for each other, but they were caught in a matrix of events and ethics that got in the way of that. He was a victim of business and the things he had to do to rise to prominence. And she felt culpable as well, though her work was social, something to do with hospitals and the poor.

They moved in black and white, through meetings, parties, and intense conversations. There was an ominous sense in the city, constant hints in street scenes and glances, that something might soon erupt, that they had little time. Things increased in difficulty, then they went to the country, to a place he had in the mountains for a long weekend, and the movie slowed down. They walked in the woods, lingered over meals by candlelight, made love, had long discussion about their future together, the details of the ways they'd extricate themselves from those things that stood in the way, their city life and its encumbrances. They came to an understand of each other. The movie marked that by a picture they took together, him pushing the timer button, rushing over to stand beside her on the deck. Then they returned to the city and were immediately drawn back in by the life they'd thought to change.

There was a Christmas party. He was the boss now, but he left early. Then, out on the cold sidewalk, he saw her coming toward him, bundled in a warm coat and hat. They'd not seen each other in months. They shook hands, then embraced. The camera held them for a while, then lifted above their heads and slowly scanned the facades of the city's buildings until it paused at a wall of dark windows, a dim light in one. It moved in then, to the window and through it, and there they were again, their coats off, sitting on a couch, her head on his shoulder.

TOBY OLSON

The camera moved around and behind them, showing only the backs of their heads now and the television screen they were watching, a disaster movie, or a documentary, about earthquakes. Buildings tipped and fell on the screen. There was smoke and fire, a slowly collapsing bridge, cars swallowed by fissures in the streets, a maelstrom at sea. The television sound was off, and the elements of disaster passed on the screen in silence.

But then their bodies and the couch began to shake, a vase fell from a shelf. There was a deep rumbling, and the TV rocked, a floor lamp tilted, shaking the shade. The camera passed over these things, ice cubes tinkling in their glasses, a broken figurine, the picture they'd taken in the country. It wasn't clear whose apartment they were in, which one had put that picture in a frame on the glass table.

Jen shifted as the movie ended, a fixed image of a smoky, dark sky. She was snuggled up against me, her head on my shoulder. She'd fallen victim to her busy day and had been sleeping there for close to an hour. I had my arm around her, my hand on her elbow, and when she moved, a sweet scent of the last remnant of her fading period rose up from her lap.

I got up, her blood in my nostrils, and turned off the television set. Then I lifted her, struggling to do it gracefully, and carried her into her own room and put her to bed.

14.

Over breakfast Jen told me the difference between a J and K valve and the workings of a two-stage regulator. Michael Higgins had taught them that. He'd showed them how to read their submersible pressure gauge, and to get them in trouble had taught them skip-breathing as a way to conserve air. He'd dived with them, looking for clues, and when one of the young men had gotten disoriented because of carbon dioxide retention, he'd brought them all up, had the young man describe his experience, then had gone over why skip-breathing had caused this.

"What about nitrogen narcosis?"

"Not yet," she said. "But isn't it like getting drunk?"

We finished eating by seven-thirty, and while Jen went back to her room to read over the day's lesson, I took a walk on the beach. It was a beautiful California morning, clear and cloudless skies, a slight nip in the air, but no breeze. Good enough for here, I thought, but though its scent was gone from the still air, I was wondering about the smog inland.

I dropped Jen off at the Main Beach parking lot at quarter to nine, told her I'd pick her up at four. We could talk then for a while, and I could take her stuff back to the hotel. She'd be going to the volleyball game at five. I offered to help carry her gear to the lifeguard tower, but she refused, saying she had to do these things herself, learn to be an efficient diver even on land. I watched her as she trudged over the sand under that heavy load. Her limp was prominent in her struggle, and I realized I'd almost forgotten that she had one. Then I drove back to the hotel and called the police station.

"I found the sheet," Sanchez said. "The rest of her stuff too."

The building was a corrugated metal structure that sat on a low, bare hill behind the station. A new blacktop drive curved up from the street to it, but we took the brick steps that started at the station's back door. Sanchez went ahead of me, the sharp creases in his tight uniform distinct at his triceps and below his knees. His hair was short and black, and I could see the sunburn line where his dark neck rose above his collar. I'd taken him for a desk man, but he was lean and light on his feet, and if it wasn't in his job to get exercise, he certainly got it somewhere else.

"Was it difficult?" I asked.

We'd reached the padlocked door and he'd inserted the key, was pulling the heavy door open.

"No," he said. "You'll see. It was a common box, and clearly marked. Right where it should be."

Inside, the walls were lined to the tall ceilings with cardboard boxes on metal racks, and there were rows of additional racks running halfway down the center, also piled high. Ladders of numerous sizes leaned neatly beside the entrance, and as we crossed to one of the four large tables that stood in a row near the room's center, the high lines of suspended fluorescent lights were still flickering on. The tables were empty, but when we got to the second one, Sanchez reached under to the low shelf and pulled a box out. I saw the name Rennert on the end, a date, and two rows of neatly written numbers.

"It's the system," Sanchez said, catching my glance.

The sheet was folded neatly at the top, and Sanchez lifted it out and spread it over another table, tucking it carefully at the corners, as if he were making a bed. He looked up at me as he smoothed the fabric.

"Thick," he said, "and tight. This is good quality."

"And the color," I said. "A fast dye. How long in the water, do you think?"

The sheet was lime green, still vivid and rich. There was a rusty blotch the size of a man's head near the center, where the bowl of the hips would be, thick streaks spiking down from that and changing to a lighter color where they ended in bloody splatters on the green fabric.

"The lab said only a few hours. Didn't you read that in the file? But that was just a good guess. Not something that comes up often, salt water and dried blood, I mean. They couldn't figure a time when the blood got there. But it had to have been ten to fifteen hours at least. It could have been days, though, months, longer even than that."

"You know the case," I said.

"Well, I guess so. Maybe I do."

"And she didn't have her period." I was looking down at the faded blood.

"No," he said.

I'd asked him to bring a tape measure. There was one in a file cabinet beside the ladders, and once he'd gotten it I helped him turn the sheet to get its width flat on the table. I saw light as we lifted it, places where the lab had snipped out pieces for examination. He held it in place, and I tucked the tape in under the fitted end until I found the corner, then reached to the other, smoothing the sheet out as I went. I marked the tape with my thumbnail, then brought it out of the corner and looked at it. Then I looked up and across the table to where Sanchez stood. He was watching my face, as if he were looking for something. I started to speak.

"I know," he said. "It isn't right."

"When?" I was looking hard at him now. "Couldn't it be shrinkage?"

"Yesterday. Just after you left. Maybe you said something. I don't know. But I don't think that's it. Salt water and no heat. And we're talking forty-eight inches. Isn't that what you got? That's six under a double. And these are *good* sheets."

"So. What do you think?" I said.

"I've no fucking idea. It comes out of nowhere. Maybe something that *should* have been gotten, but so obvious a thing. I looked back through the file. Nothing about it there."

"What does it mean to you?"

"The whole thing? Well, I told you about high school. It was still a thorn in the department's side when I came on. I mean, it was a major case and the only one of that kind that went unsolved. The state police got into it a little, and that was an irritant too. As if we weren't competent. Not me, I wasn't here then. But it hung on for a long while, even after I came. It still does."

"A hobby?" I said.

His smile was slightly twisted.

"Sure, that's what it is," he said. "Maybe more than that."

We folded the sheet, and he put it beside the box. Then he reached into the box, took out a clear plastic bag, and placed it at the end of the table where the chair was.

"This is it," he said. "All of it. Feel free."

I sat down in the chair, opened the bag, and slid the contents out. A comb and brush, a nail file kit, a few pens, a box of hairpins and some cheap costume jewelry, a soft cosmetics bag with bottles and tubes of lipstick in it, and a half dozen postcards showing scenes around Laguna. Sanchez was standing at my shoulder.

"No savings or checkbook? What about clothing?"

"No," he said. "The clothes were gone through, then listed and disposed of. You might wonder about the postcards, someone to write to? But they were stuck up at the edges of her mirror. To look at, I guess."

"Not much of a life."

I wanted to feel Susan Rennert there again, in the way I had while looking at her picture. I lifted the brush up and smelled it. It was clean and had no scent. It had been a very long time ago, and her presence had left even her objects now.

"Not much of one here, at least."

We put it all back in the box and rested the sheet on top. Then he took the box and left me at the table while he went back among the metal racks and filed it. I was standing at the door by the time he got back, and after he'd locked up, we walked the blacktop drive down to the parking lot where I'd left my car. I opened the door, then turned and extended my hand.

"The thing is," he said, squeezing it with a tight grip, "I'll be looking into this as best I can. Anything you get, I could use that."

"I'll be in touch," I said, then got in and started the car. I saw his stiff, starched back through the rearview mirror as I turned around. He was heading toward the station door.

15.

It was eleven-thirty by the time I reached the Santa Anna Freeway and started northeast, leaving the cleansing sea breeze and that feel of salt in the air.

It had taken me a while to get there. I had the crude map I'd copied from the magazine on the seat beside me and a larger, detailed one that covered all of Los Angeles and Orange counties. The former noted the freeway exit, and there were arrows at the corners, one pointing at L.A., the other toward San Diego. The larger map was dense with streets, and I'd been unable to find Blevins when I'd searched for it.

The freeway traffic was light, but I was unused to the speed and drove in the slow lane, cars shooting past me. I'd never had much use for speed, not even as an adolescent. My father had given me the old Oldsmobile freely once I'd gotten my license, but I had learned his ways. He always traveled secondary roads, keeping his eyes open, and would stop for anything that caught his interest. Seeing the world, he'd say.

I kept an eye on the off-ramp signs. Towns I remembered from my youth, but had never been to. I had a good long way to go, and I settled into the seat and began thinking about Jen and me, and incest.

I wondered if that was part of Carol's concern, but I couldn't really think so. Even when we'd spoken about Jen's period, there'd been no hint of that. I was a man who had fallen into a relationship with a young woman. It was no real help to call her a girl, though she was that, or a daughter, either, something only in name so far. I was adopted and couldn't really see my mother in her. I could see Carol, though, a hint of her ways remembered even after sixteen years, that brief but intense passion between us.

Could such feelings be natural? I thought Jen had my eyes, at least something in them that I understood, maybe a way of humor or its gestures, but how would that act as censor? Love of self found tangible in another might well push toward union. But we were moving in that direction, I knew, almost as a proposed contract we'd agreed upon: her letters and my acceptance of them. I'd be the father to her daughter, both facing that empty space of years between us as a neutrality, no guilt or blame.

And I knew I had not thought of her in that way, but I still had to watch myself, the warmth of her body and her sweet smell as she'd slept close to me on the couch like a baby, the intense fatherly power I'd felt in the shower while tending her, curing her of that dream and her menstruation, as if they were illnesses of childhood. It was as if I'd been on the brink of something with her, could have stepped back a little and looked down at her, sprinkled her body with talcum, changed her diaper, wiped her nose. I could have blown smoke into her aching ear to soothe it in the way my father, who was no smoker, had done for me. I could have made a spoon of myself, held her in bed and sung her through some injury in the way of my mother. I wanted those years I'd lost, the taste and touch of her child's body. But she was no longer a child. I wondered if any father could do that, if there were those who had seen the physical in their daughters as a kind of beckoning and had tried a returning only to find themselves in the company of a woman, and in ruin.

She was too good to be true, and though I had no reasonable model against which to measure her behavior, that was troublesome to me as well. Did she stand forth as an actress guarding some privacy that I had no perception of, a daughter playing the part of a daughter in the way that I was, sometimes, acting out the ways of a father awkwardly in my ignorance, though she was more successful at it, given her past rehearsal of appropriate lines? An adolescent from a fifties movie, a light musical in which rebellion was no more than joking, something resolved gracefully well before the lawn party, in ponytail and still virginal costume at the final scene?

She had reason to be very good, as I had, but we were in the movie and without the advantage of audience, and I wondered what we looked like from the outside: a sweet cliché? Or might I be seen as some manipulated fool, she as the calculating ingenue, transparent in her machinations? I thought this, not for a moment believing it. At least I didn't think I did, or didn't want to.

I came up into a hazy smoke and saw the sign ahead, *Monrovia,* still a good distance from Los Angeles, but in the "area," as the map had said. The smog reminded me of smudge, my blackened face when I'd returned, still in grade school, from my paper route. Tall, skinny palms along the roadside dipped a little, shaking their tufted tops, evidence, I hoped, of a cleansing breeze. Two miles to the off-ramp and my eyes were burning, the green sign darkened to a dirty brown and just barely visible. I reached to the circulating fan and shut it off.

The ramp descended, then opened at its end into a narrow boulevard. A sign gave a two-digit number and pointed the way, and I continued in the slow lane, close to a curb and sidewalk now. There were numerous traffic lights, with no clear synchronization. No left turn arrows, either, and smoky cars waited in long lines in the center lane, weary, it seemed. Only occasional horns, and those like foghorns, their sound hollow in the thick air.

Blocks of one-story stucco stores, dirty pink and from the thirties; metallic gas stations set back from the street on blacktop where stone-and-cactus yards had once been; fake stucco two-stories, insurance and check-cashing offices named in dim neon. I passed a dark hole in a line of simple frame houses, saw men stacking cinder blocks, passed a concrete steer, its hooves planted in red painted gravel, lawn mowers and small tractors through glass behind it.

Few people were on the sidewalks, and those I saw moved slowly and held handkerchiefs over their faces. I saw a woman in a surgical mask, a nurse in dirty white pushing a green oxygen tank behind an old man gripping the rails of a walker.

The smog wasn't lifting, but was thickening, and though I drove slowly, I was halfway past the boarded-up restaurant before I caught the sign, paint peeling in curls from its elaborate gothic letters. I pulled over at a broken parking meter, its glass face shattered, and looked across to the restaurant's corner, saw the street name on the concrete post. They'd boarded the place with thick plywood long ago, and it was scarred and covered with graffiti.

I reached for the crude map, checked the street name against that on the post, then figured what seemed the best route to Blevins. It would take me off the boulevard after a few more blocks, back into what I guessed was a residential area. I traced the route with my finger, then put the map on the seat and pulled out into the street.

I had to wait a long time at the corner. There wasn't much traffic, and it moved slowly, but the smog made for a kind of sluggish care, spaces between the moving cars, but none large enough to squeeze into. I waited through four light changes, then after an old, smoke-spewing pickup, I cut behind its exhaust and went through a cloud of smoke and crossed the boulevard.

The street I entered was straight for the first block and held a failed commercial wish for spillover from the main drag. I passed a closed grocery store, a house with the name of a Mexican restaurant over the door, a car down on its axles, and a tilted refrigerator in the dirt yard. There was a garish rug shop, fake mosque-like turrets in blue stucco; a day-care center, remnants of halloween figures hanging from tape in its cracked windows. There was no

TOBY OLSON

one in sight, and after I'd paused at a useless stop sign, I crossed a side street, and the one I was on bent off to the right, became a street of one-story houses, set back a little in dirt-and-stone yards; I saw untended palms, their roots lifting the concrete slabs of the sidewalk where they'd been planted in careful rows. I couldn't see to the street's end, just a wall of smog in the distance, and when I looked in the rearview mirror, I saw the same thing.

At the end of the street, I stopped and checked the map again, then turned right into a sand-washed road. There was curbing and a sidewalk to either side, but beyond them no houses, only low sand hills where houses might have once been. The road was black-top, but the sand had drifted into it, and I could hear a faint shush-ing under my tires. At the road's end, the sand hills to the right fell away and a broad dirt drive descended into a compound of some kind. I could see prefab buildings and dark heavy equipment off in the distance, hazy through the smog. I was at a crossroad, and at the corner to my left I saw the stone marker, *Blevins Street* carved into it. I turned left, and in a hundred yards came to a high dirt embankment. It cut across the road and ended it. There was noth-ing but low scrub, cactus, and twisted willow at both sides.

I sat there, looking into the dirt rise, then opened the car door and got out. Smog entered my nostrils, and my eyes burned. I reached to my pants pocket, but there was nothing there, so I got back in and opened the glove compartment. Jen had left a thin scarf there, and when I pulled it out, one of my mother's necklaces fell from it onto the carpeted floor. It was a beautiful thing, silver and some green stone, and I thought I remembered it under my mother's smile, hanging over black fabric between her breasts. I gathered it up and tucked it back in the glove compartment, then lifted Jen's scarf to my face, a sweet smell, and got out of the car again and headed up the embankment. I was looking down a steep slope to a freeway, hazy cars moving at great speed, the drone of their engines dampened by the smog that obscured sight of them.

Beyond the freeway was a low valley, dark shapes of hills rising up in the distance. At least I thought it was a valley. All I could see was a dense smog cover that started at the freeway's far side. I thought there were buildings on the hills, but I couldn't tell if they were houses or other structures. I heard a sound and thought for a moment it was coming from below. Then I heard it again, behind me, and I turned.

She was standing beside my car, and for a moment I thought I was seeing Susan Rennert, that same tight hair pulled back across her scalp. But it was not hair. It was a blond bathing cap, the kind women used to wear. I'd sucked in smog through Jen's scarf, and I raised my hand to the woman, coughing and sneezing, working to slow my breath down.

"It's something," she said, reaching to the cap at her temple as I started down the embankment toward her. "I hope I didn't startle you. For the smog."

Her hand moved to her high collar, checking the button. She wore a long raincoat, her legs below it encased in tights, and dirty white gloves. There was something on her face, a slick lotion that gave it the look of porcelain. I guessed she was close to sixty, maybe older than that, crow's-feet cracking the second skin covering at the corners of her eyes.

"California," she said, smiling as I got close to her. "Why in the world do we live here?"

"Is it always like this?" I asked. I was only a few feet from her now, glancing from her face to the bulge of her ear under the tight cap.

"This?" she said. "It keeps the hair clean. Not always, but you can count the good days. I get crazy staying in. You're not from around here, are you?"

"No," I said. "Well, yes, a long time ago. Before all this."

"I can remember that," she said, a wistful and fleeting smile.

"Blevins Street?"

"This is," she said. "A part of it. What's left. But no, I'm back near

TOBY OLSON

the boulevard." She pointed behind her, wiggling her gloved fingers. "That's changed too."

"Where's the rest? Can you tell me where the rest is?"

I'd lowered the scarf in asking her, felt that acrid sting in my throat, and quickly touched my eyelids, covered my nose and mouth again.

"Of course," she said. "It's properly isolated now. The freeway, they put it in years ago. It's down there, on the other side, in the valley."

I watched the way she breathed, very shallowly, her lips only slightly parted when she spoke. I thought I saw something over her nostrils, a kind of thin filter, something unnatural covering her eyes. Contact lenses? I couldn't be sure.

"Is there a way from here?"

"Well, obviously, there must be. But I haven't been there since the freeway. We didn't even go there back then, of course. Outsiders, I mean."

I didn't know what she meant. She'd lifted her head in saying it, what I thought was a gesture of disapproval. It was hard to tell though. Her porcelain face was doll-like, empty of all expression.

"Well," I said, "I guess it's the boulevard again. There must be a way there."

"I'd suppose so," she said.

I asked her if she wanted a lift, but she declined. She said she was out for a walk. Stir-crazy. She still needed some time. She was climbing the embankment as I turned the car around, and I saw her looking down to where the freeway was as I started back the way I'd come.

It was twelve-thirty by the time I reached the boulevard again. The smog had thickened, and though I had the vents closed, I could smell the smog leaking in at the window seams. I'd tied Jen's scarf behind my neck, wore it as a cowboy mask, but I had nothing for my eyes and few tears. I had to blink constantly, force myself to focus through the dirty film on the windshield. The traffic was still light, though it was lunchtime, and I saw no one on the sidewalks now. I turned the radio on, searched through Spanish and Vietnamese music looking for my language. I caught a phrase or two before the station faded, something about precaution and respirators.

I reached a major intersection, four lanes crossing the boulevard, and though I could not read the sign under the dim and smoky halo of light, I turned left, hoping to cross over the freeway or go under it. I drove slowly, guessing at the distance. It was hard now to see beyond the curbing on either side. Even the few cars that passed me going the other way were no more than shadows. In a while I judged I was far enough, though I'd not seen the freeway or known the nature of my passage beyond it. I edged over into the middle lane, hoping there was no one behind me, and at the first stoplight turned left into a narrow, winding street.

The street descended. I thought I was going by houses, trees of some sort fronting them. I watched the curb to my right, caught the glow of occasional dim lights beyond what I guessed were yards. I came to a corner and pulled over to the curb. I had my headlights on, but they were useless. Still, when I flicked to the bright beam, I thought I saw a stone marker near the edge of the sidewalk. I opened the door, leaving the lights on and the motor running, and moved in my mask toward the corner, squinting through the acrid sting to find the curb, then stepping over it and onto the grass verge. I found the marker and knelt down beside it, my movement stirring the dead air. I felt the burn of a chemical wash at my neck and chin, and I held my breath as it drifted to my nostrils, an acid etching. My lids felt like sandpaper against my pupils as I blinked and worked to focus, reading the carved vertical letters on the concrete post. Then I was up on my feet again, still holding my breath, stumbling toward the dark shape of the car's hood.

Back in the car, I turned the overhead light on and lifted the crude map. The street was there. It ran in a way that would inter-

TOBY OLSON

sect Blevins, but stopped short of that. Still, the direction was right, and I reached up and turned the light off, then pressed the accelerator and turned left, my brights finding the street's edge, which I hugged close as I moved slowly along. Then I came to the street's end and stopped.

There was nothing before me but what looked like a thick wood, trunks of eucalyptus, what I thought were berry vines twisted at their bases. Nothing to my left either, a house maybe, but I couldn't be sure. To my right seemed the only passage, a few feet of blacktop petering out into a dirt road defined by weedy growth on either side.

The road was narrow and without clear boundaries, and I drove down the center of it, keeping my eyes where the headlights' beams washed along tall weeds at the brink in a dirty wash.

The road bent to the left in a short while, and where weeds had been on that side, a dark embankment now rose steeply up to a height I could not measure. The road straightened, hugging the embankment's edge, still descending, and after a few hundred yards I saw black clouds ahead, the smog no longer settled evenly throughout the air, but churned by a wind from somewhere, various in its density, at least over the road's surface. It still hung in a thick, dead, and impenetrable bank to either side, but I could see farther into the distance ahead now, and I felt as if I were moving through some tunnel.

I slowed to a crawl, watching the roiling smoke. I'd stopped blinking and I felt fresh tears at the edges of my eyes, mucus in my nostrils. The smog clouds had lifted a little, and now there was a wedge of dim light under them, only a foot or so, but a space of clearer air between their churning and the road.

They seemed to be receding as I approached, but it was not that. The distance I could see ahead was increasing, as was the brighter space, and I drove slowly on, my headlights sneaking under the clouds, picking up stones in the road, then some metal structure. I touched the brakes, then rolled forward at a slow walking pace. The clouds reached the car hood, and as I inched forward, they continued to lift until they were flooding over the top half of the windshield. I slipped down in the seat to where I could see between the spokes of the steering wheel. I could see the clouds' thick undersides, dark as a rippling black blanket, and below them, in clearer air, I could see the metal structure where the road ended and a narrow strip of blacktop turned off to the right. It was some sort of retaining wall, red-painted steel beams in a crisscross pattern, huge bolts sunk into the earth, holding it in place. I pressed the brakes, came to a stop, and looked out the window to my left. Though the smog was still thick and heavy there, I could see the dim outlines of a similar structure against the high embankment. I looked down to its base. There was a clear hole in the smog there, smoky clouds rushing into it, a pipe or a tunnel.

I looked into the rearview mirror, saw the clouds rolling over the trunk lid, drifting back until they joined the smog wall. There was nothing for me there, and I turned right, felt my tires bump onto the blacktop as they left the dirt.

I was still well down in the seat, had only a six-inch space of vision. The clouds were thicker and moving faster now, fanning out over the roof and to the sides when they hit the windshield. I could see the lines of the car's hood clearly, the metal shining, and beyond the emblem at its nose some source of light, or at least clear air. Then, quite suddenly, the hood dipped. I came over a brink, saw the steeply descending road below. The clouds lifted away, and the windshield cleared as I followed the road down, touching the brakes as I descended.

Blevins Street. The name was etched into a concrete pillar of the same kind I'd seen earlier, maybe three feet high, tapering into a pyramid shape at the top. It was set in the middle of a well-tended bed of flowers, darkly wet wood chips mulching the base of each bouquet.

TOBY OLSON

At the bottom of the hill the road had turned sharply right to run parallel to a thick stand of tall eucalyptus trees. I'd rolled the window down, sucked in the trees' sweet, decaying scent and the clear air. They'd ended at the edge of a large brick building that I thought at first was a school. Then I'd seen the brightly painted sign above the door: *Blevins Street Community Center*. I'd passed it, then stopped at the far corner, where Blevins Street itself began. Then I'd pulled over and gotten out of the car.

I stood at the mouth of the street, where a curbed teardrop island holding various small cactus shapes separated it into two lanes. Beyond that, the street narrowed, then turned sharply left, going back behind the eucalyptus stand where I couldn't see. Before the turn, there was a house to either side, but not California stucco or frame. These were brick houses, deep, narrow, and rectangular, with flat roofs, of a kind built in the Midwest or East. Both had been converted into commercial places, a combined drugstore and market on the left, a coffee shop directly across from it. On its near side was a small gas station and repair garage. One of the two bay doors was open, and I could see the rear of a car up on a rack, a figure moving around under it.

I looked at the long buildings' brick sides, a few small windows set into them. The bricks had been carefully pointed, and there was no bellying out or crack lines. These were not old houses, though their design came from the past. A dull and filtered glow shone evenly on their sides, but their roofs held shifting patterns of light and darkness.

I looked above the roofs to where the smog clouds were rolling, as dark as thunderheads filling the entire sky. Their path was toward the steep roadway I'd come down, and when I looked up that way, I could see the top half of the road beyond the tips of the eucalyptus trees. The moving smog clouds picked up speed there, the road rising up toward them. They funneled down and moved even faster where they touched the top of the road, seemed to bounce in chunks off the blacktop as they shot over the brink and headed for that pipe or tunnel where I'd stopped. Below the brink, the road was bright and from my angle shining, and when I looked back above the eucalyptus trees themselves, I saw leaves and twigs tumbling in the air, a stiff clean wind blowing them. The treetops were still, untouched by that wind, which followed the path of the smog, holding the clouds up, it seemed. Under them, the air was sweet and clear and held a scent of flowers.

"Don't shoot!"

I jerked my eyes down from the dark sky ceiling, startled, and turned and saw him standing there at the curb beside the stone marker. He had his hands in the air, had lifted them from the handles of the aluminum walker he stood behind, and was smiling. I blinked, then felt the edge of fabric at the bridge of my nose. Jen's scarf was still in place there, the tip of its triangle flapping below my chin. I reached up and pulled it down around my neck, returning his smile.

"I forgot it," I said.

He laughed, his hands back on the walker now.

"You've come from the outside." He turned his head, tilting his face up at the sky. "What do you think of that?" Then he looked back at me, must have caught my curiosity. "Cherman," he said, exaggerating his accent.

"Is it always like this?"

"Historically?" he said. "No. We were like the rest. But since they put the freeway in, we get days like this. It wasn't bad way back, but it's pretty shitty up there now, isn't it? Even when the wind doesn't come, it's not too bad here."

"On the outside," I said.

He shuffled his feet. He was a small man, well into his eighties, I guessed, but with hard and angular German features and a short gray haircut, flat on the top, shaved close over his ears. His narrow eyes looked suspicious, but he'd been smiling and laughing, his jaw loose. Now he was watching me closely as he spoke.

"Well, they cut us off, you see. The freeway did. We were well on our way even then." He glanced behind me toward the community center. "Then some others came, and now we have what we want."

"Where from?" I said.

"You have questions?"

"No, no," I said. "It's not that. Quite a trip, though. Is there a phone? Something to eat?"

I glanced at my watch. It was after one. I wasn't going to mention Susan Rennert, not yet.

"Well, of course!" He smiled again. "This is a public place! Chermans from Chucago. Most of us, anyway. From other places too, back east."

"Well," I said. I had more questions, but I held them back, unsure of him.

"You can get a bath," he said. "A German bath."

"A bath?"

I reached up to my brow, felt the grit there, then looked at my fingertips. They were brown with smog; small luminous particles, like glass shavings, blinked near the nails.

"And it gets beyond your clothing too," he said. "Back there, just after the turn." He pointed down Blevins Street. "There's a sign."

Then he picked up the walker, turned it and pointed it toward the community center, beginning to end our conversation.

"Poker," he said, looking over my shoulder at the building.

"I hope you win," I said as he began to move, lifting the walker ahead, then shuffling up to it.

"I will," he said. "I always do."

I turned and moved to the car, and when I got in and saw the open window, I reached to the handle to raise the glass against the smog that was no longer there. It came up awkwardly, a scraping of grit down in the mechanism close to freezing it, and the glass itself was almost opaque, streaked with brown and that same faint sparkling I'd seen on my fingers. I could see the wavy outlines of the man's slow movements through it. I cranked the window back down, with effort, then turned the ignition key. The windshield was streaked as well, but not nearly as bad, and I had no trouble driving the fifty yards or so to the small garage.

I parked at the pumps, heard the bell, then saw the man duck under the bumper of the elevated car he'd been working on. He wore blue overalls, was wiping his hands on a red cloth as he approached. He came around to my window, put his hands on the door frame. He was tall and had to bend down to look in. His face held that same bulky, Germanic look as the old man with the walker. He started to speak, then glanced in at the windshield. Then he lifted his hands and turned them over on the sill, showing me his palms.

"That's it," he said. "The window. Right?"

"And some gas," I said. "And can I get a wash job? Is there time?"

He stood back from the car now, wiping his hands with the rag again.

"The window first," he said. "That will take an hour and a half, maybe two. The wash. I can have it in under three."

We both looked at our watches. It was one-thirty. I had to meet Jen at Main Beach at four. But that was only for an hour. She'd be going to the volleyball games from there. I'd remembered money this time, and she'd taken a change of clothes. I'd pick her up at eight, in the parking lot, just like yesterday. I'd have to call. Figure something.

"Is there a phone?"

"Next door," he said. "The coffee shop. Mine's broken." He pointed to the side of the building, a pay phone, the receiver hanging down from its silver wire.

"Okay," I said. "Let's do it."

He looked at his watch again.

"Four-thirty," he said. "No later than that."

He had me drive into the second bay, and when I got out on the concrete floor, he was already facing the side wall, uncoiling a thin hose and attaching a long metal wand to it. The wall was lined

TOBY OLSON

with rows of small cylindrical objects resting in an egg crate structure. They descended in size from left to right and resembled large bullets. Each had a circle of petal-like scallops attached at the tip, then folded back and held tight against the cylinder with a rubber band. He removed one, then looked over his shoulder at the car door and shook his head.

"The keys?" I said.

"In the ignition. You can leave them there." He'd replaced the bullet-like object, then taken out a smaller one.

"What are they?" I asked.

"These?" he said, holding the cylinder up between us. "These are fans." He removed the rubber band and the scallops unfolded, forming a small open umbrella at the object's tip. "They're spring loaded. They'll bend in either direction."

He lifted the fan blades above the cylinder to show me, gathering them in his palm until they were no thicker than the cylinder itself. I just stood there, looking, not sure of what to say, and he continued.

"There are circular knockouts under the bottom of the door frame. The sizes vary with make and model. I don't know why. What we do is we knock them out. Then we use this gizmo," he lifted the thin wand. "It's a sprayer. We use high pressure, a solution of water and oil. We slip it between the rubber and the window, then flush the hell out of it. The solution drains through the knockout holes. Then we get the right fans, usually three or more. They pop open once they're up in there." He used his hand on the thing to show me. "They bend the other way so we can get them out. It's that part that takes the time. Even with the oil, we have to get it very dry to prevent rust."

I looked at the wall behind him. There were hundreds of little fans there.

"All this?" I said. "It must happen often."

"The smog," he said. "It's a common thing." He looked above my eyes. "Your face. Do you wanna use the bathroom?"

16.

I could see the low, black sky of moving smog clouds through the high window, and when I leaned forward over the sink, I could see where earth met that sky, the top of the narrow road where I'd started down into clear air. The metal nose of a car poked through as I watched, then dipped over the brink as I had. Then I could see the whole car, shining green in the filtered light, as it slowly descended and went out of sight behind the eucalyptus trees.

I looked back to my hands, thick brown water running from them as I soaked and wrung Jen's scarf, the bright color coming back to it after many rinsings. I started to wipe my face with it, but felt the scratch of metal particles on my cheek and pulled a handful of paper towels from the dispenser. I'd unbuttoned my summer shirt, and I wiped wet paper over my chest and up into my armpits. Then I fished out my comb and lifted my hands, feeling grit at my waist as the shirt pulled up from where it was tucked in. The comb came away thick with hair, and when I rinsed it, I saw that same faint sparkling in the smoky water swirling across the porcelain at the drain. I buttoned the shirt, then left the bathroom and headed for the coffee shop, passing beside the pumps and the open bay. The man was there, and I saw him push a handle at the wall, then saw the thick streams of dirty brown water bouncing off the concrete floor under the frame of my car's open door.

The coffee shop was really a small restaurant, entered through the front door of a house. It seemed to run the whole length of the place, a counter to the left, tables along the wall on the other side, and in the back, beyond where the counter ended, what looked like a small dining room. It was dark back there, a thick velvet cord hanging from free-standing silver posts that blocked the way.

A bell tinkled when I entered, but no one answered the sound, so I moved to the counter and sat on a swivel stool halfway down. Pitchers of water rested on trays, glasses upended beside them, spaced out along the counter's length, and I reached out and filled a glass, drank it all, then filled it again. There was a soreness in my throat, and though the water soothed it going down, it was back again soon after I'd drunk.

Still no one appeared, though I thought I heard something, a dull bump, water running through pipes in the ceiling. A carpeted staircase ascended near the left of the door, and I guessed the owners lived above. I drank again, looking at myself in the narrow strip of mirror that ran above stacks of plates, silver, and glassware. My hair was dark and looked oiled, and I could see a sooty brownness at the edges of my nostrils and ears. I looked at the wall above the mirror. There were pictures cut from calendars there, a framed dollar bill, some photographs. The pictures showed winter scenes, towns and mountains. In Germany, I guessed. But the photographs, large and professional-looking, held scenes of half-demolished buildings and the construction of new ones. I thought I saw the restaurant itself in one of them, a finished structure fronted by raw dirt, manufacturers' emblems still on the windows.

"It's this place," a voice said.

She came from the far end of the counter, not the staircase, and I guessed there was carpeting back there. I'd not heard a sound. I was up off the stool, had my hands on the counter's edge, leaning forward as I looked at the photographs. I sat back down, turned, and saw her lift a piece of the counter and move along behind it toward me. A heavy woman, maybe sixty or sixty-five years old, her hair gone mostly gray, but frosted a light

TOBY OLSON

brown at the tips. She wore a white uniform, no makeup, and I could hear the shoosh of her stockings where her thighs met. She grabbed a menu from a stack of them, then rested it on the counter between us.

"Coffee?"

"No, please," I said. "Tea? Herbal?"

She blinked, looking at my ear. "Oh, you've been in the smog! We have camomile. Very hot and soothing."

"Perfect," I said. "And a sandwich? Tuna or chicken?"

"I've a hot brisket. With gravy. How about that?"

"Perfect."

She worked directly across from me, and I watched her thick shoulders, her back. I started to ask her about the photographs, but she had something else in mind.

"You know," she said, her voice slightly muffled under the hiss of the tea kettle as it came to a boil, "you could use a bath." She turned and smiled, the cup in her hand. "I could call Edna?"

"You're the second one," I said. "Edna? The place around the corner?"

"Oh, you know, then."

"No, no, I don't. Someone mentioned it to me. An old man."

"In a walker?" she said. "Henry. He's always out and around."

"Well, I'm convinced, then," I said. "But do you really have to call?"

"Yes, yes indeed," she answered. "There are still some who work here, go outside. Business picks up early in the afternoon. Best have an appointment."

She put the tea down, then turned back to work on the sandwich, but she was still talking.

"I'll call, then. What time?"

I looked at my watch. It was quarter to two. I had to do something about Jen. "What about four?" I said.

"I'll check. I don't see why not."

"And the phone. Where is it? I mean, can I use it, get some change?"

She turned toward me again, the plate in her hand, the sandwich flooded with dark gravy, carrots and mashed potatoes at the edges. "Eat first," she said. "While I call Edna."

The phone was on a small round table in the rear, not a pay phone, but she said I could get time and charges from the operator, leave cash. The connection was bad, and I tried again, but still Lin's voice was scratchy on the line. She said she couldn't help. She was tied up. "Right through the evening. The fucking Avalon trip. I'm lucky to get out of here by ten!" Her voice sounded odd. She seemed surprised that I'd called, and to ask something of her, maybe suspicious, but curious too. "Where are you?"

"Well, I can't get back in time," I said, knowing that if I left right then I could. "I'm tied up."

"That's interesting," she said. I heard her faint laugh. "Why not Tod? You could try him."

"Tod? I don't know about that. Why Tod?"

"I *told* you," she said. "He's really a decent person, even with all that money. I'm sure he'd be glad to help. I can give you the number."

I took it from her, wrote it down on the small pad beside the phone. Then I sat there, looking at it. The tea and meal had helped, but my throat was still sore, and now I felt the taste of bile rising. Oh, what the fuck, I thought, and dialed the number.

He was there, and when I told him my name without mentioning Jen, he knew who I was immediately.

"Oh, hi! How's Jen?" he said.

"That's why I called."

I told him about the volleyball finals, her diving class. He knew of the former, and was enthusiastic about the possibility of meeting her, going there with her.

"Just to watch after her," I said. "Not to go after her."

I wanted to drag back the words as soon as I'd said them. Either he didn't hear, or he ignored them.

"Sure," he said. "I can do that. We can eat there."

"She has money," I said. "And have her at the parking lot at eight?"

"Absolutely," he said. "No problem."

"It's four o'clock, then. At the Main Beach lot. And Tod," I said. "Tell her I'm sorry. Everything's okay."

"Glad to do it," he said.

I hung up, then lifted the phone again and called the operator for time and charges. Then I returned to the counter. The woman was behind it, sitting on a stool, a cup of coffee in her hand. She rose as I approached.

"Pie?" she said. "They're homemade? I've got apple and peach."

"Sure," I said, sitting down across from her. "Peach. And maybe a cup of that coffee?"

She put a fork over a napkin beside the pie, then filled my cup and her own and sat down again.

"It's slow," I said.

I knew she'd be the one to ask about Susan Rennert, but I wanted to do it right, take my time. I had a lot of that now, didn't have to be back until eight.

"Well, it's Tuesday. Always on Tuesday. Stuff at the community center."

"I only saw the old man."

"Henry. Yes, he's always late. Whoever was going was already there, quite early, and for most of the day."

"Those photographs," I said, looking beside her head. "What's that all about?"

"Oh, well!" she said. "That's the whole thing really. The street, you see. Blevins Street." She turned on her stool and looked at the wall. "When the freeway came we were cut off, quite totally. But then we'd been a community anyway. Most from eastern cities, Chicago, some from Milwaukee and New York. My parents were from New York. Germans mostly, but not all. I'm Polish. The houses were old here, dilapidated you could say. There wasn't much money early on, but we were hard workers. We became prosperous. Somebody got the idea, after the freeway. To build these houses. Like the ones back east. In that manner? Stone houses. Some had more money than others, so it was done from a common pool. Blevins Street, we're really a kind of cooperative. At least so far as the houses are concerned."

"And the smog?" I said.

"Oh, my, no!" she laughed. "Just a fringe benefit! But it *is* interesting, isn't it? The way it funnels under. We joke sometimes, about those on the other side, the boulevard. That's where it goes!"

"I met a woman up there," I said. "Out walking. She had something on her face, a kind of protection? Something slick, like porcelain."

"And a bathing cap?" she said.

"Why, yes! How did you know that?" I had a cut of pie near my mouth, but lowered the fork.

"That's Pearl," she said. "She used to live here, a long time ago. It got hard for her. She left and found a place above. Did she seem bitter?"

I thought for a moment, chewed the pie, then lifted the hot coffee to my lips. "I think she did say something. I'm not too sure."

"The way it goes," she said, dismissing the woman with a shake of her head, but I didn't let it go.

"What about *her* house?"

She looked hard at me then, searching my eyes as if I'd caught her in something. I thought she was tracing our conversation back, looking for some way in which I'd manipulated it. She lifted her cup, still watching me over the rim as she sipped. Finally, she seemed convinced, and the tendons in her thick neck relaxed.

"You haven't been down the street yet?"

"No," I said. "I just got here."

"Well, you'll see it. It's on the left near the end of the block. Are you going down there?"

"I thought I would, before I left. It's that I'm not from here. Los Angeles, I mean. I got lost," I lied. "All that smog. And I'm in no rush. The good air here."

She smiled then, proud, I thought.

"It's the only old one left," she said, disapprovingly. "Seems we can't get rid of it. The Reuss place."

I put the fork down, steadied my hand beside the cup. "Does the name Rennert mean anything here?"

She looked hard at me again, a smile lifting the side of her mouth.

"I thought you were lost," she said.

"Well, yes. But that woman. She mentioned that."

I was lying again and I felt my face flush, like a child soon to be caught out.

"Oh, well," she said. "She would. Even after all these years. It *was* Rennert, before Reuss. He changed it when he got here, from down south somewhere? Maybe he'd left something behind him. I don't know. But we kept it to ourselves here. That was our way. Still is."

And that's why Susan Rennert's past was lost. Such a simple thing, I thought. Her father had been beating bills. He'd just changed his name, had a place where he could be safe with that, here at Blevins Street. But she had taken the name back then, for some reason. I wondered when, and why.

"That woman," I said. "Pearl? How about her?"

"That's it," she said. "She owns it. At least I think she does. It's confusing. We had a lawyer here quite long ago, but he couldn't find a way. Then we gave up on it."

"A Rennert?" I asked.

"Pearl? Yes, a cousin, I think, of the old woman. She lived there, a long time ago, even before I came. But not a Rennert, or Reuss. She was from the woman's side. I forget the name."

"Does she come here?"

"Who?"

"Pearl. Does she ever come down here?"

"Oh, God, no! She wouldn't be very welcome! Not at all!"

I thought to press on but decided against it. It was two-thirty. I'd been there close to an hour. I had the bath appointment at four, and

I wanted to see Blevins Street, have enough time for that. Still, I asked her if she knew where Pearl lived, if she thought she might remember the last name.

"Just curiosity," I said, seeing suspicion in her eyes again.

"It killed the cat," she said.

The smog moved slowly over Blevins Street and was lower now, the dark blanket slightly tilted, so that houses in the distance appeared farther away, smoke brushing their roofs, then rising as those billowing clouds came toward me. I could see dusky trees where the street ended.

I stood at the opening, having passed beyond the brief commercial district and *Edna's Bath,* a wooden sign hanging from porch beams to my left.

Her house was like the others, a brick rectangle with a flat roof that seemed to taper slightly toward the rear, giving a sense of motion, like those renderings of speeding locomotives I'd seen among my father's papers when I was a child. Each house had two stories, but the top one ended short of the front, and below a square stone porch protruded like a train's nose or a jutting, Germanic chin. Some were open, stone pillars at the corners supporting flat roofs, but others were completely enclosed, the porches real rooms, to sit out on in any weather. The houses faced each other across Blevins, small, careful yards fronting them, defined by low, clipped hedges and rows of topiary bushes cut in shapes reminiscent of artichokes. Behind the houses, on both sides, hills of brush and wildflowers rose up, and when I looked back and over Edna's roof, I could see those eucalyptus tips, then the top of the road where the smog rushed out. I was at the very bottom of the small valley, Blevins Street tucked in there.

There was no one in sight. I thought I heard the creak of a screen door, a window being lowered, muffled sounds of electrical devices or voices beyond walls as I passed houses, glancing up their brick

TOBY OLSON

steps to porches, or looked across the street into driveways with
cars parked in them, small garages at their ends. The sidewalk was
clean, the grass that edged it had been carefully clipped, but up
ahead, beyond leaf and branch shadows staining the narrow concrete, I saw a rougher place, weeds spilling over the sidewalk's
verge and spiking up through twisted cracks.

I stopped for a moment, looked up to the row of roofs ahead.
Each had a short chimney, identical to the others. They seemed a
purposeful measure, light diminishing in the glow that touched
their bricks as they grew smaller, given my perspective, and the
tilted smog ceiling came down to meet them at the street's end.
There was a break in the line a few houses up, no chimney there,
and I stepped from sidewalk to curb, crossed the street at an
angle, then continued along the other side until I was across from
the ruined section of sidewalk and could see into the overgrown
and untended yard beyond it to where the house sat, deeper back
than the others.

It was pink, or at least had been. Paint had peeled and blistered
on its stucco sides and along the edges of its once-graceful archways.
There were three of them, in a wall running the length of the house's
front, and beyond them was a wide low porch or patio, a dark and
heavy door visible through the central arch. It was a modest house,
but I guessed it had once looked ample, even prosperous. It was set
well back on its lot, and I could see the remnant of a stone walk
moving in a handsome curve from the sidewalk to its central arch.
Now the larger, harder houses to each side seemed to press it down,
to oppress it even. It was a typical California house in a Spanish style,
much like all those others I'd seen in Hollywood and towns above
the coast. Still, there was something else familiar about it, something
particular. I knew it was the Rennert house, but that wasn't it.

I stood and looked at it for a long time, pictured the yard in front
as it might have been, that curve of walk, cactus, palm, and stone-
mulched plantings, bougainvillaea possibly, lilac and yucca. Had

there been walls defining the yard, running out to the sidewalk from the house edges, low, imitation adobe? Nowhere on Blevins Street were there California plantings now, but for that stand of eucalyptus I'd passed coming down. Were all the other houses once like this one, before they'd demolished them? I looked to the street's end and beyond it, into that smoky growth of brush and vines, tree trunks, above which branches and the dark shape of a hill disappeared into the low smog blanket. Then I started that way, not really making any choice to do so.

I found the section of curbing just a few yards beyond the street's ending, down a thickly overgrown and steep slope that ended in a small arbor or glade. I was completely below Blevins Street, had passed down through wisps of smog that sheeted from under the low-hanging clouds, then came again to a pocket of clear air. I could smell the smog, just a faint bite at my nostrils, no burn in my eyes, but when I looked up I could see that thick covering, no more than twenty feet above my head. It was darker than it had been where I'd stood across from the Rennert house, but still there was light, though the various colors—the orange vines, and the greens and reds in the leaves—were dull and just barely distinguishable. The vines formed canopies where they twisted at the trees' trunks, and it was under one of them that I found the section of concrete that had once been a street and the high curb with that thin rectangular drain cut into it where the two joined.

I got down on my knees, ran my hand along the edge of the drain opening, then lay down, my legs in the weeds and my chest on the street remnant. I looked into the drain, gripped the edge, and slid forward until I had my head and shoulders through, my arms hanging down, hands pressing against the cool concrete wall that descended into the earth. Darkness, but in a few moments my pupils dilated and I could see the floor of the chamber a good five feet down, the curved walls, the edge where the viaduct turned and headed away, a spill of dirt and concrete rubble there, where the passage had collapsed. I

TOBY OLSON

could imagine myself near that corner, just beyond it and out of sight, soon to come into the light I'd been following, then to climb up and slither through the curbside opening and into some new and promising world. I pressed my hands against the descending wall, knowing I could still fit through if I worked hard at it. Then I heard something, a rustling in the brush behind me, a quiet snort.

I pulled my arms up to my chest, dug my toes in and reached beside my head for the opening's lip, then pushed back and slid out of the chamber, turning as I rose to a sitting position, my back against the curb. The dog just stood there, panting, looking at me. A large golden collie, his ears perked, small flaps at their tips. I said his name, *Santos*, but he didn't respond. Then I extended my hand. He looked at it, then stepped slowly forward and smelled it. He allowed me to scratch his long nose, then he stepped back, looked at me again, then turned and moved away toward the ascending hill. I watched him go, then got to my feet and followed after him. When I reached the edge of the street again, he was gone.

I didn't head toward the mouth of Blevins but dipped over the hill again and moved through brush and among tree trunks to my right. I could see the upper story of the last house on the block from there, undulations in a smog cloud brushing the tip of its brick chimney.

The house lot ended in a wood-fenced yard, behind it a garage, then a narrow alley, garbage cans near a gate. I could see down the alley, other fences and cans, a low storage shed, the metal T of a clothesline. Beyond the alley, the hill started up, low scrub there and wildflowers on the embankment. I saw a cat moving close to the row of fences, but no people. I climbed up to the alley's ending and followed the cat's path, my feet on soft blacktop, past garages, gates, tall wooden fences I couldn't see beyond. Then I reached the break, stopped at a garage end, and looked around it.

The yard behind the California house was the same as in front, weeds, but here there had been a pond. It could have been a small swimming pool, but it was hard to tell. The rectangle was lined with broken tile, rusted metal that may have been the support for a diving board. The hole itself was full of rubble, hunks of plaster and brick. I saw pieces of faded plastic and porcelain, the stucco torso of some figure, a sand hill near a corner. The yard around the pool had become a kind of dumping ground, a sink and toilet, broken appliances, a car fender. Along the brick wall of the abutting house were remnants of a narrow fenced enclosure, a collapsed wooden structure at the alley end of it, a ramp leading into its low open doorway from hard-packed earth. I thought it might once have been a dog run.

The rear of the house echoed the front, no covered porch, but a low stucco wall with a curved archway at its center, the door and boarded windows of the house itself a few feet beyond.

I moved around the garage edge, hugging its side. Then I looked across the ruined yard to the stone wall of the house beyond it. The windows there were hung with curtains, but anyone who chose to look out would see me. So I left the garage and walked directly through the yard, past the pool and through the archway. I had nothing, no implement, and I looked for one. There was a small pile of plaster below one of the windows, and I saw a piece of metal pipe sticking out of it. I moved to it and pulled it free. I was facing the window, and without second thought, I forced the pipe behind the thick plywood square and pulled back. It came away with little effort, and I had to drop the pipe and grab it before it fell. The pipe banged on broken tile at my feet, but I didn't pause or look behind. I rested the piece of plywood against the building at the window's side. There was no glass or frame, only an open hole, and I turned around and boosted myself up on the sill, then swung my legs in and dropped to the floor.

I was in the kitchen, had landed where the sink had once been. There were pieces of plumbing near my legs and a row of wooden cabinets on the wall across from me. It was dark, but light outlined a doorway to my left, and I made my way through it, down a narrow

TOBY OLSON

hallway toward the front of the house and into the living room. There were two large skylights in the ceiling. I moved under one of them and looked up. I could see the moving smog clouds, their black billowing.

There was little in the room, a broken coffee table, a built-in window seat. The floor was dusty red quarry tile, lifted in places above its grouting. There were dirty squares on the wall where pictures had once hung.

I went to a doorway in the corner of the room, down a curving hallway, at the end of which was a door. It was darker there, and I had to search for the handle. A bedroom, light leaking in at a window's edge, no furniture, only a dusty pile of rubble near the room's center where pieces of the plaster ceiling had fallen down. There was a narrow door off in a corner, and when I opened it, I was facing into a shallow closet, a thick wooden dowel suspended from a low shelf. I pushed the door flush against the wall, but it was still too dark to see inside, so I went back to the window, managed to raise the sash, then pushed at the plywood's edge until more light entered. Then I went back to the closet and leaned inside.

It was empty, only dusty webs hanging above the shelf and something dark on the floor off in a corner. I squatted down, reached in, and touched it. It was a corrugated flap of cardboard, part of some discarded box. I dropped it where I found it and was rising up when I saw something else, what looked like scratches or markings on the four-inch piece of pine that had been nailed along the back wall to support the shelf. I gripped the door frame, still squatting low, and leaned in under the shelf for a better view. The hanging wooden rod was in the way of my vision, and I had to lean in farther to see back behind it. Then I had them.

They were faint stroke marks, clearly intentional, scratched in with a thin nail or some other instrument. Four strokes, then a crossing one, making five. I ran my hand over them, feeling the shallow grooves, wiping the dust away, and to the left I touched others, then felt the same configuration on the right. I moved deeper into the closet then and found more of them. I counted ten clusters, a tally of fifty, and two single ones where the row of clusters ended. Someone had squatted here, as I was now, and made some accounting. Or it had been a child who had done so, standing up in the dark, I thought, feeling along the wood as I had, finding the right place for the next stroke.

The closed-in porch at Edna's Bath was a waiting and reception room, and beyond it, after an ascending staircase on the left, the entire ground floor was a large open rectangle, cubicles closed off with plastic shower curtains lining both sides. Edna wore a stiff white uniform, like a nurse might, and a cheap red wig. She was all smiles, but quickly efficient as she ushered me into a cubicle, pointed to the locker and the stack of thick towels on a metal table beside the tub, the shampoo, brushes, and soap.

The tub was claw-footed and huge, and attached to the spigot that rose at its side was a thick red hose, a good four inches in diameter. She reached over and turned the metal handles and a heavy rush of water flowed out in a wave over the porcelain.

"If you need anything," she said, "just use the bell." It was a real bell, silver, with a chain and a ring at the end.

I hung under the water, my hands gripping the tub's lips. Then I rose up, felt metal particles flood down over my cheeks. I dunked myself again, then squeezed shampoo into my hair. Smog suds stained the water, then drifted toward the drain. There was some sort of circulating system, and the water constantly refreshed itself.

I used the thick hose, the brushes on my feet, hands, and arms. There was a long-handled one, and I scrubbed my back with it. Even the twisted grooves in the scar tissue in my side were lodged with grit. My hair was thick with residue, and my fingertips burned a little as I dug into my scalp. I blew my nose into the washcloth, saw that slight luminescence in small flecks of blood. I soaped and dunked again and again, blinked my eyes under the water, used the

TOBY OLSON

special lotion soap Edna had pointed out on my hands and face. Then, in a while, I put my head back on the tub's broad porcelain lip, hung suspended, my hands drifting on the surface, my eyes unfocused on the white plaster ceiling.

I'd been no more than twelve, and with friends had discovered the system of viaducts that ran under Los Angeles and well out into adjoining communities where they drained into the broad open washes in times of heavy rain and winter runoff from the San Gabriel Mountains above the city. California had been in drought then, and during one long summer, we'd explored the viaducts, central passages that were often a good five feet high, ten or more from wall to wall, with narrower cement passages we had to crawl into, which opened into curbside drains and came up under manhole covers in the centers of streets.

I'd been alone when I'd ridden my bike to Montebello, to a place my friends and I had found, a square, brush-hidden opening at the side of an old wash. We'd not entered it, had been heading somewhere else, but it was something we'd planned on. Then one day I'd decided upon it and had gone there on my own. I'd taken my bike into the opening with me and had found a place a few yards in to hide it. Then I'd worked my way along the dark tunnel. I had matches, a canteen, some candy in my small pack.

The floor of the passage had been strewn with rubble, shards of cement and wire mesh I could see in the dim light from the opening, but in a while, when the passage turned, I could only feel it under my feet as I hugged the cool wall and moved carefully along in the dark. I lit matches, saw red brick in the ceiling where the cement had broken free. The passage narrowed as it turned, and my hair brushed the ceiling. I felt brick dust on my cheeks. I went on in darkness for a while, then had light again, a dim glow that revealed my feet, the skeletons of brush that had somehow blown deep into the passage. The light was coming from ahead, and beyond a last turning I saw its source, a glow at the broken edge of the cement wall that had been built to seal my tunnel off.

There was room to crawl through, into a newer and larger viaduct, one I traveled for an hour or more, passing numerous tunnels that branched off to both sides. I counted those on my left and looked carefully at my place of entrance. Each intersecting passage held light at its mouth, and I knew they were drainage passages that rose up to streets. Most were too small for me to enter, but then I found a broad and easy one. I could stand in it, though bent over slightly, and I took it to its ending, where it opened into a small underground room, four walls and that sunlit narrow slit, up and before me, the curbside drainage opening, down which the rain would spill. I pushed my pack into the slit and onto the street's edge. Then I climbed up and slid through.

I was on my hands and knees at the end of a street, rows of pink stucco houses, yards of gravel and cactus, small palms along the sidewalks, and I remember seeing her watching me, then the dog moving from her side. She stood in the yard a few houses down on the right. The dog's tail was wagging. By the time he reached me I was on my feet, felt his wet nose as he pressed his muzzle into my palm. Santos.

And I remembered her name because it was Estelle, like Stella, the kind of name my mother spoke of, wistfully romantic and of the gone days of the theater.

"From El Monte?" she had said, her eyes wide with wonder. Over ten miles away, and how could I have possibly . . . And that was my romance for her, at least that I could feel it as such and find a way to talk to her. She seemed my age, but a woman as I experienced her. Yet I'd come magically up from the street. El Monte was as much a foreign country to her as Blevins was to me. She introduced me to her dog. I caught the smell of her, like my mother, but different, cheap perfume and adolescent sweat. She took me to a room and kissed me there, put my hand over her breast. The house seemed empty but for the two of us. I gave her candy. She sucked on it, then pushed it between my lips with her tongue. She said she'd be an actress and would someday sing for me. I held her gaze without blushing. We didn't speak of our families or our lives, as if they were some past that we were beyond together. Just an hour, and though I had no watch I glanced at my wrist, acted as I thought a man might, my father, said I had to go. We kissed as if I were leaving on some long journey, into voyage or war. She touched my nose with her fingertip and laughed. She even held a hankie, and I saw her wave it from the yard as I slid into the side of the curb. I raised my own hand, a kind of salute, before I dropped down into the ground under the street.

"A collie," I said.

I was standing beside him, looking down at the translucent skin of the packing pressed along the doorframe where it met the clean window. Sun glistened on the door and hood, but when I looked up, the smog clouds were still there, thick and moving in billows as they had all day. I could smell Edna's eucalyptus shampoo in my hair. The pads of my fingers were soft now and free of grit, and when I breathed in, my nostrils felt moist and clear.

"Hot wax," he said. "It's cooled now and sealed. You'll have to heat it up, when you want it off. A hair dryer? Something like that. But the windshield. I couldn't do anything with that. It's a rental car?"

"Yes, it is."

"Well, you can take it back. You can see okay. Just watch the sun."

"What about the dog?"

"A collie? It's strange, really, for years now. They just keep coming back. Like something in the genes, I guess. Pups of the ones she raised here. Maybe *their* pups, even."

He had the bill in his hand, a large damp towel draped over his shoulder. He removed it and dabbed at the fender as he spoke.

"Who?" I said.

"Her name's Pearl. I don't know the last. That one old house? Down the street? It's there she raised them. A long time ago."

"Do you know where she is?"

He looked at me, tossed the towel back over his shoulder, then looked above my head beyond the stand of eucalyptus toward the hill where the road went into smog.

"Up there somewhere. That's all I know."

He told me not to touch the window or try to roll it down, said something about the seal. He'd cleaned the inside of the car as well, and when I got behind the wheel, I smelled wintergreen.

The windshield seemed all right until I left the San Gabriel River Freeway and picked up the San Diego. After leaving Blevins Street, I'd been traveling through thick smog the entire way, and it had made no difference. But on the San Diego, the smog had begun to lift and dissipate, sun washed over the glass, and I could see the pitting, so thorough that at times the windshield was almost opaque. I had to lower the visor, move to the slow lane, and navigate by watching the white lines at the freeway's verge. It got even worse when I turned west on the Laguna and headed into the setting sun. It was close to seven by then, and I pulled over and checked the rental car directory that was in the glove compartment and found the closest place.

They sent out a skinny kid with short red hair. He wore a dirty white T-shirt and jeans that were too loose for him. He kept grabbing at his belt, jerking them up.

"That's right," he said. "No question about it." He moved around the car, checking the windshield from various angles. Then he saw the packing.

"What in the fuck is that?" he said.

"Hot wax," I said. "It's set. You'll have to soften it. A hair dryer?"

"Hair dryer? Where in the fuck will I get a hair dryer?"

The new car was the same make, but a different model, a sporty one. I drove it back to the hotel and parked it in the lot. Then I went up to my room and changed, stuffing my gritty clothing into a plastic bag. The message light was blinking on the phone. Sanchez again, asking me to call him in the morning. It was quarter to eight by then.

TOBY OLSON

17.

Jen was full of her day again, the diving and the volleyball, and I knew I'd have to wait to tell her about Blevins and the things I'd found out there, that I'd known Susan Rennert, however briefly, in a childhood magic. I remembered Jen's dream, that I had killed the woman and had not. It had seemed like nothing more than a nightmare. But now I knew I'd even touched and kissed her, however innocently and only as a boy, had done an imitation of myself as older, in a time when even the romance of murder might seem possible.

They were standing at the edge of the parking lot when I drove up, Tod in chinos and an expensive raw silk shirt. Jen was barelegged in her wet suit top, her diving gear nowhere in sight. I felt a twinge of guilt at failed responsibility. I'd made no plans for that. But Tod had handled it. He'd taken the stuff to his place down the beach. He'd have it at the lifeguard tower the next morning, in time for her lesson. He stood in the sand looking after us as we drove out of the lot.

Now we were on my balcony, sitting in a soft sea breeze.

"What do you think?" I said.

Jen had showered and washed her hair, and while she was doing that, I'd ordered up a sandwich and some nuts and a couple of sodas. It was too late to call Carol, so I'd written a reminder on an envelope and stood it against Jen's phone for the morning. I'd brought in the necklace Jen had left in the car but had said nothing as she'd tucked it away, a little guiltily, I thought. She sat beside me as I ate and told her about Blevins Street. Then we'd taken our sodas and gone out to look at the stars, not many, but a clear sky and a gibbous moon.

"About the dog," she said. "Santos? Wouldn't that be the next step?"

"Yes," I said. "To find that woman Pearl."

"And *Rennert: why Susan?* number five on your father's list. You remember, for sure? That she was Estelle?"

"I'm sure it was. And there's that other name, Reuss. Her father must have changed *all* the names. She was just a baby then, when he ran out of Encinitas and those bills."

"But how do you know it *was* her?"

"She came back to me. Seeing the place, remembering. I think it explains the dream that night, mine at least. That she was somewhere back in my mind. It's why I've been so drawn to her, by those photographs. It was as if I'd known her. And I had!"

"Well, but the age would be wrong, though. You said you were the *same* age. But she was over two years older than you. Fourteen at least."

"So I was a little off." I said. "My memory. Does it make much of a difference, twelve, fourteen, even sixteen?"

"You bet it does!" Jen said, then caught the sound of her own words, that mocking of adult wisdom, and laughed.

"About this Tod," I said, turning toward her, exaggerating the seriousness in my voice.

"Oh!" she said, dropping the "Bill" from it this time, as if it were becoming too much of a thing.

We heard the drone of a small plane, the sound receding across the water in the west.

"Catalina," I said.

"Do they have an airport there?"

"Could very well be a seaplane."

"Is the boat big?"

"The one we'll go on? No, not too. You'll get a feel of the sea."

"Good," she said. "I can't wait!"

TOBY OLSON

I drove Jen to the Main Beach parking lot at quarter to nine the next morning. She'd called Carol before leaving, and they'd spent a good ten minutes on the phone. Tod was waiting near one of the benches with Jen's gear, and she let him carry it down to the life-guard tower for her. I'll have to watch that guy, I thought, laughing to myself. What did I think? That they were fucking under the stands at the volleyball match? I was playing the foolish father again, enjoying the game and the fact that I really wasn't worried, maybe a little jealous, though, that I'd left something undone with Susan Rennert on that day. I shook my head to clear such quirky thoughts, then left the parking lot and headed back to the hotel and called Sanchez.

"A four-foot," he said. "That's what they call it in the trade. Or a three-quarter. They're just forty-eight inches wide. A double's fifty-four."

"And a queen?"

"That's sixty. Far bigger."

I told him about Blevins Street, that I might have found the Rennert house, but I didn't mention the fact that I'd broken into it. I told him about Pearl too, said I was going to try to find her.

"You say she's an older woman?"

"A strange one, I think. Not too old. But sixty at least. And there's something else."

"Wait. I'm going to make some calls. I'll check on tax roles, build-ing permits, things like that. I can probably get the maiden name that way, at least dates of ownership. And some computer checks as well, broad-based stuff. We'll throw a net out, see what comes back. You can call me this afternoon, around three, no later than five."

"That quick?" I said.

"That quick. Now what was it, this something you mentioned?"

I told him about the King of Norway Line, the dots my father had inserted beside those entries in the traffic schedules. I had my notes of the dates of passage, and I read them to him over the phone.

"Right," he said, "that may indeed be something. I'll get onto it."

"And one other thing."

"Go on."

"Could you check the weather on the day she died? The moon, wind, and tides?"

"No problem," he said.

I hung up, slipped my notes back into the file, then took them to the glass table and removed my father's list again and read through it.

1. Look into blossom gradation and etching.
2. Go over it with Bev again.
3. Laguna: check local newspaper morgue.
4. Leonard has batteries.
5. Rennert: why Susan?
6. Could it really have been Housewares?
7. Weather: moon, wind, tides.
8. The question of the sheet.
9. Write letter to Billy.
10. The History of the American Theater
    (TAT: Its History) what?
11. Time longer than Rope.
12. Go see Blevins.

I had a handle on seven of the twelve. I'd try to find Leonard this evening, and it was possible that Jen could find something out about number ten at the El Monte Museum, where my mother's papers were stored. That could make it eight. Then there were two and nine, something to do with family, and reading them I had a strange feeling that Susan Rennert was involved in that, if only that I'd met her when my parents were still alive. *Go see Blevins.* It read like an order now, as if my father had written the list for me, to tell me what to do when I found it.

I spent the rest of the morning organizing things. I took my soiled clothing down to the hotel laundry, then checked through all my diving gear in the car trunk. My tank was only half full, and I drove over to the dive shop for air. When I got back, I checked all the hoses and the regulator. Then I went to the hotel dining room and had a light lunch. It was one o'clock when I'd finished, and instead of going back to the room, I walked to the Coast Highway, crossed it, and dipped into a few shops on side streets. The sky was cloudless, just enough breeze to soften the heat, and after I'd picked out a few things—sunglasses, film, bottled water, a Laguna Beach T-shirt for Jen—I found a bench at the edge of a small park and sat in the shade and watched the tourists.

It was three by the time I got back to the room, and after I'd called the El Monte Museum, checked to make sure of its evening hours, I lifted the phone again and called Sanchez.

"It's Kapuscinski," he said.

"That's an odd one."

"Not in Poland, it's not. It's common."

"So a cousin, then? On the mother's side?"

"A sister."

"At Blevins they thought she was a cousin. But it's Pearl, right?"

"That part's right. In the phone directory. She's the only Kapuscinski in the area where you were."

I waited for him to continue.

"The house on Blevins? It was community property. Reuss, the husband, died. The deed held Cora Kapuscinski. Then, when she was gone, it was Pearl. It still is. The husband's name was George. I haven't figured just when he changed it yet from Rennert, but I'd guess right after Encinitas."

"I would have thought the daughter, Susan. That she would inherit."

"It stands to reason."

"And the mother? When did she die?"

"In 1963, in May. But she didn't. I mean, die. She disappeared.

The house was tied up then for five years. Pearl paid the taxes. It was her name in the will."

"How old was Cora?"

"She was sixty-two, a missing person. There was nothing much to be done. It was checked out. In a perfunctory way, I think. Then it was tied up in the courts."

"The age seems odd," I said. "Almost twenty years between the two sisters. What about the contents? Was nothing left to Susan?"

"That's another thing," Sanchez said. "There was a break-in. Just a day after Cora disappeared. I have a skimpy report. Pictures were taken off the walls. And maybe some other things, but there's no way to tell. Nothing was trashed. It was right then that Pearl stepped in, started to pay utility bills and taxes. But no, the will doesn't mention Susan. Everything went to Pearl."

"The date," I said.

"That's right. Just over a year before the Susan Rennert drowning."

He'd checked the King of Norway Line but had come up with nothing. Only that the ones my father had put dots beside were all on the same course, a cruise from Long Beach through the Channel Islands and down to the tip of Baja.

"They'd go around to La Paz for a stopover, then steam back."

"Catalina?" I said.

"No, not in those days. Most everything was aboard ship. They'd anchor near the harbor at Avalon and watch the lights."

"And what about the weather?"

"You mean with Rennert? Full moon. A stiff wind coming in from offshore throughout the night. The tide was high at six A.M. the morning they found her, quite high."

"Did the name Estelle come up?"

"Estelle? Where did you get that?"

"When I went to Blevins Street," I said.

"Somebody mentioned it?"

"Just a name," I said.

TOBY OLSON

I heard a rustle of papers, Sanchez breathing, then his voice again.

"No. That name isn't here. And I think I would have remembered it, a name like that."

"Is there anything else?" I asked.

"I don't think so," he said, then paused, then spoke again. "You know, there's nothing for me to do here. I mean with the Pearl business. No cause to look into that. And even if there were, I'd have to turn it over to a station in Los Angeles."

"I understand," I said.

"Right. But *you* can, I mean, go over there. When do you think you'll be going?"

"Tomorrow."

"Okay. Here's what you do. You call me when you get close to the place. Then you call me again after you leave. We'll give it a certain time."

"I'll do that," I said. "Probably in the late morning."

18.

When my father was in his electrical phase, he built a power clothesline for my mother. Attached under the back porch eaves, the rope ran over a pulley to another that was bolted to a square post sunk at the fence edge no more than thirty feet away. He'd set a metal button into the floor below the rigging, and when my mother would step on it, the bodices of her dresses and the hips of my father's pants would lurch to the side, the flowing skirts and limp legs lingering in a kind of dance lean before they swept back to hang straight again, like poised, erect bodies. Sparrows would rise from our avocado tree, startled by movement and the whir and clatter of the mechanism, and my mother would look up to see them, startled a bit too, then over to where I stood, a grin spreading across her face when she saw mine.

On the inside wall beside the back door was a row of switches, a black one to engage the clothesline power and a dozen colored ones for the lighting of various pathways through the house. There were similar switches near the front door and in each bedroom, a special one for the illumination of those model planes hanging from my ceiling. And my father had installed strips of theater aisle lighting bought at some going-out-of-business sale along the baseboards running from my bed to the bathroom. He'd rigged them to pressure switches under the carpeting, and they would blink on just ahead of me, a trail constructing itself, as I staggered half asleep in my pajamas, touching the walls, making my way toward some relief in the night.

Lights lining our brief driveway, automatic spotlights washing across the front door as we drove up, lights activated inside as we stepped onto the porch. And my father had not stopped at lights. Stopping was not in my father. He'd moved onward to small generators, to experiments with magnets and propulsion. In the garage, he'd simulated earthquakes, had tested the concrete of our house foundation using a model and serial explosions. My mother would shake her head, then smile vacantly, as the house rocked. Then one day a small crack appeared in the foundation below the front porch, and when my father saw it, he shook his head and smiled too. "Well, that's it, Bev," he said. "No more of that for now."

The crack was still there, though the porch wasn't, and I could see the upper branches of the avocado tree through a brown haze beyond the roof peak. The garage had been ripped away, and where it had stood, a green corrugated roof covered a flagstone patio outlined by large, earthenware planters spilling over with bougainvillaea and cactus. They'd painted the stucco pink, added a metal shed to the side of the house, and the front yard was overgrown with prairie weeds and wildflowers. A battered pickup truck sat in the drive, and on the post of the white mailbox, its red flag up, the name *Olivares* had been stenciled.

I'd dropped Jen off at the El Monte Museum.

"You're getting California," I'd said, as we were driving inland from Laguna.

Her hair had turned to straw and her nose was peeling. She'd belted her new T-shirt with a colorful Mexican rope and wore a pair of loose cotton pants and sandles. Her lips held the dull shine of a moistening gloss. Her dress seemed thoughtless, yet certain. Confidence of a woman, or of a child. There had been no Tod around when I had picked her up after class, and I was shocked to feel so pleased about that. We'd grabbed a quick sandwich at a deli before heading out.

"Oh, Bill!" she'd said. "I could live here."

TOBY OLSON

"The diving?" I'd asked, and she'd turned quickly thoughtful, looking away from me and out the window, where the haze was thickening into a serious smog cover as we got farther from the sea. The palms lining the freeway seemed petrified in their stillness beyond the smoky window glass. She turned back and looked over at me, then looked down at the dashboard.

"No, it's not that," she said, then glanced out the window again. "And it certainly isn't *that*. I mean, of *course* I like the diving. I love it. But what will I do?"

"Is it Tod?" I said, the words uncalled for, jumping out of me.

I looked quickly over. She'd turned and was looking at me. Her eyes blinked and her cheeks flushed, darkening her sunburn. Then a smile started at the corners of her mouth, and after I'd looked back at the road, I heard her light, bubbling laugh.

"Tod?" she said softly. "No, no, it's not that. I mean, he's very nice and all. But I meant all this. Coming to California, with *you*. God, Racine! What in the hell will I do there?"

"It's not over yet," I said, knowing that was nothing that could help just then.

"But it *will* be."

"I'll come and see you, I said. Often. I might even move out your way."

I'd had no intention of doing that, of leaving the East. "But you won't," she said. "I know you won't. Move, I mean."

"What makes you think that?"

"We don't really know each other. Do we?" Her voice was plaintive, asking me for the right answer. It was easier than I thought it would be to talk like a father.

"Well, I think we do know each other. At least enough that we're headed in the right direction. It's something new for each of us. I mean, I'm your father. I've never had a daughter."

"Are you sure?" she said. The joke was pure, not a hint of bitterness or irony. "There could be hundreds of us out there!"

I laughed, then reached across and took hold of her knee and squeezed it. "Not possible," I said. "There was no one else like your mother. And yet . . . "

I sat across from the house for a good fifteen minutes, reconstructing it in my mind. The blacktop road had been dirt when I'd lived there, and my father had devised an oil coating to keep the dust down. The houses to each side of mine were still there, but they too had been changed, made more rambling and colorful, and the owners had let the growths around them loose. Everything was tended, but not tamed in the way of my father. I lingered, trying hard to bring the house back, myself in it. I was right there, after all, and I thought something should happen, that I should see something, maybe walk across the road to it and touch it. There was that thin crack line in the foundation, that glimpse of avocado tree, but that was about all there was, and even those two visible evidences of my past seemed different somehow. Was there something inside? A remnant of wiring, a hint of some scent deep in a closet? I could picture the back porch, the small garden plot where I'd planted squash. I thought of my mother standing there, the way she'd turned and smiled at me, her ingenue of a farm girl ready for song. Then I started the car up and for a moment thought to just drive away, head back to the museum and get Jen. The taste of the past was bitter, perversely present, and I thought if I found Leonard I might find myself too close to the dead.

At the end of Burkett Road was Doan, the name carved vertically into the same kind of thin concrete pillar I'd seen at Blevins Street. I turned at the corner, heading in the direction of the broad concrete wash I'd played in as a child. The road was a short one. It ran flat for a few hundred yards, then dipped over a steep hill and dead-ended where the wash embankment abutted it. It was narrower than Burkett, but here the houses were set well back, behind high, wild hedges, deep among walnut and eucalyptus trees. Dusk

TOBY OLSON

was coming on, and smoke hung in feathery wisps high in the road-side trees ahead, a fire down in the wash, brush, or someone burn-ing rotted hay. But that was from my childhood, when there had been a stable down there. Now it was smog. The radio had predicted some dissipation, a light breeze coming in the evening and blowing throughout the night. It would clear the air a little, but not enough to matter, and by noon the next day the pollution count would be nearing the warning stage again.

I recognized a configuration on the left, at the mouth of a drive-way cut into a curb. A low fire hydrant, exactly as it had been. Leonard would be two doors down. I pulled to the curb and parked, then got out and made my way along the road's edge, feel-ing the dirty breeze at my ears. There was no sidewalk, no other cars in the road, and once I passed the hydrant, I saw the squat stucco pillars at the edge of Leonard's drive, their rough white sur-faces peeking out through the vines that almost swallowed them. I turned in between them, stepped from the blacktop onto packed dirt. The driveway was long, and fifty yards back I could see the edge of the peaked roof. I was halfway down the drive when the lights came on, a row of lanterns set in the brush to either side, no more than a few feet between them, but a dim glow only in the fail-ing evening light. Then I heard the music, just a hint of it, but enough so I could pick out the tune, "Blue Moon," coming from the house back in the trees. The music grew no louder as I approached, and even when I'd stepped to the brick walkway leading up to the front door, it remained at a far distance, as if it were coming from somewhere behind the house and not in it.

A screen door, the inner door behind it open, and as I stepped up on the brick porch and a light above the door came on, I could see into the house, a dark entryway, just a dim glow in the room beyond it. I could see the edge of a couch, the frayed arm of an easy chair. I reached out and knocked lightly on the screen door's edge. It was thin and unstable and tapped against its frame, so I knocked more firmly on the frame itself, then waited. There was nothing. Then I heard something, a door closing, a cough, then a shuffling of feet.

He materialized out of the darkness, a small man with a shuffling gait I recognized immediately. I could see him loping up the drive to my parents' house, remembered my mother standing at the front door, beckoning. But he had only lifted his arm, waving her off, and headed for the garage and my father. Maybe he had nodded to me, but I couldn't remember.

He came toward me now with the same resolve and intention, his head down as if he were watching for obstructions in some unfamiliar place. He was almost touching the screen when his body lurched and he pulled up, and before he lifted his face to look out through it, I saw the soiled dome of his bald head, grease streaks where he'd run his fingers absently through the few remaining wisps. When his head came up and I saw his eyes, they were blinking, working to focus, as if he wasn't sure just where he was. I thought he might have been thinking about something on the way out and had forgotten where he was headed. The blinking stopped then, and he saw me, and his face stilled. I recognized that face, an absence of expression that I remembered from thirty years before. The skin beside his eyes was still smooth and free of wrinkles, but slightly translucent now, and his thin nose was lined with the veins of an alcoholic. He was wearing loose coveralls over a dirty white T-shirt. I bent forward slightly and looked through the screen at him. Like the face of a fetus, I thought, only able now to name what had troubled me in his presence when I was a child. My father had let me watch them at the worktable, had even invited me in as a helper. But I had never known about Leonard, what he was thinking.

"I don't want anything," he said, the voice distant and without inflection, as if recorded for some other occasion.

"Leonard?" I said. I had the Rennert file and the list in a large manila envelope in my hand, and I saw him look at it, then back up at my face, blinking again.

TOBY OLSON

"Yeah," he said. I'm Leonard. *Mr.* Leonard."

"I'm Billy," I said. "From around the corner. A long time ago."

"Billy." He said it flatly, neither question nor statement. Then he lifted his hands and wiped his palms on the bib of his overalls.

"Yes," I said. "The house on Burkett. My father. Don't you remember my mother? She was an actress."

It was nothing that he should remember, and I didn't know why I'd said it, as if to push my mother forward, to bring her significance up to him, something he had probably never considered. And yet that did it, causing his eyes to widen.

"Billy? Andy's boy? Is it Billy boy?"

He reached out and pushed the screen door, and I had to step to the side quickly to avoid being hit by it. His hand was small, but his grip tight when he grabbed my elbow and shook my arm. I touched his shoulder briefly. He was smiling, but I could see nothing at all in his eyes.

As I followed behind him through the dark living room, he spoke about the lights and the music, how he had them switched. "Especially the music," he said. "That old tune. I got it wired to fade as you come on. A nice trick." He didn't seem to be talking to me, though I was the only one there. Then he said, "Old Andy's boy. Billy boy," though he didn't turn.

He took me to a small sitting room at the rear of the house, pointed to one of the tattered easy chairs, then turned without speaking and shuffled out the door. I sat down, the envelope in my lap, and looked at the wall a few feet away. It was covered with deep shelves, and on them, butted tight against each other, were various electrical panels, banks of toggle switches, and what looked like amplifiers. Heavy wires ran down the wall behind the bookcases, and when I turned in my chair, I saw that all the walls were outfitted this way. Some of what was there was clearly stereo equipment, but most of it seemed designed for heavy electrical work. A few shelves had been cut away in the bookcase to my right, and in that space was a massive breaker box, the door removed. There must have been a hundred breakers at least, more than half of them engaged. Above the box was an old master switch mechanism, an inverted U with a thick wooden handle, and above that a complex electrical scheme had been taped to the edge of a shelf. I thought I saw pencil markings at places along the thin lines.

"Your father's dead."

Leonard stood in the doorway, a can of beer in each hand. He lifted them as he spoke. Again it was neither question nor claim, and then he stepped into the room and reached a beer out to me.

"My mother too," I said.

He crossed to the other chair and plopped down into it. It was large, with heavy upholstered arms. Only his toes touched the floor. He looked like an old child.

"All this," I said, lifting the envelope, gesturing to the wall behind him.

"It's a living," he said. "I do a little repair. I have no wife in the way. Never did. What's that?"

His hand was in a fist on the chair arm, his finger extended and pointing at the envelope in my lap.

"Do you remember?" I asked. "My father? My mother?"

"Shit, yes!" he said. "Your father and me. We had a few things going from time to time. He had ideas."

"This," I said. "My father had a file. You're mentioned in it."

"Gimme," he said, but he didn't move, and I had to get out of my chair and hand the envelope to him.

His cuticles were black with dirt, and I worried that he'd soil the documents. But he was careful as he took them out of the envelope, then rocked himself to the edge of the chair and spread them on the floor at his feet. I watched as he took a pair of thin, wire glasses from a pocket in his bib, settled them carefully on his nose. Then he put his hands between his knees, as if to avoid touching the papers, leaned over, and gazed down at them. I could see the square that

214   TOBY OLSON

was Susan Rennert's photograph, the list beside it on the carpet.

He sat there for a good long while, his lips moving. He was reading every word. "Bev again," he mumbled, "Rennert."

"Leonard has batteries," I said.

"Of course. I can *see*."

He said it sharply, glancing at me over his glasses, then dipped his head again and continued to read. He'd moved to the clipping now and was staring intently down at the photo. I sat silently and waited, and in a while he was finished. He sat up at the chair's edge then, rolled his shoulders, rotated his neck. "My fucking back," he said. "Don't ever get old."

Then he stood up and stretched his whole body, his arms above his head, the beer can in one of them, stood on his toes, then dropped his arms and waved his hand over the papers. I'm to pick them up, I thought. He stepped over them, jerked his head for me to follow, then shuffled toward the doorway.

He was already in the kitchen, standing at the sink. I'd gathered up the papers and followed after him, guided by the light that flooded down a narrow hallway. He had his hands on his hips and was grinning, waiting for my response.

"You surely do," I said. "Have batteries, I mean."

"You bet your ass," he said.

The kitchen was square and large and flooded with dirty fluorescent light. The counter to each side of him was thick with dishes and pots, and electrical coils and small generators as well, and off to his right, under a curtained window, a small wooden table held the remnants of his last meal: soiled plate and paper napkin, a glass and a fork, and beside them a gauge of some kind, bits of colored wire sticking out from it, something he'd been working on while eating.

There were two straight-backed chairs, one draped with clothing. The cabinet doors above his head were grease smeared, loose on their hinges. Two stood open a few inches, and I could see tools, ribs of motor parts, and coils of wire on the dark shelves inside.

Thick wire ran on the floor at his feet also, snaking up beside his legs to enter holes drilled in the cabinet doors under and beside the sink. One headed across the linoleum to the baseboard, where it was held in place by heavy staples and nails before it too disappeared into the wall through a hole.

I stood in the doorway, could see through the narrow slit where the curtains joined above the table that it was getting dark outside, smoky shadow fronds of some growth, the dark trunk of a eucalyptus. A black wire ran up the wall under the curtains' edge, and I traced it back down to the floor, watched its progress among the others, the way it twisted through their knotty braiding, then reappeared, heading like them toward the room's center, where all rose up like trained cobras reaching for the charge of food at Leonard's batteries.

He'd clearly made them. They sat on a thick metal plate, itself slightly elevated above the floor on solid cinder blocks. There were three of them, each a broad rectangle rising a good six feet above the plate, and they were contained in a kind of black rubber, something painted onto the surface like rough stucco. Together they formed a six-foot square, and when I stepped through the doorway and a little to the side, I could see no more than the crown of Leonard's head above them.

"Careful with the wire," he said.

His voice was slightly muffled, something more than the bulk between us causing it, and when I stepped among the wires and got closer to the batteries, I felt the hair on my arms rise up, an acrid bite in my nostrils. And I could see something, faint smog-like waves undulating above the terminals. There was something in their scent, slightly lemony.

I could see Leonard's face again. He was smiling and nodding.

"It *is* lemon," he said. "Something I found out. Just to cut the smell. Now, why don't you go over there. Mind the wires. This'll take a while."

I crossed carefully to the chair and sat down before the remnants of Leonard's meal. Then I turned the chair slightly so I could watch him.

"If there's a problem," I said, a little nervous at the unknown prospects.

He had turned and squatted down and was reaching up under the cabinet to the left of the sink. He had moved into it up to his shoulders, and his voice was even harder to get than the last time. I saw his foot tap impatiently on the floor.

"No, no, it's nothing. It's about time for it anyway." Then he came out and climbed to his feet, pulling himself up at the sink's edge. "This *fucking* back!"

He had a wrench and a heavy gallon container in his hands, and he rested them both on the floor at the batteries' side when he got there. Then he shuffled to the corner of the room and got the small stepladder, brought it back and settled it near the batteries, and climbed up to the second rung. His back was to me, and I could see his elbows move as he fussed with something on the surface.

"Just checking the juice," he said.

I saw the aura along his shoulders and neck and at the tips of his ears before I saw the flash, a thick blue flame that shot above his head, then quickly vanished. I felt a slight vibration through the chair's seat, heard the fork click against the plate, and smelled lemon again. Then I looked to the ceiling above his head. It was scorched, and a wisp of blue smoke hung there. There were other scorched places as well. A demonstration, I thought, he's done this before. His own pleasure probably. I couldn't imagine he had friends. I was his catch for the day, something rare.

"Your father wasn't really my friend," he said, as he climbed down from the ladder and reached for the jug and wrench. I stood up at the chair's side so I could see the batteries' surface. I counted twelve terminals, eighteen corks sticking up from the mouths of ports among the tangle of wires. Some of the terminals were bare.

He climbed back up on the ladder, pulled a cork out, then reached for the jug he'd rested beside the wrench on the ladder's small shelf. I waited for him to continue.

"Your mother," he said. "We weren't friends at all. It started up again because of electricity, music too. Show tunes. Your mother, she was la de da, in the *theatah*, you know."

There was more than a joke in his voice, and I stiffened as I heard it.

"But your old man. He brought something over to get fixed, and I showed him this. It wasn't this big then, but it was still something. Music was on, and we talked about that. I've got a collection. So there was dinner, over at your place. He was working on something, propulsion, I think. We went over things. Possible forces and controlling them. And the music. He borrowed records for your mother to hear."

"Can you say what the thing was? Any more about it?" He was removing corks, pouring in liquid. "What about the date?"

"Well, that I'm clear about. If that list was made near the time of that newspaper clipping. I wasn't here. I was laid up. I wouldn't forget *that* date. I was in the hospital for three months."

"What happened?"

"We don't talk about that. Let's just say some wires got crossed. But he didn't see me then. And then, when I got out. Well, you know, they were dead. But we had fucked with electricity before that. For a while it was thick between us. Work, I mean. Figuring things out. But for that one time, we didn't talk about other things. It was the music then, but *only* then. That time I came over for dinner."

"But you were over at other times." I'd stepped away from the chair so I could see what he was doing. He had the wrench in his hand now and was moving wires to empty terminals. "I remember."

"Oh, sure," he said. "To the garage. Years before. Your pop had a lot of good shit there. Junk too. But some curious stuff. I got a few

TOBY OLSON

things out of him." He waved the wrench in the air behind him. "There, in those cabinets. I'll bet there's still something there. But I hadn't seen them much since you were a kid. Wasn't he working on other things then? Gliders?"

"Anything I could know about?"

"I doubt it. He wouldn't lose what he didn't need. And your pop had a way of needing most everything. A kind of pack rat, wasn't he?"

"That's true," I said.

"Old Andy," he said.

"What about the woman in that clipping?"

"Nothing. I don't know nothing about her. But then, I was in the hospital. I told you that."

"Right. But it could have been earlier. Something at dinner?"

"No, just the three of us. Three happy people. Your mother danced! I still remember *that* shit. The drinking too."

I didn't know what he was talking about, but I didn't like it. I had an urge to move over to him, just a small old man clinging to a ladder, to kick it out from under him. He must have been well over eighty.

"How old were you then?"

"We don't talk about that," he said.

He climbed down from the ladder, folded it, and stepped carefully among the wires as he moved it back to its place against the wall. Then he put the jug and the wrench on the counter beside the sink, picked up a dirty dish rag, and stood there wiping his hands, not looking at me, but over at the batteries.

"Propulsion, you said?"

"Yeah, I'm pretty sure it was that. Something about that. Hydraulic? But it must have had something to do with the electrical. Else he wouldn't have come here."

"So that's it? All you can tell?"

"What about the letter?" he said, dropping the dish rag in the sink. "Wasn't that on the list? Didn't you get it?"

"I don't even know that he wrote it."

"Ah, well," he said, shaking the subject off. "Let's get down to *this* business."

He moved to the end of the counter where it met the frame of the back door, squatted, and opened the cabinet below it. I could see the cylindrical, ribbed shape of what I thought was a generator from where I stood, and when I moved over to stand above him, I could see that it was large, filling the whole space revealed by the open door, extending back under the counter toward the sink. My shadow fell across him, and he craned his head and looked up sharply.

"Move back!" he said. "Gimme some light!"

I stepped to the side and watched as he fiddled with a petcock, took up a small can he kept under there, and squirted some oil into the small opening. I watched him run his fingers over the side of the housing, feel places where wires were attached, check the tightness of other connections. Then he reached up for the counter, gripping the edge. His knuckles whitened, and again he looked up at me.

"*Can't* you give us a fucking hand?" he said.

His voice was almost plaintive, and I reached down to his thin arm above the elbow and pulled him up to his feet. We were standing close together now, and looking down, I watched him roll his shoulder as he had before, rotate his head again. He shook himself, moved from foot to foot, then he looked up at me, a coy smile at the edges of his lips.

"A breath of fresh, smoggy air?" he said. "I can get you another beer?"

I shook my head to the latter, and he turned slightly, still looking at me, and moved to the back door, opened it, and stepped through. I followed him out onto the small stone patio, its edge defined in the darkness by only the dim shapes of a few low ceramic pots. I could see nothing at all beyond them. There were two cheap plastic lawn chairs there, and he moved to the side of one of them, adjusted it, then beckoned for me to sit down.

220   TOBY OLSON

"You just sit here," he said. "It'll take a little while. But I'll be back."

I heard the door close behind me, then in a few moments felt a slight vibration and heard a deep, constant hum. The generator, I thought.

I looked out into the darkness, waiting for my eyes to adjust, and soon I could see into the distance, the silhouette shapes of tall eucalyptus, filaments of berry vine winding up their trunks. And the shadows of brush and various shrubs too, and maybe some manmade structures. It seemed a very deep yard. I could see no end to it, nothing but a wall of darkness a good fifty yards off. I waited, but there was nothing.

And I thought I'd learned nothing. Surely nothing about Susan Rennert. Only propulsion. And what could that mean? And I had learned little here about my parents, either, though I held back the thought of some difficulty between them and Leonard, a certain distaste.

I recognized then that I had no objective view of my parents at all, no other view, at least. There were no relatives, no friends that I'd even spoken to about them. There was only me, the way I'd seen and had come to see them, in memory, since their deaths. I'm not through here, I thought, not nearly.

Over the hum of the generator, the sound of which I was losing as it drifted toward white noise, I could hear the faint wash of a light breeze high up in the eucalyptus, the shush of bird wings occasionally, and moments of chirping. Maybe there were other things, nocturnal ground animals in leaves, the muffled buzz of insects. I felt a slight chill, though it was warm and no breeze reached the patio where I was sitting, and when I touched my forearm I found the hair there had risen again. There seemed another sound then, but not a sound, a quality like light rising slowly up out of darkness. The yard was still dark, but there was something in it now, a kind of static energy; it had silenced the breeze, seemed to have stopped even the flap of bird wings.

Everything seemed poised, some powerful potential waiting. Then it began to materialize.

I was gazing off into the distance, to the wall of darkness where the yard ended, and I began to see color there, a faint blue emerging, a small ragged cloud of it that spread slowly out from a center. It was cloud-like in its texture, like a kind of dry liquid, wisps of smoke or waves of plankton in sea water, an expanding cloud that spread to the sharp right angles of its finalized figure, a vertical rectangle of swimming blue color imbedded in the wall of darkness, pulsing. It was the size of a playhouse door, but higher than a door should be, ten feet above the ground at least.

It stayed there a good long while, intending that I enter it. But I was reading it, an abstraction of changing organic shapes that were really just faint color changes, shadings of blue. It had a quality like faint neon defining its edges; still I thought I saw its smoky substance drift in wisps beyond them slightly from time to time. Then it rotated and elevated, came to the horizontal near the wall's center.

I could hear nothing. The generator was gone, all sound seemed sucked from the yard or frozen there. Then I saw the blue figure vibrate slightly and felt the wash of a different light touching my lids. I looked up and a little to the left, and there was another rectangle, a green one, high in the eucalyptus. It was moving down toward the other, and as it slowly passed over leaves and the structure of limbs, they were apparent in it. The same cloudy milkiness as in the other figure, but the changing skeletal shapes of the tree, as if x-rayed, leaf capillaries, a vision through bark to the limbs' arteries and veins.

Then I saw another, this one blood-red and rising up out of the ground off to the right. And a yellow one had risen up from behind the central blue one, the two now forming a kind of Rothko painting. Then there were others, some moving down from the treetops, others stationary and materializing in the air as the first one had. They were figures like those in the canvases of another painter, Mondrian, but motivated into liquidity and motion, and for a while

TOBY OLSON

they seemed to stay at the same distance from me, fading and disappearing, then coming to life in other places. But then a purple one materialized in the air no more than twenty yards to my left and began moving toward me. I gripped the metal chair arms.

It was as if I were sitting in the front row at a movie, very close to the screen. The glow from the rectangle extended beyond my body before it reached me. I saw a human shape in it, then recognized that it was I. My arms were up, my hands reaching to hold it back. Then I was in it, its light surrounding me, my fingers feeling for its upper edge. I touched a band of coolness. Then it was gone away behind me, and when I could see out in the yard again, there seemed to be hundreds of them.

Some had moved over others now, their colors mixing, and a few were slowly rotating, turning to the vertical, back to the horizontal, then sliding off to right or left, fading away as they reached the yard's sides.

At times I thought I saw patterns of movement, something analogous to a musical score, or music itself, a melody forming as rectangles echoed the shifts and undulations of others, a shape moving slowly on a plane toward the center, then blinking and fading out as another rose from the ground below it, came up to take its place. Then another, high in the trees, turning.

Others came close to me, but only that first one reached me. They'd approach, then rotate slightly in the air, drift off like sailboats tacking away, and I began to see that the pattern of their movements might be more than what I'd experienced on a flat plane. Maybe there was something to be known as they moved away from me, or came toward me.

It was while I was concentrating on that way of seeing them that I began to catch the words, or thought they were there. A brown rectangle drifted out from behind an orange one in the far distance, then slowly crumbled, its last cloud fragments forming the word *time* before they were gone. I saw a red blink briefly to my left, a momentary aura, like that from a flashbulb, *rope,* the word seemingly on the very surface of my eye before fading. And *check,* and *blossom* written on the skeleton of a eucalyptus branch, and *question.* They were all words from my father's list, and I could only imagine that I was seeing them.

I could tell it was reaching the end, or a dramatic change of some kind, before it got there. Some quality, like a growing vacuum in the air. The space between the rectangles was slowly shrinking, and though they were still shifting and fading, they were all moving toward the center. And as they did so, others appeared and took their place at the yard's periphery, then moved inward also.

They were forming a block of color now, their edges touching each other, melding. Those closer to me were moving back, covering, then melting into the ones behind them. Some turned in the air as they receded, then came to the horizontal as they joined the grid. They were coming together where the wall of darkness had been, and as I watched them, the hum of the generator rose up behind me again, louder and more powerful than before. It was laboring, and I began to feel a deep vibration in the stone under my feet, thought I heard a creaking in the structure of the house behind me.

The glowing rectangles drifted inward from both sides, from above, and out of the ground below. They slid into empty spaces at the edges, slowly forming a square that I knew would cover the whole back of the yard when it was completed. As each joined the grid, its shape melted and its color faded or intensified until it complemented those it connected to, until there seemed no distinction of shape or color at all.

I found it hard to focus, to fix my eyes in one place. No longer was this a pattern of various details, it was becoming a oneness, and my gaze could only drift beyond any intention, swimming over that liquid surface that had completed itself without my being aware of its finishing.

TOBY OLSON

I felt lifted, pulled forward, and thought it must be a trick of perception, that I was following my dreamy eyes out to that wall of color and light, to join it and lose myself in it. Then I realized that I had actually lifted. I felt the chair runners tapping on the brick, sliding forward toward the patio's edge. I pushed down hard with my feet, felt grit slipping under my soles, held tight to the jiggling chair arms. Then, suddenly, everything became still, no generator, vibrating house, no movement. I felt a rush of air come over me from behind. The wall of colored light seemed poised.

Then, at its center, I began to see something, a figure in the far distance, taking shape in the smoky color. And the colors were fading, the wash of hues melting into a real liquid, becoming a sea, and the figure was swimming in that sea, moving toward me. I could see its arm, her arm, as it reached out in a labored stroking, her forehead, wet hair stuck to her cheek as she turned her head for breath. She was deep in rolling waves, and at times only her hand was visible, her arm foreshortened behind it. Then she'd be up on a crest, and I'd see her breasts for a moment, the short sleeves of her soaked dress. The wall of light was a movie screen now, but more real than that, though the swimmer seemed to be getting no closer.

Is it Susan Rennert? I thought. Is it Jennifer? I pushed on the chair arms and started to rise. Then the figure was fading, the wall of color returning. It was there again for a long moment, then it began to crumble, until there was only that first blue rectangle, its outline clear again. It pulsed in its liquid hues, like a slowly beating heart, then it too drifted away into darkness.

"That last part's tricky," Leonard said. "It takes more than just energy."

We were back in the small room again, Leonard in his chair, a can of beer in his hand. I'd turned another one down. He'd been on the porch behind me for most of the thing and had touched me on the shoulder a minute or two after it was over. I was just sitting there, looking out into the darkness. I had questions, and I could tell he knew that, but I hadn't asked them yet. His face held the hint of a smile, and he was kicking his heels against the chair legs above the floor, enjoying me, my hesitancy and discomfort.

"Tricky," he said.

"They seemed to be actually moving. The ones that came toward me."

"Yeah, I know. It's projection and mirrors. But there's something in the light also. I can't really explain it. Something."

"You mean it's too hard for me? Too technical?"

"Well, yes, probably that. Maybe something else too."

He took a long swig from his beer, then wiped his chin with the back of his hand. He knew my questions, but he was waiting me out. I looked at my watch. The museum closed at ten-thirty, and it was close to nine. Only a ten-minute drive for me. I'd told Jen I'd get there early, so we could go over things before it closed. I didn't want to give him the benefit, but I had little time.

"I thought I saw words off and on."

"Did you?" he said.

"Yes. But I must have imagined it."

"You might have," he said. "But actually you didn't."

"And the film?" I said.

"Yes. Well, that was just lucky. That I had that clip. I've hundreds of them, but that's the only one with swimming. I got the words from that list you showed me. The one your pop made."

"But how?"

"Computer," he said. "That's another thing I do."

"For how long?" I said.

"Since the beginning, the fifties." He smiled. "Just another thing I do."

"My father," I said. "I don't think he was involved in that."

"Andy?" he said. "Oh, God, no! He didn't have the skill. He was just a tinkerer."

TOBY OLSON

"He was pretty damn good at it." I could hear my child's voice, defending my father.

He shifted in his chair, crossed his short legs and grinned at me. It was a stony grin, and it faded away before he spoke again.

"You know, Billy, it's probably a good thing to know some facts about one's parents."

"Is it?" I said.

"Oh, yes," he said. "Especially on the chance one has them wrong. Your mother, for example."

"What about my mother."

"Well, there's no name for it, except something like silly drunken bitch. But that's not something we'd have said in that time. So it really doesn't fit."

I wanted to get up out of my chair, go over and take his thin neck in my hands, and choke the life out of him, the little bastard. But I was also fascinated. He was the first one I'd ever spoken to who knew my parents in any way, and I had to hear what he thought of them. I couldn't figure just why he was saying these things, what he had to gain by it, and that was something else I wanted to know. He'd changed for me in the time I'd been there. He was no longer just Leonard with batteries. I thought he might be a genius of some sort, if a twisted one.

"What *does* fit?" I said.

"No name, but all that pompous shit about the *theatah*. I saw her in a play once, some Norwegian crap. She really wasn't very good at all."

"How could you tell?" I wanted to pull the words back, not to tangle with him. I wasn't sure what I might do.

"Well, maybe I couldn't." He seemed slightly offended. "But we had dinner. We talked a few times. Your father kissed her ass. And she *liked* that. Keeping him on a short leash. When she was around, there was nothing else to talk about, just her, you know. Just her fame."

"And my father?" I said.

"Andy? He was okay. Just okay. He didn't really know what he was doing. Just fucking around here and there. He never stayed with anything for long. She was in his hair, your mother. Maybe he needed time, and he couldn't get it. But maybe he just wasn't up to it. That's possible too."

It was coming to me now, his motive, and I thought it was a tortured one. They were both long gone, but he hadn't forgotten. I reached for some sense of particulars.

"A woman," I said. "Have you ever had one?"

"What the fuck does that mean! A wife? Not one of those."

"Somebody else's?" I said.

"You mean your mother? Oh, God, no. She would have none of that. I mean, she wouldn't have. The perpetual virgin. What do they call them, in the *theatah?*"

"Ingenue," I said. "An ingenue."

"That's it. One of those things. But usually not a drunk. Like your mother was."

I'd had enough, as much as I could take or get.

"So," I said. "With the other. All I've got is propulsion. That my father was involved in something like that. When you two were working together. Is that right?"

"Except that we weren't together. I was advising him."

"Right," I said, pushing up out of the chair. The envelope I'd brought with me was sitting on the end table at my side, and I picked it up, opened it, and checked through the contents."

"All there?" he said, climbing out of his own chair.

"Yes. Yes, it is."

He led me toward the front of the house, but before we got there he stopped at a door in the side of the hallway.

"Would you like to see something?" he said, turning in the half darkness toward me.

"Why not," I said.

He pulled the door open and went into what seemed like a closet. A light came on, and I followed him. We were in a kind of

TOBY OLSON

anteroom, nothing there but a long white lab coat hanging on a hook. There was a glass door opposite the one we'd entered, darkness beyond it, and I could see a light switch to its side.

"This is the heart of the thing," he said.

He reached up then and flicked the switch, and the room beyond the glass door was brightly illuminated.

It was about the size of the room we'd sat in, but here the walls and ceiling were painted a dead white. There were two metal desk chairs on rollers, back to back, each facing a bank of white computers, their screens and power centers covering the entire expanse of walls, a continuous shelf fronting them, lined with keyboards and grids of toggle switches and colored glass leads. At the end of the room were printers, an enlarger, and a color Xerox machine. The floor was clean white tile, and white track lighting hung from the ceiling.

"The glass has been antistatically treated," he said, touching the door. "I can't let you in. It's a matter of dust. Delicate materials."

"I'm sure," I said.

The place was a white oasis in the otherwise filthy house, and I wondered if the lab coat had been enough for him earlier, of if he'd programmed the light show from another place. I thought to ask him but decided against it. It was getting late.

"There'll be a constant light going out," he said, when we got to the front door, "and no music. That's only for coming."

"That's fine," I said. "I can make my way."

When I reached the front porch, I turned to face him, not knowing if I would shake his hand or not. But he had closed the screen door and was standing behind it in the half darkness, looking out. I waited for him to speak, but he left it to me.

"Well," I said. "Thanks for the information, and for the show."

"And the past?" he said. I couldn't see his face clearly, read his expression.

"Maybe," I said, lifting my hand in a half wave. Then I turned and headed down the lighted driveway toward my car.

On the way to the museum, I thought about the things he'd said. His words had come up from a deep bitterness, some unfinished business with my parents that he'd been unable to shake. Maybe there was more to the story than I'd gotten out of him. Maybe things I should have gotten. But that was not really what was bothering me. It was more that his judgments were a torquing of the reality I'd come to think of as the truth, an exaggeration only of those qualities in my parents that I remembered. He'd turned it, then put a negative face on the excessive. And they had been excessive, both my mother and my father, and I wondered just how far I'd have to push my own memories to see them in his way.

19.

Jen was sitting at a table near a bay of leaded windows, a cardboard box to her left and papers spread out before her. A floor lamp stood at the table's side, and I could see her flushed cheek and peeling nose in the glow of light. She'd pulled her hair back tightly and tied it with a rubber band. She held an open folder in her hands, and her lips were moving as she read.

She smiled when she saw me, shaking her head to clear her hair out of habit, then tapped the table. I took a chair from the far end and pulled it up and sat down beside her.

"How was Leonard?" she whispered, leaning toward me.

I could smell the ocean on her arm, see remnants of salt crystals there. She'd been sucking mints, and I could smell that too.

"Interesting," I said. "But I didn't get very much. I'll tell you later."

There was a woman sitting at a desk near the entrance, an older man and woman reading in chairs near library stacks across the room. Otherwise, the place seemed empty. I could hear a clock ticking. There were carpets over the hardwood floor, machine-made orientals with frayed fringe. The place seemed a little down at the heels, but it was neat and ordered. A board on an easel near the front desk held pinned-up flyers and lists of upcoming events. The history of El Monte, I thought, how complex could that be? I felt I'd been there before. Had it been the water department, the place I'd come for my bike license? What Leonard had said was still with me, that possibility of a changed past. I felt myself reaching for some stable aura, some quality of nostalgia that could verify memory.

Jen was beside me, though, and speaking now, and I shook off the past for her healthier immediacy.

"I did," she said. "But there's so much. Your mother was really involved in all this. The theater, I mean. There's a whole history of her life here. She's in everything!"

I thought of the things Leonard had said.

"And my father?"

"Oh, yes! There are pictures of him too. You can almost date when they met, I think. But look what I *did* find."

She reached among the papers, still talking.

"I've been through it all once and three-quarters. I'm putting it back in the box as I go. Here it is. Three of them. But look at this one."

She held up an eight-by-ten photo, leaning to the side again so we could both look at it.

It showed a street and sidewalk glistening with a recent rain. A crowd of people in evening dress were standing before the glass doors of a theater lobby. I saw my mother and father in conversation off to the left, other couples and small groups, people talking and smoking. The marquee was a lighted band at the photo's top. *History of American Theater,* it read, and below that, *Eugene O'Neill— The Emperor Jones.*

"Number ten," Jen said. "*The History of the American Theater* (TAT: *Its History) what?* It was almost the first way. But he wasn't sure."

"A series," I said.

"But there's something else."

She put the tip of her finger near my mother's waist. My mother's hand was resting on my father's forearm, which he'd raised, tucking his wrist into the fold above his tuxedo button. He was leaning toward her, listening, most probably nodding, but his eyes were on another couple near the curb in front of them. I looked where he did, but could find nothing, just a man and a

232   TOBY OLSON

woman older than my parents, the woman's shoulders draped with a light fur wrap, tails and heads of animals hanging along her arms.

"No," Jen said. "Your mother, back here." She moved her finger, making a circle around my mother's head and torso. "Don't you *see* it?"

Then I did see it. My mother wore a tight black dress that hugged her breast, arms, and shoulders, and rose to her neck. Her hair was short and designed to curl under at the sides, to frame her face, leaving her garments untouched. Her lipstick seemed blood-red, and I thought she'd dusted her face to whiten it. She wore a thin silver bracelet, loose at her wrist, modest as a piece of string, just a touch of something at a distance. It was the necklace she was showing off.

"Here," Jen said, and touched the back of my hand with a magnifying glass. I took the handle and held it up to the photo. It was one of the necklaces I'd given to Jen, stones set into silver ovals, each separated by a link in a thin chain. At the bottom, between the slopes of my mother's breasts, hung a kind of medallion, a circle of small stones set in a silver disk.

"It's one of yours," I said, still holding the glass up. I imagined it around Jen's neck, the medallion deeper, between her higher breasts.

"Your mother," she whispered. "She's not wearing a bra, you know."

I could see that possibility.

"Fashion of the times," I said.

"I'm not sure. Maybe it was just Beat. Something like that."

"Bohemian," I said. "You've got the times wrong."

"I don't know," she said, "but there's something else."

She released the edge of the photo, reached out and shuffled through some others on the tabletop. I looked again at the image, the tilt of my father's head as he listened. They looked good together. It must have been intermission. She was telling him about O'Neill, the play, about the ones she'd acted in. And I was sure he was learning things, adding them to that storehouse of information in his mind. He'd write some of them down before long. Then he'd go to books and records. Finally, he'd know everything. And looking at my mother, I felt I was hearing her voice, that I was my father, looking elsewhere but listening.

"Here they are," Jen said.

She'd found three other photos, and she had shuffled and stacked them in a certain order for her presentation, then turned them face up on the table.

"The lobby?" I said.

"They all are. Check this first one. See what you can find."

It was a kind of game now, a girlish one, but I knew she wouldn't drag it out too long, that new woman in her. I turned my wrist and looked down at my watch. It was ten now; we still had a half hour. The woman at the desk coughed quietly.

The shot of the theater lobby showed a loose group of people headed for double glass doors, the entrance to the theater. It was near the end of intermission, but there was still time. A small crowd had gathered off to the side, and some in it were turning, men with drinks held up to miss bumping the arms and shoulders of others. Near the doors coming in from the street, I saw my parents again, my father's hand at Bev's elbow now, guiding her. They seemed in no hurry. My father was smiling, the lift of his head suggesting he'd spotted something, or someone, across the room. I looked there, but could find nothing, just a small cluster of people in a tight circle, their shoulders brushing as they gestured in animated conversation.

"Here?" I said, putting my finger on a woman's waist. Her body obscured a poster on the wall behind her, O'Neill again, the word *Electra* beside her shoulder.

"No, she's *here*."

Jen took my finger and moved it to a man's upper arm. He was part of that grouping at the concession stand, one of those holding up drinks. He was in profile, in the act of stepping away.

"See, that's the edge of her dress, just there to his side. She's

TOBY OLSON

bending over, getting something, I guess. It's some kind of textured tool. You'll see."

She tugged at the photo, pulling it free of my fingers, then lifted the second one.

My parents were beyond the doorway now, and my father's hand had risen. He was waving to someone across the room, still smiling. He'd moved a little ahead of my mother, though he still held her elbow, and I thought he was urging her forward. She was looking at his face now, her own face out of view. He may have spoken, or she was acknowledging the pressure of his hand. She may have seen his wave and understood.

"Back at the drink place now."

I'd been searching for the object of his attention, somewhere near the woman obscuring the poster. Only moments had passed since the taking of the previous shot, but people had shifted and moved. The man at the concession stand was gone now and another had taken his place, his back to me, and at his side the woman had risen up from the table of drinks.

It was Susan Rennert. She was wearing a dress not unlike the one my mother wore, but of heavier fabric and with a lower neckline. Her hair was shorter than in the photos from the newspaper, and it seemed darker in color. But it was clearly her, though something in her posture and the way she held the drink denied that. I recognized that I'd constructed some attitude for her, made it up out of very little. Still, I couldn't figure her standing in just that way. She seemed quite sure of herself, comfortable in the surroundings. I felt heat rising in my cheeks at the sight of her, and I looked away.

"Look again," Jen said.

I'd dropped my wrist to the table, the photo with its stiff backing still between my fingers, and was looking over at her. I think I was smiling at the discovery, as much that she had made it as that it had been made at all. Maybe it was a fatherly kind of smile. At any rate, she wasn't buying it, not then. Her look was serious, even severe, as if I'd overstepped the rules of our engagement. She'd lifted the magnifying glass, and was offering it to me. I saw her nose twitch, getting at the itch of her recent burn, the flaking scales rumpled along the bridge. I took the glass from her hand and lifted the photo in the air again.

And there it was, the necklace, not identical to the one my mother wore, but very like it. The discs were smaller, and they alternated with thin cylinders, but the stones seemed of the same kind, and it was silver. I thought it was longer than the other, but it might have been the shape of Susan Rennert's neck and torso. I couldn't be sure. I looked again. Was it really her? There was something asymmetrical about her face, though the same broad forehead and chin. *Rennert: why Susan?* I thought of my father's list and was still uncertain.

"Can you tell where it comes from? The origin, I mean?"

"I don't know about jewelry," she said. "But I'll bet it has an origin. I can't believe it's new, a copy, you know? Your mother's isn't, that's for sure. The stuff you gave me. Silver might be American Indian. But I don't think those stones are turquoise. Even in black and white they seem darker than that, maybe red?"

"From India?"

"I don't know. But there's more. Look at the last one."

I picked up the remaining photograph from the table, the magnifying glass still in my other hand, and looked into the same space. The play was over now, and groups of people were moving out the doors leading to the street. Some lingered, though, at the lobby's center and off to the side. The concession stand was in view, just a long card table close to the wall, empty but for a few crumpled napkins and some glasses, and beside it, close to the now-visible poster announcing the next play, I saw my mother and father. They were standing to either side of Susan Rennert, facing her. My father was smiling, his hands open, making some point, and in the palm of my mother's hand, which she'd lifted to Susan Rennert's chest, was the

TOBY OLSON

medallion at the end of that woman's necklace, the small disks and cylinders dripping through my mother's fingers. She was looking at it, feeling and turning it, and Susan Rennert was gazing down to where my mother held it, an awkward look of pleasure on her face.

On the way back to Laguna, we talked things over, but not before Jen had some things to say about the new car. All they'd had was a sporty model when I'd dropped the other off, bucket seats and circular dials set in the dash, a tachometer. I hadn't even checked the name. Cars had meant little to me over the years. I'd had a truck, a four-wheel drive, in Corpus, which I'd used for fishing trips to Padre Island, but at most duty stations I'd footed it or used taxis. My father had taught me how to drive, but I'd seldom had use for the old Oldsmobile, had traveled mostly on my bike, all the way through high school.

Traffic was thick on the freeway, and I'd had to goose it to make our way into the flow. The eight coughed a little, then kicked in when we reached thirty.

"Not bad," Jen said, when we were up to speed. "And I like the seats too. I could get around in this one. I wish I had my license."

"You're old enough now, in Racine, I mean, aren't you?"

"Sure."

"We could have done that," I said. "Instead of the diving lessons. Some driver's education."

"Oh, Dad," she said. "I've *had* that. Last semester. You *know* I even have my learner's!"

It was Dad this time, completely natural, and I let it pass without gesture or comment.

"Maybe after Catalina. We'll still have some time. We could find places away from traffic."

"Not much time," she said. "I'll be going back."

"You should call Carol again. Too late tonight, but maybe in the morning before the class?"

"Where will you be going? Still to that island?"

"Bonair," I said.

I wasn't sure about that anymore, the idea of just heading out after this was over. There was nothing I had to do. A few bills and other business back at Mrs. Venuti's in Philadelphia. Nothing else in that city for me.

"But I may not. I might stick around in the Midwest for a while. My friend Aaron? I told you about him. Near Madison?"

"The farm," she said.

"That's right. Maybe visit him for a while."

"Then you can come and see me again."

She said it like a fact, and I knew it would be that, and I wondered what my dealings with Carol would be like.

The traffic lightened as we got closer to the beach. It was late and a weeknight, and few were headed down that way. I turned the air conditioner off and opened the vent. The stale air we'd been recirculating to keep the smog away washed out as a clean sea breeze entered.

"So you went through everything?" I said.

She'd told me that already. I'd wanted to take my mother's papers out of the museum, at least those photographs, and had talked the museum woman into letting me borrow them. But not the papers. I'd have to come in the daytime, talk to their director. "Yes," Jen said. "The playbills, all the pictures, even the scripts. They were marked up in the margins, the way they taught us in drama when I was in the play."

"I didn't know that," I said.

"It was nothing." She didn't want to be the schoolgirl. "There were a number of fan letters. I made a list of the names, but there was nothing familiar. I read every one of them."

"Do you think she *is* Susan Rennert?"

Jen had taken the newspaper clippings out of my father's file as soon as we'd left the museum. She'd looked them over while I was getting us to the freeway.

TOBY OLSON

"It's real hard to tell. She could have done something with her hair. And dressed up like that, who knows?"

"Maybe I'll find something out tomorrow," I said. "From that Pearl woman. She's her aunt, after all."

"We've a short day, tomorrow. From twelve to two we're going to look at slides and a movie of Catalina. The diving places? Then we're done until eight the next morning, when we catch the boat."

"I'll see her in the morning. Back by noon, I think. When you're done, we can shop a little, anything you might need for the trip."

"It's only two *days,* Bill!"

"You have something else to do?"

"Well, I *do* need some lotion, for the nose!" She touched the tip of it with her finger. "And maybe some little thing to wear over there. Is it a fancy place?"

"It could be. Depending on how *you* dress."

"Oh, fiddlesticks!" she said, tapping her finger on my knee.

It was eleven-thirty by the time we got back. Both of us were yawning, yet we both spoke of a shower at the same time. We laughed, but something passed between us, I thought, recognition of that other shower. It seemed so long ago, yet the focus in our dreams, Susan Rennert, was still very much with us.

"Then a drink before bed?" I said. Jen was standing in the open doorway between our rooms. "I'll call down for cocoa, maybe some cookies?"

"Oh, that would be wonderful!" she said.

We were both in our white hotel robes, sitting at the round glass table in Jen's room, our cocoa cups before us, a dish of chocolate chip cookies on the tray to the side. I could smell the conditioner she'd used on her hair, which was softer now, a shine in her waves. She'd rubbed something onto her nose, and it was moist, the flaking no longer evident.

She'd pulled the table over close to the bed and had spread out my mother's necklaces on the coverlet. There were twelve of them, three rows of four, and I saw immediately that each was a variation on the others, similar stones and silver work.

Before we sat down, Jen had lifted one of them and arranged it on the white rectangle of a hand towel that she'd smoothed out on the table. She reached for a cookie and took a bite of it, then sipped at her cocoa. The photographs rested beside my knee on the bed.

"This is it," she said. "The one your mother was wearing. It's not so different from the others. See these links?" She lifted one of the silver disks, and the thick chain of connectors tapped against her nails. "They're silver too. And it looks to me like they're very well made. I don't know, but I think this is good stuff. Expensive. Old, but in very good shape."

"I wonder how much," I said. "My parents weren't rich."

"Well, I don't know," she said. "Maybe not *very* expensive. But this is not costume stuff. Could she have been collecting it? I mean, there's so much, and it's very much the same."

It made sense to me, collecting, but if that were true, I was sure my father had had a hand in it. I wondered if there was a file in one of those boxes in storage, a jewelry file.

Jen lifted the necklace in her hands, the disks resting on her fingers and the medallion hanging along her wrist, and held it up for me to see. I looked at it, then nodded, and she got up and returned it to its place on the bed, picked up another one, and brought it back to the table. Before she'd finished spreading it out, getting the disks and medallion flat and in line, the whole in a clean oval, I knew what I was seeing, but I waited for her to speak.

"Well, it *is* the one," she said, after a sip of cocoa. "That Rennert woman was wearing it. Look at the photo. I'm sure of it."

The photograph was turned up on the bed at my knee, and I looked down at it.

"I can tell," I said. "The links."

"But not only that," Jen said. "These disks?"

"Go on," I said.

TOBY OLSON

"The way they're etched and cut, bent, or whatever name they give to doing that. They're roses, I think, rose blossoms. And the little stones or jewels? See them peeking out? Doesn't the size change? I mean, both the blossoms and the stones."

"I get it," I said.

"Chalk another one up, the first one. *Look into blossom gradation.* This must be it."

"It certainly opens something," I said. "But who the hell knows what?"

"At least some reason for your father making the list at all."

"But what about etching? That was part of it: *Look into blossom gradation and etching.*"

"I've looked into that," Jen said. "At first I thought it was the blossoms themselves, the way they're cut. Isn't that etching? There's nothing at all on the backs. But then I found something. Hold out your hands."

She reached beyond the cup and cookies and lifted the necklace, then swung it over and dropped the heavy medallion and the blossoms near it onto my open palms. She held the other end at the clasp, her fingertips on the chain links to either side of it.

"Look closely," she said, lifting the clasp and turning it.

It was a tiny silver box. A loop at one side held the chain, and a slit cut in the other held a delicate spring-loaded mechanism for locking and disconnecting. Five sides of the box were smooth, but on the sixth side, the back, there was an intricate etched figure. It was very small, but the lines were clear and deep: a coat of arms, or a crest. Something like that. I could see a bird at the top, a raven or a crow, then a broad horizontal stripe. Below that were crowns, three of them forming a triangle.

"We can get a magnifying glass," Jen said.

I was squinting, moving my head back and forth a little, working for a clearer focus. Then the clasp was shaking, and when I looked up Jen was in the middle of a deep yawn.

"Wow!" she said, finishing and tossing her head.

"That's enough," I said. "We can get into it tomorrow. Come on, I'll help you stow this stuff. Then it's to bed."

"Okay," Jen said, her lids drooping when she looked up at me. She was still holding the necklace out in the air, and I took it from her and put it back on the towel.

"And in the morning?" I said

"I know, I know. I'll call Mom."

20.

I felt a damp nose poke at the edge of my hand, and when I glanced down I was looking into the dog's calm eyes and I scratched the bridge of her muzzle. Another was curled on a scatter rug at my feet, a thick billow of white at belly and crotch. She'd taken the other two with her. At least they'd followed her, one to either side, a male and a female. "Don't worry," she'd said, when the collies had crowded around her at the door. "They're well-bred." Then she'd laughed, and the dogs' heads had tilted up to look at her.

The trip to Montebello had been easier this time. The smog was lighter, and I could see into storefront windows. There were more people on the sidewalks now, only a few with handkerchiefs held to their faces. It seemed a typical morning. The radio said the breeze was holding on longer than expected. Now they had it dissipating in the late afternoon. Then the smog would be back again, just as dense as before.

I could hear her tinkering in the kitchen. I took the envelope and tucked it against the chair cushion at my side. The living room was small and very neat and a little old-fashioned. There were anti-macassars on chair arms, a tall breakfront holding crystal. The prints on the walls showed meadows and farmhouses, and each pictured a collie, running or standing beside a structure. A floor and table lamp were lit. The two windows were thick with a smoggy residue, and I could see where fiberglass had been stuffed between the sashes. Heavy, half-pulled drapes filtered the dirty light. The dog on the scatter rug lifted her head, her eyes following mine as I looked around.

"Did you find Blevins Street?" she said.

She'd come back carrying a TV tray holding a teapot, mugs, and a dish of cookies; the dogs were still at her side, and she nudged the one sitting on the scatter rug with her toe. Then she set the table in its place, left the tea to steep, and went to the couch and sat down, the dogs circling, then collapsing at her feet.

She wore a thin cotton dress with long sleeves. The dress was buttoned to her neck, and her legs were encased in dark stockings. No longer did she wear her bathing cap, but her hair was pulled back tight. It looked oiled, and there was some shiny substance on her cheeks and forehead, a thinner shell than the one I'd noticed when I'd met her in the smog.

"Yes, I did," I said.

She crossed her legs, made a spider shape with her hand, her fingertips on the couch arm. One of the dogs heard the scratching and its ears lifted.

"And the Reuss house. You found that too, I guess. My house." I heard the remnant of an accent.

"Actually," I said, "I was there once before. Years ago, when I was a boy."

She blinked but seemed otherwise unmoved by the information.

"It's been years ago for me as well."

Her eyes lost their focus for a moment; something was coming back to her. I waited for her to have it, and in a while she uncrossed her legs and pushed up out of the couch and moved to the TV table and poured our tea. She held up one of the mugs.

"Nothing," I said, and she reached it across to me, then poured milk into her own and went back to the couch again and sat down. She took a sip, looked over the cup. She's waiting; she has a story to tell, I thought, but she wants prompting. I wasn't ready just yet.

TOBY OLSON

"There was a dog," I said. "Back then. I saw another one the other day when I was there. His name was Santos. I mean the one years ago."

"Oh, my," she said. "That *was* a long time. This one," she slid her fingers over the end of the couch arm, pointing down. "His great grandson. And even *he's* pretty old."

"You raise dogs?" I said.

"I did, once," she said. "Not anymore. I've just these four now, and that will be the end of it. It was never something I planned or bargained for."

"What about that other one, on Blevins Street?" I said.

"Probably more than just one," she said. "It got out of hand in the beginning. I had to give them away. People on the street there? They were good about that, at least."

"They weren't good about other things?"

"That's another story." Her face tightened a little. She didn't have to think back. It was right there for her.

"Anyway," I said. "The time I saw that dog? There was a girl, about my age then. And I think I remember her name was Estelle, not Susan. That's the confusion. Something I'm trying to figure out. Susan Rennert?"

"You're right about Estelle," she said, looking over the rim of her cup as she raised it to her lips. "They were sisters."

I'd had the idea ever since my visit to Blevins Street but had not acknowledged it. I'd wanted her to be Susan, that girl so long ago, to in some way account for those strange desires, the way I'd been drawn to her photograph, the way she'd entered my dream. I felt a certain deflation, a need for air.

"Twins," I said.

"Who?"

"Susan and Estelle."

She smiled a bitter smile. "That was the idea. But no, not even full sisters really. It all came down on Cora. I can't really blame her. She's gone now, and that's it. She was my sister."

"But I heard, you know, when I was down at Blevins, that she was your cousin."

"Oh, I see," she said. "It's him, that fucking German. He insisted upon that, because of Estelle."

"And Reuss?" I said. "Is it right he took that name early on, to escape from debt?"

"He was always in such trouble. It was a good thing he had Cora, what *she* had. Otherwise he would have gone down for sure. But, yes, you're right. Reuss was the name for many years, since Estelle's birth, at least."

"But she was Susan Rennert when she died. Not Reuss."

"So was Estelle," she said. "I mean, they both took the name back again, once they left. Maybe to cleanse it all away. I don't really know."

"Where is Estelle?"

"Oh," she said, something forming briefly in her cheeks. "I don't know. But that's not really surprising. *She* never knew."

"What?" I said.

"That I was her mother."

Her words must have registered somewhere, maybe in some stiffening or in the pores along my arms. The dog on the floor beside me rose quickly to his feet, his head cocked to the side and close to a level with my own. He was looking intently at me, waiting for me to speak or to do something. I understood what she'd said but couldn't fit it into anything. The small, accumulating confusions had risen into a larger one, and I had no sense at all of the significance of her words. I looked back from the dog's face to hers. I held the mug of tea, resting on the chair's arm, and I noticed it was shaking. I started to say something, not knowing at all what it might be. Then I saw that she was about to speak again, that she was ready now. She was looking toward one of the windows across the small room, and I knew that for her it opened onto another Blevins Street.

TOBY OLSON

"I remember you," she said. "Santos was a child then, a pup, but he was big. He was always roaming, and it was a bother, but he was sweet, and I couldn't find it in my heart to punish him. That day, you came right out of the street. I was watching from the window, looking out for Santos, and I saw you, then Estelle did. I remember the two of you talking, right there on the sidewalk in front of that lousy house. He never would go along with changing it. Then, when I got it, I wouldn't, either. Where was Susan and Cora? I'm not sure. But he was dead. Almost two years then. He'd left his dirty leavings.

"But I came to love those dogs, though I knew nothing much about them. He never did, just that he wanted them, his kind of greed, and once he had them and the want was gone, *they* were gone for him. But they were there, and somebody had to take care of them.

"Just like he'd wanted boys, that iron German head of his, but even had that happened, it would have been the same, like the dogs. As it turned out, it was Susan, of course. They were living in Encinitas then. Cora had come over years before, with my father, then he'd died. I and my mother were still in Warsaw. She was an old woman, and ill, and just before *she* died, the letter came. It was in Polish, the only language I had then, but for a little German. It said they would soon be moving to Los Angeles, that I should join them in Encinitas, then go there with them.

"What money there had been came from my mother's family, and it was not really money, but objects, furniture and paintings, some jewelry, crystal and silver things, linens. It all went over ahead of me, once Mamma was dead. George took care of that, Cora translating for him, I guess. I doubt it could have been legal then, in 1938.

"That was when it was. I was just eighteen, the younger sister. It all went to Encinitas, as I was supposed to do. That I didn't I can't blame Cora for. She was older, almost twenty years. A little too old. But George wanted that boy and had forced her pregnancy. It would be a difficult one, and would of course become even worse when she had Susan, a girl. Cora was a little dull witted, as she'd always been. She was rather hard, and crude. They said she was my father's child, in Poland. Something that got whispered. My mother had married below herself, and I was more like her. Neither of us knew a thing, about life, I mean.

"George met me at the train station in San Diego. I'd docked in New York, then came across the entire country by rail. I was an immigrant, no English, and all my belongings in the rack and pressed down under my knees. I saw the country out the train window, still it was like traveling through a tunnel when it came to experience. Just the plains passing, then the mountains and desert, and up into the lushness near this coast. I'd found a way to sleep during the ship crossing, and I wasn't tired. I was ready to get there and stay put, to see my sister, but George had other plans for me.

"He took me to a place in the city. I remember sailors in uniform, and those I knew who were sailors, even though they wore civilian clothes. I could tell by their shoes and haircuts. They passed in and out of bars. And there were women on the streets, and men standing in front of dark doors, placards showing half naked women to their sides; they were calling out, enticing sailors in, and cars moved slowly along the street. It was summer, and the arms of men extended from open windows, and when the cars pulled up at the curb, women would go over to them. And I with my bundles and with George carrying one of them, his free hand holding me at the elbow, urging me along the street, people looking at us with little interest, then our turning in through a glass door, climbing flights of narrow stairs. There was a stove and sink in the room, a bathroom down the hall. I remember the coverlet, rust stains where it touched the brass headboard.

"He gave me to understand I should go to sleep, spaces between his German words. He'd be back in a while with food. I didn't feel tired at all, but I did sleep, falling deeply into dreamlessness, only to be awakened into sounds from other rooms, not knowing what time it was. Then I drifted off to sleep again, and in the morning he woke me. He'd brought coffee and hard rolls, and while we ate at the small metal table, he told me we'd be staying there for a few days, something about transportation, that we'd have to wait a while before going to Encinitas, to Cora and my new home.

"Then he was courting me. It was the strangest thing. For while I was an immigrant, I was not that kind of fool. And I think he knew this. He just ignored it. Later he was to tell me it was for the child, for him to be born out of some appropriate joining, since I was young enough, so that he might be normal, something like that. He wasn't excusing himself. He told me he might have just taken me. I had no choice in the matter. And it was then that he also told me there was nothing for me to do or say about it. Only the story. That he'd discovered me this way, the day he'd met me at the station. Some boy my sister didn't know, from Warsaw.

"He took me out to dinner, on bus tours in the city, a day trip to Coronado Island, where he asked to see a bridal suite and squeezed my shoulder as we stood in the doorway looking at the large white bed. He even took me dancing, at a bar where sailors went. Music that was unfamiliar, but he did a waltz with me. 'Of course,' he said, his bitter breath against my ear, 'we'll raise the child as if it were our own, your sister and I will. Our two boys. He'll never know the difference, and they'll be like twins.'

"You'll wonder that I didn't fight him, that I accepted him, though I didn't. But I was alone with him, and I was nowhere. I didn't know the language or the country. I had nowhere to turn. And I felt there was one way only to get to my sister, his way, and that our stay in that limbo would continue until I made the decision. That it was *my* decision and not his.

"I tried to leave him once, at a time on a sunny day while he was gone. But I only got to the corner in that foreign city and didn't know which way to turn. So I turned back and went to the room again. And it was on that day that he impregnated me. I was a virgin, and he needed a lubricant. He said words he thought were the right ones, those spaces between them so I would understand. It was like some poorly acted play. He went through the motions, then looked down intently at me, as if I would know something in my body, then he shrugged, and I knew he'd do it a few more times, just to make sure, which he did, just a few other days, then he left me to pack the few things I'd taken out of my bags. He was in his car, waiting at the curb, when I struggled with my burdens out the door.

"Of course, they were not twins, and they were not boys, either. But I don't think that made any real difference. He wanted something, then he had it, then he was through with it, no more than a few months after their births. They came just a week apart. I was early, and Cora was late. First Susan, then Estelle, my daughter. And I could not tell Cora of the real circumstance. She never hated him, as I did, but I think she hated the product of his greed, though she could never have admitted that. She was stern with both of them, one more than the other, thinking it nothing but the right way to bring up girls, the way our parents had brought us up. She'd never been the favored child. It was I who was that. She reminded my father of the past he'd put behind him and suggested to my mother that he hadn't quite managed to do that. They too were stern, and I guess Cora learned that as the appropriate way of a family.

"Right after Susan's birth, we left Encinitas for Blevins Street, and it was there he took the name *Reuss* and gave it to both Cora and Susan. Then Estelle was born, and he gave her that name too. Then he died. And in my head I said good riddance to the son of a bitch, and Cora was left with a family she hadn't wanted. The girls were six years old then, very twin-like in their looks but not in their connection.

"From the beginning, it was as if they knew the secret difference in their sources, and like us, their sister-mothers, had no more than a civil use for each other. And not so civil in their childhood. They fought over things, until they were old enough to stand separate. Estelle came to my side then, her face fixed in a bitterness beyond

TOBY OLSON

her years, and Susan, crushed by her father's distance, her mother's resentment, climbed down into doggie holes.

"I mean that literally. I'd see Cora find her in a corner of the run, hugging into the earth where the collies had dug their shallow coffin troughs to lie in against the summer heat. And then she'd punish her, though never physically. It was standing in that closet for many hours, not talking to her for days on end. Those kinds of things, not even some stimulant of imagination for the child, punishment that could fit a crime.

"And Cora had no imagination, either, when it came to her own retribution. When George died, the street tried to help. He was German, after all. He'd been selling off our mother's things, gradually and with care, putting that money aside until he had enough to change the house, make it Chicago German like the others.

"The street association offered a good deal, workmen to build the house, materials at cost, but Cora stood firm against it all. It was George's wish, and she bore down against the street as if they all were him. She had the money. In his arrogance, he'd kept it in one of my mother's vases on the mantle, even when he was gone away on what he called 'business,' which was often. When he was there, he was also gone, from all of us, even as he sat in his chair reading the paper.

"And she bore down too against Estelle and against me. After George was dead, she waited. She seemed to want Estelle at the right age, both vulnerable and aware. I didn't know she was waiting. Maybe I would have said something, but then she told Estelle she was not her child, they were not twins, she was adopted. She said it one night at dinner, our only daily gathering. The girls were nine years old then, and I saw what it did to Susan, who sat across from me, the way that vacancy that became permanent took shape in her face. I remember thinking, she wants her closet now, that dull darkness. Then I turned to Estelle and saw the hate, for her mother and for her sister too, but not for me. And I wanted her. I can't say

I loved her, but she was all I really had. I had no sister, no country anymore. I'd had no lover. But I had a daughter, and I feared I'd lose her if I told her that.

"So Cora had her children, those awkward twins. As with the house, she seemed to need to have them so the rejection of them, of George, really, could remain constant. There was no thought of moving, of selling the house to those who were waiting, back there in the East, to come to the new Germany of Blevins Street.

"Did Cora soften at the end? I can't be sure, but I can't forgive her. What she did to those children. After she disappeared and the will was opened, I found she'd left it all to me, the house, my mother's belongings, a good deal of cash and securities. I'd brought a little with me from the other side and had saved that. I had enough to buy this house without selling the one on Blevins, and I've not sold it even now. Every time I think I might, I think of Cora. I guess there's something there. Maybe it's *my* way of getting back at George, keeping him turning in his grave. I don't know.

"But I've gotten ahead of things. After Cora disappeared, I sat in that house alone. I *did* call the police, and after a few weeks I called a lawyer. I'd called Susan. She was working as a chambermaid in some hotel then. She came home for a day, wandered around the house, a vague look on her face. Then she left. Then, in a while, when Cora was deemed permanently gone, dead, I guess, I received my inheritance, and in a week I was gone. I was here. I'd tried to reach Susan once again, to share the money with her, but she was gone from her job and apartment, and I couldn't find her. I had movers empty what was left in the house. There had been that robbery, just the day after Cora's disappearance, and there was little left to move. They'd taken everything of value, even the good furniture, just pulled up with a moving van. People on the street thought it was me.

"Estelle? She left home when she was seventeen. She just packed up her clothes one afternoon and walked right out. She said

TOBY OLSON

good-bye to me, even gave me a kind of hug. I don't think she said a word to Cora, nor to Susan. When she was gone, Cora acted as if she had never been there. There was no word spoken in the house about her. I remember I tried once and Cora shut me up, then turned and left the room. Susan was there, and when I looked at her, I saw something in her face. Then she too was gone, in a similar way, without speaking to either of us. She left by the back door, and I watched and saw her standing at the fence. Maybe she was gazing at those coffin troughs. I don't know. Her face was turned away.

"It was Cora, then, and it was me. We lived as if in different houses. We'd sit together for lunch, but there would be no real talking. The empty chairs remained, but they urged neither of us to a proper subject. She'd closed off from them completely, and I knew there was no hope for it. At times I felt like a little girl, sitting there, as if we were back in Poland, before George and the start of it all. But that never lasted.

"Susan called from time to time, but it was always as if she'd gotten a wrong number. I'd hear Cora's voice, asking nothing, only responding in clipped phrases to the things Susan was saying. I imagine Susan's questions came from an empty wish for magic change, that she knew it was empty even as she spoke her first words. They confirmed it, and the calls were quickly over. I never heard anything from Estelle. When she was gone, she was gone.

"Then, of course, Susan died, a year after her mother's disappearance, about that. She drowned, but you know that, I suppose. I wasn't shocked to see her name as Rennert in the newspaper. Estelle had been calling herself by that name, and not Reuss, for months before she left.

"For me, the family was over then, and I just settled in here with the dogs. They were really all I took of value from that place. They're all dead now too, but these are their relatives. It's funny that you should come here. I've been thinking about selling that place, just recently I have. Can it be fifteen years? Even more than that? I think it's about over for me now, even that bastard George is. All the anger is just that it lasted such a long time. What I do now is take care of these few dogs. They, in turn, keep me company."

I knew that right then she was wondering what she'd done with her life, not all of it, but the time she'd been here in this house. It was getting close to a generation, and as she spoke of the dogs and her story ended, she looked away from the window and let her eyes roam over objects in the room. She noted things as a stranger might, as I might, sitting there with her. Even the animals at her feet drew a quizzical look from her.

I wanted to say something, that I understood perhaps, because I did. Hers seemed the kind of questioning I'd been thrust toward since Jennifer, her letters, and the beginning of all this. My years in the Navy, the whole of my adult life up to then, had come to seem no more than a waiting time, and though I could mark the movement of years by travel to various duty stations—Carol in Corpus, coming close to drowning that time with Aaron—change was not part of that movement, if change is development, a constant twisting outward into a new self. Not even my clothing had changed, neither uniform nor civilian, and though in the few pictures I had there were various stripes on my sleeve, at one time a mustache, a broader lapel, the face under those slightly differing hairstyles seemed that of a virgin, someone untouched by the experience out of which the photo had been cut.

She was looking down now at her own unchanged garments, her smog clothing, that costume she'd taken on since leaving Blevins over fifteen years ago. Before that, she'd been in the place of her story, in that bondage, and however tortured that life might have been, it remained a richer complexity, though only in memory, than the stasis she was sitting in right now. It's the same for me, I thought, that time before I left home to see the world, at least the

TOBY OLSON

one underwater. Still, her family story had a vividness and logic to it that I'd begun to question in my own, certainly since Susan Rennert and my father's list, even more since Leonard and his blunt judgments. Maybe that was why I was doing this, to find the right narrative.

"What was that again?" I said.

She'd gone away in thought, then I'd gone, but she'd come back before me. She was looking at me, the cup no longer in her hand. She must have risen and placed it on the small table between us. It sat there, and I leaned forward in the chair and replaced my own. The dogs were looking at me.

"I was saying about your coming there, to Blevins Street, when you were a child. That time with Estelle, when I saw you through the window. Could that be coincidence?"

"I don't know," I said. "But I used to do that, go down into those tunnels. I'd come up in many places. My father. He had maps, but I didn't use them. I guess I liked the mystery. Or I didn't know about the maps, not then."

It was more than she was asking for, or at least she was asking for something else. I wasn't sure, but I was still back there a little, not quite with her yet.

"Well," she said.

The dogs had put their narrow snouts between their paws and had closed their eyes.

"But it's something else," I said. "The reason I came here." I'd lifted the envelope from between the cushions and put it on my lap. She was looking at it.

"Susan. Something about her death? I can't imagine, it's been such a long time."

"Well, yes," I said. "But there's something else too. Do you know anything about her death?"

"No, I don't know. No one came, and I never called. Maybe I should have. There was only that one little notice in the *Times*. I had no reason."

"To identify the body?"

"Was that something?" she said. "I didn't see anything about that in the papers."

I thought it must have gotten beyond Laguna. The police had made some effort to find out about her past.

"But I don't read the papers," she said. "Only from time to time. And it could well have been a time when I was busy. With the dogs, I mean. Some pups? It would have been around that time."

Her hand reached down, and the collie to her left lifted her muzzle and touched her fingers.

"Could be," I said. "But there is something else."

I opened the envelope and slid the pictures out. I'd brought my father's list and the Rennert clippings too, but I left them inside. It was just the two photographs, and though I didn't want to shock her, I needed her objectivity. I thought I knew what she'd find there.

"This might be difficult," was all I said, holding the photos on my lap for a moment before I got up and handed them across the table to her.

They were face down, and she took them from me with both hands. I watched her closely as she turned the first one over on her lap. Her head was down, and I couldn't see her face, but I could see her finger as she moved it over the surface, not touching it, but searching through it. Then her finger stopped, and I saw her head move back slightly. She looked quickly up at me, blinking, then back down at the photo. She'd come to some recognition, but she wasn't speaking. I thought she might be holding herself together, knowing that if she did speak she might come apart a little. I waited, giving her time, then saw she might be waiting for me, that it would be easier that way.

"Who is it?" I asked.

"Well," she said, in a flat tone, controlling herself. "It's Estelle, you must know that. But she's a grown woman. Do you know when this was taken?"

"The poster," I said. "On the wall behind her, a few months before that."

256   TOBY OLSON

"She'd have been twenty-six then. The year that Susan died. That's a long time ago."

"As long as you've been here."

"Not quite," she said. "But almost."

"And the necklace?"

"I see it."

"It's clearer in the other one."

She pulled the other photo out, turned it and placed it over the one she'd been looking at.

"Who are these people?" she said.

"That's my mother," I said. "And my father."

"They know each other."

"I don't think so," I said. "At least not yet. I think they just met there. But I can't really be sure of that. They're both dead now, my parents, I mean. But what about the necklace?"

She looked hard at the photo. Then she got up, stepped between the dogs and took it over to the dirty light at the window. She stood there for a while, one hand pushing the curtains to the side as she held the photo up and gazed at it. When she returned to the couch, she had some things to say and some questions too.

"It belonged to my mother. Cora had them all, many of them, among the other things. I haven't seen it, though, since Poland. I knew Cora had them, but she never took them out. And maybe it was George who had them, some of the things he was selling over the years. I can't be sure. The robbery, as I told you, they could well have gone there. But Estelle, how in the world did she get it? Do you know where she is?"

Her hand rested flat on the photographs in her lap. She'd leaned forward slightly, urging the right answer, one that I couldn't give her.

"No," I said. "I don't know. And I don't know how she got it."

She leaned back, then looked over at the window. Drawn again to Blevins Street, I thought.

"Your mother's father," I said. "What did he do?"

"What?" she said, bringing her eyes slowly back to my face.

"In Warsaw," I said. "Was he a rich man? I mean, the value of that piece. Do you think it's valuable?"

"It wasn't Warsaw," she said. "He traveled. He even went out of the country. That was rare then, as you can imagine. It was nothing we talked about, in the family, I mean. Only that when he died it all came to my mother. She was an only child, and his wife, my grandmother, was gone. I never knew her. He was an old man already when I was born. I don't know the value of this thing, just that there were more like it. I don't remember my mother ever wearing it, or the others. I guess it could be valuable, enough for George to sell for money, to travel places to do that. He did it for the other things, the linens, art things, and silver. At least, I think so. But who knows where he was going? Other women? It might well have been that, or some other shady business. Maybe the selling was only some lie, an excuse for his absence. I don't know."

"But it's not Susan. In the photographs, I mean."

"Oh, of course not. Of course it's not."

"They look alike."

"Daughters of sisters," she said, a slight smile on her face. Then the smile faded. "They were manufactured twins. They thought they *were* twins until they were nine years old. It's no wonder. But they were not alike, not the same at all."

She stood in the doorway watching me as I left, the way Leonard had, and Carol before him. Aaron and Bev would have done the same, I thought, had they not risen early for their fishing trip with Jason. In each case I'd come back into their lives, or come for the first time, but with information about them, a stir for memory, and I'd taken something away with me—Jen herself, as I'd left Carol—or left them with things they'd thought settled cooked up again. I knew it was nothing in the case of Aaron, only a little with Leonard, about whom I was unconcerned, though he'd brought me a new concern, stirred up my own past for me. Pearl, though, had expectations, and I told her before leaving that I had things to do and that I'd keep in touch, let her know should I learn more about Estelle. She needed to ask for that, or I needed to say it, I wasn't sure which. I thought too that she needed to leave it where it was before I'd come to her with those photographs.

I had nothing at all to do, and after I'd spent a pocket of change at a pay phone calling Sanchez, telling him I was out of there and would call again, explain things when I got back, I headed down the boulevard toward the freeway, under the blanket of smog that now hung still over the low buildings. It was just after noon by the time I joined the flow of traffic. I stayed in the slow lane, the air conditioner on low power, and thought things over.

I had the reason now for my father's list. He'd known Estelle, and when Susan Rennert had drown, he'd thought they were the same person and had begun looking into things: *Rennert: why Susan?* He'd known her by another name, the first one, at least. Had he been someone else, I might have had to assume that he and my mother knew Estelle in more than a casual way, more than enough to have purchased or in some way acquired that necklace. Maybe some of those other pieces of jewelry I'd given to Jen had come from her as well. But my father was like that. Any puzzle he came across could grab his interest, and once he was into things, he wouldn't quit until he had an answer or saw that one was impossible.

But for the bloody sheet, the drowning of Susan Rennert could well have been an accident. Maybe it was that, the sheet no more than an odd coincidence, something left on the beach by someone else. The tide had been coming in. It could have been lovers in rough love on the sand, leaving it there, not menstrual blood, but blood from a fingernail or some sexual instrument cutting a surface vein. Then the tide came in, and Susan Rennert came in with it, had fallen from some boat, or drifted back upon the tide to come near the place where she had entered earlier to drown herself. And the sheet drifting into surf or out on swells beside her, then coming in to the shore again as she had. Something like that, I thought, really so very simple.

But there was something new now, that necklace, and how Estelle had come to have it. The robbery, of course, that seemed the obvious answer, though Pearl hadn't even known that the jewelry was still there at that time.

But it was Jennifer who was waiting for me and not Estelle. She'd be there with her diving gear at the edge of the parking lot, flushed with the prospect of our coming trip to Catalina. We had little time left together, just a few days now, a week at most. Still I couldn't shake free completely from that story of Blevins Street. I could feel the close space of that closet, see Susan Rennert standing there in the dark, making those careful marks, a too-adult accounting. I could smell Pearl's collies on my fingertips and clothing, and their scent stayed with me all the way back to Laguna.

21.

We passed under the shadow of the *Queen Mary*'s hull as we steamed slowly away from the dock at Long Beach. Jen stood in the prow, tall as the boys there, and the old man's head was near her shoulder. His hand held her elbow as he pointed, the *Queen*'s massive super-structure climbing into a hazy sun. She turned and grinned brightly at the others, all the students gathered there, and inside their teacher fussed with the diving gear, leaning tanks against the bulk-head, draping wet suits over them.

On our way back from the beach, I'd filled Jen in on Pearl and what I'd learned from her.

"Two of them," she'd said. "That takes care of number five, *Rennert: why Susan?* Your father thought she was Estelle."

"That seems right. And that leaves only the blossoms and the etch-ing. We can take the necklace into Los Angeles and find some jeweler there. We'll have a couple of days at least, when we get back."

"And don't forget Billy's letter," she said. "There's that too."

Jen was in the shower then, and I was on the phone.

"Well, maybe, ese," Sanchez said, when I told him my half-baked theory about the sheet. Then he asked if I was satisfied with that.

"I don't think so," I said.

"There's certainly something fucked up about that investigation. There's nothing about a sister there."

"Weren't they looking elsewhere?"

"Sure," he said. "They were looking into murder, not so much about her past. I wonder why she changed the name? Back to Rennert, I mean."

"I think that's a long story."

"At any rate," he said, "I can't see letting it go. There's still her death. Being sure of accident, or suicide, either one will do. But I want those photographs."

I said I'd leave them in an envelope at the hotel desk. "Okay," he said. "But why don't you forget about it for now. You and your daughter. The diving's good over on Catalina. It's a little crowded, I guess, this time of year. But you should enjoy yourselves, good seafood. You can check out the seals."

Our boat was the 9 A.M. express, and we were on the road by seven-fifteen. Jen had called Carol while I'd carried our gear down to the car. Then I'd sent Jen to check us out and had called Mrs. Venuti in Philadelphia. Our suitcases sat in the center of my room. We had reservations for Tuesday at another place, the one where Lin worked. She said she'd take care of things, someone to fetch our luggage, and she'd see to storing it until we returned.

There was little for me in Philadelphia. A couple of Navy things had come, another travel brochure from the Antilles. There was a postcard from Aaron and Bev, and I asked Mrs. Venuti to read it: a few words about fishing and that they hoped I was having a good time too.

"What about your son?" I said.

"Larry?" He was her only son, but she made it sound as if he'd just come to mind.

"Who else?" I said.

"He's doing very good. He has two articles coming out, one in *October,* the other in *Raritan.* I told you about his new executive position? His book is also soon to be published by Oxford."

The names spilled out familiarly. I thought she must have written them down, then memorized them. She was a good mother, respectful of the specifics that brought her pride.

"That's great," I said. "Say hello for me."

TOBY OLSON

I'd met him a few times only. He lived in New York City but taught at a university in Philadelphia. His mother kept his room ready for him those nights when he worked late and stayed over. I'd hear him moving around on the third floor, the faint sound of girl groups from the fifties on his stereo.

"And you?" she said. "When are you coming back?"

I told her I wasn't absolutely sure just yet.

We had reservations to fly to Racine, and I didn't know how long I might be staying there. I thought I might go back to the farm and visit Aaron and Bev. We had ten days before our flight, but no more than three or four after we returned from Catalina. We'd deal with the jewelry in that time, see about the etching on the clasp. We'd also have to do something with my parents' things in storage. And maybe there'd be other things. I'd be talking to Sanchez, finding out what he might have learned about Estelle.

I told Mrs. Venuti it could be a few weeks. She said she'd pay the gas bill, other utilities as they came in. Jen was back, waving the room receipt as I hung up.

Now I stood at the fantail watching the sea, that long ago remembered dip at the apex of the v-trough where the screw churned. I'd been a landlocked sailor for the most part, serving in repair at docking, but there had been maneuvers at Guantanamo, a few salvage operations in the Gulf off Corpus, and I remembered sailors lost in moody meditation looking aft. Lovers and family, memories of land legs on lawns and sidewalks, a Formica table in some diner underneath the steaming coffee mugs they held at the rail. And I too had had such moments, flickering pictures of my parents in the passing kelp and turbulence.

I looked out to the v's dissolution, a blue swirl of oil on the calm surface beyond it, and above that the changed and receding skyline of Long Beach. A breeze was pushing out from land, and smog had come down from the basin in its dirty wash. It hid the tops of buildings, extended out beyond the shore itself to form a canopy that ended in a smoky line over the last oil rig at the edge of the harbor. I thought I saw the place where the Pike had been, that skeleton of a roller coaster. I'd gone there on my bike when I was nine or ten, a long trip, and even now I felt a little guilt. My parents had been worried and had searched for me. But now there were only buildings where the Pike had been, offices and hotels. I pushed back from the rail, then turned and headed forward. We'd passed beyond the North American plate by then and were over the Pacific Tectonic. Catalina would be safe from earthquake and smog.

"How far do you make it, sailor?"

Jen's hair had drifted in the breeze to cover one eye. It was as if she were winking, but her pointing finger was shaking slightly with excitement, something beyond such jaunty joking. I could see the massive casino in the distance at the point, white dots of moored boats at the edge of the harbor to its left, and I remembered that one time I'd been to Catalina with my parents so long ago, and how it had felt then to be steaming slowly toward what seemed a very foreign place. I looked over at Jen, sharing something of her anticipation.

"Another fifteen minutes," I said. "At least that. We won't see Avalon, the town, for a while at this angle. Is your stuff ready?"

She leaned forward, her face in the wind, hair blown back over her ears now. She was like a figurehead, her back arched to catch the full blow. At first I thought she hadn't heard me, but then she was nodding. She had her ankles crossed, her weight on one leg. I held the rail too, standing beside her. Gulls drifted out ahead, then rose above us on stiff wings. Then, in a while, the engines cut back. We could see the balcony pillars and red roof of the fat, arrogant casino, people standing on the balcony and waving. Jen lifted her arm, laughing. Then we steamed around the point and came into view of Avalon Harbor. It was thick with lines of boats bobbing at their ordered moorings. We moved slowly around them, heading for the dock at Cabrillo Mole.

TOBY OLSON

We had adjoining rooms at the Zane Grey, each with its own terrace, small stone patios that overlooked the harbor and the town. Jen was delighted with the transportation that was waiting at the dock. There were few cars in Avalon, and most people got around in golf carts. One came with the room, and after we'd unpacked, Jen took the wheel and drove us carefully down the winding streets to Pleasure Pier, where the other students had already gathered. She called out to the old man as we pulled up. The boys were helping Higgins load the launch, a large inboard with a small wooden cabin and benches at the gunwales.

They'd be heading north along the leeward shore for a few miles, rocks and kelp beds, around forty feet of depth. Then they'd cruise a little farther, to a deeper place where they'd see yellowtail, bass, and lobster. It was eleven, and they wouldn't be back until five. Higgins had stocked food, and they'd go into one of the small bays along the shore and have a picnic and a lesson around two. There'd be a dinner at a harborside restaurant in the evening. I was invited.

I stood at the dock and watched them as they steamed away. Jen stayed in the stern and waved back at me. They moved out slowly, and in a while the waving became awkward. I pushed my hand toward her in the air, releasing her, and once she'd turned away and joined the others in their fussing with the diving gear, I left the dock and headed to the mouth of Sumner Avenue, where I'd parked the golf cart. I had to pass along Crescent, the pedestrian mall edging the harbor. It was thick with tourists dipping into gift and clothing shops and bars. I had the whole day ahead of me and nothing to do. I thought I'd head back to the Zane Grey and read, but I was itchy, and halfway there I changed my mind, turned into Avalon Canyon Road, and headed past the golf course toward the canyon's end, to see the Wrigley Memorial and gardens.

The old man wasn't buried there, though the place was tomb-like, a somber and ostentatious stone structure up on a slight rise. Wrigley had controlled the whole island until it had gone into con-servancy, and there were pieces of it that were still in the family.

The gardens spilled out at the memorial's entrance, and I wandered along the winding paths, reading the names of shrubs and flowers printed on metal plaques until I got hungry. Then I chugged back to the golf course, where I ordered a sandwich and iced tea at the outdoor snack bar.

I had the tea at my lips when I recognized I was in something like mourning. It had all ended too quickly, that daily anticipation, and now nothing. I had an urge to go to the pay phone at the snack bar's side and call Sanchez, but I knew the idea was ridiculous. One of the island's sight-seeing buses moved slowly by. People at tables around me were in animated conversation, and I was missing Jennifer. Dinner, I thought, as I lifted my sandwich. It was getting on to three o'clock. Maybe I could read for a while, take a nap. I finished eating and headed back to the Zane Grey.

"Tomorrow it's the underwater park down there, two shipwrecks and some cliffs and pinnacles. Then, in the afternoon, we go around to the backside. Isn't that it? To learn about currents and see abalones and things. Then at night we have the big cookout. Not here, of course, but up the coast."

She was dressed all in white, a long cotton shift with a high neck and embroidery at the sleeves. It was gathered at her waist with a white cord. White tennis shoes, and white barrettes above her ears to hold her hair back. She wore one of my mother's necklaces, and the silver disks hung away from her breasts slightly as she touched the adobe terrace wall and looked down to the harbor. She was careful to stand back from the wall a little, not to brush it with her hem, a gesture of adult concern, but her enthusiasm for the day's activities and those of the coming one made her seem like a child playing dress-up in women's clothing.

"They *do* call it that," I said. "At least in the East, they do. I don't know about here. But it's abalone. There's no *s*."

"Oh," she said. "Jimmy's from the East."

TOBY OLSON

She pushed back from the wall and turned, and the necklace settled between her breasts, the large medallion's apex close to her waist.

"The old man? How did he do in deep water?"

"He did fine. Everyone did. We had such fun!"

Her eyes were bright, and I saw a slight darkness on her lids, a touch of blue makeup. Her nose had shed the dead skin from her burn and was smooth again. She was looking at me. "What?" I said.

"It's the color. Your shirt and pants. They don't really match!"

I could hear her giggle as I went inside to change.

The restaurant was on the harbor side of Crescent Avenue. It was seven and Friday night, and the place was crowded with day-trippers. The last boat to the mainland wouldn't leave until eleven, and they were getting the most out of their visit.

We had a reserved section, two large tables at the end of a broad outside deck that rested on pilings driven in at the water's edge. We were a little early, but the old man, Jimmy, was already there, his back to the harbor, arm resting on the low railing. He waved when he saw us come in from Crescent. There was someone beside him, and I felt Jen touch my shoulder. It was Tod, and she was moving out ahead of me, winding through the crowded tables to get to him. She was standing beside his chair, holding his hand in awkward formality, and as I approached, he pushed up from the chair and let her hand go. I extended my own when I reached him.

"Fancy meeting you here," I said.

"Mr. Stewart."

He took my hand in a firm grip, as awkwardly formal as the way he'd held Jen's.

"It's Bill," I said. "You can call me Bill."

"I'm only here for dinner," he said. "I'll catch the last boat."

It seemed uncalled for, a quick explanation, as if he'd been accused of something. Then I recognized my look might have prompted him. He flushed, dropped his eyes for a moment, then forced them back to my face.

"This is fine," the old man said. "Our diving helper."

I looked down at him. He was tilted back in his chair now, both arms up behind him on the rail. His eyes held mine, and I could see he read the situation perfectly. He smiled a forgiving smile, but one that held a bit of sternness too.

"Well," I said, looking up at Jen. "Celebration of the day's activities. Let's get champagne!"

"That's the ticket!" It was Jimmy, his voice very loud, and those at other tables turned to look at him.

Jen sat at the table's end, Tod beside the old man, near her elbow, and I sat across from them, facing the harbor. There was no champagne, so we ordered sparkling cider, three more bottles when the others got there. I gave up my seat to the single woman and moved to the far end of the table. It took a while for everyone to order. Things kept getting interrupted by talk of the day's events. These divers had many things to say to one another, and I was not part of their conversation. Tod wasn't either, but he was talking to the other young men, and he seemed to belong there more than I did.

Michael Higgins stayed tight in among them, telling his sea stories, exaggerating in ways appropriate to such adventures. They all turned toward him and toward each other, and I leaned back in my chair after we'd eaten, a bourbon and water in my hand.

From where I sat, I could see along the harbor's shoreline for a good distance. The sun was almost gone, but the figures of strollers lingering on the casino walkway were distinct, though turning into dark sticks as light sunk down behind the hills above Avalon. In the past, the walkway had been a quarter mile of covered passage, a kind of winding arbor, lighted from its adobe archway at the town's center to where it spilled out near the casino entrance at the point. All the big bands back then, Kay Kyser and the rest, six thousand people drifting over maple, white oak, and rosewood to the dreamy sound sheets of Kenton in the forties.

268   TOBY OLSON

The walkway was dark now and open, just a concrete path, but the lights of the dominating casino still seemed to beckon, the glow from its circular balustrade washing over those boats that bobbed at mooring under its shadow. From where I sat, I saw it over water, but the harbor between us was thick with the twinkling of lights. There must have been three hundred boats there. I counted seven arcs moving out from the harbor's shore to the mouth of Avalon Bay. They were pleasure boats, large and small, a few good-sized yachts that were bright jewels on the dimmer, night-lighted chains.

The restaurant was slowly emptying out. The Catalina Express sat waiting at the Mole. But at our tables, the divers were still in animated conversation. I saw Jen touch Tod's shoulder, tug at his sleeve. Jimmy had his back to me, his elbows at the table's edge, facing them, talking. The young men were gesturing, explaining something. Higgins had ordered pitchers of beer and soda.

I might just as well have been miles away from them. I could hear the quiet slap of water against the pilings under my feet, and when I looked out over the lines of moored boats, I saw the one that had caused the swell, something large, outlined with strings of fairy lights, drifting in between two others in the terminal chain. There was a sudden dim wash of light, like distant summer lightning beyond the casino's roof out to sea. It flickered, then remained constant, forcing dimensional shadows over the high shoreline hills beyond the town. It's the flying fish, I thought, remembering those charter boats that cast bright lights at the shore to confuse the fish, make them rise up from the sea and fly. And the bright eyes of the island fox might be waiting there, drawing them in as well, then lifting them off the shoreline rocks with its teeth, their paper-thin wings beating against its muzzle. "The food chain's perversity, Billy. But the fox doesn't know that": my father's voice coming back to me distinctly under the drone of conversations at the table's end.

I must have been twelve years old. At least I was old enough to feel some reason in my desire for a uniform like the one my father wore. And my mother had her own, something she'd put together from her store of theatrical costumes, the small green Wave cap set jauntily on her head.

She'd pulled her belt tight, getting the military jacket to flair out a little at her hips, and she'd found a pair of oxfords that had some lift. I watched her turn to the side and check her calf in the floor-length mirror.

"I understand perfectly, Billy. It's something any reasonable man would wish for."

My father glanced to my mother's legs, a faint smile at the corners of his mouth.

"But you see, this is the trick of it. That you be the child tourist and we the guides. You'll be playing someone much younger. Maybe nine? That in itself will need a kind of uniform. You're far too mature to go as you are."

"Acting!" my mother called out, turning in the kitchen doorway, her palm held out in a dramatic gesture, and my father nodded in agreement, the slick bill of his policeman's hat catching sunlight at the window.

I left them there, then rummaged around in my room until I found an old pair of knickers, a striped jersey, and saddle shoes, and when I was dressed and had returned, we crowded tight against each other and looked at ourselves in the mirror.

We caught the boat to Catalina at San Pedro. It was a slow boat then, the trip two hours, and after I'd helped my father lug the suitcases from the car down to the dock, we'd lifted them aboard, then slid them along the wooden deck to where my mother had secured window seats.

She'd gone ahead, and I'd heard the whisper of her green cotton stockings as she stepped up to the gangway. Her entire uniform was green, as was my father's, but for his hat, which was dark brown.

TOBY OLSON

They both looked very official, and I hoped I looked the part of the summer tourist child I was playing.

It was mid-August, the boat was full, and though I was the only boy in knickers, I saw others who looked as innocent and vulnerable as I. Some caught my stare, bright-eyed, but I refused to give them any satisfaction and quickly looked away.

My father made a kind of curved wall out of the suitcases, forming a little chamber for us at the window. We had some legroom and privacy, and once we'd passed beyond the shoreline sights and entered open sea, my father told me the story of the buffalo, my mother nodding and smiling at the familiar exactness of his details.

It seemed that in 1924, when the moviemaker William Farnum was filming Zane Grey's *The Vanishing American,* fourteen buffalo were brought to Catalina Island for the film. "These were not cowboys," my father said. "Not by any means. They were easterners decked out in cowboy garments, most probably stiff and new ones. Only the stunt men could sit horses properly, and once the filming was over, they surely got a laugh out of what happened. A failed roundup. All those actors and extras yelling Who-Ha! in the way they'd heard it done in cowboy movies."

The buffalo were left to roam, and in a few years, they'd multiplied. "Then, and no wonder, given Wrigley's ownership of Catalina, his promoter sensibility," my father said, "other buffalo were introduced. That was around 'thirty-two, I think?" He blinked at my mother, chagrined at not having the exact date, and she touched his arm reassuringly.

"But there's a good number of the woolly buggers now, Billy. Could be four hundred, maybe more. They get a count periodically, but they can never be sure."

"What about us?" I said, looking up at him as I twisted the baggy folds of my knickers, getting them straight.

"Ah!" my father said.

He'd lifted his index finger to his lips and was hitting it softly against them, his eyes moving to the others who sat beyond our makeshift enclosure. He'd taken his policeman's hat off, and the webbing under the crown had pulled his hair up into a thicket of spikes. He looked a little crazed, but I'd seen him that way before and wasn't worried. I looked to my mother. She'd removed her hat as well and was touching her jacket collar, feeling the silver bars she'd pinned there as evidence of authority. My father's words were thick with intrigue.

"Don't the walls have ears?"

Our boat came to its docking at the Catalina Island Mole, and my father left me with my mother to guard the suitcases while he headed down the pier and along Crescent Avenue. The town was crowded with tourists, but we could see him clearly as he limped along in his tight-fitting olive uniform, sun glinting off the bill of his hat. Then our view was blocked by Pleasure Pier, and we sat down on the edges of our suitcases to wait for him.

"He won't be long," my mother said, but she sat at the end of her suitcase facing along the dock toward the busy avenue as if he would.

She crossed her legs, her green cotton stockings stretched to a light lime over her knee, and she put an elbow on that knee, her chin resting on her loose fist. Her cap sat back on her head now, and her look was one of boredom, or resignation.

I was confused for a moment, then I got it. It was a theater or movie still, much like the many we'd shuffled through in our quiet evenings: a young woman was sitting at the edge of a suitcase in a bus or train station, or was resting at the shoulder of a dusty road after a bus had pulled away. She was waiting for something, a beginning or an ending. She wore traveling clothes, and I thought her hat sat at the same jaunty angle.

My mother turned to me and winked, somehow knowing of my recognition. Then, without removing her hand from her chin, she extended her index finger and pointed to the side, toward Crescent

TOBY OLSON

Avenue. I looked there and saw my father coming, his face distorted through the ripples of the plastic windshield.

The golf cart had a canvas awning, and when he got abreast of us, I saw the fringe and fabric balls hanging where the awning draped over at the edges. The cart's sides were open, and he'd pulled the safety belt tight around his hips. He sat up straight, almost military in the seat, and as he passed us and turned his head, the bill of his hat hit the hanging balls and they bounced off it. Then he was making a broad turn, almost too quickly. I saw the small wheels rise above the pavement. Then the cart was lurching toward us, skidding to a stop only inches from my mother's dangling foot.

"*At* your service!" my father said, then reached for his belt buckle and climbed out.

We loaded the three suitcases behind the engine. There were luggage straps there, and my father took some time in securing them. The rear of the cart squatted from the weight, the front end lifting up until I could see the shock absorbers above the wheels. We climbed in, and the front settled.

"Kind of tight," my father said.

I was squeezed between them on the seat, and I guessed my father's hip was hanging out in the air. He belted himself tightly, made sure my mother did the same, then he lurched the cart away from the pier, drove slowly among the walking tourists until he crossed Crescent Avenue, then picked up speed as he headed along Catalina and jogged over to Eucalyptus.

We gave the town a wide berth, chugged along those twisting roads that led into the foothills behind and above it. Then we were driving steeper and narrower roads, passing the Zane Grey Hotel and Ada Wrigley's Chimes Tower.

My father leaned forward, intent and careful, negotiating the narrow byways and blind turns. But he often looked to the side as well. It was his way. As urgent for destination as his driving seemed, he just couldn't help it. He slowed down when curious sights presented themselves, and once, at a yard-sale sign, he even pulled to the shoulder and parked. But then he shook his head, looked behind us, and pulled out again.

"There are things to see here, Billy," he yelled over the grinding engine. "But they'll have to wait for another time."

Then we were beyond the town and climbing higher, the road edge at my mother's side a descending cliff of scrub oak and tall pine. I saw her look down there, my father glance over at her and laugh. He dropped a hand from the wheel now, sure of the machine, and I saw him reach to his bill and adjust his hat. Then, after a while, we rounded the last turn.

There was a break in the tree line there, and the whole town of Avalon, the harbor, and the casino displayed themselves below us. My father pulled to the narrow shoulder and stopped, and the three of us looked at the sight, the shuffle of buildings as they meandered down to the straighter streets of the town, the white Wrigley summer house, now the Inn on Mount Ida, tucked into hills in the distance.

"Well, it's quite beautiful," my mother said. "Don't you think so, Billy?"

I was about to answer, but my father jumped in ahead of me.

"Bev," he said, "that may not be something a boy of his age would consider. What is it? Eight, nine years old? We better play it close to the vest now. Look up there."

He was pointing away from the town and up the road to where the edge of a white kiosk was visible, a metal gate running out from it, blocking the way.

"It's the entrance," he whispered, though there was no one there to overhear us. "Entrance to the wilds! Only controlled tours get beyond it, and officials. Which is what we are."

My mother pulled at her clothing and adjusted her hat. I put on the beanie my father had insisted I bring along and fished the purple jawbreaker out of my knickers' pocket. He nodded and winked

TOBY OLSON

as I popped it into my mouth, then jerked his own hat down tight on his head. Then, when we were ready, he pulled back into the road and headed for the gate and the kiosk. I could hear his voice only faintly through the clatter of the golf cart engine.

"A lad of importance," he was saying. "An *important* lad." He was practicing. "This boy is here for research. A member of the family. Permission has been granted."

"We have a boy sent out from the mainland!"

He called the words out loudly, once we'd stopped and seen the uniformed man at the kiosk door. He wore the same green my parents wore, but the emblems at his shoulders and the cut of his coat were different. My father reached to his own chest and took hold of the metal shield there. It was something he'd gleaned from his store of such things, a badge of certain authority in Yugoslavia.

The man headed for the gate, then saw my mother's hat and paused for a moment. Then he moved to the cart's open doorway on my father's side.

I felt my father's knuckles tapping at my knee, and I lifted my saddle shoe to the dash, displaying my knickers' fold and the white sock below it. The man leaned on the edge of the awning pipe and looked in.

"Yes!" my father said. He spoke so loudly that the man lurched back and released his hold. "Her hat! It's the new uniform! *This* is the lad, the one here beside me!"

The man looked in at me, his dark brows lifting at the corners, and I wet my lips and gave him what I thought was a sweetly purple and girlish smile. He recoiled slightly as I grinned at him in the silliest way I could manage, then he turned and went to the gate, swung it open, and let us through. We traveled along the main road for a while, and once it had turned from blacktop into dirt, my father found a section of shoulder that was wide enough and pulled to the side.

We were high on a ridge that wound along the leeward shore of the island, and beyond my mother's green knees the land fell away into steep scrub, greasewood and elderberry that climbed down through rocky declensions to the edge of stony cliffs overlooking the sea.

"Keep belted," my father said as he stepped from the cart. It lifted slightly from the loss of his weight, and my mother and I were tilted toward the steep decline. Then he worked at the awnings' connections, had my mother reach up and disconnect the ones above her head, until he could roll the thing back on its tubular frame and we could see the sky.

"Where are the buffalo?" I said as he climbed back in, but his answer was lost in the cart's clatter as he hit the peddle and we rumbled back onto the road.

We proceeded along the ridge for a good fifteen minutes, and once, in a broad valley in the rolling hills that descended more gradually to our left, I thought I did see buffalo, a gathering of dark specks in the far distance. But my father was looking the other way, below us to the right, and I didn't touch him or say anything.

Then we descended slightly. I could see the ridge rise up again ahead, but at the bottom of our brief decline, my father slowed and turned off at a narrow road, its mouth lined with cottonwood, and headed down toward the sea.

The road was no more than a jeep track, and my father had to cut to its sides to avoid rocks and ruts. I felt the frame bottom out, saw the wheel jerk in his hand from time to time. He looked over at us with wide eyes in mock horror as the cart jumped into roadside brush, our bumper hooking vines of sweet pea and woodland star. My mother had her hand on her head, holding her hat, and with her other arm she held the dashboard stiffly. She was looking straight ahead. My wrists bounced on my thighs. I was cushioned between my parents, their bodies softening the shocks, and I let myself be tossed, bumped like a baby in a fine buggy.

In a while we were deep in a narrow canyon. A stream ran close to the road beside us. Then we were climbing again, the golf cart lugging down and moving at a crawl as we ascended. We came to a

TOBY OLSON

tight turning where my father had to stop and back up, drive down into the shallow stream itself to make the angle. Then we came up out of the ironwood trees that had shaded us, my father pointing at them and saying something we couldn't hear. We were out in the sun again, and in a hundred yards had climbed to the crest of a hill, beyond which the shallow bowl of a tiny valley spread out at the cart's nose. It was there my father pulled to a stop.

The clatter of the engine died, and I could hear the sea, dull breakers in the distance. Rocks rose at the valley's far side, no more than fifty feet away, the last ascension to the cliff's edge. We were very high up, and I knew there'd be a steep drop to the narrow beach and surf.

"Indigenous!" my father said, his voice loud now that the engine sound didn't dampen it. He'd unbuckled and jumped down from his seat, then limped to the cart's rear, and was working at the straps that secured the suitcases.

"What's that, Andy?" It was my mother, her voice thin and a bit shaky. She was patting at her uniform jacket, adjusting her skirt and hat. She'd unbuckled her seatbelt too, but wasn't quite ready to touch ground yet.

"Why, the ironwood!" my father called out from behind us. "Catalina Ironwood. Only here."

He had the suitcases out on the ground by the time my mother and I climbed down. We were looking at them, but he was standing erect again and pointing toward the rocky rise at cliffside.

"Over there, Billy. That's the place. That big one, halfway up."

I pulled my eyes away from the shiny metal surfaces and looked where he pointed, at a broad shelf of rock, the worn-away top of a massive boulder, most of it swallowed up in the ascending hill.

We all three helped in lugging the suitcases across the valley floor to the brink of the rock rise. We must have been an odd sight, I in my knickers and beanie, my mouth still purpled from the jaw-breaker I'd thrown away, my mother, her Wave hat askew now, the seams of her green stockings twisted. She kept fussing with her clothing, smoothing her lapels and skirt, and my father chuckled as he watched her, sweat dripping from under his hat bill.

"Me too!" he said at one point, releasing the handle of the suitcase he was dragging along. Then he lifted his hat and settled it on his head, took his sleeve in his palm, and reached to his chest to shine up his metal badge.

"Oh, Andy!" my mother said, but she was laughing, and she struck a theatrical pose. Her hand was high on her hip, and the other shaded her eyes as she sighted out over the tiny valley like an Indian scout or a sea captain looking for a safe harbor. "If they come, they come!" my father laughed. "You'll be ready, Bev. Beautiful as usual. Isn't that right, Billy? I do love her in that uniform."

I reached down and adjusted the baggy cuffs of my knickers, then touched the top of my beanie.

"I'm ready too," I said.

There was a small ledge down below the larger one, only a few feet up from the edge of the valley floor, and it was there we left the smallest but heaviest of the suitcases. My father took one of the others and began moving up the escarpment, pushing it ahead, then climbing up, then dragging it for a few feet, then thrusting it forward to a new perch. When he reached the higher ledge, he left the suitcase there, then scrabbled down for the other.

"I'll need help with this next one," he said, when he was beside us again. He winked at my mother. It was the lightest of the three cases, and though it was made of metal, I couldn't see why he'd need any help with it.

"You go up a little, Billy. I'll push it to you."

I climbed ahead, finding the going was quite easy, even in my saddle shoes. There were jagged rocks and twigs to hold onto, a kind of natural pathway between boulders, where rain must have washed down. I held the suitcase until my father had climbed up beside me, then moved up another few feet and waited. In five

TOBY OLSON

minutes we'd reached the ledge. The crest was no more than thirty feet above us now. I felt my father's hand on my shoulder, then jumped a little as he yelled down to my mother.

"Oh, Bev!" he called out. "We're going to check the top!" Then his voice was softer, almost a whisper in my ear. "A member of the family," he said. "Permission has been granted."

He set out ahead of me, turning every few feet to see that I was following, was keeping up. The climb was steeper, but no more difficult, and before I knew it we were standing beside each other on a narrow pathway among boulders, those behind us smooth, but those at our chest rendered jagged by wind and rain. My father stood in a v where two of the boulders met, then he stepped carefully to the side and let me look.

We were two hundred yards at least above the narrow beach, a small, square inlet off to the left. Spray rose in clouds as giant waves hit a rock formation near the inlet's center. A gust of wind rushed against my jersey, and I turned to the side slightly as it pushed me back. Then I looked out to where the sea darkened beyond the waves. I thought I saw something at the far horizon, a faint crenellation touched by a pencil line of haze, a web of swirls near the center.

"Long Beach," my father said, "and the roller coaster at the Pike." I saw the shadow of his arm in the corner of my eye as he pointed off to the left. "And that would be San Pedro, where we started from." Then he was silent.

We stood there for a while, looking out. A broad ribbon of kelp drifted in the swells a good distance from shore. A cloud of gulls floated over it, settled on beating wings, then rose up again and scattered. I saw what I thought was a small seaplane. It was like a child's toy suspended in the sky. Boats moved on the quiet sea under it, but just a few, their sails like curved petals from white roses as the wind filled them.

My father waited there silently until I had enough, and only when I turned and let him know that did we start back down to the ledge again. I followed behind him and could see my mother below us, her hand at her brow as she looked up into the sun, judging the progress of our descent.

When we reached the ledge, my father slid the smaller suitcase into brush at the side, then opened the other on the ground.

"It was for something else entirely," he said. "And there's too much wind up there. Best skip it this time around. We've got enough to do right here."

I looked down into the open one and saw the tangle of thin aluminum tubes, some connected through bolted sleeves at their ends into flexible joints. He'd gathered a handful of these by the time I'd found a place for myself, a small perch of rock a few feet up toward the summit. I waved down to my mother as I settled in to watch him, saw the glint at her wrist as she waved back.

"Well, Bev's put her jewelry on again," my father said. I couldn't figure how he'd noticed, bent down over his work that way.

He was tightening the small bolts, attaching lengths of thin cable with loops at their ends, forming some drooping and unclear structure that swayed at his thighs, sections bouncing off his knees. Then he gripped a tube in each hand, gave the whole thing a jerk, and it snapped into the shape of a low tripod. He settled the tripod firmly at the ledge's center, then fished around in the suitcase again, coming up with a metal hammer and four stubby spikes.

"Pitons, Billy," he said, as he pulled the cables taut and drove the spikes into declivities in the rock. "For climbing." The hammer sent a loud pinging into the air, and I saw my mother's head jerk up at the sound. She'd been leaning over, looking at something on the ground. My mother was no nature lover, and I figured she'd been searching for something to occupy herself. She had an object in her hand and was turning it, glancing up to us from time to time. She'd tugged her Wave cap down to the bridge of her nose.

"Dear old Bev," my father said, shaking his head between hammer strokes. "Your mother's a *very* good scout."

TOBY OLSON

The structure rose up quickly from the tripod at the ledge floor. My father would form a star cluster of rods and connectors, then reach up and settle it above another. Then he was climbing the thin tower, stepping up on those horizontal rods that formed a ladder. Soon he was twenty feet above the ground, and after a few more feet, the tower swayed a little with each ascension. It grew thinner as it went up, and when he was a good thirty feet above, he hugged it against his chest as he climbed, the next star cluster held out in the air at the end of his extended arm.

He grinned down at me as he attached the final section, something different from the others, a kind of propeller with small metal boxes at the blade tips. He took a length of cable hooked to his belt on that last trip, and I watched as he busied himself with attaching it. He still wore his policeman's hat, and I could see wind ripple at his buttoned sleeves as the tower drifted in the air while he worked.

Then he was finished and descending, unraveling the coil of cable through the open tunnel at the tower's center as he stepped carefully from rung to rung. There was a good fifty feet of cable left in his hand when he reached the ledge again, and he waved me down from my perch and handed it to me.

I stood above him as he squatted and locked the cable's descending length in place, passing it through a pulley device near the tripod's center. Then he was on his feet again, rubbing his hands together and limping back toward the brink of the ledge, looking up at the tower, checking everything.

"Okay, okay," he said after a while, then turned and looked down to where my mother stood, gazing up at us.

"We're coming, Bev!"

I followed behind him as he snaked the length of cable out, stopping once to lock it through a piton spike with a hole in it, which he then drove into a rock.

When we reached the second ledge, he put the last coils of cable on the ground beside the remaining suitcase and opened it up. He started to squat beside it, then hesitated and turned to look down at my mother.

"Would you like to come up, Bev!" His voice was much louder than was necessary. She was only thirty feet below.

"Oh, no!" she said, smiling, her hat brim touching her brows. "I'm looking around here. I'll be okay."

"Well, okay, then," my father said. "But you've got only these few steps up if you need to get here. Is that right?"

"Oh, yes," she said. "Not to worry, Andy." Then she lowered her head and turned and began searching the ground again.

"Now this is it, Billy," my father said.

I'd squatted down beside him and was gazing into the suitcase. It contained what looked like a small generator that was wired in above a mechanical structure.

My father reached to the suitcase sides and pushed in, and the whole mechanism snapped up a good foot above the rim. He reached under the skeletal structure that had extended to support the generator and removed a crank with a wooden handle. It was very much like the one we'd used for kite fishing, and he must have guessed I saw that, because he turned toward me, shaking his head and grinning.

"Not near the amount of work, my Boy! Not this time. You've only got to keep the propeller turning. Which will be easy. Just a constant speed. This," he pointed to the little generator, "this will provide the juice. Low voltage all the way. Even it you touch the cable, it's only a weak shock. It's sound, Billy! Just the right frequency and pitch. Those little boxes at the prop's end? They'll catch the wind and transform it. Into sound! Like a dog whistle, but electrified. That's what we're after. We won't even hear it. Not a thing!"

He attached the handle, then pulled the cable taut. It ran from the back of the mechanism up to the piton, then farther up to the pulley at the tripod base. Then it ascended the tower's center to the propeller.

TOBY OLSON

He was standing over me, looking up the escarpment, the bill of his hat shading his eyes. He had his hands on his hips.

"Okay, Billy," he said. "Let's give it a try. But do go easy at first."

I reached for the handle and began to turn. There was some resistance, but soon there seemed nothing. Then I felt the handle pulling at my fingers.

"Too quickly!" my father said, and I pulled the handle back a little. But in a moment I had to push again.

There was a bit of lag. The cable had to catch up with itself, and I with it. Then I began to get it, could turn smoothly, just a minute force against my palm, and I looked away from my hand and watched the cable torque as it snaked up the escarpment to where it rose vertically at the tower's center. The propeller was circulating, and but for a dull squeaking at the tripod's base, I could hear nothing.

"That's something," my father said. "A little oil." And he climbed back up the escarpment to the higher ledge. I saw him kneel where the cable entered the pulley, and in a few moments the squeaking was gone.

He didn't come back, but he looked down at me, his arm moving slowly in a copy of my cranking motion. He stood at the tower's side, and high above him the propeller turned steadily in the air. He looked up at it for a few moments, until he seemed satisfied. I watched as his head lowered again and he began to scan the hills off in the distance. He could see farther than I could, much farther than my mother down below, and as I settled into the slow cranking, I glanced back and forth between them.

I was the crucial pivot in the activity, or at least for a while I thought of myself that way. But even though the cranking was much easier than that other time, when my father and I had gone kite fishing, I began to feel a slight edge of resentment at being held in tight action on my little ledge. I couldn't move, pause, or alter my focus in any significant way, and I started to think of myself as a kind of trapped worker, only a slave to my father's whim.

I didn't have such words for it, but as the sweat rose at my jersey collar and dripped down from my beanie rim, I wished for some uniform of authority, like the one my father wore, and not those silly knickers. I pulled my eyes away from where my father stood, his legs stiff and spread a little now, hands on his hips, and looked down to find my mother.

She was nowhere in sight, and my hand lurched on the crank handle. Then she was there again. She'd leaned down close to the escarpment, had picked something up. She turned it at eye level, then looked up over her shoulder to where I was, lifted it higher, and presented it to me. Her hat sat square on her head now, and wisps of hair had drifted down from under its rim. They were caught in sweat on her slick brow. We were together, below the light breeze that cooled my father, and even as I squinted to recognize what she was holding, a stone or a piece of metal, I knew she too was subject to his plan, though easier in her role than I was.

This was no place for my mother, a woman of the theater, but she'd found a way to use the time to her advantage. Even in holding up a useless stone, there was a smile of discovery and surprise on her face. Maybe she was a Navy nurse on the beach at Pearl Harbor, only days before the seventh, wholesome and innocent, ironically foreshadowing the coming attack.

I kept turning the crank, glancing up to the slowly spinning propeller from time to time, and in a while I began to recognize that we were in a moment that was common to many of my father's developing plans. It was a time that had slid into moratorium and beyond any anticipation. There had been the mad fun of all that preparation and deception, and now there was just nothing, and there would be nothing. Half of what my father attempted came to nothing, though the attempt itself always seemed valiant, full of confidence and sureness, and he was never daunted by his failures.

I squeezed the wooden handle tighter, though I kept a constant speed. I tried to urge some completion, feeling anything at all would do. I watched a large shadow as it climbed slowly up the metal tubing of the tower. We were well into afternoon now, and my father had tilted his hat back a little. Then I saw his hand come up and cover his shield, the other flutter in the air at his side. He made the crank-turning motion again, then stepped close to the ledge lip and leaned out, staring off into the distance.

A rush of pebbles and dirt flooded down the escarpment as his toe jutted over the edge. His eyes followed them for a brief moment, his mouth in an o. Then he looked at us, wide-eyed, his finger at his lips, then reached out and pointed toward the low hill that rimmed the tiny bowl of valley where my mother stood. I looked down and saw her drop the stone. I didn't think she'd seen my father pointing. She must have heard or felt something, for she was looking intently out over that natural enclosure she stood at the edge of and toward the rising hill, her hands clasped together at her uniformed chest.

I saw a rustling in the elderberry at the hill's crest, heard a twig snap. Then leaves were falling as the giant woolly head pushed through the branches and came into view. A leaf had stuck to the buffalo's wet, black nose, and it shook its head, blunt horns bright for a moment in the sun, then snorted deeply and blew the leaf away. It pushed through to the shoulders, then dipped over the hill's brink, branches closing behind it, and stepped down carefully until it reached the valley's edge, where it pulled up, shrugged its widow's hump, then exhaled in a long snore and settled on its stubby legs facing toward the center.

Then the others were coming, each breaking through elderberry and holly as the first had, and soon they were rising along the whole arc at the crest, stepping down daintily among sweet pea and Indian paintbrush, those following coming into view above them.

The breeze stiffened slightly, lifted my beanie, then shuffled it to the back of my head, and I could smell them, a dark and dusty scent rolling up the escarpment to my ledge.

They kept coming. For a while, the whole shallow hillside was full of their slowly meandering figures as they descended. The ones lining the crest were forced to wait their turn, and those reaching the bottom at the valley's edge had to push up between others in the front row. Then they began a second row, snouts pressing between rumps, tails flicking at the touch.

I looked back across the open area of the valley's shallow floor and down the escarpment under my feet. My mother was pressed against a boulder at the hill's brink. I could see the peak of her Wave hat, the bridge of her nose. She'd lifted a green knee, one foot up against the boulder at her buttocks. Her hands were in the air at her chest, and she was rubbing them together slowly, looking across to where the buffalo no longer roamed but were still and waiting.

The hillside was thick with their bodies now. There was no more room for descending, and they stood in jagged rows, as still as those lining the crest and the floor at the valley's edge. They had the appearance of a dark audience in an open amphitheater, quiet and attentive, maybe even expectant. But then some were shifting against each other, and I saw a few heads rising, wet snouts scenting, and I heard something.

It was my father, a quiet whistle above me, and when I looked up and saw his hand turning in the air with some urgency, then looked above him to the still propeller, I recognized I'd stopped turning the crank, had gotten fixated on the sight below. I pushed hard at the handle, saw the propeller jump into its spin, and looked down quick enough to catch all the buffalo heads jerk up in unison, all woolly chins lifted toward the tower. I looked up there. My father was pushing his hands down toward me, and I pulled back on the handle slightly, slowing down, and in moments I had the right rhythm again. When I looked back, the buffalo were as still as statues, their eyes milky but focused, all gazing into the empty space at the valley's center, into which my mother then stepped.

I expected "Home on the Range," but it was not my mother's choice. I knew it would be something, though. She stepped out in the way she often did in our small living room at home. She had a way of making that space seem larger, like two spaces, so that my father and I in our easy chairs felt like a front-row audience just beyond the footlights. She'd do a show tune, or a monologue, and sometimes we'd read the male parts for her, though she wouldn't act to us, but as if some lover or father were standing before her. And he would seem to actually be there, at least I'd imagine him, at times with understanding, but often with a pure resentment that found its way into my words.

"You did that one quite well, Billy!" she'd say to me afterward. But I'd have felt my voice as a disembodied thing coming automatically from a place on our living room stage beside her, and I could take no credit for my acting.

My mother would always be dressed in appropriate costume at such times, and as I watched her mincing steps as she moved down to stage center, I saw she was making the best of what she wore now.

The hundreds of buffalo remained perfectly attentive, shoulder to shoulder, and the unblinking eyes of those in the front row followed her movements with what seemed a human anticipation. She turned around once in a slow dance at the valley's center, then paused, her palms opening at her hips, head coyly to the side, and began to sing.

We lost her first lilting words, other pieces of the beginning lyric. Then the song organized itself as her voice strengthened and drifted up the escarpment to us.

". . . little me, with my proper up-BRING-ing. . . . Well sir, all I can say is if I were . . . I'd be SING-ing. And if I were . . . I'd START . . . blowing my lid. And if I were a bell I'd go DING-dong, ding-dong, ding."

I looked up to my father at the tower's side, and though his hand still turned in an urging copy of my cranking, it was losing its rhythm as he watched my mother dance. It kept breaking out of its circular motion, rising up, then down in syncopation. It was as if he held a conductor's baton in his fingertips. He was grinning, and up above his head the propeller turned at the same slow pace.

I saw it was all up to me, and though I watched my father begin to imitate my mother's steps, then looked down to her as she lifted her arms and dragged a foot through yellow pansies in the drama of her song, I kept the crank turning at a constant speed, knowing it was I who held the audience in place, though it might be my mother who held them in thrall.

It was when my mother had moved into a few words of monologue between verses, words I wasn't sure were in the original but couldn't hear well anyway, that the first one landed. She'd moved up a few paces and was speaking to the rows of buffalo, her hands in dramatic gesture as she leaned a little forward. It alighted on the back of her uniform jacket, a cigar-shaped thing with broad gossamer wings, then fluttered up to a purchase in the fold at the crest of her Wave hat, its papery wings beating slowly against the fabric to the sides. It was as if she wore a small propeller, much like the one I'd torn from my beanie against my father's wishes before we'd left home. My mother hadn't noticed the thing was there, was moving back into the song again, and I looked up to see if my father was aware of it.

A dozen were pressed against his arms and legs, the transparent filament of their wings lighting up as they beat through the path of the sun, and he was picking them off with his fingers and dropping them to the ledge, where they bounced and shuffled against his toes. I saw a thick cloud come over the cliff edge above him. He must have heard them, for he turned that way, and one struck against his hat and knocked it off, and others banged into his chest, forcing him back to the lip. I watched him as he extended his good leg and braced himself against the onslaught, then saw his hat as it rolled down the escarpment toward me like a pie plate. Then I felt something at my wrist. A flying fish had landed there, its wings rigid

and elevated as it moved in the circle of my turning, the salty wetness of the sea holding it in place.

I heard my mother singing the last words of her song, and
when I looked down at her, I could see fish flying past, skipping
through pansy and woodland star near her feet, some landing on
the backs and heads of the buffalo. All but the one still riding the
crest of her Wave cap had missed her, and if she saw the others,
she gave no evidence of that. She was at the finale, and there was
no stopping her now.

The fish seemed to come in squadrons. I felt them bumping
into the baggy folds of my knickers, their scratchings against my
jersey back. My father would get the best of them, then another
thick wave would dip over the sea crest and he'd be at them again,
dancing like some ancient Catalina Indian in feathered costume on
his ledge, swatting his chest and arms in ritual gesture, kicking out
and turning.

I kept cranking, the flying fish like a fancy bracelet at my wrist,
disappearing, then coming up to show its lustrous wings. And I
think I might have continued cranking forever. It was as if my
mother's performance and the flying fish and the buffalo were all
driving me. I'd lost all sense that it was the other way around, that
it was I who was the stage manager. I heard my father's voice then
from above. It was calm, though the plaintiveness in it held a bit
of urgency.

"Billy," he said. "That may be enough now. You can stop turning."

But I couldn't stop. I was watching the fish come into view, the
way its wings pressed down as it reached the crest, then lifted as my
hand dipped over on the other side.

"Hey, Billy," my father said softly. "May I have your attention?
Your mother's finished her number. You can stop now."

I was able to stop then, but not before the fish fell away at my
wrist. I saw it drop to join the others fluttering in the dust around
my saddle shoes. My hand slipped from the crank, brushing the last

remaining fish from my knee. The crank continued on its own for a few more turns. Then the wooden handle came to rest in the air. I looked up to the tower's top, saw the still propeller, then looked back to where my father stood.

He was picking flying fish from his chest and arms as if he were picking lint. He bent, lowered each one to the ground, then rose up again and pulled away another. He must have felt my look, for he glanced down for a moment. His head was shaking with chagrin, but he was smiling. Then I heard my mother's voice.

"What in the dickens is this, Andy?"

And when I looked down to where she stood, hands on her hips and looking up at my father, I saw that the flying fish was still sitting on her head, its wings fixed now in a stationary v. Beyond her, the buffalo were leaving, heading slowly up to the hill's crest, some waiting for places in the crowded lines, much like respectful patrons in no rush to leave the theater. Most carried flying fish on their heads and backs, and I wondered if they'd release them into the sea when they reached the other side of the island, knowing all the while that that wasn't possible. The fish would be dead by then, as would the dying legions of those others beating softly on the ground around us.

My father gave it a good go, but we were too far above the sea, and urgency was not a strong suit for him. He took his jacket off and spread it on the ledge, then looked for the ones whose bodies still held life. He had a slowly seething pile before long, and I watched as he lugged the bundle up the escarpment to the crest where we had stood. He leaned into the cut between rocks, and I saw his shoulders slump as he looked down. His limp jacket hung over his arm when he reached the ledge again, and he draped it over a rock, then started to dismantle the tower.

My mother had climbed up to my ledge in the meantime, and I saw that the fish had fallen from her Wave cap. There was a darkness under her arms, wisps of damp hair pasted to her forehead.

"That was very good," I said, and she smiled at the compliment.

"Rather weird, though." She laughed softly, her eyes above my head, watching my father. He had taken half the tower down by then, working quickly.

"Andy!" she called up to him. "They were only fish! Just fish!"

He was holding a tangle of metal tubes in his hands, an intricate star cluster.

"But beautiful. And alive," he said softly, his voice bell clear in the afternoon air.

The lights' glow in the harbor at Avalon came back into focus, and I saw again those seven arcs of mooring. Now there were absences in each jeweled chain; even dim cabin night-lights had been turned off. Over the dial of my watch, I saw a wash of phosphorescence in water flooding against the pilings at deckside. It was ten-twenty, and when I lowered my arm and looked down the table, I saw Jen leaning across it.

A wave of hair hid her expression, but she was clearly intent, listening to what Michael Higgins had to say. Tod was beside her, and I saw him look at his own watch, then lift his beer glass and drink what was left in it.

I could remember a moodiness in my father in the days following our Catalina trip, and my mother's attempts to lift him out of it. He'd left one of the suitcases behind in his haste to get us back to Avalon in time for the six o'clock boat, but I don't think that had much to do with it. I couldn't bring up the details, but as I sat there watching the focused intensity in the divers' conversations, I thought of Leonard's blunt comments, and was troubled by distant textures.

My mother had opted, quite reasonably, for the theatrical, and I thought I remembered a chain of evenings in which she'd performed for us. I thought too that she'd gotten caught up in that, in preparation and rehearsal, and I could remember the look on my father's face when she announced each evening's program. He suffered her self-involvement gracefully, and though he became his old self again before long, I thought she'd had little to do with that, had very quickly been performing only for herself.

I could remember the image of my mother's gestures as she spoke Blanche's lines. My father's hands held his knees, and though he watched her from beyond the footlights with attention and respect, something in his posture told me he wished he were elsewhere, alone with all those foolish feelings and his sentimental regrets.

22.

The next day passed in a haze of empty events. I'd awakened with the residue of a dark dream, one in which my parents were alive again and happy, and I was aware, in guilt, of their impending deaths. Jen had called Carol in the early morning, and I'd overheard their conversation from my patio as I sipped coffee. "Yes," I heard her say. "It's *perfectly* safe." There was a pause, then, "No, it's an island. A kind of resort." Carol hadn't asked to speak to me.

I had Jen at the dock by eight, and once her diving party had steamed away I realized I had the whole day ahead of me, and even the night this time, with nothing to do. Because of the cookout, their return time was uncertain, and I wouldn't be waiting at the dock. Jen and I had agreed to meet back at the Zane Grey, whenever we both got there. When I returned to the hotel, I organized my diving gear, then wrote a postcard to Aaron and Beverly. Then I settled in on the bed with Grey's *The Vanishing American,* which I'd found on the small bookshelf in my room. The prose was muscular and simple, and I made it through the first few paragraphs, then fell asleep with my finger between the pages. I woke close to noon and stumbled into the shower, and by one-thirty I was back in Avalon again.

The town was crowded with tourists, day-trippers from the mainland and a good number who had come in on launches from a cruise ship sitting at anchor beyond the harbor's mouth. It was large and imperious, well out of scale with Avalon's quaintness, though the casino at the point stood placidly across from it, as sure of itself as the ship was.

I ate at the same place we'd eaten at the night before, lucky to find a small table, inside this time, in a shadow near the kitchen door. I ordered a green salad and iced tea, then munched at the limp lettuce and let the loud voices of the tourists keep my mind away from useless thought. They spoke of scented soaps and Catalina pottery, their trips on the glass-bottom boats, the absence of smog, and the clear water: you can see right down to the bottom! A child wept insistently across the crowded room.

It was three by the time I finished eating. The restaurant emptied onto Crescent Avenue, and there were dozens of shops and hotels there and a few bars with tables out on the street in front of them. The tables were crowded with tired tourists taking time out to drink and watch those still with energy as they passed by. I had to work my way through walkers. I thought I might try the shops, find something for Jen, for Carol too; it seemed right that I bring back a gift, as well as her daughter, though it was hard to imagine what might be appropriate.

The shops were as crowded as the street was, and though I poked around for a while, brushing against women in large sun hats, men in visors, I found nothing that seemed appropriate for Carol. I bought a white golf cap for myself, the letters of Catalina ironed-on above the bill, and a fat bar of lavender soap for Jen. Then I entered the Chamber of Commerce, also on Crescent, and picked up maps and brochures. I wore the hat and carried the soap in a droopy plastic bag as I headed through the crowds to where I'd parked the golf cart on Metropole. Then I headed back to the Zane Grey again.

I slept, then woke up and tried to read, then fell asleep again, and when I awakened for the last time it was dark, and by the time I'd showered and dressed it was eight-thirty, and I chugged the golf

TOBY OLSON

cart back to Avalon for dinner. I'd found a restaurant in one of the town's brochures. It was off Crescent, near the Via Casino archway. White tablecloths and crystal, and the food was good, but I had little appetite and only picked at the salmon. I knew the problem: Susan Rennert, all that unfinished business.

It was ten by the time I returned to the hotel, and once I'd unlocked my door and turned the light on, I saw a folded piece of paper on the floor at my feet. It was a note from Jen, written carefully under the hotel's logo, a stylized rendering of the writer leaning against the building's edge.

Bill, we got back early, it read. *Exhausted. But it was fun. I'm going to bed. See you in the morning, love, Jen.*

I folded the paper and placed it on the end-table at bedside. Then I went to the small desk, intending to write a note of my own, but changed my mind. She'll sleep, I thought. I crossed over to the doors leading to the balcony, opened them, and stepped out to the adobe wall. The lights of Avalon displayed themselves below, and beyond Crescent Avenue, out in the harbor, the seven curved necklaces blinked dimly, night-lights of the boats at mooring sending faint shimmers down over their gunwales, a dull sparkling like starlight on the shifting surface of dark water near their hulls. I was wide awake now, feeling the need of a drink before I tried sleep again, and I left the Zane Grey in my Catalina hat and chugged back down to Avalon in the golf cart.

I found a single stool close to the middle of the bar. Two young women sat to my left, and the men hitting on them were standing pressed against them, one with his back to me, waving a bill at a bartender for another round. There were two bartenders, both in blue aprons and white shirts with rusty-looking anchors printed on them. The place was called the Rusty Anchor, and there was a real one hanging over the mirror above liquor bottles on the wall behind the bar. Various nautical photographs lined the mirror's lower edge, and I could see old pictures of Catalina, both the town and the harbor, between bottles, and above them, a good portion of the room behind me. The place was thick with tourists, men and women in their early thirties mostly, here from an evening cruise ship. Outside, Crescent Avenue had been almost empty. A young couple had passed me, arm in arm, her head leaning into his neck, and I'd heard voices from the open window of a hotel above the street. The day-trippers had departed, leaving the town to lovers and drinkers, most of them in dark rooms or cabins in boats out in the harbor, or in party bars like this one.

The bartenders were busy, but I was in no rush. I took a twenty-dollar bill from my wallet and placed it on the bar, then looked between the bottles at the photographs.

There was one picturing the point before the casino had been built. Another showed the harbor, mostly empty, just a few boats at anchor. I saw a night shot taken from above the town at a distance, those flickering necklaces on the water, a craft at each mooring. There must have been close to three hundred of them, illuminating both the edge of town and the sea beyond the harbor's mouth. And there were close-up photos too, the facades of old buildings and the Via Casino archway, sterns of pleasure boats at mooring, their names visible: *Chuck's Folly, Spindrift, The Stellar, Adam's Rib,* and others that I couldn't make out.

"Hey, partner. You've lost your *i*."

It was one of the bartenders, a man in his late thirties, with bright red hair. He'd wiped the bar with a damp rag, then flipped a cork coaster down in front of me. He was looking above my face, and I reached to the cap's bill and took it off and turned it. It now read *Catal na.* The letter *i* had fallen away.

"Would have thought you'd know that trick," he said familiarly.

"Right," I said. "How 'bout a bourbon and water, about half and half."

He blinked at me. "Right you are," he said, then turned to the shelf at the mirror and lifted one of the bottles.

TOBY OLSON

"Busy," I said, when he'd turned back and was pouring the drink.

"You know the story. Day-trippers, and now the cruise ship. The only tippers are those who wanna impress the girls. Give me weekdays anytime."

He'd leaned across the bar and was speaking intimately. Aren't I a day-tripper too? I thought. He seemed to know something that I didn't. I nodded in agreement. Then he pushed back, winked, and headed down to where others were waving their fingers to get his attention.

I lifted the drink and sipped it. He'd poured Wild Turkey, though I'd not asked for it. It was in a tall glass, a double, and over not much ice. I'll have to take my time with this, I thought. And I'll have to tip well too.

Someone had dropped some coins in the jukebox, and now the Beach Boys were singing the Catalina song softly in the background. Though the place was crowded, voices were muffled by the porous wood and fabric covering the dark walls. I could hear the click of glasses, the occasional scrape of a chair being shifted, and under the music and laughter I could hear conversations too. The men standing beside me were proposing a get-together after the cruise was over, and the women seemed interested. Someone behind me was telling a story about Mexico and another cruise. I heard a ship's horn in the distance. "That's the hour call," somebody said. "Time for another round."

I lifted my drink again and looked in the bar mirror. There were a few empty tables now, and people were moving toward the door. But there were others ordering again, flirting with the waitress as she wrote things down on her pad. Then I looked back at the photographs.

There was a space now where the Wild Turkey bottle had been. The bartender hadn't put it back, but had left it below the bar in front of me. I could see one of the photographs more clearly, one that showed boats at mooring. There were four of them, each with a white numbered buoy in the water at its stern, two numbers, one indicating mooring row, the other placement within it. They were large inboards, yachts, really, and each had its name lettered across the stern. On the left was a squat, fiberglass cruiser, something that looked swift. It was called *Descanso*, named for the first bay north of Avalon. Then came *The Emma, The Stellar,* and at the end was a low ebony craft, *Dark Dream*. There were no more than a few feet of sea between each boat, and there were lines running from cleats to the white buoys, holding them in place. Each had rubber fenders hanging down from the gunwales, and I imagined they were anchored at their prows as well. Above decks and through their riggings, I could see the next line of boats, and beyond that the mouth of the harbor, then the open sea.

I looked back at their names, the various scripts that had been chosen for christening. *The Descanso* was printed in a twisting gothic, *Dark Dream* looked like something from a soap opera credit. Then I looked at the square letters of *The Stellar*. They were fainter than the others, and there seemed something wrong with the spacing. They needed a coat of paint, and I had to squint and lean forward a little to identify the nature of the script. It seemed slightly and intentionally retrograde, something from the fifties. The boat's stern above waterline looked like mahogany or some other hardwood, and I could see lines where the planks had been joined, cutting through its name. One of the bartenders passed in front of me, blocking my view for a moment, and when he was gone, I looked back at the letters and saw them for what they were. It was not *The Stellar* at all. What I'd seen as some of the spaces were faint hyphens. I'd been seeing TH E STELLA R, but now I could join the letters into other possible words, TH E-STELLA-R, and if I changed one letter, I'd get what I knew was the real intention: THE ESTELLE R.

"Now it's the *a*."

TOBY OLSON

The redheaded bartender was standing in front of me again, blocking my view. He'd wet his finger in the sweat from my glass, then pressed down on the bar and lifted the letter. I saw it at his fingertip and reached for my hat again. It now read *Cat 1 na*, the spaces similar to those on the boat's prow. I had a crazy thought that he could put the *a* over the last *e* in the name I'd constructed, correct my mistaken reading.

"They just stick them on," he said. "The place goes away over time, like the memory of it. People end up with a nice white hat, like a clear conscience."

"Where did you hear that?" I said. I was wishing he'd move to the side a little, so I could see the photograph. The ice had melted in my drink, and he was looking at it.

"You know how we are," he said. "Island fever. A lot of time for thinking. Can I freshen this?"

"No," I said. "That's enough. I'll just sip it."

He looked up at me, searching my face for something, then shrugged and headed down the bar, giving me back the photograph.

I heard the cruise ship's half-hour horn, the sound of chairs being pushed back from tables. People were standing at their bar stools now, digging in their pockets for money.

What I could see of the boat seemed orderly. The brass railings at the gunwales were shining, as were the inboard's exhaust ports, and the deck gear was covered with dark tarps and lashed in place. But the low wheelhouse, obscuring my view of the boat's prow, was in need of paint and repair, like the letters, and I thought I saw grunge at the stern's waterline. The wheelhouse had a curious shape. It rose square from the deck, but its roof was curved, and there was a dip at the curve's center. Seen from the stern, it had a shape reminiscent of a valentine heart. Something to do with the wind, I thought, or just some aesthetic move.

I climbed off the stool and stood there, waiting for the bartender to come back. He was busy ringing up the bills of the cruise ship travelers, and I had to wait a while. Then I caught his eye, and he moved down the bar and stood in front of me again. "Nine-fifty," he said, looking down at my half-full glass, then over at the twenty.

"Fine," I said. "Keep that. But there's one thing, that photograph? When was it taken?"

He turned and looked at the mirror, then stepped back to the shelf of bottles and lifted his hand, watching me as he moved it along the row of pictures. I nodded when he got to the right one, and he looked at it for a moment, then turned back toward me.

"Well, it's hard to say," he said. "But I can tell you one thing. That boat, *The Emma*? It went down a good fifteen years ago or more. I've only been here five, but it was a big deal, a whole family went down with it, and there's a plaque at the Yacht Club. So it's got to be that far back at least."

"What about the others?"

He turned back to the picture, leaning down a little for a good look at it. Then he was shaking his head as he rose again and faced me. I didn't wait for him to speak.

"Good enough," I said, then tapped the bar in thanks and headed for the door, looking back for a moment when I reached it. The bartender was watching me, hands on his hips now, and I pulled the bill of my cap down and stepped out into night on Crescent Avenue. Then I headed toward Pleasure Pier, where I could see the light in the public phone booth in the distance.

It could have been a coincidence, but I didn't believe that. If the bartender had been correct about the date, then the time was right. TH E-STELLA-R had been moored here when Susan Rennert had drowned, at least when my father had been looking into that. But that had been sixteen years ago, and the chances that the boat was still here seemed very slim. Still, it was something I had to find out about, and the best way to get that information was from Sanchez. It would be an easy matter for him to learn things, both about the past and the present. It would only take a call or two.

I had no change in my pocket, but I had a credit card. I knew Sanchez wouldn't be in, not at this hour, but I hoped to get his home number.

"It wouldn't do you much good, anyway," the duty officer told me after refusing to release it. "He's gone for the weekend, fishing, I think, and with the family."

"Will he call in?" I asked.

"I can imagine that," he laughed lightly. "He's tenacious, and he did feed the computer before he left. He may well call for the information."

I left a message, getting him to read it back to me slowly before I let him go.

"Are you a cop?" he said, once he'd repeated it. "You certainly act like one."

"No," I said. "Not that. Just a friend of his, a civilian." I hung up, then lifted the phone book that dangled at the end of a metal chain. There was no Rennert on Catalina. Then I left the booth and headed back toward Crescent Avenue. Another letter fell from my cap. I saw it flutter away in the dim light as I left the pier. Now the hat read *Cat l a*.

23.

A narrow beach ran along Crescent Avenue, separating it from the harbor, but only to the south of Pleasure Pier was there a place for swimming. To the north, dinghies had been pulled up on the sand, secured there by ropes tied to metal rings in the low seawall. I sat on a bench at the wall's edge facing the water, thinking things over.

Why Catalina? My parents had brought me here, but there was no other connection that I knew of. We were a good long distance from Laguna Beach, though I had a boat now, and Susan Rennert had drowned. Many facts were before me, and I knew I'd have more if I had my father's file and list. But the facts just sat there, waiting for the story that could link them.

I could see activity on boats in the first arc of mooring, no more than fifty yards off. People stood on decks, drinks in their hands, and some helped with the securing of dinghies that had made their way out from shore for the night. There were other benches to either side of me, lovers sitting close together, watching the lights. The casino was aglow out at the point, and over at Cabrillo Mole, the last boat to the mainland was taking on passengers, the line slowly shrinking as they climbed aboard.

My tennis shoes shifted in the gravel, my toes at the seawall edge, and beyond them, just a few feet away, people moved among the dinghies, strollers close to the gentle wash, but some untying the small boats and sliding them into the water. One man climbed aboard, unsteadily and clearly drunk. He huffed as the little boat wobbled, then lost his balance and stepped out to right himself, soaking his shoe. He swore loudly, jerked his leg out, and plopped down onto the wooden seat, then fished for the short oars at the locks. I heard laughter off to my left, and when I looked there, I saw four kids sitting on the seawall. They were nudging each other. It was their night's activity, watching the antics of drunkards as they made their awkward way to those expensive boats out in the harbor.

I had my eye on something, an old wooden thing, green paint peeling away on its hull. It was pulled up close to the seawall, its prow pointed toward the water, and I could see its name, *The Pelican*, stenciled in near the prow's point. Most of the other dinghies sat askew on the sand, recently pulled up, but this one had settled in, and I thought it must have been there for a while.

I was beyond the lights at the edge of Crescent, still their glow washed down over me and the narrow beach. It was darker there on the sand, enough to obscure the faces of the strolling lovers, but it was light enough to see most any activity. I waited, hoping for a time when I might find myself alone, but I got nowhere with that. Drunkards and groups of loud revelers came along the sand, struggled with the boats, and climbed into them. The kids on the seawall remained there, watching. I heard the horn from the mainland express at Cabrillo Mole blowing last call. People were thick at the railings, getting their final glimpses of Avalon.

Two middle-aged couples stood down on the sand in front of me, the women in long beach dresses. They were laughing and arguing as to who would be ferried out first. One man pulled the rope loose from the ring below my feet, while the other, dressed in a blue blazer, jerked at the stern with his fingers. "My shoes!" one of the women called out as the slow wash touched them. I got up from the bench then, stepped to the seawall, and jumped down over it to the sand. They all looked up at me as I moved to the boat's prow and helped them slide it down into the water. There were thank-yous from the women, waves from the two men as they rowed away. The

304   TOBY OLSON

women turned from me, watching their husbands as they drifted off, and I moved back to the seawall where *The Pelican* rested and untied its line. There was only one short oar slid under the seat, but the dinghy was small and narrow, and once I'd gotten it down to the sea's edge and had climbed aboard, I could use the oar as a paddle. I looked back once, saw the women waving, then dug the oar down deeply and moved out into the harbor.

I made the first arc of mooring in just a few minutes, and once I was close to the boats, I turned to the side and paddled along their sterns, where names looked down at me: *Lustra, Blue Boy, Cal's Catch, The Angelino*. There were fewer lights now, and not much activity. One man looked at me from the rail as I passed his boat, but he said nothing, and I could hear voices from cabins below deck as I passed others. There was little space between the boats, no more than fifteen feet, and the glow of night-lights was enough to read the buoys by. They were white cans, the numbers in black above water-line, and when I got to twenty, I dug the oar in and moved up between two boats, heading for the next row. I could see into port-hole windows as I slid by, saw a man in a bed reading a book, a woman, naked from the waist up, leaning over a table.

I crossed open water, came to a space of darkness where the boat's dim lights couldn't reach. But the water sparkled there too, and when I looked up, I saw the cloudless, starry sky, a distinct sliver of moon. Off to the left was a wash like the Milky Way, but it was only the bright lights of the casino, which stood like a massively garish jewel out at the point. Then I drifted close to the sterns in the next row, found a way between two boats, and paddled on, the wash lifting into low waves as I got closer to the harbor's mouth.

The boats bobbed at the moorings now, and I had to dig the paddle in to avoid their hulls as I passed through to more distant arcs. Then I reached the one I was after. I was close to the center of the harbor now, parallel to the point, and I paddled toward the spectacle of the casino, checking the names on the hulls above me as I slid beneath their shadows. I saw the number 2-23 on the white buoy, the same as in the photograph in the bar. Then I saw the name.

The stern was higher than I thought it would be, and I had to look up toward the sky a little to read it, TH E-STELLA-R, the paint faded and rippling slightly where the letters crossed joints in the wood. I could see the brass railing aglow in the sky above it, but that was all I could see, and I dug the paddle in and backed off a little, then made my way between the boat and the one to the left of it, a white sailing craft with no lights shining from its deck. The port side of TH E-STELLA-R was lower than its stern, and as I paddled along it, hugging close to the hull of the white sailboat, I could see the edge of some object at the brass railing. A soft rectangle rose up there, something covered and lashed down. No light shone in the row of ports below decks, and when I drifted past the wheelhouse, I saw that its windows were dark also. It was a much larger craft than I'd imagined, a good sixty feet or more. I thought it might be ocean-going, though it clearly needed some repair. Caulking had crumbled and fallen away between boards in its wooden hull, and as it lifted and sank back down in the wake, I saw barnacles and a rusty accretion below the waterline. It was an old craft, but in its time it had been a luxurious one.

I rounded its prow, drifting under the mooring line, then made my way down the other side, between it and another dark boat, this one with a high and intricate superstructure, fitted out for serious fishing. Again there were no lights visible in TH E-STELLA-R's ports. I'd passed no moored dinghy, nor had I seen one up on the deck, but I couldn't be sure of that. It could be amidships somewhere, out of sight.

I passed around the craft once again, moving slowly, lifting my paddle from time to time to listen. A dull, distant hum came from the bowels of the sailboat, some sort of generator, I thought, but I could hear nothing from TH E-STELLA-R, only the slap of water against its hull. Then I passed under the high prow again and reached out for the taut mooring rope, holding myself in place. I

TOBY OLSON

worked to untangle the dinghy's thin nylon line with my free hand, then attached it to the metal oarlock on my left, securing the other end to the thicker mooring rope of the larger vessel, then pulled the dinghy in tight against it. Then I stood carefully on the dinghy's rocking seat, reached up, and took the rope in my hands and began to climb, my head reaching starlight at deck level in just a few moments.

I looked along the deck's surface toward the wheelhouse, just the broad rectangular window that faced the prow visible from my angle, the rest cut off from view by a low wooden housing of some kind. But once I'd gotten my leg up and was squatting against the bulkhead at the prow's v, I could see more of it, the way the front wall curved a little, and the dip at the center of its low roof. Starlight washed over the wooden deck and the tubular brass railing that seemed to encompass the whole craft, rising a foot or more above the gunwales. The deck was low, and once underway, one could stand safely at the side, the rail rising to waist level, and watch the sea pass by.

I could hear nothing but the occasional splash of water against the hull, and in time I rose from my squat and started down the deck's center, my tennis shoes in starlight, until I reached the side of the low wooden housing and could see the brass hinges and clasp on the far side, a door there, entrance to the cabins below, but no light leaking around the frame.

I was only ten yards from the wheelhouse, and once I'd gotten to it and had seen the entrance door in its side, I continued on for a few feet until I had sight of the stern section behind it and the covered and lashed-down rectangle I'd noted from the water below. There were five of them, each of awkward shape, upper surfaces uneven from objects pushing up under the dark coverings. Two thick lines were coiled neatly near the stern, and I saw the edge of the anchor line, the figure eight where it was gathered at a cleat. I turned then and headed back to the wheelhouse.

The door was latched, but not locked, and it swung open silently on oiled hinges. A dim yellow light came on above the prow-facing window, something wired to the door, and I could see clearly enough as I entered and stepped down, pulling the door closed behind me. I'd seen a small, goosenecked lamp extending over a broad, sloping map table, and once the door was closed and the yellow light was off, I crossed the cabin and reached out for the switch, my hand visible in the starlight that flooded in at the front window. The light was a spot, and its beam cast a large and distinct circle that covered most of the table but lit nothing else. Still, starlight bathed the cabin, and I could see the map drawers and the doors of cabinets lining the walls. There was a railed shelf to the left of the prow-facing window, two white coffee cups sitting on it.

The map table rose up gradually in front of me, ending at a brief section of bulkhead below the window, and at the edge of the light, I could see something affixed there, some document under thick plastic. I reached for the neck of the lamp, forcing the light back a little, until I could see it clearly. It was a license of some sort, rows of numbers and letters, some official stamp, and a name printed near the center, *James R. Mooney*, and below the name, above lines designated for the address, *TH E-STELLA-R*. The name meant nothing to me, but it was a name at least, something for Sanchez when the time came.

I bent the light back, then reached for the first map drawer and pulled it open. A few sheets curled up at the edge, and I slid them out, then placed them on the table under the spot. They'd been handled and used, how recently I couldn't tell. There were dates penciled to the sides of charted lines, but no years given, and there were other numbers, degree designations, and some I couldn't identify. Each map depicted the sea and a section of coastline to the south of Catalina. There were ten of them, and the last and most southerly one documented land below Acapulco on the coast of Mexico.

I was looking down at that one, studying a place where I thought figures and lines indicated the boat had come ashore, when I heard something, wood creaking, or a tap of metal. I jerked my head up, seeing the reflection of my own face there in the window, and was shocked for a moment, thinking it was someone looking in. Cloud cover, I thought, as I looked back down at the map. Starlight no longer brightened the cabin beyond the spot.

Then I heard the sound again, and at the same time recognized that my reflection had been grinning at me. I looked up to the window. My face was still there, and as I gazed into it, I saw a hand come up and tap at the glass near its cheek. Then it was grinning in at me again, and I knew it was not my face. Still, it was that, and as it moved back and disappeared, I turned from the table toward the door. I was sure none of it had happened, but then the door was opening, and I felt the hair rise up on the back of my neck. He stepped down into the cabin then, his face coming up as he reached the floor. It was myself again, that face I'd seen each morning in the bathroom mirror, but it was grinning at me, and those familiar eyes held something foreign and slightly wild.

"Hey, brother," my own voice said to me. "Fancy meeting you here."

24.

Even now I cannot bring back the quality of those first moments with any accuracy. I know I thought of the bartender, his odd familiarity, and recognized the reason for it, that he'd mistaken me. I thought of Leonard and of my parents and of Susan Rennert too, but I couldn't quite place them in events, and I felt the narrative of my past life coming to a kind of stasis, then crumbling, all the pieces to be put aside for now, so that some other, alternative, and more rational story might begin. And I thought of Jen, her image afloat in terrible guilt for just a moment. Then I thought of those letters falling from my Catalina hat. I'd been tricked into buying it, whatever the cost, and I imagined it above my brow, the remaining letters scattered in disarray across the bill, only a white and empty space now at the crown.

I walked behind that back I'd seen in clothing store mirrors. I'd started to speak, though I had no words, and he had lifted his hand up, still grinning, and motioned for me to follow, then had turned my face away from me and stepped back up and through the wheel-house door. Out on the deck, we were both in starlight again. There had been no clouds, only his figure outside the window, blocking the glow. Then he was ducking, descending the ladder at the low open door in the housing I'd passed earlier, and I was a shadow copy of his movement, climbing down behind him. He wore a blue terrycloth robe, tennis shoes without socks, and the edge of the robe flicked at his calves as he led me along a narrow passage to a door, which he opened, then stepped over the sill.

I followed him. We were in a large and opulent living room with a curved bar at the end. Two imitation leather couches faced each other, a glass-and-metal coffee table between them, and there were two chairs, each pushed against wooden wainscotting at the bulkhead to either side, under window ports over which curtains had been pulled closed. A large figured carpet covered most of the floor. Its design was geometric and modern, something from the fifties, as were the couches and chairs. It was all very much like my parent's house had been when I was a child. When we were children, I thought, still quaking at the idea of it. I wanted to ask him something, but again I didn't have the words. He left me standing near the doorway as he crossed to the bar at the room's far end, and when he'd gotten behind it and turned, giving me my face again, he was smiling, lifting his open palm.

"Sit down," he said. "I'd imagine bourbon? Wild Turkey?"

I looked at him, then nodded and moved to one of the couches and sank down into it, my legs shaking as I pressed my knees together.

Then he was sitting across from me, our drinks on cork coasters on the table between us. He crossed his legs, and I noticed that I'd crossed mine in the same way. I'd pressed my hand into my side but only knew I was doing that when I saw him look there. Then he pulled his robe open and shifted in his seat. The hair on his chest was as thick as mine, but touched with gray, and he was more muscular through the shoulders. I saw the indentation under his ribs, then the hatching of scar tissue, those familiar twisted braids of white flesh.

"We were joined there, you know."

His voice held a strange nostalgia, and for the first time I could find something that was different from my own in it.

"What do you mean?" I said, knowing exactly what he meant, but needing some talk and acknowledgment, some time to get myself back to where I was, what I was doing here, and what was still to be done.

312   TOBY OLSON

I thought of Jen curled up in her bed at the Zane Grey. Would the phone message light be blinking in my own room? I saw the boat's name on a piece of wood above the bar, TH E-STELLA-R, the letters bought at some store and tacked in there. His name was James R. Mooney, but he was my brother, and I couldn't quite figure what that meant just yet, not here, and I hadn't even begun to consider the past, my parents, their part in this, and where I'd been before I'd come to them.

"Oh, *you* know," he said.

I'd forgotten my own question, then it came back to me in his studied answer.

"Siam. Chang and Eng. It's not *so* surprising, really. Is there any pain?"

"Yes," I said. "At times."

"It may well be a cost," he said. "There are others, for me there are."

He looked steadily over at me, his face in repose. And I saw that without talk or expression, we were truly identical. His lips were mine. His nostrils had the same shape. I saw the slab of my forehead, the way his brows extended slightly, and then my eyes. They were set deep in their sockets, wider apart than I'd ever noticed, and the prominent bones and brows that surrounded them suggested a penetrating look they did not have. Bright blue, but an almost dull-witted vacancy, some profound guarding, behind which duplicity seemed to lurk. *Could I really look this way?* I thought, and I shuffled through memory: myself in uniform, the gaze of some wary recruit, his eyes shifting, then looking away. I wondered how Jen had gotten beyond this face. Only his hair was a little different, cut carefully and a bit longer, but the same mix of graying blond above the same ears.

I was finding some differences when he spoke and his face became animated, but I was finding similarities as well. At times it was like my mother acting, as if he were acting, getting my own way with expression and tone of voice, bringing things up to me that I had seldom noticed, yet recognized. But at other times he was missing that, though only slightly, as if he were acting out some caricature, doing it to ridicule me or simply for the fun of it.

"I don't understand this," I said, not wanting to let the words out but unable to stop them.

He sipped from his drink, then looked above the glass at me. "But you will," he said, glancing over my shoulder and toward the door where we had entered, then back at my face.

"Okay," he said, looking into my eyes. "You can come in now."

I heard footsteps and a brush of fabric, and I turned my head to the side, catching sight of her slipper and bare leg as it came through a fold of black silk. She wore a kimono, the large garish figure of a curving dragon on the back between her shoulders. She moved to the other side of the coffee table, then sat down on the couch arm, her robe falling open above her crossed knees. Her left arm hung carelessly down near the couch side, and she held a small pistol in her hand.

She may well have been Susan Rennert had she been alive, but I knew she was that other, dark half-sister, Pearl's lost daughter, the mysterious Estelle. I almost laughed in my growing hysteria, thinking of her in that dramatic way. She seemed dressed for the part, the pistol only a kind of theatrical prop dangling from her fingers. Her hair was pulled back tight, as in Susan Rennert's photo, and I thought of Jennifer and our twin dreams and the bleeding, and felt the pressure of my penis against my pants leg.

"Steady as she goes."

It was Mooney, and when I looked from Estelle's face to his, shocked once again by what I found there, I saw a strange concern in his eyes. I'm shaking, I thought, or doing something else, but I didn't know what.

I looked over to Estelle sitting on the couch arm. The same nose and high cheekbones, those thin, light brows and broad forehead. I could see my father's mistake: *Rennert: why Susan?* They

314   TOBY OLSON

were very much alike, the same expression, thin lips, and slightly pointed chin.

And I was drawn to her, sitting there with her dark robe open, her long white legs and milky thighs. I saw the prominent bones at her ankles above her slippers and wanted to reach across the glass table and touch them. Then I looked up and caught her twisted smile, her eyes pushing me away. They were not Susan Rennert's eyes. They held something entirely foreign to what had drawn me and continued to. They were deep but impenetrable, as if coated with unwanted knowledge, and I thought they might be searching · for a permanent blindness. I wanted to hear her speak but feared the sound of her voice, that it would take me back again to Blevins Street, that day she'd touched and kissed me so long ago. We'd been children together, and I felt my face flush in that knowledge as I looked at her, maybe even remembered her, though there was no such recognition in her eyes.

Mooney had risen while I was watching her, had come around the back of the couch to stand beside her. It could have been me, standing there with Susan Rennert, everything undone and perfect.

"Billy," he said, pulling me away from staring. "It will all be clear in just a little while. But there's something else, something we have to do now."

He touched Estelle on the shoulder and she rose, then handed the little gun to him.

"Why don't you change," he said. "And bring the photo." She started toward the bulkhead door behind the bar.

"And the wig," he called after her. "You'd better wear it." Then he turned and smiled at me and lifted our glasses from the table. Mine was untouched, but the ice had melted away. "I'll just freshen these," he said, then went and stood behind the bar again.

I watched him as he raised the bottle and reached in the silver chest for ice. He'd placed the gun at the bar's corner, and though there had been no threat, it rested there as evidence of one. Still, that needed acknowledgment, something sane through which to define the circumstance.

"Have I broken any laws?" I asked. "I just came aboard. I haven't taken anything."

"But we're brothers!" he said, as he tipped the bottle and poured the bourbon, watching it flow. "My house is yours, and this *is* my house, though I had another here once."

He picked up the gun and put it in his robe pocket, then lifted the two glasses and came back to the couch. I could see myself in the way he walked, edged along the coffee table, then sat down.

"Yeah," I said. "But what about that?"

"The gun?" he said. "That's nothing. It's really only a toy. It could do some damage, though, if one isn't careful."

He was smiling across the table, and I doubted I'd ever smiled so much in such a short time. I saw a crazy version of my face looking at me but didn't want to name it that. Maybe he was only a little nervous, though he seemed relaxed enough. There was some plan here, and he'd organized it, and I knew he'd give me nothing right then, not until he was ready.

"Okay," I said, trying to gain some control over things. "So you live here?"

"*Only* here," he said. "We had a house in Avalon, but that's gone now. We've had many good years on this boat, Estelle and I. Travel, you know? But there's always money, and it has a way of running out. It's done that."

He smiled at me again.

"But things are looking up! Have you had problems? With money, I mean?"

It was a real question, odd that he should be asking such a thing, as if we'd just met in some bar or restaurant and he'd overstepped propriety.

"Don't you know?" I said.

"Well, no. I don't know everything."

"Well, no, then, I guess not."

Our voices echoed each other.

"That's never been something, of concern, I mean. The Navy took good care of me."

"A diver," he said. "That's something I know about, through your parents."

He was teasing me, but I refused to bite. I just sat there looking at him.

"But you're lucky," he said, finally. "About money."

Money, I thought, Mooney.

I saw the door opening in the bulkhead, then Estelle came through it. She was dressed in jeans and a dark cotton shirt, and she wore tennis shoes. She'd picked clothing that hid her body, and she'd gathered her hair up in a bun on the top of her head. I saw the brown wig hanging like some dead animal near her hip, gathered in her white fingers. She held a large manila envelope in her other hand. She acknowledged my stare with a faint smile. She'd put on lipstick, a light thin line, but no other makeup. Mooney had turned in his seat.

"Perfect," he said. "Come, sit here beside me."

He took the photograph out of the folder and placed it on the glass coffee table facing me.

"This is it," he said. "This is the one we want."

It was a picture of that necklace, the one Jen and I had given the most attention to. It rested on some dark fabric, and no light glinted off the disks and stones. Each metal blossom was distinct, as were the links that joined them and the intricate clasp.

"And we'll need your daughter too," he said. "Jennifer, isn't it? Just for a little insurance."

He was not smiling this time when I looked up from the photograph to his face.

"No," I said. "That isn't possible."

"Well, it is," he said. "Actually. Estelle will be getting her. It's not going to be a problem."

I saw myself recognize motion as his face grew alert, some familiar tightening at the edges of his eyes, and knew I was rising up from the cushion. Estelle was rising too, her hands pushing out in the air in front of her chest. Mooney reached into the pocket of his robe, but he didn't bring the gun out. He knew my judgment of the situation before I did. There wasn't any chance. He could fire before I even reached my feet, and I sank down again as he spoke.

"Now, now," he said. "Really. There's absolutely nothing to worry about."

He was lying through his teeth, and he saw I knew this and was waiting. He smiled again, letting me know that.

"Okay," he said, when we'd all settled down. Then he turned to Estelle, his hand still holding the gun in his robe pocket. He spoke to her, but his eyes were on my face, his words attempting reassurance.

"Be gentle," he said, "when you wake her. No urgency. Just that her father has learned something important and needs her help. Tell her you'll be going out to a boat in the harbor. It's about Susan Rennert, should she ask, but you don't know anything more. You're just a messenger. And tell her her father mentioned someone named Tod. That should do it."

Estelle had risen from the couch and was heading for the bulk-head door, and I started to speak, but Mooney was finished with her and now spoke to me.

"Never mind that," he said. "We'll be getting to that soon enough."

25.

"Do you believe in coincidence?"

We were sitting in lounge chairs on the deck, and his voice came to me out of the half darkness. It was my voice, at least the same pitch and inflection, the way I'd heard it speaking from a tape recorder from time to time. I'd lost his face to shadow, though, and that was something; I didn't have to confront the constant shock of it, and I could focus on the content of his words.

He'd left me in that opulent living room, locking both doors with a key before he went, and before I could figure any attempt at getting out, he was back again, dressed in shorts and a dark blue cotton shirt, two light blankets over his arm. He had me carry the bourbon and glasses and the small ice chest and had followed me up the ladder we'd come down earlier. Now our drinks rested on a low table between us and he'd covered himself with one of the blankets against the light breeze.

We were sitting in starlight, and I could see it sparkling on the dark deck beyond my feet and on the tip of his elevated tennis shoe, where he'd crossed his legs at the ankles. We sat beside each other, facing slightly inward, and I could hear him breathing between sips of his drink. Jen rose in my mind, a frustrated rage that I could do nothing with. Rage at myself as well as at Mooney. That it was I, her father, who had carried her into this thing. I wanted to strike out at myself in his body and had to grip the metal chair arms to keep from rising. I knew there was nothing I could do. Mooney was talking, and the image of Jen drifted away into the night.

"Well, *I* don't believe in them," he said. "But that's where it all started. I mean, finding you. I knew *about* you, of course. I'd found that out years ago, but not where you might be or what you were doing. Then Estelle went to the theater. Something she's quite interested in, actually. Acting, I mean. Do you know the rest?"

"Tell me," I said, hearing my voice as if he were still speaking. I could see the ridge of his nose, a hollow where his eye was.

"Well, it's simple. Estelle had one of her mother's necklaces on, and *your* mother, she was wearing one very much like it. They met and talked about that, and your mother was quite interested. She was an actress, wasn't she, quite theatrical? Self-involved? Estelle said that. We were interested in selling the necklaces. We had quite a number of them, and we'd had a few appraised. We'd had to be careful about that. I mean, bringing so many in for appraisal. And we of course missed the important one. I sent Estelle back with them, to your house, actually. Your father had given her their number. Your mother bought four of them, at a good price. Not too much, but we wanted to be rid of them at the time.

"Then things got social. They had tea and cookies, and your mother brought out pictures of you, as mothers will.

"You can imagine her shock. Estelle, I mean, when she saw my face in them."

"This was a long time ago," I said.

I lifted my glass and sipped at the tepid mix, just a hint of bourbon now. The glass shone in the starlight, and I felt the breeze in my hair. How social it all seems, I thought, just sitting out on the deck and drinking. The rail was no more than twenty feet away, and I thought I could make it over the side quickly enough. But Jen was in it now, and I knew I'd have to wait it out. I wondered how much the necklaces had cost. Was it my mother's thoughtless indulgence? They'd never had much money, but she'd always gotten what she wanted. A brief image of my father materialized on the starlit deck. He was sitting at his workbench in the garage, head in his hands, something about my mother and despair or longing, then he was gone.

"Well, yes," he said, "a while ago. And I never did pursue the matter. Of you, I mean. I might have, but Estelle and I were long gone then. We had some money, and it went a long way in Mexico. We even bought a little house there. Mostly, we were aboard this boat, though, traveling. The goodly TH E-STELLA-R. For many years, in fact. But now we're back again, and there's no more money, not just yet, at least."

"How much is the thing worth?" I said, thinking of that first entry on my father's list: *Look into blossom gradation and etching.*

"Eight hundred and fifty thousand. Of course, that's at discount. Our part of it, Estelle's and mine. God knows what the buyer will get. It *is* Estelle's after all, her mother's."

That wasn't true. Her mother was Pearl, but neither Mooney nor Estelle would know that. She'd held it close and in secret, yet another useless deception in those tortured lives. At least it was something I knew and they didn't know. I'd save it; maybe I could use it later.

"What about Susan?" I said.

"Well, she's dead, of course."

I felt that strange longing for her once again, even in the face of that absolute. I could never have her, and still I couldn't shake free of her. I thought it might be something in my genes, and in his too. I thought of that dream Jen and I had shared: Susan, deep in the water, then waking up to Jen and her bleeding. She'd dreamt I'd killed her, and yet hadn't. It was blood here too. Mooney had her sister, and I wondered if Estelle held the same power for him as Susan did for me.

"It was down in Mexico," he said. "Guadalajara, and just by acci- dent. We were in a bookstore, browsing. And there it was in a book, right out of royalty in nineteenth-century Poland. It was part of some loot or other, lost for a long time. I don't know how it drifted down to Estelle's mother. Her grandfather possibly? We'll never know.

"But we cruised back again, to here. Then we found out your parents were dead, that you were in the East. We were out of money anyway, so we stayed here."

"How long ago?" I said.

"That we came back? Why, just weeks. I had plans to come for you, a trip to Philadelphia to see you. Isn't that the place? I'd been looking into things, that house in El Monte and where you might be now. Then *you* came. I don't mean here, but in that tourist restaurant on Crescent. Estelle saw you there and saw your daughter wearing one of the necklaces. She even got a handle on that Tod boy. Just another coincidence. I guess I'd better start believing in them."

It was that, and yet it wasn't. I'd been searching too, had trailed my father through his list, looking for Susan Rennert. Then I'd found Blevins Street and Estelle through Pearl's story. Mooney was still talking, his head resting on the chair's back, and I thought he was looking into the stars. I looked there too. The casino lights had dimmed now, and the sky was brighter. I could see the Big Dipper, Orion, and the shimmering flood of the Milky Way. I thought I saw the North Star but wasn't sure of it. There were no clouds, but occasional wisps of fog drifted at the gunwales. I pulled the thin blanket up, covering myself to the shoulders, just as Mooney had done. We were two still and identical figures there, like aging twins on the deck of a fancy cruise ship. And as the boat rocked in the gentle swells, I imagined we were moving, setting off down the coast in this pacific ocean for parts unknown. I seemed to have the meaning in his words a moment before he spoke them, as if it were I who was doing the talking, telling a story I already knew.

We were in a town on the far West Side of Chicago, next to a wealthier town from which his mother would return in a gray uniform after cleaning the toilets and carpets of the rich. His father would be waiting, jobless then, and drinking, and Mooney and the three children would have ordered the house and set the table, then dressed themselves properly for the evening meal.

"He was not really my father, nor Carolyn my mother." It had been the first foster home, and they'd taken him in for money, the older children resentful from the beginning. Before that, it was a place with many children eating in rows at a metal table, being awakened in the night for a look or something he had said in the day, but he was only six by the time he left there, and he didn't remember it well.

Then he was eight, and there had been trouble, he'd been beaten for talking, and he was lifted out and placed in a home in the city proper, then moved to other homes, until he had no life in any of them but was traveling with other children his age, a gang of them who owned certain blocks in the city. High school for a while, then living alone in a room in Cicero, near the freight house where he worked.

Then he'd quit that place and headed south, down into Texas, where he met a Mexican woman who was twelve years older than he was and learned some Spanish and a way to make money, bringing people up and across the border. Then after a while he was out of there too and into Oregon, then back south to a town in Utah, and by the age of twenty-one he'd settled himself near Los Angeles, where he met Estelle. I'd been traveling also, but in the bosom of mother Navy, in a life devoid of care.

"It was Estelle who sent me to find my parents. I'd settled only because of her, and I was listening. She had a job in a good clothing store, and commissions, and I didn't need to scuffle for money. Her life had been at loose ends too, but she thought I needed a source."

And so he'd gone back to Chicago, had found a way to open the file, and had found us together in it. "But that was only the first shock. I found her then and got the other."

She'd been sixteen when we were born, and I imagined us floating in her womb, sharing some intricate piping of the kind my father might have devised to join us under our fragile ribs.

"She was thirty-eight years old and small and almost like a child herself, and though I was only twenty-two, I'd been around, and it felt as if we were the same age, like brother and sister. She had long black hair, a dark woman married to a Swede. I saw us in her eyes, though a different color, and he'd been fair about it all, had left the room so we could be alone. Our father had been a little older, son of a grocer she had worked for. I tried to find him too, but without luck. She didn't know a thing about us after our birth. The shame of that, made worse because of our joining. Her parents had simply put us away somewhere. Those were her words for it."

"Is she still alive?" I said, hearing my voice as an echo of his own, as if he'd asked himself the question.

"I suppose so. I don't know. Seeing her just put it all behind me, except for you, and that was a new thing entirely. We didn't keep in touch. There was no information about you, just some feeling that I wasn't alone in where I went and what I did. A parallel life? Just something going on somewhere, as I was going on. I can't explain it, really. I had no thought to find you, as I had her. That didn't seem to matter."

I'd found a star as beacon for our slow rocking, and I let my gaze slide over it. Wisps of fog would intervene from time to time. Then the sky would clear again, my star a bluish gem and dimensional, a little closer than those others in its matrix.

Mooney was still talking, of Estelle now, and the things she'd done for him. Her magic, I supposed. I was feeling that common hollowness in hearing of a love one doesn't share. Yet hearing it was undoing that strange passion I'd felt for her sister. It had been a borrowed passion somehow, one delivered up to me from brotherhood. I didn't think I'd ever had that feeling of a second life as he had spoken of it, but then I'd not known of his existence. Still, I'd

324   TOBY OLSON

come under his influence, through Susan. I saw myself in that dream again, masturbating in the bathroom, looking at her picture. Then I thought of Jen, and for a moment I was frantic and had to grip the metal arms to steady myself.

I'd drifted away from his talking, and I had a strange desire for return, as if there was some safety there for both of us, but I couldn't find the way. I was wondering about my parents, what they might have known of this. Had they known anything about Mooney? My scarring had been my "birth emblem," and my mother had made a romance of it. That I was struggling out in anticipation, knowing she was waiting. She'd have a little song then, something about mothers and children.

"Susan," Mooney said, bringing us back to the telling, "she was the favored daughter, Estelle the adopted sister. Really, they just drove her out. And that father of hers, another son of a bitch, like fathers I had known. We had a lot of things in common."

But the story. It's not Pearl's, and he surely had it wrong. Yet I knew that if Susan Rennert were here, she'd tell yet a different one, so I settled in again to listen.

Once Mooney had gone east and found our mother, then had returned with a certain peace for himself, it was Estelle who had gotten restless, feeling there were things undone for her as well. She'd left home with a pure hatred for her mother, little feeling at all for her aunt Pearl, but time had softened things, and she was speaking of the few good times she could remember. Her mother's faults were developing into matters of character. Just a strong and certain woman who'd had a hard life and was doing the best she could, not much time for children. So she'd called her, just picked up the phone one day.

And her mother had seemed glad to hear from her, though her voice sounded reserved and a little cold. She didn't say much or volunteer anything, but she agreed to a meeting, that they might spend some time together. Her mother had said there were a few things to talk about. She would tell Estelle when she saw her. Estelle and Mooney were living on Catalina at the time, but not on the boat. They had a small house in town, and the boat was being used for fishing trips, an enterprise that was failing because of fuel costs and maintenance.

"We're talking well over fifteen years ago, but this is a large craft, really inefficient for day trips, even longer ones. I'd have to fill it with people, and there weren't that many around then. Estelle worked in a gift shop, but the wages were low, and we were just getting by."

They met her at Cabrillo Mole, where the boat from Long Beach docked. The plan had been that she'd stay the night, maybe even a few days, but she carried only a small bag. She was older, of course, but her face held that same intractable and dogmatic sureness, familiar after all those years, and Estelle was like an awkward child when she introduced Mooney. Her mother just looked at him, not even nodding, then looked over at the casino and at the town of Avalon, as if they were just as she had expected they would be, places only for pleasure, something she disapproved of. If she thought they'd be staying at the house, she showed nothing at all when Estelle said they had a boat, it was a surprise, and they'd be spending their time there and would maybe even cruise out to sea. If she wanted to do that. Whatever she wanted. They could do anything at all. But her mother just looked into her face, seemed quite clear about what she saw there, as if nothing had changed between them, and Estelle had to turn away.

They went out in the dinghy, all three of them crowded into it, and her mother sat with her hands in her lap, as if in some chair at home. Climbing the ladder at the gunwale took some time, and she accepted Mooney's hand without comment, as if it were her due.

It was over dinner that she began talking, speaking of the people living on Blevins Street, mostly judging them, what they had done with their gardens, what had happened to children who had

TOBY OLSON

matured, then returned with satisfactory jobs, wives and husbands, children of their own.

It was a beautiful, moonlit night, and they ate out on the deck at a table covered with a white cloth. Mooney had strung lights in the riggings and had bought good wine, though Estelle's mother didn't touch it. She said nothing at all about Pearl or Susan, nor did she speak of Estelle herself, things in the past. Yet everything she said was an accusation, what others had done that had not been done by Estelle.

"It was a common enough thing, I guess. The disapproving mother. But for Estelle it was more than that, though I didn't know it until it was too late. The depth of her hate, and her rage at how she'd deceived herself, thinking the hate might have left her, that things could be as they had never been. Then her mother had reassured her in her hate, and while she was doing that, Estelle slowly tore her napkin into shreds."

She'd actually brought the papers with her, and she'd taken them from her cheap purse and smoothed them out on the table where her plate had been. She'd pushed it aside, the cold poached salmon Estelle had taken such care with. She'd continued her talking and had moved from considerations of Blevins Street to the Polish American veteran's fund, then to the monument they planned, a plaque to the war dead and a statue of soldiers rising above it. Everything, she said, would go to that. She was old now, she said, though she was only sixty-two, and she tapped the papers with the fountain pen she'd dug out of her purse. Everything. She'd filled the papers out, and all that remained was the signing. And right there, she signed them, looking at Estelle before she found the right line, signed, then looked at her again. Everything.

"There was no idea that there was much, of course. That wasn't the point. Just that she'd come here to do that, had made a plan for it. And that she stayed afterward. She excused herself, just as if she were at home, and went down to the cabin Estelle had prepared for her. We were left sitting there, alone with our dessert and the candles guttering. Later, I'd heard Estelle talking, her voice muffled but rising."

He'd reached over in the bed for her, but she wasn't there, and he'd come awake recognizing that she was speaking from her mother's cabin down the passageway. He'd not heard her mother's voice, but then had heard Estelle's grow into screaming and a kind of thud and a scuffling and another voice calling out, almost ethereal. He'd slid from the bed and grabbed his robe and had stumbled down the passageway to the open door.

He saw Estelle at the foot of the bed, her hands in fists at her sides, leaning over at the waist and screaming "You are not my mother!"

Then he'd stepped through the doorway and had seen her. She was on her back, the covers thrown to the side, as if she were rising. And she *was* rising, at least her legs were bouncing on the sheet and her chest was heaving as she struggled to rise. But she couldn't seem to take her hands away in order to push up. She was pulling at the handle, but the knife wouldn't come out. Blood was seeping through her nightgown, and though she looked down at her hands and at the knife in her stomach and at the blood, she looked up also as she yanked at the handle. She was looking at Estelle. There was no surprise in her face at all, nor disappointment, just a pure effort and resolve that she would soon remove the knife and then get up, and when she did, Estelle would get a lesson in how to behave properly.

They'd disposed of her body on the way to Long Beach, a sea burial without ritual. Mooney had taken care of it, wrapping her in the bedding, then tying her tight with rope and the anchor chain, the anchor itself tied over her chest and stomach.

"She really wasn't my mother," Estelle had said afterward. She'd been hysterical, shaking and talking rapidly for the first hour, rehearsing the memories of the ways her mother had put her aside from the very beginning. "I'd been left with Pearl, as if *she* could be a mother. It was Susan who was the only daughter."

Then she'd quieted down after a while and had come to an insistence that was very much like her mother's: now they would go and get the things that were owed to her.

They'd docked the boat in Long Beach, then taken a taxi to the truck rental place. Estelle had known the way. Over the years, she'd gone back to Blevins Street, had driven by the house. She'd never really gotten free of it. They'd taken her mother's keys, and Mooney had burned the purse and her suitcase and those few pieces of clothing on deck on the way over. He'd made a low and smoldering fire, just a few wisps of acrid smoke rolling out behind them. It was early afternoon when they reached the house, Pearl had been away, at work, they thought, and once they were inside and Mooney had seen what was there, they'd taken their time.

"The jewelry and silver, and there were paintings and small pieces of furniture. And we found cash and old documents. There were books and letters with official seals, signed photographs, coins, a dozen tablecloths sewn with gold thread, four ivory cameos, a music box with a dancer on the lid. We filled the truck, and when we got back to Long Beach, I loaded it, and we ferried it all here. We took most of it below, all but a few pieces of furniture, which we lashed to the deck. Back there," he said, "behind the wheelhouse."

And it struck me that Cora hadn't told Pearl of Estelle's call, though they were living in the same house, just the two of them and without daughters. She was not the mother. Her sister was, and yet she seemed to have robbed her of her child without thought, even that second time, though with a dark enough motive to suggest clear reason.

His gesture as he nodded toward the stern was only a fleeting ripple in the light blanket. I'd turned my head on the chair back and was watching him, that profile that was identical to mine but that was ceasing to surprise me. Each time I'd give up pieces of my face to him, then watch them re-form into an expression that was not mine, though very like it, but from that past of his, a different way of seeing things or of being in things. He must have felt me watching him, for he turned his head too, and then we were looking into each other's eyes in moonlight, both searching for something and not finding it. It was too dark for me to see his pupils, and he blinked and squinted slightly, working to get mine. Then he gave up and turned his head into profile again. He wasn't finished yet, and I looked back up into the stars and waited for the rest of the story, the part I'd come there to get.

It was close to a year later that Susan Rennert found them. "I don't know how," Mooney said. But she'd been looking in that year, now that their mother was dead and might not stand between them, and had called the house from a pay phone on Crescent Avenue. The listing was in Mooney's name, not Estelle's, so she must have asked around once she'd reached Avalon. He'd been out with a fishing party and had found the two of them sitting in the living room, their hands in their laps and leaning toward each other, talking like sisters when he came back in the early evening.

At lot had happened in that year. They'd sorted Cora's belongings. Mooney had developed contacts, and they'd been disposing of things.

"It was the paintings, mostly, some woodblocks and lithographs. They brought a lot, all from the same buyer. He was someone I'd found through people in a fishing party. Just a name, and I'd managed to get it without suspicion."

But even the furniture, silver, and linens had been worth something. And the music box had been a gem. They'd gotten fifty-thousand for that.

And as things had gone and money had replaced them, Estelle had brightened up. It was as if she were replacing her past and her mother, dross into gold, and each dollar was another brick in the growing edifice of justification she was building for herself. "She was not my mother," she'd say, "but she did own me." And now things were reaching a kind of balance that seemed ethical: a reward

TOBY OLSON

for toil in a wasted life, as if they had entered the heaven Cora had often spoken of. And when Susan came, Estelle was glowing with the perfect understanding of an evangelist, and Mooney had thought this too would be a setting right, lost sisters coming together again at the end of travail.

"But there were your parents too in that year. Estelle got restless, island fever, and she went off to the theater wearing one of her mother's necklaces. There was so much coming in then that we didn't think to sell them. I'd gotten appraisals of some of them, and they were worth some money, but Estelle was wearing them, something her mother had never done, and we just put them aside for later."

Until my mother had seen that one on her at the theater, and had wanted it. Her collection. And then Estelle had gone to my parents' house for dinner, and my mother had taken those pictures out and shown them to her, and Mooney had learned about me. He'd sent her back, then, with some other necklaces, and for information. "There were six of them, and your mother bought them, and I found out where you were, the Navy, somewhere in Cuba then, I think. It might have been a time to search you out, send a letter at least, though that felt funny and I'd have rather found you in person, faced you as we've done now. But then Susan came only a while later, and we needed a different plan."

She'd spent the night in their house in Avalon, the two of them staying up past three A.M. talking. And in the morning, when Mooney had come to the table, they were still talking, and with a euphoric intensity he didn't think could last. They were making plans for themselves. They'd contact Pearl, go back to Blevins Street to see her. Susan would leave her job, move out to Catalina to be near Estelle. And Estelle talked as if it could all be true, speaking quite honestly, as if there were nothing dark between them, no secret at all that needed to come out. Not even the practicality of Mooney stood between them. They'd be two loving sisters again, though they had never been that, both constructing a fiction of the past. And it seemed it could be the actual and true past, so long as their talking assumed it. They'd affirm it by being close to one another in the present.

And they'd gone shopping the next day in Avalon, had bought dresses of identical cut but in different colors. They'd bought sun hats and scarves, underwear and the same shoes, and they had taken lunch at a place overlooking the harbor, still talking. They'd left the preparations to Mooney, steak and wine, a fancy salad and a light lemon tart for desert. They'd be dining and sleeping aboard TH E-STELLA-R that night. "What a perfect name!" Susan had said. "Can we both be stellar?" They'd worn their new dresses, Susan's a light yellow, Estelle's blue, and Susan had carried a small purse.

It was a clear evening, and the sea was calm, so Mooney took the boat out of the harbor and steamed south and toward the mainland, heading below the offshore oil rigs, then finding a place of anchorage about a mile off Laguna Beach. The sky was cloudless, a breeze had blown the smog away, then left, and as they ate and drank, the boat circled slowly at anchor, and they saw the distant lights on the mainland as they blinked on, replacing the last glow of daylight as the sun went down behind Catalina, out of sight, behind them.

Estelle and Susan were still talking, and they'd talked enough now that they'd exhausted both the future and those few bright moments they'd managed to find, soften, and twist into pleasant memories from their past together. They were edging now into other things, their mother and Pearl, even their father and the way he'd been with them, and they were bringing back meaner moments, the way they'd had to sit silent at dinner, that intractable coldness when they'd tried to speak to their mother of adolescent things, blood and romance.

It was Susan who was finally able to speak out and name their feelings, though she whispered the words, as if her mother might be there, below deck and listening. She still wore the sun hat she'd bought in Avalon, though it was growing dark now and she had no

TOBY OLSON

need of it. Her words leaked out from under the brim, almost too softly to be heard.

"She was a cruel and inhuman woman, and there were many times I wished her dead."

Estelle listened intently, as if she knew the words were coming, or at least hoped for them. And when they did come, she exhaled, breathing the last remnant of her mother out of her lungs. She held her fork up, the lemon tart dripping between the tines in the candlelight, and she smiled at Susan once the words were out in the air between them. Then she lowered her fork, pushed her chair back from the table, and stood. "I'll be right back," she said. "I have something to show you." Then she headed for the low housing, stepped quickly down the ladder and out of sight.

"I didn't know a thing. How could I? Susan just sat there, her eyes following Estelle, then looking over at me, curious, once she'd disappeared. We heard her knocking into things below us, opening drawers, and we just sat there waiting. Then she returned."

The sheet came up the ladder ahead of her, and they could see the solid dark stain and the lighter bloody redness of the star spire smears radiating from its center as it licked the edges of the housing, then billowed out and opened in the night air. Estelle held it up at the fitted corners like a flag, her smiling face coming around its edge as she reached the deck. She raised it, stepping toward them, then waved it until it drifted out over the table like an awning, its corners snapping above the plates and silverware, shaking the candle flames.

Susan pushed her chair back and stood, her little purse clutched in her hand, and Estelle came around the table behind Mooney, who lost sight of her for a moment. Then she was there again, moving toward Susan, the sheet now pulled to her body and gathered against her chest and stomach.

He couldn't see Estelle's face, but he could see Susan's, a look of wonder in her eyes, her mouth open. She didn't understand, not yet, but she was beginning to get something, just a glimmer of what this had to do with her.

Estelle approached Susan. Mooney himself was rising, knowing he had to stop her, stop the words, at least, but they were already spoken by the time he got to her. She handed the sheet over to Susan, as if it were some keepsake, then had fallen back against Mooney's chest as he reached out to her shoulders and pulled her.

"I killed her," Estelle said, her voice calm and measured, "for both of us."

It might have ended there, been some crazy joke, even, but Mooney could see the recognition in Susan's eyes. He started to speak, to undo it all, but there must have been something in his eyes too.

Susan looked at him, then back to Estelle. She held the bloody sheet now in her fingertips, up at her shoulder, then looked down to where it trailed on the deck. Then, in the candlelight, he saw her glance to the rail and knew that he had looked there too and that he'd be heading there to stop her. He'd have to push Estelle away first, but even as Susan was moving, Estelle's gravity was too much for him. She'd fallen back from that perfect moment, exhausted by her spoken revelation, and she was like a lodestone on his chest, her fingers hitting his eyes and forehead as she reached up over her head to right herself, then rolled away from him and staggered toward her chair.

Susan had reached the gunwale and was climbing it. Her purse hung down from her wrist on its metal chain, and the sheet fluttered against the brass railing and her thin dress, which also fluttered, its yellow fabric mixing with the congealed red. Her hat had shaken loose and lifted, and as her hair rolled to her shoulders and bounced, the hat floated over the side and down to the dark sea like a tossed dinner plate. Then she was standing on the gunwale, the rail against her shins, and was looking down and back at them.

Mooney was reaching out for her. "I might even have touched the heel of her shoe." But she had risen above the rail, the bloody

TOBY OLSON

sheet draped at her shoulder now, gripped tight at her breast and spreading out over her thighs and calves as she dove. Her right arm was a stiff and extended wedge for her entrance, the small purse dangling from her wrist. She entered night's darkness before reaching the sea, and then she was lost to them completely.

"I had lights, and there were stars. The sea was down, and I steamed in circles for a while, but it was no good. She just disappeared there, where she'd entered darkness beyond the boat's hull. I gave it a full hour. Estelle sat at the table. She didn't weep or say anything, and after I'd given it up, I put her to bed before heading back to Avalon. She was sleeping so deeply when we reached our mooring that I just crawled in beside her. We spent that night on the boat, and in the morning we prepared for leaving."

I could see her striking out for the lights at Laguna Beach. She had the problem of the sheet and purse, but the tide was coming up and moving in, and that would be a help to her, as would the calm sea and stars. She may have gripped the purse in her hand, a thoughtless thing, and tied the sheet around her neck and let it trail. She'd need both arms for stroking. Would the sheet be evidence? I couldn't think that. It was her life, after all. It would have been something else, her mother's blood against her back, the only thing she had now to count on. Maybe her mother's will, that it could in some way soak into her and help her in that impossible journey.

I wondered if she might have made it had she let the sheet go. I'd never know, and I imagined it was nothing she'd considered, either, not even as her lungs were filling and she was sinking, only to rise up again near morning, carried in to shore on the last of the swelling tide, just as night-lights from those fine hotels along the beach were blinking off.

"The bed," I asked, softly, "Is it a four-footer?"

"What?" Mooney said, his question hollow and perfunctory. He was too much in the ending of his story to make sense of it.

I heard his chair creak and looked down from the stars again to see him pulling the blanket to the side and rising. I heard a clunk at the hull. He was at the rail then, where the ladder was, and looking over, and I saw a white hand at the gunwale and watched as Mooney reached out for it. I knew it was Estelle, though she was changed dramatically by the dark wig, something my mother might have worn for acting. Still, her chin was lifted, her face bright in the starlight at the rail, and she looked remarkably like those pictures of Susan Rennert. Mooney turned slightly, holding her hand as she stepped down to the deck, and for a moment it was me there, somewhere in the country with Susan, helping her over a stile in our romance.

Then I heard the ladder knock against the hull, and in a moment Jen was there, looking down and watching her step as Mooney helped her over. She thought it was me, and only when she glanced up and saw me rising from the chair did she turn and see his face.

"This means you're my uncle," Jen said.

Mooney looked hard at her for a moment, then lifted his hands slightly, and laughed.

"That's right! That's right!"

"So you shouldn't do this."

It was Estelle who was laughing then, and when I looked over at her, I saw that everything I'd heard had been behind her but was coming back a little now, in this recollecting circumstance. It had been close to fifteen years, after all, and they'd been in Mexico, another world entirely, absent of any reminders, but for the money, which had been translated into their new and different life, though now it was gone. There was a promise of more, but it was untranslated: fact of her mother's jewelry, a reminder. And I had Pearl, something that could twist it all, when the time was right. It was the first time I'd heard Estelle's voice, and the sound of it was foreign to my imaginings of Susan Rennert. There had been no voice there at all, only the look of her, mute and without character. Her laugh came close to hysteria, and I wondered which of the two I should worry about more.

"I'm *serious*," Jen said, looking across the couch toward Mooney.

She was dressed seriously, jeans and a sweatshirt, and her hair was tied back with a piece of ribbon. The sleep was still at the corners of her eyes, but she was fully awake and energized. She'd taken it all in quickly, after just a little shock, and I found myself proud of her, though I knew there was no place for such parental romance here. She could be my daughter, though, and my partner. We'd worked together, and we were a good team. Guilt bit at my throat as I thought of Carol, back there in Racine. I could see Jen's vulnerability in her almost prim posture, hear it in that stern tone she'd used on Mooney. Both were a mimic of adult disapproval, the way of an ingenue on a stage. My mother might have stamped her foot in making the point, "I'm *serious*," turning the scene slightly comic, stealing it from the older actor standing beside her.

Estelle's head jerked to the side slightly as Jen spoke, and she stopped laughing. She'd taken the wig off and had even brushed her hair out while we were sitting there, as if it were the only natural thing to do and we were that familiar.

She sat beside Mooney on the couch across from us, back in that opulent living room below deck. She'd gone to the bar to make drinks when we'd entered, but Mooney had stopped her. There would be no drinks this time, or small talk. The photograph was on the table between us, and Jen had recognized the necklace immediately and had looked at me, blinking.

"If you think . . ." but Mooney interrupted me, his voice rising above my words.

"Look," he said, "we're brothers. It's only the necklace. That's all. We get that, and we're gone. But she'll have to stay here." He looked at Jen, who was still staring at him, and corrected himself.

"You'll have to stay here. Just for a few hours."

His voice had turned gentle, like that of an uncle, and he'd leaned across the table and touched Jen on the knee. I couldn't tell if he was faking his concern, but I didn't think so. It was that voice of mine again, the one I'd heard on deck, emerging purely from his own at times while he was telling his stories. I thought for a moment that it could all be finished now, he could be a brother and an uncle, that we could all settle in and talk about our separate lives together.

I looked over at Estelle. Her face was a mask, and she was gazing above our heads, clearly somewhere else. Then I looked at Jen. She'd pressed her knees together at his touch and was gazing intently into his face, looking for me. I wasn't there, and it was clear she wasn't buying any of it.

"We've been through the place."

He was looking at me again.

"The Zane Grey, I mean. And we know it isn't there. We're betting it's back at Laguna, where you were staying. Maybe even El Monte."

"How do you know that?" I said.

"Laguna? I checked with your diving party. That was easy. And why else would you be out here in California? You have the one necklace, after all."

He was guessing. He knew nothing about Jen or our recent meeting. He'd asked nothing about my life once he'd finished his own story. He thought he knew enough, that mine had been better than his. I'd had parents, at least. He knew nothing about my empty wandering, those lost years in the Navy, how much of the feel of that I'd heard in his telling. But then, I'd not known of it, either, not until Jen had come to me and I'd looked back to take stock.

But he was right about the necklace, and his look told me he better be right, for our sakes. It was a look I'd seen before, cutting through the moments of our strange and growing relationship, erasing them completely, but only for a moment. It said none of

TOBY OLSON

this, even our joining in the womb together, meant anything. They'd gone a long way, he and Estelle had, and they were on the other side of any family relationships that could censure them. He'd kill me in a moment, Jen too, and only then would he figure the consequences, just as he had with Cora and Susan Rennert.

I wondered just what it might be like to fight with him, to touch his body in some struggle for whatever weapon he threatened us with, but it was a self-indulgent wondering, weirdly brotherly. At any moment, I thought, he could come apart, or Estelle might, and then Jen might come apart. I had nothing but our twisted history to work with, and once I was gone, Jen would have little of that, only that I was her father, he her uncle, issues she might raise, but in the face of this look of his, they would count for little. Just the necklace, then, only that as a lever, until he had it and it wasn't that.

"Okay," I said. "What is it, then?"

Jen's hands were in her lap, and she stared over at me, what I took as a look of disapproval on her face that I had given in so easily. Then I saw it wasn't disapproval, but something else. Her pupils dilated slightly, telling me something. That I should hang on? She had control of herself now, no longer the ingenue, just sweet sixteen and with a secret she was centered in.

"It's this," Mooney said, touching the edge of the photograph. "It's three-thirty now. You'll catch the seven o'clock boat to Long Beach. It's an hour from there to Laguna. Is that where it is?"

"No," I said. "El Monte," feeling Jen's look as I lied to him.

"Okay. That's another few. It'll be rush hour going there. Let's say you catch the six o'clock to get back here, in by seven. You have a golf cart?"

"Yes," I said.

"You'll have a pass, and a map too. We'll lay here for the day. Then we'll anchor in the inlet that I've marked. There's a road in. You'll come down to the beach. We'll bring her into shore in the dinghy. You can wade out, and we'll settle it there."

"Why not here?" I said.

"Just in case," Mooney answered, "and we'll be leaving from there, anyway. And one other thing." He looked over at Jen and grinned broadly, then his brow darkened. "I'm serious too. Don't fuck it up."

They led me up to the deck. Jen insisted that she come along, and before I stepped down over the prow, she moved against me and hugged me. Mooney and Estelle stood back a little, giving us a moment.

"It's all right," I said, my mouth at her ear.

"I know," she said. "I'll be all right."

Then she said the one word, quickly and in a whisper, then pushed away from me. Estelle moved up beside her but didn't touch her, and all three, like a family, watched me as I climbed down the mooring rope to where I'd tied *The Pelican*.

26.

The water at my prow was a dark soup as I paddled in. Cloud cover had drifted out from the California coast to hide the stars, and I wondered if there was smog in it. They were thick clouds, and they reminded me of that smoky blanketing at Blevins Street.

It was four-thirty and still dark when I reached the harbor, and after I'd pulled *The Pelican* back up to shore, I climbed the low seawall, then stepped the few feet to Crescent Avenue. All the stores and bars showed vacant windows to the damp street, and I was alone as I walked quickly toward Metropole and the golf cart. It was the only vehicle parked at the curb, and once I'd wiped the sheen of water from the vinyl seat, I backed it out, its motor clattering in the pre-dawn silence. At one turning, I could see down over the dark town and the harbor. The casino lights were off now, and the building was only a faint hulk at the point, and though I looked out to where I thought *TH E-STELLA-R* might be, I could see nothing beyond the first necklace of blinking stern lights near the shore.

Once inside my room, I went immediately to the adjoining door in the darkness, then stepped into Jen's room and threw on the wall switch. I could see the evidence of her quick leaving, covers thrown back, a nightshirt draped over the footboard. Her day's gear was piled on a chair and on the floor beside it. She'd brought her wet suit, mask, and snorkel back, but not her tanks and regulator. They'd be gathered with the others for tomorrow's trip beyond the harbor's mouth. Today's trip, I thought. I reached down into the pile of clothing, her swimsuit, pants, and shirt, and there it was, tucked against her hat. She'd said "sack," and it was just that—a heavy canvas bag with strap and drawstrings she used for a purse.

It was down near the bottom, under a hankie, wallet, and sunglasses, and wrapped up in a scarf. She'd forgotten it was there and had taken her sack with her on the diving outing, and when Mooney had searched the room while I was sleeping or away in Avalon, the necklace hadn't been there, though the other one was, a pile of linked disks still on the bedside table, where Jen had left it after that first night's dinner. There was a candy bar beside it.

I sat at the table in my own room near the terrace doors, looking at the phone. If only Sanchez would call, then we could make a plan, could take them in the harbor or while they were out on the sea. He'd know a way to do it, to get them quickly enough, before Jen was injured. Or at least I trusted he would. I opened the terrace doors, and I could see the thick cloud cover, black billows against a lighter slate that promised dawn. It would stay dark for another hour or more, then the sun would start to show, coming up over Long Beach and Laguna. I had the map spread out on the table, the necklace resting in the open scarf beside it. I made a cup of instant coffee, and I sipped at it between bites of the candy bar.

The inlet was no more than a few miles up the coast from the harbor, the Bay of Avalon, and though the map was small, it was detailed, and I could trace a way for myself on main and secondary roads into the interior and down to the sea.

It was the only advantage I had, that I was not expected before eight o'clock that evening. I could get to the inlet before them, then find a place for myself. I could get into the water with my tanks, move out to the boat unseen that way. I had no idea what I might do then. But it was surely better than nothing.

Mooney was trusting me as if he knew me, and it suddenly came to me that the whole telling of his story had something to do with that—that I should come to understand him and learn what he was capable of and take him seriously. It had been an egocentric wish. He didn't know me at all, not even the facts of my relationship with Jen. And it was that egocentricity that was the problem, the way it edged him into uncertainty. I didn't know him, either, or what that self-involvement might push him to.

I got up and went to the phone then and called the police station in Laguna. The voice that answered was sharp and clear, in contrast to the sleepy fuzziness I heard in my own when I spoke.

"Not that I know of, but he could have checked in. There's some stuff here on the computer."

"I left a message. Earlier," I said. "Yesterday?"

"Yeah. I got that right here. About an Estelle Rennert, a boat with her name on it?"

"That's right," I said. "But there's more now."

I made it simple, just that I'd found her and a man named Mooney and that Jen was with them. Then I located the inlet. I had no name for it, only the distance up the coast from Avalon.

"Is this trouble?"

"No," I said, the word coming out of me quickly. "Sanchez will understand, if I can get him the message."

Jen's safety was a wish only, and I kept thinking of Estelle's wishes, that she might have a mother, then a sister, and what they had come to.

He said he'd be there for a while yet, then he'd pass the message on to the day shift.

I put on my swimming suit, a pair of khakis over it, and a thin sweatshirt. Then I went to Jen's room and searched out two thick rubber bands for my ankles. I only had tennis shoes, but they were good ones, and I had thick socks. My Catalina golf cap rested on the bed where I'd dropped it. *Cat l a* looked up at me from the crown, the last letters holding, and I lifted the cap and placed it on the table beside the other things I'd gathered there. I had the binoculars, Jen's underwater camera bag and three of her scarves, a T-shirt, a length of nylon rope, my abalone bar, and the two-edged sword knife I often carried when diving in unfamiliar waters.

I hoisted my tanks, flippers, and wet suit onto the bed and checked the air and regulator. I was as ready as I could think to be, but before leaving I went through Jen's room and my own to see if there was anything else I might take. I found only a small mirror in the bottom of Jen's sack, and I packed that along with the necklace in her camera bag. Then I emptied her sack out on the table and shoved the rest of the stuff into it, and when I was finished, I lugged everything down to the golf cart.

I could see into the first hint of dawn now. The clouds had stopped drifting and were hanging, black and ominous, over the island. Still, they had some color at their edges, just a hint of dark gray where the soon-to-be-rising sun lit them. And I could see the shadowy casino's shape more clearly out at the point as I chugged up the steep and narrow road that led into the hills of Avalon, high above the Zane Grey and the town and harbor.

The gate guarding the entrance to the interior was down. Dew drops had pearled, then flooded across the cart's plastic windshield, and I could see the dark, empty kiosk at roadside only dimly as I pulled onto the shoulder across from it. It would soon be day, and I'd have passed the entire night without sleep. I felt a slight aching in my wrists. From paddling *The Pelican*, I thought, knowing it was more than that. It was in my shoulders too and in my thighs, and I felt it through stiffness in my neck when I leaned out at the cart's door for a better view, seeing that I'd have to edge up the side hill at the gate's end to get around the checkpoint.

Once beyond the gate, I could see for a good distance ahead, but almost nothing where the morning fog was rolling thickly up the roadside to my right. I knew the sea was there, but I didn't know how far away it might be. The road ahead was dead straight, and the fog drifting across it was almost white. I could see shafts of

TOBY OLSON

sun in it, coming down at an angle from the direction of the coast and the mainland.

I clattered on straight for a good fifteen minutes, riding the slight crown of the road at its center. Jen kept entering my mind, all those dark fantasies rising up toward hysteria, and I had to punch at the wheel, bring my fist against my thigh, to push them away. Then the cart bounced from blacktop to dirt, the road narrowed, bending to the right and descending.

In the first minutes of descent, I was remembering my mother and father. The cart shuffled in rocks and loose soil as it had on that day so long ago, and I could hear my father laughing as brush caught in the axles and was ripped out by its roots. I could see the buffalo coming over the crest, and I imagined they were standing at the roadside now, off in the fog, watching me as I bounced slowly through ruts and washouts.

In a while I could see brush and low hills off at a distance, and after a sharp turn, I could see through the fog, up into the cloud cover above. The sun was behind the clouds, which were moving over the island swiftly, toward the open sea. I could see the place where they ended, the clear morning of a bright, unfiltered sun. Then I lost the sight line, just a v of sky between rocky crests, and the road dipped down again, then straightened, and I was at the bottom of a deep canyon, steep hills of brush and rock rising up on both sides, pine and honeysuckle, what I thought was ironwood, and lupine near the bases of stunted oaks. The hills rose close against the road, and after a few minutes I reached the place of its last turning. It was a tight turn, and I had to back up once, edge the cart into brush to get around. The rising hills were even steeper there, the only growth some scraggly bits of scrub peeking from between rocks. A dry streambed ran along the road on my left, and once I'd ascended slightly, I saw the sea, whitecaps off in the distance, then the edge of the sand beach.

I was still in the canyon. What I took to be the inlet was only a sliver of sky, sea, and sand, the rest cut off from view by the canyon walls. The beach kept growing deeper as I got closer. Then I reached the edge of the canyon's walls and pulled to a stop. The road ended in sand at the brink of the beach, and I could see the whole of the inlet and what would be facing me.

It was as if a massive and blocky u had been cut from the shoreline and I was parked at the center of its base. The beach spread out to either side at the canyon's mouth, then ended where high, rocky cliffs moved perpendicular to it toward the sea. I judged they extended for at least four hundred yards until they turned and became the shore that faced the open ocean. Out beyond the inlet, waves rolled in from the sea, a line of whitecaps gaining speed as they funneled toward the u's mouth. They rolled in for a hundred yards or more, then settled and pushed up only into a light spray where they broke against a tower of rocks rising as a safe harbor near the inlet's center. I couldn't see the base of that rocky rise from where I'd stopped the cart, so I climbed out and stepped into the sand, then trudged up to the beach crest. Then I saw the gentle wash of surf where the rocks formed a small island, the largest one, a massive thing, towering many feet into the air. It was covered with green lichen, slashes of white veins where it had fractured ages ago, bits of it falling away to form the corona of smaller boulders extending out for a good twenty yards at its base. There were shallow caves and pools among those rocks, and I knew that would be the best place for me. I'd just have to hide the cart, then lug my tanks down to the water. I could swim out from there.

When I turned to head back to the cart, I saw that the rise was even steeper where the canyon opened at the base of the u, the inlet's shoreline, where I'd parked. Sand washed against spills of rocks along the beach, and from there the wall on either side rose into cliffs and ended in jagged peaks. I had to crane my head back to see the tops.

On the right I saw nothing, but on the left, far down the beach, I noticed a deep declivity that started high up on the stone wall,

TOBY OLSON

irregular shadows in the rock face, a cut that ran from near the crest down almost to the beach. There were large, tortured boulders on the sand below it, rubble running from the cliff base down to the water and into it. A giant piece of the cliff had fallen away, perhaps centuries ago, and what was left seemed a kind of twisting vertical valley, a deep wound descending.

I reached the cart, then went around to the rear and loosened the straps that held my tanks in place. Out through the windshield, the inlet and the sea beyond were a fuzzy shimmer as sun washed over the rippling Plexiglas. There were only a few clouds in the sky now, and they were high up, white and fluffy, just sitting there. I though it must be close to six-thirty, maybe later.

I had the first tank almost free when I caught a flash near my wrist, then quickly looked up and through the windshield. It came again, a slice of light in the vague image, and I stepped to the cart's side so I could see the inlet clearly.

And there they were, the tip of Mooney's craft just coming around the point, a sheet of light where sun hit the side window of the wheelhouse. They were running parallel to the inlet's mouth. Then I saw them turning, the boat's prow pointing toward me now, that distinct white wash where it cut into the oncoming swells, riding them, as it entered the safe harbor.

I stepped back quickly to the cart's rear, pulled the loosened strap tight again, then jumped into the seat, jerked the cart into reverse, and hit the accelerator.

Then I was bouncing backward down the narrow canyon road, yanking the wheel as I slipped into ruts, working to keep myself from sliding over the edge, down into the dry riverbed just inches from my wheels.

Once I was facing back the way I'd come, I worked my way around the tight turning, then stopped in the middle of the canyon road and got the map out. My hands shook where I held the paper over the steering wheel. I'd been very close to getting caught, and I wondered what Mooney would have done had he seen me. Was it like him to do this, arrive so much earlier than he'd said? Had something happened, or had he simply been guarding against the possibility that I'd betray him? I had no way of knowing, no real hint at all of how his mind worked. I couldn't trust a single thing so long as Jen was with the two of them.

The beach was out now, and that cut in the cliff face seemed the only way. To come down from above, at a place where they surely wouldn't be looking, and to keep that island and its rocky tower between us as I descended. I could cross the beach unseen then, move along that spill of broken-away cliff. And once in the water, I'd be all right. The cut had looked at least possible, and I had that length of rope.

I had time too, plenty of it. It was really the only thing I had as an advantage—that and coming at them from underwater. They wouldn't be expecting me till evening. They too had been up all night and would surely soon be sleeping, at least one of them would. I hoped they'd let Jen sleep, give her a proper bed of her own, and not the one Cora had spent that interrupted night in so many years ago. I was sure she'd lie awake, waiting for me, and once again I felt myself slipping toward panic and had to force my mind back to what I needed to do.

I folded the map and tucked it under Jen's sack where it was belted tight on the passenger seat. Then I pressed the accelerator. The cart's clatter was loud in the waking morning, and birds lifted and scattered high on the canyon walls. The cart lurched forward, then steadied into a slow progress as I released the pedal a little, moving ahead at the pace of a quick walk. I climbed over rocks, slid through rain ruts as I made my way down the twisted canyon road, then rose slowly out of it, up into bright sun and a fresh breeze blowing in from the sea.

It took me an hour to find the right spur. I parked where it

TOBY OLSON

ended, in a rough circular area, tall grass and weeds obscuring its perimeter, and once the engine had ground down into silence, I could hear the distant pounding of the sea. It came from beyond the rocky escarpment that rose up near the cart's nose, nothing but empty blue sky beyond its crest, about fifty yards above.

The climb up the rise was an easy one, over steep rocks and larger boulders serving as stepping-stones. I saw little growth in the sandy interstices but used Jen's rubber bands anyway, gathering the cuffs of my khakis into knickers at my ankles against possible snares. I took the binoculars out of Jen's sack but left everything else in the cart. I needed to see where I was and where I had to go.

At the crest, the escarpment flattened into a sandy trail perhaps six feet across and tucked down between a jagged, chest-high wall at seaside and rounded boulders nearer land. The sand was powdery, and I saw its surface stir into thin veils as the breeze gusted for a moment. It's come all the way up here from the beach, I thought, been pounded into thinner grains, and I stepped across the path to the cliff's edge to see how far up I was.

I was standing high above the u-shaped inlet, near the angle where the beachside cliff ended, then became the southern wall defining the down-coast side. I could see the northern wall across from me, a good half mile away. I couldn't see the cut at the narrow canyon mouth where I'd parked the cart earlier, but I knew it was down below me to the left, and once I'd slipped into a space in the cliff wall and leaned out, I saw a sliver of sand, though most of the beach was out of sight, obscured by a slight humping of the face below. Still, an edge of that spill of boulders was visible, off to the left of where I stood. No more than a hundred yards of sandy path, and I'd be above it.

I looked out over the water. That single spire of rock rose up from the island corona at its base, and beyond its tip, in clear view, was Mooney's boat, drifting at anchor. Sun washed the dark hull, causing it to glisten, and a square sheet of brighter light flashed on and off, sun reflected in the wheelhouse window when the boat shifted.

There was no one on deck, or at least I could see no one. The wheelhouse blocked my view of the starboard side, and I was too far above to know for sure. I lifted the binoculars, and the boat jumped forward, even the fittings on the brass railings clear enough to distinguish. I could see the anchor lines, coils of rope on deck near the prow, and in the stern those dark covered objects. But the wheelhouse window facing me remained opaque. The entrance door in the squat forward housing was closed, and I was sure they were below decks.

I wondered what they might be doing. Would Jen be sleeping? Mooney would be smart about that. They'd need their rest, he and Estelle would, at least. He'd have locked Jen up. I felt the pressure of the binocular cups against my eyes. I was looking at the hull, trying to see through it, imagining.

I lowered the glasses after a while, then just stood there, looking out. The line of surf at the inlet's mouth seemed gentle and benign. It rolled in, then collapsed, and there was only a faint spray washing along the lower surfaces of the small rocky island. The boat turned slowly as it drifted to the ends of its tethers at both prow and stern anchor lines. I scanned the distance from the island to it. Not far, I thought. Then I traced a line from the island toward the shore below me. It seemed about the same, maybe a hundred and fifty yards or a little more. I'd just have to manage a way down, then cross that expanse of beach unseen. Once in the water with my tanks, I'd be invisible. At least until I reached one of the anchor lines. My hand shook where I touched the rock.

The tanks were aluminum alloy, each holding eighty cubic feet of air and weighing a good thirty-five pounds apiece. That was far more air than I'd need, too much of a burden, at any rate, and once I was back down the escarpment and at the cart's rear, I removed one of the tanks from the dual harness, disconnected its hose and rigged the regulator for single use. Then I unbelted the harness

TOBY OLSON

from the cart's carriage straps and rested it on the ground, securing the tank I left behind in its place.

The sun's heat had grown stronger. I could feel sweat beading on my back as I loaded my wet suit, Jen's sack, and the other gear into the vacant harness space where the tank had been. I pressed my flippers in, then the coil of rope, then stripped away my sweatshirt and folded it over at the top. Then I strapped the awkward bundle tightly in place. I'd left the T-shirt and my white Catalina cap on the cart's seat, and once I finished packing up, I put them on, tugging the cap's bill down against the sun.

The harness balance wasn't bad at all. The wet suit was heavy, and I had other weight too. Still, the tank was heavier, and I could feel it pulling me to the side, the strap tugging at my left shoulder as I struggled up the rocky rise again. I slipped once, almost fell, and had to grab for rock to the right of myself, my left knee glancing off a boulder's edge. There was sharp pain, then dampness there, and when I reached the crest and was standing on the sandy path, I leaned over under the weight on my back and saw the blood spots soaking through my khakis where they stuck to my knee. I pulled the fabric away and saw my pants leg fall and billow, become a knickers leg again, the cuff bagging over where I'd gathered the material at my ankle with Jen's rubber band. Then I rose slowly under my weight and started down the path.

It was when I reached a place where the rock crest to my right was lower that I looked out again. Here the crest was even more jagged, waist-high spires of pointed rock with open cuts between them.

I could see out to the rocky island, its near side in shadow, sun touching its jagged spires. There was a light blue at the feathery tips of spray, fans of the rainbow's spectrum I could see through, and beyond its peak, almost on a straight line from where I stood, the boat lay at anchor in full sunlight. It was the size of a child's toy, but a large one, as big as a child, and I lifted the binoculars from my chest and sighted over the island's central spire to where it drifted. I could see the curved trough of the wheelhouse roof, textures in the canvas that covered the roped-down objects in the stern, even the creases where the boards of its deck were joined. There was no one visible, and when it turned on its tethers, I thought I could see angles of blond wood through the wheelhouse window, even the wheel itself, but no movement.

I lowered the glasses and looked down along the cliff's face below my toes. The descent was sheer for the first thirty or more feet, just a vertical wall of smooth rock, and where that ended and the slight bulge began, there seemed no purchase, either, just a matrix of milky veins in slick stone, a few stunted trees growing impossibly in thin declivities. I couldn't see the continuation of the face immediately below the hump, but below there, at what seemed no more than a short distance from where the hump's edge ended in air, the deep wound began. It meandered down through the face. I could see rock and brush in it, and a little to the right, that place where it emptied onto the beach far below. Out on the beach itself, I saw that scatter of fallen rock the size of a collapsed building in some war-torn city. It had spilled out over the beach's hump, and the last few giant boulders were half sunken in surf.

The wound snaked back and forth within the face, and it was clearly a way down, even an easy one. I'd need that length of nylon rope. It was a half inch in diameter and strong, and I had at least a hundred feet of it. That would be enough. No problem, I said to myself, mouthing the words, then crossed the path and worked my way out of the tank harness and rested it on the sand.

I loosened the straps and slid the coil of rope free. The binoculars hung out in the air as I bent over, and I took them from around my neck and tucked them down into Jen's sack, then pulled the drawstrings tight again. Then I made sure the harness straps were tight, that they held everything securely in place. My Catalina cap

TOBY OLSON

hugged my forehead, and the gust of wind that washed over me when I rose stirred only the hair that stuck out at the cap's rim near my ears. Then I crossed to the cliff's edge.

I could see gulls rise up from rock at the inlet's north border. They were bright in the sun, then darker as they sank into shadow along the stony wall, heading down in search of fish. The wall's shadow extended in a strip of darkness, staining a few feet of inlet. Then the water was blue-green in sunlight. I looked out at Mooney's boat once again. It was still in sun, its deck empty of any human activity.

I had some trouble finding a place to secure the rope. The land-side boulders were too smooth, and what brush there was was shallow-rooted and pulled away easily when I tested it. I finally opted for the crest itself, finding a thin thrust of rock high up on the left of the v-shaped opening. I had to climb into the v to reach it, and once I'd tested for sharp edges that could cut the rope, I tied it a good foot below the thrust's point, using a square knot, then another over that. The rope was smooth and waxy to the touch, and I gave it a good many tugs, leaning back on the path, watching the knots pull tight.

I'd taken two of Jen's scarves from her sack, leaving the third tucked securely around the necklace in the camera bag, and I wrapped the silk one tightly around my left hand. Then I tied the other around that. It was made of cotton and had some texture, and when I gripped the rope, it held and didn't slip. Then I got the tank harness up from the ground and found a shelf in the landside boulders where I could rest it, turn, and slip my arms into the shoulder straps. The weight seemed even heavier than before, and I had to stoop slightly as I moved away from the wall, the tank pressing down at the base of my spine. It hurt, and I moved in a circle on the path, shifting my shoulders, testing mobility. The rope lay in loops in the sand, and I reached up to where it hung down from the rock and passed it through my legs, then lifted it to my chest in my scarf-covered hand. I held the descending length in my right hand at my head, then turned and shuffled backward into the v-cut, until I felt my heels at the brink. Then I stepped over and into air.

The rope gave immediately, stretching and thinning in my hands like a rubber band, and I fell down for a few feet, then bobbed, my toes and knees banging into the slick, vertical cliff face. I looked up and saw the knotted loop open and slide down toward me on the thrust of rock where I'd tied it, watched as the tail slipped into the knot, then tightened and held. My right palm burned as inches of rope slipped through, and I gripped the length I held against my chest.

I hung there for a moment, turning, my eyes sliding over green veins in the dark rock face. The veins were tiny ridges, like lengths of worms pushing up from wet earth, and I leaned back, letting the weight of my pack pull me, and pressed my toes into the rock until I found a purchase. Then the weight I carried was pushing me toward the cliff face, and I was able to walk down it, the rope slipping through my hands as I descended.

It was my feet that told me I'd reached the hump, a sudden pressure against my soles and heels, then a slight slipping as I shuffled among loose stone, then came to firmer rock. I was still hanging back in the air, the pack pulling at me, the rope a taut line extending up the face. There was wind now, quick gusts that pushed me, turned and lifted me a little, so that I had to spread my feet apart, at times only my toes touching as I skipped from side to side along the hump's curve, playing the rope through my fist, still descending, pushing off, letting the rope slip, then bending my knees when I touched the rock again. Jen's scarf was shredding, and when I looked down to see how many coils were left at my chest, I saw strips of scarf waving in the wind above my hand like flames.

I pushed off again. The pack's weight brought me back with force, but I was getting used to that, my toes touching, then my

TOBY OLSON

heels, ready for the next thrust. Then it ended. My toes didn't touch, and before I could straighten my legs, my knees hit the rock, and I thought I'd broken something. I could feel wetness through the sharp pain, new wounds. My feet were kicking out in air, and I let the rope slip through my fist.

Then I was below the edge where my knees had hit, a smooth arc of rock just inches from my face, and under it, that darkness in which I was foundering. I looked down along my chest, past my damp knees, my knickers' folds and feet, and saw the vague floor. Then my legs were rising, the pack pulling me down, and in moments I was hanging horizontal, inside the cliff face.

I let the rope slip again, its braids taking fluttering strips of Jen's scarf up with it. My heels touched, then my legs and the pack. I was on my back, the pack holding me in a half-sitting position, gazing into darkness. I felt the rope slacken and looked up its length, past the archway above to where it disappeared over the hump. It swayed loose in the air now, snaking back and forth across my vision.

Then I saw it shudder, felt a coil forming on my chest. The rope was coming down, telescoping into itself. I could feel its weight grow on my body, and when I looked down I saw the way it was covering me, an intricate weaving, like some strange garment or cocoon, dressing me from my collarbone all the way down to my shoes. I could hear it hiss in the air above me, then heard a deep rumbling and looked back up.

The jagged spire of rock was there, the rope still tied to it. It was tumbling out and away from the cliff's hump where I'd descended, and it turned in the blue sky, the size of a falling man, as it came down toward me. I jerked my head to the side involuntarily and felt a rush of air as it sailed past.

Then the rope was racing through my hand, the coils flying away from my chest and legs. I squeezed it, Jen's scarves ripping away from my palm, and felt my body slide along the cave floor toward the edge. It was taking too much time, long enough for me to know I'd go over if I managed to hold on. Then the rope's tip slipped from my fingers, and in a few moments I heard a dull thundering far below. Then there was nothing but silence.

27.

I was on my back and facing into the dark cave's interior, raised up a little and supported by my rack and tank. I could see the edge of the archway opening in sun above my head and the first few feet of faceted rock that was the ceiling before it was swallowed up in shadow. I felt a breeze in the hair at my ears and reached down to the cave's floor at my side, sand again, like that above, a fine powder almost like talcum, and below it smooth, wind-blown stone. I pressed down on the floor, and as I began to rise, I felt the straps pull strongly at my shoulders, the pack slipping.

I was hanging out in the air up to my chest, and I reached down to find shallow ridges in the stone and pulled myself, rocking on my hips, until I was back into the cave far enough that I could slip out of the straps and roll over. I climbed to my feet, then looked up into the darkness. Then I turned and faced the opening where I'd entered. I could see the trail of my hips and pack, a rough road in the dusting of sand ending at the lip, and a yard-wide slice of light where sun lit the floor, almost like a warning stripe at the edge. The archway above hung out a little from the cliff face, blocking the sun, and where I stood, back at what I guessed was the cave's center, the darkness seemed complete when I turned and faced into it.

I stood there, waiting for my eyes to adjust, and in moments I could see the shape of the back wall, the way it leaned in a little as it rose up to the domed ceiling. There was a faint sparkling in shadowy juts there, light reflecting from mineral veins, oddly brighter off to the side, at the cave's rear. Then I could see more clearly, dull colors in slabs and indentations and brighter blues and greens, thin serpentine meanderings in rock.

I turned around, limping slightly, fabric pulling at my knee. My Catalina cap brim blocked the bright sun at the opening, and when I looked down, I saw the dark oval of blood staining the tan khaki. It was drying, but still wet when I touched it, and bending over, I could see that it extended below my shin, running down in star spires into the billowing at my knickers' fold, a few domed drops at the toe of my tennis shoe. I touched my knee. It was tender, but the patella seemed intact, and when I lifted my foot and bent my leg, the pain was just a little stronger, though I felt a seepage where the fabric pulled away clots. I shuffled across the sandy floor then and moved carefully out into that strip of sunlight at the cave's lip and looked down, knowing immediately that I was in deep trouble.

There was nothing but a sheer face below me. The cut was there, but it was a good hundred feet down. It moved off at an angle to the left, then back to the right again, where it disappeared. Below it I could see that rocky rubble, the terminal boulders, where they sank into the surf. They seemed a mile away, as if I were viewing them from a low-flying plane. I saw a brief length of my rope, like a piece of white thread. It was draped over a sunlit rock. The rest had disappeared into shadow where the cut deepened.

I knew I was putting it off, calculating the perspective from above, trying to figure out how I'd been fooled. But it wouldn't have made a difference anyway. I'd lost the rope, and even a few yards of sheer descent would be impossible. But it was Jen there, pushing up from where I was trying to hold her down, and I lifted my eyes then and looked out to find Mooney's boat in the inlet's waters.

It was off to the left, well beyond the spires of the rocky island, and once again it looked like a child's toy bobbing peacefully on an opalescent sea. It drifted a little as I watched it, displaying itself, then drifted back as it reached its tether ends, its hull darkening

TOBY OLSON

gradually as it lost the sun. I could see the north wall of the inlet beyond it, that shadowy stripe on the water still at its edge, which even as I watched lightened a bit, and when I looked up into the blue sky, I could see high thin clouds drifting away from the sun.

I pulled at my cap's bill, blocking the new glare, then looked back to the boat again.

My focus was clearer now than it had been, and though the boat was far down and away, I could see the distinction between wood, metal, and fabric. Then I saw motion, something moving at the gunwale, and I stepped back from the cave's lip, turned and headed for Jen's sack to get the binoculars.

It was slightly brighter in the cave now, its rough, domed shape distinct, and as I moved to my pack near the center, I saw something in a dark corner at the back wall, a faint wash of light there, coming from behind a rock, not out of it.

I squatted down at the pack, warned by that tug of fabric at my knee, and freed Jen's sack and spread its mouth open. I thought I could smell her, something dark and sweet rising, but it was my own blood, a seeping again where my pants had pulled more clots away. I climbed stiffly to my feet and moved back into the sun at the cave's lip, then lifted the binoculars.

It was Mooney, and he was fishing. He was standing at the rail holding a long bamboo pole out over the water. He too wore a golf cap, his face obscured under the brim, and a pair of khakis and a T-shirt. I could see something in the water, a bobber, I thought, and when I looked back, I saw his head come up, my own face squinting out into the sun for a moment before he turned. I followed his gaze. He was looking over his shoulder, across the deck between the wheelhouse and that low stairway enclosure. Estelle was there, her back to the rail, dressed again in that colorful silk robe, feet crossed at the ankles, leaning against the gunwale. She was brushing her blonde hair out in long and deliberate strokes. I looked away from her, then back to Mooney. His head was down again, watching his bobber. Then I scanned the entire deck, knowing that Jen wouldn't be there. They'd have her below, locked away from this strange domesticity. Fishing. Why not, I thought. There's nothing for them but this waiting, and it's me they're waiting for.

I lowered the glasses and looked along the sheer cliff face to either side of the cave opening, then far down below, where the cut began. It was all impossible, and I turned and moved back into the shadowy interior.

The sun's glow touched my tank in its harness and Jen's sack on the sandy floor beside it, just a dim wash reflecting off the cave's stone lip. Beyond that, darkness deepened, until my eyes found luminescence at the back wall, those veins of various mineral deposits defining the shadow shapes of rock formation. To the left, back in a corner, the shapes were more distinct, the veins recessional and dull, their finish matte and their colors clearer, blue and sea green. I could see an ascending shadow there, a place where rock seemed more dimensional, and I headed for it, turning my Catalina cap as I went, positioning the bill above my neck.

It seemed like a passage, at least I felt my face flush at the prospect of one. But it was not a passage, just the beginning of a kind of hallway, a place where the cave had extended a false rear wall, another behind it, so that I stood at the sill of a rock doorway, entrance to a narrow rectangular room, a dim arching closure above and a terminal slab about ten feet away.

Still, there was that light, a soft wash coming from the side and above, dimly mottled shadows falling in angles down the rock face, where the room ended. I limped over the sill, my shoulder brushing the wall on my right, then touched both walls as I moved to the room's end, where I found the turning.

It was just a brief cul-de-sac, another room, far smaller than the one I'd entered, and its floor was covered with earth and rock rubble. I could see the toes of my tennis shoes now, those spots of blood, and beyond them a low bush, scrub oak, I thought. It was

TOBY OLSON

green, and it was growing up through stones on the room's floor. Sunlight was in it, a breeze shook its leaves, and I looked above to find the source of both, a narrow sunlit chimney, twisting up into rock for a good thirty yards, then turning out of sight. I could feel the fresh breeze on my cheeks, see moss and clover growing on little shelves in the chimney shaft.

I had to struggle to get above the room's floor, feet spread to climb the narrow walls and elbows wedged into stony indentations where the opening began, but once into the passage, the going got easier, those shelves and rock indentations where I found firm purchase for my feet and hand holds.

I knew I was deep under that bulge in the cliff's face where I'd roped down, and as I climbed slowly up, careful of my knee, I thought I might get even higher than that, maybe even as far as the sandy path itself. I looked above at each twisting turn, but there was always another, light growing brighter, a thickening of moss on ledges and even small wildflowers in clusters, reaching up for sun. I thought of Jen and that last ascension, the one we'd made together in water. It seemed so long ago, and yet even then, at the very beginning of all this, I'd risked her life, just as I was risking it now. In all his absorbing enthusiasm and starry-eyed madness, my own father had never done that, just the possibility of small electric shocks. "Good for the system, anyway," he'd once said. I was a failed father. But not yet, I thought, and reached up into an indentation for a new grip. My fingers touched moss. It was warm, as was the stone beside it, and when I looked up again, I could see the edges of a small circle of sky.

It was blocked by something, a flat rectangle, the points of which touched the circle, so that the sky was a ring of four half-moons. The thing, whatever it was, hung in the passage, and I climbed higher, then reached out tentatively to touch it. It was metal, a faint silvery color in shadow, and where its corners touched rock, there were fittings of some kind.

I pushed at its center, but it wouldn't budge. There was a scraping above, but no movement. Then I reached into the half-moons of sky at its edges, finding it had sides, and twisted it. It broke loose, dirt and pebbles hitting my hands and arms, a clattering rush of spillage passing me, then echoing in the chimney below. Then it slipped through my hands and came to rest on my head with a dull thud. I pushed it up a little, turned it again, then found I could bring it down between my body and the chimney wall. Its end rested against my thigh, my right arm hugging it to my chest, and I was looking down at the metal grip, seeing my child's hand there as I'd helped my father lug the suitcase up that steep embankment almost thirty years before.

I gazed down at the end of the suitcase, the handle and the name of some company on a metal plate attached under it with rivets, and I remembered the moment.

He'd said the wind was too strong, then had slid the suitcase off into brush at the ledge side. And he'd forgotten it, and who knows what might have happened over the years? Wind and water, earthquake, a shifting in the escarpment itself, or maybe nothing. Maybe the chimney had been there, brush hiding it from view, and the case had slipped down into it, even as he'd pushed it to the side, then gotten on with other things, his tower and that turning propeller, the beckoning of the shaggy buffalo.

It made no difference, yet I was urged ahead somehow by my father's presence there, the fact that I was holding something he'd held, the remnant of a time we'd been involved in together, a day of technical accomplishment, though flawed. A fleeting image of my dancing mother passed by, and I looked up again, into that now-open circle of blue.

I pushed myself erect, toes wedged into rocky indentations, and let the suitcase slide down over my knees. The left one burned a little from the friction, and when I dropped the case, it banged down through the chimney for only a few yards, then came to rest at a

TOBY OLSON

tilting angle above the first turning. Then I climbed up toward the opening, breeze brushing my eyelids, and soon I was able to push my head through into bright sunlight.

I was looking along that ledge where my father and I had stood, my face at ground level. I could see sand grains, a few tiny insects, but that was all. I turned my head to the side and saw only the stubby trunks of brush growing from fractures in rock. I could tilt my head back, but just a little before my hat's bill hit ground behind me. The sky was clear and cloudless, and I made out a few birds, very high up.

At first I worked to get my shoulders through, stepped in a circle in the chimney, pushing up from various angles. It was no good. A slab of rock had shifted or fallen down at some point, and the opening had narrowed. I worked at the slab with my hands, even dug at its edge with my fingers, trying to scrape sand away. I had no idea of its size or structure, and though I pushed and shoved with all the strength I could manage, there was no movement.

I'm not sure how long I worked at it, but I think it was a good long while. I was so close, my head out in the air and safe, only a few inches for the rest of me to get there, and I couldn't find it in myself to give up. But then I did give up, finally, knowing I'd have to go back to the cave again, figure something else.

I was stiff and awkward on the way down, and once I fell, and it was only the suitcase that stopped me, my feet landing with a hollow banging on its end. Still, I cut myself deeply, a broad slice though my T-shirt and into the flesh of the birth scars where Mooney and I had been joined. I worked to keep the suitcase from damage, and that helped, a bit of concentration to keep me focused. I held it by the handle at its end, and when the chimney was too narrow for that, I worked it down ahead of me with my feet. It fell the last few yards to the floor of the small anteroom where the chimney began, and I could see it resting in rubble there below me as I worked my way down to get beside it. I lifted it then, pressing it against my chest, and made my way back through the larger room and into the cave, where I put it down beside my pack and Jen's sack. Then I moved to the cave's opening and looked down at the inlet again.

The boat was where it had been, but the decks were empty now. The central spire of the island still rose up white in the sun, but the near side was no longer in shadow. I looked across to the inlet's north wall. That shadow stripe that had darkened the water at its edge was gone, and the gulls that dipped down for fish remained bright as they skimmed the surface. At least noon, I thought, maybe much later than that. I should have brought my watch. It was just a matter of fact, and I couldn't rise up to any pure anger at my stupidity. I was tired and I was bleeding.

I reached through the slit in my T-shirt, as if into an opening in my side, and felt the sticky wetness. When I looked down at my hand, it was red. I turned and moved back to the cave's center, then pulled the T-shirt over my head and gathered it into a thick bandage and pressed it against my side. Then, holding it there, I lifted the sweatshirt I'd worn earlier and struggled into it.

There's still time, I said aloud to myself, then squatted and sat down on the sand-washed floor, then reclined. My wet suit, still in the harness, made a pillow, and I held the handle of my father's suitcase, to keep myself ready and away from deep sleep and dreaming.

TOBY OLSON

28.

I awoke in fever and with a pain deep in my side, and when I turned in the darkness, my hand came to rest in a warm pool. I pushed up from it, dizzy as I found my knees, a sharp bite in the left one forcing me to recognize delirium. I was blinking, starlight flashes in the air before my eyes, and it was only the slick surface of the metal suitcase under my fingertips that steadied me so I could rise, wobbly and uncertain, to face the cave opening.

The light was muted now, the sky beyond no longer bright but a luminescent robin's egg blue, slow shimmer of some embryonic yolk diffusing within the shell's translucency. I saw it through sweat and fever's idea dream, and when I lifted my hand absently, the moisture on my brow was joined by a stickiness. That motion clarified the pain in my side, and when I turned, focused by that momentary lucidity, the cave had materialized again, though darkly in fragmented rock facets and the disoriented tracings of serpentine mineral veins: yellow, and the lime green of some dress, my daughter's hair, another cave. I dropped my eyes from the domed ceiling and saw the yard-wide blood medallion, a dull sheen at its congealed edges, on the cave floor. My T-shirt was there, a red lump embossed at the center, and when I looked down along my body, I saw the soaking, the stain that had washed over my thigh. My sweatshirt was stuck to the wound, and I was careful not to dislodge it as I turned and limped toward the cave's lip.

Mooney's boat was still there, a cartoon clarity again, a toy boat in a toy harbor, as if seen through the binoculars I touched my chest to find, but they were not there. The hull was darker, and the rock spires on the island had been forced into distinct shadow dimensions and were gray now, drained of all color. It was still day, but the sun was sinking, had started its slow progress beyond Catalina, heading for the backside and the open sea, and I figured I didn't have much time. It must be seven o'clock, at least six, and they'd be looking out for me soon.

I had that moment, a brief urgency in advance of leaving, but then the facts came through my delirium, and I turned again, shivering now, and shuffled back to the suitcase and my pack, then sat down in the wind-blown sand on the cave floor and began working at the straps that held my gear in place, the buckles slippery in my bloody hands.

I managed to get the wet suit out and onto the suitcase lid, and after I'd carefully pulled my sweatshirt free of the clotting wound under it, I lifted my arms, was lost in a strangely comforting darkness inside it for a moment, then pulled the sweatshirt over my head. I could feel blood seeping from the cut, a cold flow on my exposed stomach, and when I looked down in the dim light, I saw the yellow fat in the opening. The jagged gouge was at least an inch wide, and it ran from my nipple through the birth scars, meandering to my hip. It was reminiscent of the mineral veins in the cave's walls and ceiling, and it too was pulsing. Maybe breathing, or heartbeat, I thought, then felt the sting of brow's sweat falling upon it. I raised my head from that fixation and reached out to lift my soaked T-shirt from the bloody pool, squeezing it, blood oozing between my fingers, then pressing it over the wound. Then, with my free hand, I fished around in Jen's sack for the sword knife, pulled it out, and rested it on the suitcase beside the wet suit. I opened the underwater camera bag and pulled the scarf free of the necklace, whose metal blossoms clicked as they fell to the bottom. My fingers touched the small mirror, and I took that out as well. I needed both

TOBY OLSON

hands, and I pressed my elbow against the wound to hold the T-shirt in place, then lifted the knife and cut away the blood-soaked side of the sweatshirt and made a folded compress out of the rest. The straps on the tank harness were detachable, all six of them, and I loosened two, then secured the compress tightly in place, the straps circling my body like belts.

I was still shivering and my hands were shaking and I was sweating profusely, my arms and shoulder and chest soaked with it, and the sweat was helping as I struggled to work my arms and torso into the wet suit top, careful to pull the rubber away and over the compress, which bulged out at my side like some strange hernia once I had that second skin in place, its tail flaps snapped tight between my legs. What the fuck am I doing, I thought, as I lifted my Catalina hat and put it on, then struggled to my feet. My pants were a strange pair of riding breeches now, a billowing at the thighs near my crotch, and one bloody leg, and those knickers' folds draping down at my ankles.

But I felt better. The pain had become a dull aching, and though I was still dizzy and sweating, I found I was more certain on my feet. Those star flashes were still there, echoing in the mineral veins in the cave's walls, but I was seeing through them as I looked down at the blood medallion and the metal suitcase beside it. I held Jen's scarf in my hand, wiping the sweat away when I became blinded, and after I'd moved the gear from the suitcase lid to the sandy floor, I squatted down and opened it, feeling a slight resistance as metal sucked away from the rubber seal.

I had no idea what I was seeing, or how much of what I was seeing I was imagining in my fever, but I saw the metal crank, its red handle vaguely visible. It was similar to the kind I'd fired those generators with, serving my father so long ago. I saw it through translucent fabric, something fragile looking, but when I pressed a finger down into it, it seemed strong and parchment-like. And through the fabric I could see other things, some attached to it, I thought: a system of thin rods and wires, finely made connectors, tiny pulleys and cables. And there was electrical material there as well, and small bulbs of the kind used to dress Christmas trees. Some of it was reminiscent of the structure my father had put together on the ledge above, but this was delicate stuff, more finely machined, yet maybe even stronger, and though it had been there many years, I could see no evidence of rust or other deterioration. I lifted an edge of fabric and saw a shift in other folds below. It seemed connected up in some way, daunting in its complexity. I was dizzy for a moment again, and thirsty now, and I slipped down to my knees, feeling that sharp pain again, and using it for focus. Then I looked up into the open lid of the suitcase and saw the scheme, a system of mechanical drawings and instructions, cross sections of parts, arrows pointing to various joints and fittings.

My father's hand was there, numerous written notations and crossed-out printing, all of it carefully done. He'd been working up to the last minute, worrying the thing, making changes, and through my sweat I could see him sitting at his bench. He'd had his head in his hands, and when he became aware of my presence, he'd lifted it and turned to me, almost sheepishly. "Billy," he'd said, "it's your mother," and though I didn't understand the explanation then, as a twelve year old, I thought I knew something now, that smell of bourbon and certain perfumes, movie magazines and the weekly insistence of her performances. More than that too, I thought, fighting against thinking, trying to stay where I was.

I pushed up from my knees and climbed to my feet, then slid the suitcase away from the blood pool toward the light that remained at the cave opening. Then I reached down and began to take up the fabric, the rods and various connectors. There was a small wrench near the bottom, and a pair of pliers to the side of the prop, and I used both, following the scheme as closely as I could as I worked to assemble the thing. My concentration was on details only. I found I couldn't look ahead, or behind, for fear of losing their intricacy. It

TOBY OLSON

was one distinct thing after another, none of them linked in my imagination. Sweat fell from my brow, wetting the parchment fabric, but it dried quickly, and I used Jen's scarf when my eyes were flooded. The pain in my side expanded, spreading out until it circled my entire waist, but it seemed to lessen in the process, to become general, a pain more thorough than any local wound.

The central structure materialized on the cave floor, the size and shape of a narrow adult coffin, though reminiscent of that box kite my father and I had used for fishing, childish in that way, light and translucent, and the underside open for most of its length, so that it formed an inverted u. The tail was separate, a conventional v, and had to be bolted on, so too the wings, which had the shape and seemingly fragile structure of exaggerated palm fronds. Each was a good six feet long and tapered to a blunt closure at the tip. The nose too was a separate section, a cone, its skeleton visible through the fabric. It was bolted on, like the tail, and there was a chest strap behind it, another where the waist would go, and toe cups taken from bicycle pedals or ski boots at the rear.

Then came the system of wires and pulleys, the electric cable and the lights and the small aluminum housing that would hold the crank, and as I fitted these in place, constantly checking the scheme and wiping away sweat, I fought against hallucination, impossible images of flight, my mother, theatrical in half-drunken gesture, and my father's failures with her and with many of his inventions, and the strong likelihood, coming through those starlight flashes vividly and tortured into many dead-end narratives, that I would, or had already, failed Jen.

The light had faded further by the time I attached the propeller, and before lifting that madly accomplished structure, I moved out to the cave opening again and looked down at the inlet. There was still sun, the towers on the rocky island softly lit, but now a broad shadow lay on the water, and Mooney's boat bobbed darkly in it. I saw movement on the distant deck, and I thought his running lights were blinking. I thought I saw a few early stars in the sky but couldn't tell if they were really there or only in my eyes. I turned then and went back into the cave to get ready, though I had no idea at all of what that might mean.

I removed another strap from the diving rack, belted it tight around my waist, and slipped the sword knife under it at my hip. Then I emptied Jen's sack and the camera bag, and when I found the necklace, I lifted it above my head and put it on, tucking it under the wet suit collar at my throat. The mirror rested on the cave floor beside the binoculars, and as I reached down for them, I caught my image in the small frame. It was not my face at all just then, nor the one I'd seen in Mooney's. It was hollow-eyed and pale, smears of blood across forehead and cheeks, and the nose seemed more prominent. There was a glimmer in those wet eyes, and though I knew it must be fever, I could see my father's look in them, that certain urge to adventure, half mad in anticipation. I left the mirror on the sandy floor, then lifted the binoculars and went back to the cave opening.

Sunlight ended at the inlet's mouth, a sheet of dull illumination running out to sea and then toward the mainland. I couldn't see the rise of buildings at Long Beach, only a dark purple stripe at that horizon. It's come down to the coast now, I thought, and even the beach towns are blanketed. Lights blinked in the smog cover, and I knew they were not there, but a matter of temperature, that fever pushing forward from my eyes.

The entire inlet was in shadow now, but for the tip of the highest island tower, a lighthouse beacon, and when I looked beyond it to Mooney's boat, I saw the winking of his port running lights and a dull glow in the wheelhouse window. A gust of wind pushed at my Catalina hat brim, lifting it, and I reached to the bill and snugged it down, then raised the binoculars.

The prow of *THE-STELLA-R* was pointed directly at the beach, and I could see Mooney clearly where he stood at the brass rail, his own binoculars at his eyes as he leaned forward, watching that place where the canyon emptied out on sand. I'm late, I thought, or almost, and tried to connect to those words, make them more than the social failing they seemed in thinking them. I could feel the sweat circling the binoculars' eye cups, and I lowered them, wiped my brow with Jen's scarf, then raised them again and found Estelle.

She was leaning against the rail at the boat's stern, as far away from Mooney as she could get. The covered objects and the wheelhouse intervened, and she couldn't see him and wasn't looking that way, but to the left and toward the island, her head elevated slightly. There was no glare on the shadowy water, and I could see her face clearly in half profile. She was dressed in rough clothing and had her hair tied tightly back in the manner of Susan Rennert, and I imagined she was thinking of herself that way, the favored sister dead now, and her own appropriation of Susan's place and attitude. Even her way of leaning could be a copy, her bored and depressed look.

I had to fight to move the glasses away from her, knowing I was about to lose myself. I was shivering and could feel a clamminess under the wet suit at my kidneys. I trained the glasses across the water, the image swimming slightly, then found the tip of the island spire still in sunlight. Then I looked back to the boat's deck, at Mooney, then to the rear of the wheelhouse. Jen was sitting there, among the covered pieces of furniture, in the same chair I'd sat in talking to my brother. She had the same blanket over her legs, or a similar one, and she was looking toward the starboard rail or over it toward the north wall of the inlet. I saw her shift in the chair, rise up a little. Then I followed her look, as I had Estelle's. A few gulls drifted on dark wings along the rocky coast, but that was all, and when I looked back, I saw that Estelle had tensed at Jen's movement, something in her hand. The gun, I thought. She's there to watch her. It was enough, and I lowered the glasses and moved back into the cave.

The contraption rested on the stone floor beyond the pool of blood, the central housing curved up a little at the end so that its tail was elevated like the stinger of a scorpion. The wings too seemed warped, a slight dipping at their tips, and forward of where the right one joined the body, the ludicrous wooden handle of the crank was a bright red against the tan, translucent skin that gave the whole thing shape.

That shape was little different from the model planes my father had flown at the Arrowhead Hotel so long ago, larger copies of the ones I'd made and hung from the ceiling of my room. Other men used gas engines and remote control, but my father had opted for rubber bands, wind, and gliding, and I remembered him limping down the gentle slopes, launching his crafts, each of a slightly different design, then sitting on the grass and scribbling notes. I thought of my mother, high at the hotel window, a playbook in her hand, the window forming her theatrical stage. She wasn't watching my father or me but was gesturing toward some figure out of sight beyond the frame.

Again I had to force myself to move. I was standing near the propeller at the nose, my mind drifting in sweat and fever. The binocular strap was an irritant, a pressure against my neck through the wet suit collar, and I took the glasses off and lowered them to the stone floor. It was darker in the cave now, and even the pool of blood was no more than a slight discoloration, a shadow emblem.

I reached down under the plane's nose to the chest strap and lifted the thing. It was light as a feather, and I pushed it into the darkness above my head, a shake and rustling in the tail and the wing tips dipping, then turned and faced the cave opening.

I was looking up into the craft's structure from below and could see the ridged cable running to the prop's center, the fabric arm supports and hand-holds along the wings. To the rear were the toe cups and their linkages. My makeshift bandaging pulled at my side under the wet suit, and I lowered the contraption down a little, seeing the ways I'd fit into it, then continued to lower it, until I could slip above the chest strap and tighten the other across my stomach.

I was bent over at the waist, and I turned to the side, feeling the tail hesitate, then catch up with me, a whispering in its skin, and I saw my shadow on the cave wall, a monstrous insect with a man hanging below it. I turned away from that image and lifted my head in order to see into the craft's nose, but my cap's bill prevented it, so I turned the cap around again. The propeller was there, visible through the transparent fabric and metal rods, and I knew that with my head down, it would be sitting in the place of the one I'd removed from my beanie on that day we'd gathered the buffalo. I looked down at my makeshift knickers, recognizing they were part of the same outfit. Then I looked out again and stepped carefully toward the cave opening, my father's contraption shuddering above me, then shuffled ahead until I felt my toes hanging over at the lip.

There was a faint sliver of moon in the sky now. Dusk was beginning, and when I looked down at Mooney's boat, I saw him standing at the prow, hands on his hips, still gazing toward shore. He turned then and headed back to the wheelhouse and entered it, and just then a breeze gusted. I heard a creak above my head, a flapping back at the tail, and felt myself wobbling at the edge, my wings billowing slightly and turning me.

I reached up along the fuselage to the crank at the side of my head and began turning it, hearing the propeller whir, as if motorized, as it came up to speed. The buzz sang in my ears, and soon the whole nose of the thing was vibrating, and I slowed the pace of my turning.

Nothing was happening. I was leaning forward over the brink, and below I could see the sheer face, the cut now a dark stain in shadow far below. I leaned out farther, careful of my footing, my shoulders hunching slightly and my left arm struggling against the wind-lifted wings. Still I turned the crank, in frustration now, much like those other times so long ago, when I had felt there was no end to it and that my father had failed once again.

The propeller steadied into a constant hum. I looked down the cliff face, then recognized I could see under the cave's lip to a place where I shouldn't be able to see, and when I dipped my chin and looked down to my knickers' folds and feet, I saw I was hanging out in the air. The angle seemed impossible; I was almost horizontal. I dropped the crank and reached out for the fabric straps near the wings' centers, then arched my back, working to gain solid ground.

Then I was lifting off, toes slipping from the cave's edge, my legs hanging down from the structure now, kicking, as I drifted slowly out and away from the face, where I hovered, the craft shaking and creaking in a stiff breeze coming at me from the sea. I looked to the side, hoping to see the cave opening, to somehow get to safety, and I must have done something with my arms, or with my legs, for I turned, and in moments was drifting along the cliff face, no more than thirty yards from it. I could see my shadow slightly ahead, a strange pliable apparition folding over rock juttings and declivities. My legs were rubbery tubes, elongated and scissoring, and I lifted them back up to the tail section and searched for the toe holds.

Then I was all the way inside my father's strange invention. I could see through the fabric hull to both sides, the cliff face passing on my left, and on my right, far away and at a nauseating distance below, shadows moving out to sea near the inlet's mouth. I pressed back with both feet. There was a slight pause, a lagging, then I dipped up quickly, felt the pressure of wind against my chest, and when I looked down, the beach was shrinking away from me, and I hit the pedals again and in a moment leveled off. Then I tried my right ankle, a slow and careful torquing. The craft turned in the air, and I dipped away from the cliff face in a gentle bank, then pulled down on the hand strap in the left wing to correct it, and was soon drifting out over the inlet toward the island spires.

There was nothing below but water when I looked down, a slightly variegated and shifting surface, swell folds cutting angular patterns, slow dissolves, and I felt the weight of my body sagging in the straps as the machine stuttered uncertainly in my awkward manipulations of its mechanisms and the wind rippled its fabric skin. Then suddenly I was above the island spires, their jagged peaks no more than twenty yards below, and I jerked at the hand holds, rocking, and somehow came to a hover, my toes pressing tentatively into the cups and my arms rotating in abbreviated circles to keep the airflow constant under the wings.

I raised my head and looked into the craft's nose. Through sweat and the translucent fabric, I could see the still prop, a faint geometric figure in stars blinking beside the blade, and the crank handle, where it hung out ludicrously in the air to the right of the cone. It's useless, I thought, knowing that made no sense at all. Never was there filigree in my father's plans. Then I looked down at the island once again, the shifting facets of its spires as I wobbled in the air above them. I could see red lichen on the stone, tiny buds of yellow flowers closed up for the night, green moss on rock shelves and in declivities. And I could see the rocky corona, far down at the spires' base, a foam of gentle breakers. I could unbuckle myself, could miss impalement in my dive, just enter the water and go very deep, only to rise up at the boat's hull. I could wait until they were looking over the gunwale at the far side. And I began to imagine the details of the play. Jen could be the ingenue, Estelle the evil sister, or half sister, and Mooney . . . ? The images began to crumble even as I was constructing them, and once I'd blinked the sweat and delirium away, I found I was looking beyond the island and down at the real boat, and I could see Estelle.

She was where she had been, standing in the stern and looking out. And Jen was there too, the length of her body pencil thin and still below the blanket. She was gazing into the sky, and I saw a stiffening as her head rose up a little. Christ, I thought, she can see me. But I knew I'd be no more than a large bird to her, unimaginable as anything else. I dipped my wing and turned to the side, looking for Mooney, the wind rustling in the fabric near my fingers, but I couldn't find him. Then I heard the distant cough and deep roar as the engines came to life, then saw something else, a blinking star in the sky among the real stars out toward the mainland.

Then I was rising, the island falling away below me, as if some massive fissure had opened under it and was sucking it down into the sea. The wind had increased in force, and I fought to work my wings and feet to break out of the tight circling I was caught in as I went up.

I was very high by the time I came again to a hover and was facing out toward the inlet's mouth. I could see everything now. The whole inlet was below me, the boat a narrow book floating on placid water, and though I was apprehensive at the prospect, still unsure of the mechanism and its strength and workings, I knew it was time now, and I'd just have to give myself over to my father's faulty skills.

I started my descent in a broad sweeping arc, one that would take me out over the sea to the right of the inlet's mouth. I could see the tiny figure of Mooney on the boat's deck off to the left as I cupped my chest and torqued the wings to cut under the wind. He was working at the prow. They were getting ready to leave, and I knew it would be only a few moments before he'd arrive at Estelle's side and loosen the stern anchor line.

Wind pressed into the taut fabric of the fuselage above, and I could see the inlet rushing up at me, and ahead, through the now-whirring propeller blades, the rocky coast approaching. I raised the right wing, lowered the left, and saw the crank handle spinning, and in moments I was sailing over the coastline and out to sea, banking in an increasingly tightening turn that would bring me back toward the inlet's mouth.

I felt the heavy force of wind pressing into my wound, the flapping of those billowing breeches near my groin and in the knickers' folds above my ankles. The waves were coming up at me, white-caps, and even the coils of kelp folding in concave curves at their crests were distinctly visible. Then I was banking in the wind's force, my left wing descending and cutting into it, and beyond the spinning crank, I glimpsed the blinking of the Christmas tree lights through the fabric along the wing's edge, those various holiday colors. "Traffic even in the sky!" my father might have said, something like that, and I understood the reason for the prop and felt a brief exhilaration in my freedom from the turning handle.

The wind was doing my work, even as it thrust me toward the waves, which rushed up to meet me, and I thought I might enter them, disappear in the way Susan Rennert had, without a splash. I pressed my shoulders back, pushed out my chest, and felt the wind like a wall against it. I could see the waves' spray, a mist above the water as I turned. For a moment there was only sea. Then I saw the dark north wall, and soon the wind was behind me, and I was moving back toward the inlet's mouth, just feet above the water and heading toward that place where the waves rose up a little as they funneled down to enter.

I looked into the heavy swells as they rushed by under me. A spray rose from the surface, coming up from a dimpling like falling rain, and I wondered if my passage was the cause of it. I felt a splashing on my face, washing the blood and sweat away, and when I looked to the side to clear my eyes, I thought I saw the last of my Catalina letters fluttering in the air, the C and then the l, blown toward the rocky wall of the inlet's north shore, now only a dark, rough shadow in the close distance on my right. I think a flying fish popped out below my wing tip, sailed along beside me for a moment, then became a bullet and disappeared in a swell.

The propeller was spinning violently now, and both it and the crank were blurs I could see through, and when I looked to the sides, I saw that the Christmas tree lights were bright and constant at the wings' edges, running lights of a plane coming in for a landing. Through the nose and whirring prop, I could see the boat's stern, the letters of Estelle's name growing in clarity and size as I rushed toward them. And I saw Mooney standing beside her there, pulling the anchor. Then I saw Estelle look up and beyond me, then down over the water's surface to where I was.

She leaned forward at the rail, then lurched back and reached for Mooney's shoulder and pointed. They were both staring at me, uncertain, but then Estelle reached a stiff arm out over the rail. I heard the popping, saw her arm rise up as she pulled the trigger. Then she was pointing into the sky, firing again, and in a moment had turned and disappeared, leaving only her name.

Mooney remained there, stiff and attentive, and the closer I got, the better I could see him, my face and hair, that certain crazed smile I remembered. I was a thing to see, uncalled for but interesting, a giant lighted insect riding the inlet's surface, coming toward him.

The craft was rumbling now and groaning. My whole body was shaking, and I wiggled my feet free of the holds, then tucked my legs up to meet my chest. My toes skimmed the surface. I was no more than fifty yards away and coming on, racing toward the letters printed on the stern, and I didn't know at all if I could stop in time. I arched my back and rotated my arms. There was a lag, and I thought for sure I'd break myself against the hull. But then I lifted, my body rising up to the vertical as I approached the rail. I was coming in like a parachutist to earth, my wings extended in crucifixion, and I kicked ahead. For a moment, I was dancing in the air. My heels skipped at the rail, and I jerked my legs back involuntarily. Then my knees banged into Mooney's chest and we were falling together, collapsing into the ruined tangle of my father's mad invention on the deck.

We were rolling in it. I heard Mooney swear, then saw my face reflected in the structure's skin. But it was his face, a twisted image through the translucent fabric, the propeller cutting at his cheek. His body was tight against me, though metal and skin intervened, and though I struggled to get the sword knife free, it wouldn't budge. Then Mooney was on top of me, the weight of his hips against my wound. I could see his head through a fold of fabric skin, his hair blowing violently. The sky was shaking and rippling all around me, and I felt the wind pressing me down into the deck. Then the weight of Mooney's body was gone, and I was ripping at the tough fabric,

TOBY OLSON

jerking my way through it, a loud metallic voice banging in my ears.

I rolled to the side, pushing up, and saw the edge of the broken wing, the Christmas tree lights still blinking as it sailed away and clattered across the deck, then struggled to my feet. Mooney staggered near my side, his hands in the air, his face looking up, and Estelle was at the far rail, standing behind Jen, her arm across Jen's throat. She held the gun in her extended hand and was pointing it at me. Her long blonde hair was loose now and blowing in a gale around her head and face, obscuring her view, and I could see the churning inlet behind her, a roiling surface extending beyond the boat's side, then ending oddly in calm water. I looked above, and there was the helicopter, Sanchez leaning out the open doorway. A voice boomed from a speaker, but its words were lost in the whoosh of the sweeping blades and engine drone. Jen was looking at me, her eyes wide but focused, and as I pulled the sword knife free and headed for the hair-blinded woman, I saw Jen dip her chin down and bite into Estelle's forearm.

I reached Estelle as she jerked her arm away from Jen's throat. She was pulling the trigger, her hand lurching, and I felt the searing pain rip at my leg. I brought the flat of the knife down hard against her wrist, then saw the gun fall and bounce across the deck, hitting the lashing of a covered object.

Then Estelle was climbing the gunwale and Jen was falling into my arms, her elbow poking at my wound and the scars under it and hurting me. I tried to push her away, to reach Estelle, but it was too late. She turned at the last moment, her hair blown back and her face visible, and though she was beautiful, her expression was enigmatic. Then she was in the air beyond the rail, and when I got there, I could see nothing in the roiling water near the hull.

29.

They kept me in the hospital at Laguna Beach for three days. It wasn't the wound, though they had trouble repairing it and said I'd have some new scars running through the old. Nor had the bullet been much of a problem. They'd cut it out of superficial flesh in my thigh; I had needed only a few sutures. It was exhaustion, lack of sleep and nourishment, dehydration, and a general draining of energy through exertion and loss of blood, and once they got some food in me and had hooked up an IV, my temperature began to fall toward normal.

"What in the hell *was* that thing?"

It was late Monday afternoon, and I was sitting up, Sanchez in a chair beside the bed. Jen had been there much of the day in the same chair, and I'd awakened often to see her watching me. She'd spent the night with Lin, and around noon Lin and Tod had come over. I was sitting up and eating by then, and I tried to chase them out, but Jen wouldn't leave. Then, at two, the stenographer had arrived, and Jen had gone off with them. They had plans for an early dinner, and she would call Carol after that and then come back.

"What is it that you'll tell her?" I had asked, knowing it was my place to be calling.

"Why, everything, I guess. Don't you think so?"

I did. The last thing we needed now was another conspiracy, and I'd just have to face her when the time came.

I waited while Sanchez read my statement. He tapped it with a finger when he was finished, then asked his question.

"Something of my father's," I said. "A little shaky in design, but it *did* work."

"We found a crank handle, among the other debris."

"That's the shaky part. I think it was useless."

They were holding Mooney on a kidnapping charge, and they had other things as well. He was wanted on an old Mexican warrant, something to do with the sale of stolen property, and there was concern too about his boat. Sanchez had finally called in and gotten my message, as well as what the computer had turned up. The link between Estelle and Mooney was there.

They impounded the boat and searched the inlet's waters until it was too dark, looking for Estelle Rennert's body. Then they'd started again in the early morning and had worked throughout the day, but hadn't found her.

"Could she have drifted out to sea?" I asked.

"Not likely, ese. The current was coming in pretty strong."

"What about her mother?" I said. "Pearl."

"Well, I've spoken to her, this morning. It'll all be breaking in the papers first thing tomorrow, and I needed to do that quickly."

"On the phone?" I said. "How did she seem?"

"Hell no! This was her daughter, man. I went over there. She seemed all right with it, some shock, I think. Trying to figure it out, you know? She'd been dead to her. Then she may have been alive. Then she was really dead. And that we haven't found her yet? I think she may be holding onto that."

"I'll see her when I get out of here."

"Okay," he said. "That's fine. When do they say?"

"Day after tomorrow. Wednesday?"

"That's right. And then what?"

"I don't know yet," I said. "I've got a few things to do. Then I'll head east."

"There's this," he said, holding my statement up again. "You may have to come back. Your daughter too."

"A trial?"

"Well, figure it out. He could be thought of as an accessory in the Susan Rennert death, absolutely that with the mother. But they're all dead, and we've only got the one body. It's his word against yours. Your daughter, of course, if it's some kidnapping deal. Then that Mexican business. I really don't think the deaths will come to anything in the end. It'll be the other, enough to keep him in for a good long while. A trial's certain, I think, but not right away. Too much investigation to be done yet."

"Jen can handle that," I said. "Testifying."

I was drawn to the idea, knowing it was a twisted wish, even a pathetic one. That this would be a definite future for us, something we'd have to do together. I feared I'd soon be losing her, that when she got back home and I had gone, it would all return to that earlier life, one that I wasn't part of. Then I thought of myself in the situation, sitting in a courtroom facing Mooney, telling the life story he'd told me. What a strange image that would be, as if I were the justified accuser and messenger of a darker self.

Jen returned in the evening. She'd be staying the night with Lin again, then would move back into the hotel the next morning. She'd called Carol, who would be flying out early and would arrive around noon. They'd share our rooms. Then, when I got discharged, we'd make other arrangements.

"I'll have to get her a present. For her help, I mean."

"Lin?" Jen smiled, tipping her head coyly to the side and into shadow. "And what about Tod? He's been helping too."

"Okay," I grinned. "For both of them."

It was dark in the room, only the dim light of a hooded extension lamp to gather us in its glow. I could see Jen's legs, her expression when she leaned forward. The light fell over my arm and side, but my face was in shadow. I was tired, and I knew I'd soon be drifting off. She knew this too, but she was staying, the daughter in repose and darkness at her father's side. She was alert, though, and was ready to rise up if I needed anything. We were quiet there for a while.

"Do you need anything?" she whispered.

I'd drifted off, but her gentle words brought me back. I didn't let her know I'd been sleeping, that she'd awakened me.

"No," I said quietly. "I'm fine. I'm okay."

Again we were silent. I could hear the faint sound of the ocean, distant motors, the constant hushed hum of the air conditioner, even Jen's breathing, then her voice, pensive and a long way off.

"Wasn't it those dreams," she said. "That you had killed her and that you hadn't. It was almost as if it came true, right there on the boat. Just almost. You didn't kill her, but she was the other one, the sister, and maybe you might have reached her. And your brother too, wasn't he the one, that other time? Dreams, and being awake in them. It all happened so very fast, but I remember."

She continued talking, and in a while her voice seemed dream-like, as if she were in my dream, one without any other content but her voice, as if I were in that cave again and she was with me, there in the dark. She had important things to tell me, and I was listening to them, but her voice kept drifting away from me, words growing fainter as they crumbled, until they left me completely and I was alone again and sleeping.

Sanchez arrived in the late morning, carrying the necklace and the official police binoculars I'd asked him to get. They were a present for Jen, to replace those I'd left in the cave. He held up the case, smiling, and I saw the town seal embossed in the leather.

"This'll do it," I said. "Wonderful."

I was sitting in a chair at the bed's side, and he pulled up another and sat down facing me.

TOBY OLSON

"I've taken care of your stuff at the Zane Grey. It's at the hotel. The golf cart's been located. The cave'll just have to be archeology."

"Estelle?"

"No, there's nothing. The newspapers are full of that, treating it like some mystery. The two sisters, both by drowning, and one missing. They'll ride that horse for a while."

"What about the necklace?" I said.

It was in a plastic bag, and he'd rested it on the bed table.

"*That's* something," he said. "Extremely curious."

He settled back in the chair, then took a small notebook from his shirt pocket and flipped through the pages, stopping to read things from time to time. Then, when he was ready, he looked up from it and told me the story.

It wasn't worth much. That was the first thing he'd learned from the appraiser. Maybe a thousand dollars or so, but nowhere near what Mooney had said. It was from Poland. That part was right. And it was pretty old too, but not of the best quality. There were many like it, imitations of royal stuff, costume in that sense.

But that was not the important thing. The clasp was. It too was an imitation, but a pretty good one, and the appraiser thought it had been done locally, by a man who was dead now. He'd been known for that, fine etching, and the appraiser thought he recognized his hand.

The emblem on the clasp represented the arms of the Kingdom of Galicia, the name given to the area of Poland that was carved out by Austria in 1772. Something like that. That kingdom lasted a few years, then Russia moved in. But in the years of the kingdom, there was jewelry, some of it at the top of the royal ladder, some a little lower down. The emblem was the same in all cases, but there was an additional scrolled figure on the stripe that separated the bird from the three crowns when the stuff was part of the holdings of royalty.

"The very top dogs," Sanchez said. He'd taken the necklace out of the plastic bag and now held the small clasp between his fingers.

"This one doesn't have it, that scroll thing."

"And what does that mean?" I asked.

"It means that if this were an authentic piece, it might run around twenty thousand, no more than that, depending on the stones and the quality of workmanship. It would be only those at the top, the ones with the scrolls, and only a few of them, that might come close to the figure Mooney mentioned."

"It *is* curious," I said. "How could he make a mistake like that?"

"He made many of them," Sanchez said. "He made one with you. That's for sure."

Carol and Jen walked in around two, and I may have been lucky to have had others there. Higgins and the old man had come over, as well as Lin on a late lunch break. Tod was there. He'd driven Jen to the L.A. airport, then had brought mother and daughter back, delivered them to the hotel, and left them there. I thought he might be a messenger.

"Was she pissed?" I asked.

"I can't really say," Tod answered noncommittally, avoiding any involvement.

The old man winked at me, and even Higgins, though he tried to remain professional and serious, was smiling. I looked over at Lin, and her eyes told me she'd stay clear of it too, at least until the lay of the land was obvious.

"Are you all right?" Carol said when she saw me. Her eyes were hard, her question empty of concern.

Lin excused herself immediately, and the old man and Higgins ambled out shortly after. Then Jen touched Tod on the shoulder, and they went down to the cafeteria for a snack. Carol refused the chair the old man had vacated, and she stood beside the bed looking down at me, well within striking distance.

"I am," I said. "I could probably leave here right now. There's no infection, and the vital signs are okay. They say tomorrow, Wednesday, sometime that day."

She waited for me to finish. I was saying more than she needed,

TOBY OLSON

trying to put it off. Then there was nothing left to say.

"Well, you're a fucking bastard then. And a son of a bitch."

"Carol," I said.

"Don't you try any of *that* bullshit. You've got absolutely no rights in this situation."

She was pointing a shaking figure down at me, and I figured she might poke me with it soon, jab it into my side. I thought to fake a flinch, something comic, anything to get us beyond this rage and into talking. Then I just opened my hands at my sides, looked up at her and waited.

She kept staring down at me. Then I saw her sharp look dissolve a little, and she turned her back, her shoulders slumping. Her voice was muffled when she spoke again, her words quieter and regretful now.

"She's made a fucking *god* of you. What did you *do* to her?"

I spoke up into her back. I was pleased and chagrined, shocked a little, but I tried to keep all that out of my voice.

"Carol," I said. "It's over now. And she's all right. She'll be going home with you. She wasn't hurt or anything."

"That's not the point," she said. "I can't talk." And then she walked out.

I was discharged Wednesday morning, but with a warning: no heavy lifting for a while and no alcohol. The stitches could be removed in a week. I could go anywhere for that.

I was dressing in the clothes Jen had brought over the previous evening when Sanchez called. Carol had come with Jen, and things had been at least civil. Jen had watched the two of us carefully, a little stiff and awkward, staying at a distance from both of us. She had to measure her allegiances. Carol had caught my eye at one point, seeing that, and had stared hard at me. They'd rented an extra room down the hall from their two adjoining ones at Lin's hotel.

"They found her," Sanchez said. "Washed up near rocks at the beach. Just like her sister."

I wondered if the rocks where she'd been found were those that had fallen down so long ago, creating that cut where the rope had been lost, but I didn't ask him. It was nine o'clock.

"Pearl?" I said.

"Just now. I called her. I think she knew already. Just needed to hear the words."

"I'm going to call her too."

"Of course," Sanchez said.

I did it right then. He'd said I could see Mooney anytime, and I told him it would probably be tomorrow. Then I hung up, lifted the phone again, and called Pearl. Her voice was empty and vacant, but not guarded. She'd expect me around six. Then I called the storage place in La Puente.

Carol and Jen were with me when I checked out. The rental car was parked in the turnaround near the hospital doors. Carol drove, Jen giving directions, and I sat alone in the backseat.

We gathered in Carol's room and went over things. They'd made tentative flight reservations for Friday, midmorning. We'd separate in Chicago. I'd fly from there to Iron Mountain to get my car, and they'd catch a plane to Racine.

"We'll be going to Milwaukee on Saturday, and for Sunday," Carol said, somewhat gratuitously, taking charge of her daughter, and Jen heard that.

"Just an overnight," she said. "Mom found out about a slide lecture there. About ship wreckage or something? Near Venezuela?"

Carol's face flushed and hardened, and I looked away.

"And I'll call my friend Aaron near Madison. Maybe I'll be there for a while. But I'll call you. On Monday?"

"You do that," Carol said. "And plan to drive over. Let's say end of the week, or the weekend."

It was not a question or request, but an order, and I could hear her resentment as she spoke the words. Yet I was warmed by the possibilities they suggested, and I watched as Jen fought to hide her smile.

TOBY OLSON

Carol and I had not spoken of the facts at all yet, and I was glad for that. Each time I rehearsed them, my complete irresponsibility rose up to accuse me. It had seemed only a game to begin with, like an adolescent novel. And the diving too had seemed harmless, most of it, just a way for a father and daughter to get to know each other, maybe another kind of drama. And I had hidden in these fictions, in the way of my mother, in order to construct a presence for myself, to play the part of a parent, and I wondered if my father had ever taken such serious risks when it came to me.

"There's something else," Jen said, that look I remembered, but directed at the two of us now. "Tomorrow night!"

"Oh, no. Tod again, I'll bet."

"That's absolutely right," she said like a teacher, and Carol caught the familiarity of play between us and remained silent.

"Yet another beach party. But a going-away party. For us!"

"If it doesn't rain," Carol said.

"Oh, Mom!" said Jen. "This is California!"

I sat among my father's boxes at the storage place but had no heart to go through them. There was so much, and though there were things still on his list that had not become clear, enough of them had.

I'd driven inland from Laguna, but not into smog this time. Wind had washed out the valleys, and it was as clear and fresh in La Puente as it was at the beach. Tod would be a chauffeur for Carol and Jen, would take them wherever they wished to go, and we'd be gathering again after dinner, for ice cream and talk. I'd passed by the outskirts of El Monte, my old house and Leonard's, but had no desire to see them a last time. My mother's things would stay at the museum. I planned even to send those photos back before I left.

The storage bin was nothing more than a long metal container, windowless and tomb-like, wooden steps moving up into it through doors like those at the rear of moving vans. It may have *been* a moving van at one time. It was hot inside, even with the doors standing open, but it was dry and clean, and I didn't think the heat would cause damage. It was mostly papers, after all, and I found myself pleased by the crowded feel of the place, those boxes tilting toward me. Not unlike my father's garage in El Monte, I thought, the way it was. The rental was cheap enough, and I wrote a check to cover the full year. I'd surely know where I was going to be by then.

When I was seated in the same chair at Pearl's house and she'd come back with the coffee, the first thing she said was that she didn't want the jewelry, not any of it. The dogs were at our feet again, and the drapes were pulled back from the windows. The room was bright this time, and though Pearl looked tired, I could find no grief in her face, but rather a release of tension, as if she'd been waiting for a long time and the waiting had been worse than the ending.

"Your daughter," she said, looking at me. "It should be hers. A daughter's. From your mother, after all."

I told her Jen would be pleased by that. She liked it, and it was something between us, father to daughter.

"You saw her," she said. "What was she like?"

She sipped from her coffee, as if it were a simple thing to be asking, as if I could tell her some truth about Estelle, something that could answer the facts she now had, that her daughter had killed Cora, her sister, had been involved too in the death of Susan. The dogs caught something in her voice, and their heads came up from the carpet. I knew I couldn't find a good way to lie to her, so I tried part of the truth.

"I think she had problems," I said. "Mental problems. I don't think she was really responsible, not for any of it."

"Your brother?" she said.

"Yes, well, maybe. I don't really know exactly what it was between them. I think he loved her, in the way he could, that he was good to her."

"How did she look?"

Again I was up against something, all those twisted happenings and her part in them. She'd combed her hair out as if nothing important was going on. Then I remembered that vision of her a moment before she'd gone over the rail.

"She was beautiful," I said. "Really quite austere and lovely. You might have been proud of her, the way she looked."

"Pride?" she said. "I think I know better than that. But isn't it over now?"

"Yes," I said. "It is for her. Can it be for you?"

She didn't answer, but she seemed to be considering the question, taking it seriously. She reached down and touched the head of the dog closest to her, the female, who lifted her nose into Pearl's palm. Then she touched the couch arm, wiping the dampness away.

"Well," she said finally, but that was all, and the word was as much an ending to our conversation as a first tentative gesture of resolve.

On our way to the door, she told me she'd put the Blevins Street house up for sale. The market was good now, and it would bring a high price.

"They'll tear it down, of course."

I was standing beyond the screen door, looking in at her. "And what will you do? With the money, I mean."

"Well, I've been thinking about that," she said. "Dogs, I expect. There's room in the back here, and I can start with a good stud and a few bitches. There's plenty of time now. Really, there has been for a while."

"Time," I said, then lifted my hand and waved lightly to her as I turned. I looked back from the car before getting in, but she'd gone inside and closed the door behind her.

It was cloudy the next morning when we met in the hotel coffee shop for breakfast, and Carol had a smug look on her face. We'd talked into the night, pieces fitting into a whole story as Jen and I had spoken. They'd kept her below deck the entire time until they brought her up before leaving, and though Estelle had checked on her from time to time, only a few words had passed between them. There'd been no mistreatment. "It was just boring," Jen said impatiently, wanting to hear my part of it, a much better story, which I told in great detail, trying to gather Carol up in it, though she remained silent and didn't comment during the pauses, just as Jen did.

Jen was looking out through the windows at the beach. Dark clouds rolled by, heading along the coast toward Long Beach. She looked at Carol, blinking. "Oh, this won't last," she said. "Not here."

She glanced over at me then, looking for confirmation.

It was two o'clock and still overcast when I reached the police station, but the clouds had thinned and moved farther out over the sea. They drifted in a thick bank toward Catalina, and I thought Jen had a good chance of being right.

They were holding Mooney in one of the few cells they had there, but they'd be moving him soon. "But not right away," Sanchez had said. "Not until they figure possible charges and jurisdictions."

The guard was shocked when he saw me, though he'd been expecting me, and he tried not to let on.

"We have him in the back," he said. "Isolated. You can talk through the bars. Or you can go inside. But if that, we'll have to do a search."

"Inside," I said, then imagined a possible story, Mooney just walking out into rain. I'd be in the cell, trying to convince them I was the wrong one.

He was sitting in a straight-backed metal chair, at a metal table, and there was another, empty one on the other side. The guard stood off in the distance, beyond the bars and in shadow. Mooney had brushed his hair and shaved, and though his drab jail clothing fit him a little loosely, he looked rested and fit. He'd risen when I entered, like a host, I thought, and there was a smile of welcome on his face as I sat down. He even tried a joke.

TOBY OLSON

"You're pale," he said. "Why not try *this* color," and he lifted a piece of fabric at his arm, then let it drop.

We sat there facing each other in silence. His face was mine, but I was no longer shocked at seeing it, and he didn't seem to be, either.

"I don't know what to say," I said.

"Well, I never gave you a chance for that. Do you have questions?"

He settled back in his chair, his fingers touching in a steeple shape, and was looking across the table, waiting for me. I felt it was I who was accused. He seemed so at home here, sure of himself, and I couldn't tell if it was madness or something else.

"Estelle," I said. "How was it that you loved her?"

That broke him. He sank back from his fragile arrogance, his hands falling to the table as he looked away, then back again after a few moments.

"That's the story of my life," he said. "Something I already told you. I never did ask you about yours, though."

"Did I . . ."

We had spoken the words in unison and without harmony. He grinned at me, and I knew he saw that same grin looking back at him.

"It was the Navy."

"Over twenty years of travel and different duty stations, up until recently."

"It seems an emptiness."

"Since my daughter, Jen. And now there's that vacant hunk of time, and before that, my parents."

"In El Monte. That's where Estelle went. She said they were colorful. I think she used that word."

"To describe them. To myself. I've been trying to understand them. We're a very large thing in this. Was it held back from me? I can't even know that, or why."

"They kept the secret if they had it. Estelle . . ."

"She was Pearl's daughter, and not Cora's. Did you know that? Could she have possibly known?"

"*That?* Impossible. Are you saying she killed the wrong woman?"

"Or the right one? What difference does it make now? Just another betrayal."

"And you're wondering about seeing your parents in some similar light."

It was true. And I imagined the recent past undone for us, that we were traveling together, back to Chicago to find our mother. I had no clear image or idea of what we might do when we found her, what sitting with her and talking might be like. What we might be like then, as sons, brothers, in her presence.

"I can only see her as a young woman," Mooney said. He was reaching inside my mind, pulling those vague thoughts up into language and some shared reality. It seemed a perfectly natural thing to have done.

"I can see that," I said. "It's like me and my parents, their lives frozen in memory when I left for the Navy."

"Can you go there?"

"To Chicago?"

"To find our mother."

I said yes, I could. I'd be in the area for a while, and I could drive over. But I could tell he didn't believe me, that there was no use trying to lie to him.

"But it might have to wait, I think. And even then I can't promise anything."

"Which is fair enough," he said. "It's not been exactly brotherly between us."

"Would you have killed Jen? Me, when I showed up?"

"Oh, God, no. I never killed anyone. I would have had to figure something. Taken you down coast, possibly, put you ashore in some wilderness. Enough time to get away. Estelle, though, she might have done that. She had before."

"I was powerfully drawn to her."

"You're speaking of Susan now."

394   TOBY OLSON

"Almost a chemical thing, beyond relationship."

"Like me and Estelle."

The dead sisters were there then, and though they were not true twins, as we were, Mooney and I were silent for a moment and in their power. I knew it was the same power for each of us, and in that sense, they too were identical.

It was I who shook off Susan first, then in a moment I saw Mooney shudder slightly and come back from the dead Estelle. Again we were silent, each waiting for the other, both knowing this was the end of it. I thought to mention the almost worthless necklace, but found I didn't need to wound him in that way. Finally, he spoke.

"Your wound," he said. "How is it?"

"It's going to be okay. But the scars will change."

"And nothing else."

He touched his own side, then rose to his feet and spoke again.

"You could write a letter."

"Yes, I could. I will, in fact."

It was the first time I'd touched him, and his grip both joined and separated us, as did the metal table. He might have pulled me toward him, or I might have done that, our grip as prelude to embrace, rather than absence. But the table was there, and I think in our way we were both glad for it, to avoid a continuance of touching that would be painful. One of us released the other after a long moment. We were both smiling. Then I turned my face away from my brother's face and called out softly for the guard.

Clouds obscured Catalina, the sun sinking into them. They were thick clouds and at a far distance, and the sun made them into a red wall and a false horizon just above the sea. It was a beautiful sight, and the Asian cook in his dark jumpsuit looked out at it through shimmers of heat rising from the almost-ready coals.

"That's certainly something," Carol spoke softly at my shoulder. "Makes me hungry," Jen said.

She was standing beside Tod near the end of the grill, her official Laguna Beach binoculars hanging down between her breasts. Tod wore his new T-shirt, black, with the lighter figure of John Coltrane silk-screened across the chest.

To me, it had seemed a too intimate gift, though I knew nothing about such things, but since Jen was insistent, I'd advised against shirts featuring other musicians, remembering the cheap soft rock that had come through Tod's windows at that first party.

"Give him someone *real*," I'd said, and she'd done her "Oh, Bill," but had agreed to it, knowing it might be our last time alone together for a while. We'd gone out shopping, something for Carol too. She'd gotten the point and had stayed behind with plans to take a long walk, see what Laguna Beach was really like. "Hungry for these burgers?" I said now. "I can almost taste the buggers."

Jen tittered, and the cook dropped a thick patty on the grill, then another. They sizzled, and Jen smiled tentatively at the two of us. "Oh my greasy, greasy burger con fries!" she said, poking Tod in the arm. Then they turned from the fire and headed off toward the surf, to look at the setting sun.

"She's very nervous," Carol said, "about the two of us."

Jen had acted a little silly for most of the day, being a child, but her hysteria was adultlike. Her frequent laughter had seemed uncalled for, and at times she had taken on a serious expression that was clearly beyond her years. Now she stood at the surf line, hip slung, acting the grown-up woman beside Tod.

"Maybe we have to do some acting ourselves," I said.

"You mean civility."

"For a while at least, for now."

"I can't forgive any of this," Carol said.

We were both looking at Jen, watching as she touched her head against Tod's shoulder from time to time. They were holding hands,

TOBY OLSON

saying that sweet summer vacation good-bye. The sun had turned the cloud bank purple.

"Of course," I said.

"But I can act. Just as you said. For her sake."

They turned then and headed back through the sand toward us. The burgers were ready now, and Jen was hungry.

"Orale, amigos. ¿Qué tal?"

It was Sanchez. He was trudging up from the surf line, wearing shorts and a sweatshirt, and there were others coming down the beach behind him. I saw Higgins and his students, the old man walking beside the women, gesturing and telling some story, lagging back a little in the distance.

"Oh, I wish I could speak Spanish!" Jen said to Tod.

"So do I," Sanchez said as he reached us. "More than a few words, at least."

He'd missed Carol at the hospital, and he smiled when I introduced them, then struck up a conversation with her. I moved away and headed down to the cooler for a soft drink. The divers had gathered around Jen and Tod, and they all sat on blankets and beach chairs near one of the fires, its flames close to invisible in the light, though I saw them begin to take shape as the sun left the Catalina cloud bank and the sky turned quickly to slate.

"Are you satisfied?" Lin said.

It was dark now. There was starlight on the sea. People were eating, gathered around the fires. I saw Carol beside Jen and Tod, Higgins's face an Irish portrait in flames. Sanchez was gone. We'd talked a little in darkness near the surf. I'd be calling him about Mooney.

"Whatever else," he'd said, "keep in touch. We'll have some good advanced notice about a trial." He'd gone down the beach then, turning back to wave after a few yards.

"Satisfied? That doesn't seem the right word."

Lin had been effusive about the flowers, but not seductive.

She'd kept an eye on Carol, figuring things out. We'd gotten her an extravagant arrangement, none of it indigenous, and had it delivered to her room in the hotel with a thank-you note. She was looking up from where she sat beside me, on the bench at the escarpment near the stairs. We were alone there, in the faint glow of the dying cooking coals.

"And Susan Rennert?"

"Well that, at least, is over. But there's a lot that was churned up in finding out about her. And some of that isn't yet."

"Maybe it never will be," she said.

"Like life."

"Until it is."

We sat there in silence. There was nothing else to say, and though I thought to ask her about her own life, if there were any things in it right now or coming up, I didn't do so. I think I felt too full of things and needed some draining, had no room at all for the life of another and the possible entanglements that might come with it. She seemed to know this, or something like it. Maybe she was feeling the same way, though I didn't think so. It had been that sense of freedom from entanglements that had drawn me to her, however briefly, and I could have nothing with her of the kind I'd had with Mooney so recently, nor with anyone else, though maybe I could have something like it with Jen. Maybe I did. We just sat there, looking out at the fires and the stars.

Carol wore the Indian brooch we'd gotten for her, a good imitation of something from a Catalina tribe. We'd found it at a shop in Laguna, and it had been an expensive thing that Jen had insisted on sharing the purchase of. It was to be a gift from both of us. Like something in a family.

Jen sat between us, my mother's jewelry folds in her lap. She and Carol were going over the pieces carefully, though they'd had them out before, back in Laguna. The necklaces shook and clattered for a

TOBY OLSON

moment as we moved through turbulence to a higher altitude, and when I looked out the window I could see the inland smog. It was coming back again, just as thick as before, and I imagined I could see it settling on Pearl's house, flooding up through that pipe above a clearer Blevins Street. Then we entered clouds, a thick, white blanket around us, and California was gone.

We parted in Chicago, and though we knew we'd be together again in just a week, Jen and I were a little frightened, as if something might happen to prevent it.

Carol stood behind Jen, giving us room, and I could see her face over Jen's shoulder as I hugged her. Her expression was placid, and I knew there was no sense in trying to read it. So I looked away and pushed Jen out to arm's length and smiled at her. She smiled back, a misting in her blinking eyes.

"Soon," I said. "Greasy burgers again, and fries!"

"Oh, Dad!" she said, not wanting any of our games now. "I love you!"

Then it was I who was blinking, Carol's face swimming in the distance as I looked away, then looked back again, at Jen.

"We'll go diving," I said. "In the Netherlands Antilles. And we'll take your mother along too. It will be wonderful. Fantastic! Just you wait and see."

30.

It was late by the time I reached Iron Mountain and the service station where I'd left my car, too late for the drive to Madison and Aaron's farm that night. So I called them. Jason answered, and I thought for a moment I was hearing Aaron's voice. Then he put Beverly on. Aaron was out in the barn, fussing around with something.

"We'll be expecting you! Around noon?"

"Even a little earlier," I said. "How are things going? How's Aaron?"

"Great," she said. "Everything's great."

The motel room was nothing like those spacious California ones. It felt tight and cramped, and I missed the sea and its ripe smell. I went to the window at the bed's foot and pulled the drapes aside, then raised it. There were woods outside, tall eastern pine and cedar beyond the parking lot, night-lights shining on needles and bark. And there was a scent too, that rich midwestern one, turned soil and manure, and not a hint of smog. I leaned into it, my hands high on the window frame, then felt my stitches pulling, a deep ache following, and a tiredness that was welcome. On the way back across the room, I considered my knee, but could feel nothing there. That's healing now, I thought, and it won't be long before the other is too. I fell asleep hugging a pillow, just moments after I'd climbed into bed.

The phone woke me at six, a cheery good morning, and after a quick continental breakfast in the lobby, I was on the road. Truck traffic was light. It was Saturday, and I chose an inland route, away from the summer vacation traffic near the lake, and made good time. I arrived just after ten. Aaron and Bev were waiting for me on the broad front porch. We had coffee there, and I told them much of the story, Beverly stopping me from time to time, making me return to earlier beginnings, until I was back with Carol in Corpus.

"And even that isn't the start."

"Go back more, then. This is too good!" said Bev.

"That's right," Aaron said. "Start where it started."

I returned to my childhood and the Arrowhead Hotel, my father flying his model planes, and then I saw Aaron check his watch. He caught my look, then shrugged and smiled a little sheepishly.

"It's not that," Beverly said. "Your story. Maybe we can hold onto it for a while, till later? We've got plenty of time, after all."

"It's a class," Aaron said. "At the Mount Horeb high school. It's twice a month. I'm teaching a diving class!"

Aaron introduced me to the dozen or so kids who sat in a row at the pool's edge, their legs dangling into the chlorinated water. They were farm kids for the most part, blond and milk-fed, and they gazed up at me with bright eyes as Aaron told them of our long-gone underwater exploits, diving for repair, and that better kind of diving, drifting down among exotic fish along coral reefs in places they had seen only in magazines. They toyed with their masks and snorkels, their flipper in a neat row on the tile floor behind them, and at times they glanced in clear anticipation at the tank and regulator resting near Aaron's feet. It was going to be their first day with that serious gear, and I'd noticed a gathering of other tanks near the pool's door when we'd entered.

Then Aaron lifted the regulator and began to explain it, and in a while the kids rose from the pool's edge and went to the doorway and their own tanks and regulators and lugged them down to the shallow end. I sat in a metal folding chair and watched them as they

402

suited up, then climbed into the waist-deep pool and crowded around their teacher. Aaron was talking then, but I couldn't hear him. I could only watch as the students bent over and put their masked faces into the water. I could see the bubbles of escaping air around their heads, and I watched Aaron as he kept his own careful watch on each of them, nudging a shoulder from time to time.

There's nothing but the tile there, I thought, possibly some scum around the drains. But they're seeing it more clearly through their masks, its geometric pattern, any flotsam floating by. Maybe they're seeing it all as fish might, or other creatures living in that foreign element. They're breathing underwater, and that's the thing, exciting even were they in some familiar bathtub back home. No chores, no homework, no hassling parents, no adolescent anxieties. Even in a pool in their landlocked piece of Wisconsin, they were in some other world entirely, and I wondered if any would be drawn to that bait and its promises, just as I had been.

Later, we sat on Aaron's porch again. We'd eaten an early dinner, and it would still be light for a few more hours. It was a beautiful summer evening, and the sparrows were reveling in the pre-dusk stillness, gobbling seed as they jumped on the decks of the large bird feeders out in the yard. We were sipping iced tea, listening to the birds' quiet clatter and the crickets in the grass. I mentioned my father's list and started to get into that, but then I saw Beverly stifle a yawn. She was losing her attention to the details of a story she'd had no part in, and she spoke as soon as she saw I'd noticed that.

"Maybe tomorrow," she said apologetically. "When you're rested and we have more time? We've got plenty of time."

"And what will you do now?" Aaron asked.

I started to look for an answer, but before I could find one, I heard the screen door opening, and Jason came out. He looked much older, more of a man now, though it was only a few weeks since I'd seen him. He was carrying something, and Aaron smiled up at him, then looked over at me with pride in his eyes.

"This came for you," Jason said. "While you were over at the pool class with Dad. I forgot all about it."

Then he handed me the flat, overnight delivery envelope. I noticed the return address, Carol's place in Racine, then the postmark. It had been mailed from Chicago, from the airport, only an hour after I'd left them there.

Inside was a note from Carol, and inside that, in its own envelope, was my father's letter. Jen had found it in one of my mother's jewelry folds, in a zippered flap at one end. Carol wrote briefly, saying I should call. They'd expect me around Friday.

I sat on the back deck of Aaron's house, overlooking the cultivated fields and the hills and forests off in the distance. Dusk was coming on, and sun lit the tree tips, turning them from green to vermillion. I was alone there, and it was quiet. Aaron and Beverly were reading, and Jason had headed off on his bike into town. Even the sparrows had settled down. It was too early for nighthawks and owls.

I can't reveal the actual words in my father's letter. They're personal and only for me. And I think too that this has really been my daughter's story and not mine. I've told it, but only in that way have I been its focus. What Jennifer was thinking, in her adolescent vulnerability and the first flush of womanhood, is the real story, and not one for me to try to tell.

She'll be rushing into the future now, of course, and will soon forget the story's flavor. And when she reaches my age and has time to look back, she may well find herself in a similar circumstance, a victim of nostalgia.

The letter was dated a week before my mother's death, and how it got in among her jewelry folds I can't be sure. Except for the tone of what my father said when he wrote of her. He must have known she would die soon and was setting her affairs in order. Maybe he zipped it in there by mistake, or for safekeeping. He too died then,

TOBY OLSON

before he could mail it to me. It was addressed to Corpus Christi, where I was seeing Carol, and where Jen was conceived.

In the last year of my mother's life, she'd been drinking heavily and he'd needed money. The theater had become even more of an obsession with her. There'd been that slippage from prominence early on, even before they'd adopted me, which he'd thought of in part as a help for her, to put her mind on something else entirely.

But now her life was slipping away too. She'd readied her materials for the El Monte Museum and was staying close to the theater through patronage, donations she would make to various acting groups, which got her invited to parties so she could dress in her jewelry and play clothing, make personal appearances, and be talked about. He'd had to sell that necklace near the end, and he'd substituted an imitation, even a fake clasp. It had brought fifteen thousand dollars, just enough, and she'd been too far gone by then to notice the difference.

There was not a word of regret or frustration in what my father wrote, but it was his mention of the necklace, bound up in my mother and the theater, that got him to Estelle Rennert, and to me.

He'd been sure when they'd showed Estelle those photographs, her shock at seeing me in them, that my brother was alive and probably close by and would soon know of me. That's why he was writing. He'd put it off for a while. Then Susan had drowned, and though her death was a puzzle of sorts and he was looking into it, he knew it was time. He'd considered going over it with Bev again, but by then she had failed almost completely.

They'd found me, through his study and research, in Chicago, and they'd traveled there together, only then to learn that I was a special kind of twin and that my other self, my brother, was gone away forever. That was the understanding, though the adoption had been a private matter and there were no papers, something that had bothered my father, who was in love with papers and the information written on them.

But it was a circumstance my mother was drawn to immediately, the drama of a crucial family secret, like those protected by women in plays she'd had parts in, the ingenue, desperate for discovery, innocent in confusion. And she'd held it as a secret in our lives together, something to be acted out when she fed and tended me, then later spoke to me, a mother's secret that could darken and enrich her life, keep it theatrical, a deep and hidden poignancy in her relationship with me.

It was time to give the secret up now, and he was telling me, and though when he wrote of my mother's failing health his words seemed to carry his own death too, near the end they brightened, and he referred to the letter's enclosure in the old way, that one I remembered from many conversations with him, those about experiment and discovery.

The enclosure was a carefully wrought mechanical drawing, and like the one I'd seen below the suitcase lid in that cave on Catalina, it was marked by entries in my father's hand, alterations and adjustments. When I saw it I knew that Leonard and his batteries had nothing at all to do with Susan Rennert, though they appeared on my father's list. They were there in the way he'd been there and were part of a larger matrix, one that included my mother and his desire to keep both of them alive in the only way he knew how, through the power of invention and through the theater.

It was a rendering of a thrust stage, a mechanical one, driven by hydraulics and electricity. Behind it were open curtains, and I recognized the doorway to my parents' bedroom close to where they joined. The stage would come forward from the bedroom, extend into the living room, and would stop its motion only a few feet from the easy chairs. There were bulbs circling its oval edge, others pointing down from above, and I saw figures that were actors' marks in places on its surface.

And I could see my mother there too, in costume and theatrical makeup, standing on that stage and gesturing toward someone who

406

TOBY OLSON

was absent beside her, acting out her part. I could see her profile, then her full face, the smiling ingenue, as she turned and looked out into the darkness to where my father and I were poised attentively in our easy chairs. I knew she'd soon be stepping close to the footlights, holding imaginary roses in her arms. She'd bow deeply, waiting for evidence of the audience she couldn't see. There'd be a hushed silence, then the sound of our enthusiastic applause filling the room.

I moved the mechanical drawing to the side and looked down at my father's list where it rested on my knees. It was almost complete now, each entry having yielded its secrets, all but one. I looked up from the list, then out to where the cultivated field started near the foot of Aaron's deck. The sun was leaving, and it sent its last wash across the furrows, lighting the late crop that was still budding, giving it the cast and appearance of a complex carpet.

And as with any carpet of value, there has to be a flaw or an absence, a place to let dark spirits out and the healthy light of the future in. There was one on the list. It remained a puzzle, but for me it held promise as well. It was something Jen and I could talk about in just a few more days. *Time longer than rope.*